Madeleine Roux received her BA in Creative Writing and Acting from Beloit College in 2008. In the spring of 2009, Madeleine completed an Honors Term at Beloit College, proposing, writing and presenting a full-length historical fiction novel. Shortly after, she began the experimental fiction blog Allison Hewitt is Trapped which quickly spread throughout the blogosphere, bringing a unique serial fiction experience to readers.

Born in Minnesota, she now lives and works in Wisconsin where she enjoys the local beer and preparing for the eventual and inevitable zombie apocalypse.

Praise for Madeleine Roux:

'The chief reason to read is Sadie herself...She's a fascinating figure...It's her leap-first-think-later bravery and constant struggle to match up to the parental role thrust upon her that keep you hooked' *SFX*

'Madeleine Roux's novel is one of the single most exhilarating reads you'll find this year' www.sassisamblog.com

'*Allison Hewitt is Trapped* is just fantastic...This is no ordinary zombie novel. It's fresh and original and I just loved it' www.bookchickcity.com

'The plot...rises above the "same old" due to its unflagging energy and momentum. The central protagonists, and particularly the character of Allison herself, are depicted with discomfiting realism; fallible, damaged, and as capable of truly dreadful acts as of selfless ones. Overall, this is a great read, and a worthy addition to any zomfan's personal library...Read it, absolutely' www.zombiefictionreview.blogspot.com

'I've got only great things to say about this book. It's a keeper. One I haven't stopped thinking about since I finished. One that will live on my bookshelf forever. I loved it!' www.ysfetsos.blogspot.com

'This one rocks and shows the sub-genre is indeed maturing...If you only plan on reading one horror novel this year, then look no further' www.beyondscary.com

'Adrena

D0176889

Also by Madeleine Roux and available from Headline

Allison Hewitt is Trapped

SADIE WALKER IS STRANDED

MADELEINE ROUX

headline

Copyright © 2012 Madeleine Roux

The right of Madeleine Roux to be identified as the Author
of the Work has been asserted by her in accordance with the
Copyright, Designs and Patents Act 1988.

First published in Great Britain in 2012 by
HEADLINE PUBLISHING GROUP

First published in Great Britain in paperback in 2012 by
HEADLINE PUBLISHING GROUP

1

Cataloguing in Publication Data is available from the British Library

ISBN 978 0 7553 7917 0

Typeset in Goudy Old Style by Avon DataSet Ltd,
Bidford-on-Avon, Warwickshire

Printed and bound in Great Britain by
Clays Ltd, St Ives plc

Headline's policy is to use papers that are natural, renewable and
recyclable products and made from wood grown in sustainable forests.
The logging and manufacturing processes are expected to conform to
the environmental regulations of the country of origin.

HEADLINE PUBLISHING GROUP
An Hachette UK Company
338 Euston Road
London NW1 3BH

www.headline.co.uk
www.hachette.co.uk

For my family, friends and professors

'You'll get back to where you came from.'

– William Golding, *Lord of the Flies*

'I can't make this.'

'But Jason . . .'

'There's just no audience. No one will want to read this so no one is going to make it, especially – *especially* – not me. I'm sorry Sadie, but it's not gonna happen. The pictures are great, maybe some of your best, but it's too soon. Way too soon.'

'You said things were changing,' I said. A whining note crept into my voice. 'We could run just a short issue, a teaser. Maybe see if there's interest . . .'

'There won't be. It's a waste of my time and – sorry – yours too.'

Jason was a genius, a penny pincher and – sometimes – an idiot. Most successful people are. But I thought he would go for it, I really did. My sketches sat spread out in front of him, panels and whole pages with empty speech bubbles where words would eventually go. Well, with Jason's latest decision, make that where words would never go. With his green light, that would have been someone else's job – a writer's job. Me? I'm just Sadie Walker, illustrator. I handle the art, the 'way too soon' art that apparently nobody wanted to see.

At least Jason had given the pages a good look-see. He

tried. His fingertips were smeared with pencil lead when he peeled them away from the drawings and raked them through his thinning gray hair. With a little sighing laugh I gathered up the pages and stuffed them back in my folder. I'm not sure what I expected. It's not like life was a series of triumphs these days. Just managing to eat and not smell like a sewer was a big accomplishment.

I turned to go, one corner of my drawings sticking out, a blood-drenched ax peeking at me like a winking albino eye.

'Well, thanks anyway,' I said. 'Maybe next year.'

'Probably not.'

Jason's apartment, his 'studio,' sat on the western edge of what's left of Capitol Hill in a cozy and crooked brownstone nestled against the east side of Melrose Avenue. The whole place reeked of corn beef hash from the abandoned diner downstairs. He said something I didn't quite catch as I shut the door and made my way down the cramped hall to the stairs that led into the diner's storeroom. It was empty now, stale and spotted with months-old coffee and ketchup stains. Nobody had eaten there since September, when The Outbreak started. The chairs and tables and fry baskets were still overturned from when things went bad, and the kitchen doors remained cocked open, showing the messy, pillaged shelves and countertops beyond.

With the portfolio of sketches close to my chest I stepped back outside. A stiff wind caught a few street pamphlets and sent them wheeling down Melrose; cold for April but not unbearable. March was worse, colder, and the food was leaner, making every drop of blood in your veins run a little bit slower. Nothing like hunger to intensify a chill. There were two bus lines up and running now and the pamphlets said there might even be three by the end of

April. Who could guess? Two was all we had and even that felt like a luxury.

Leaving Jason's studio, I considered just how lucky I was to still have something, however small, to remind me of what I used to be. 'Illustrator' didn't mean much now. My friend Andrea joked that I took my old job too seriously, that the only job that mattered now was survival. But I'd go mad, completely nuts without those pages, even if survival really was the only thing worth fighting for.

The view here looking down to the waterfront was mostly unobstructed. The Space Needle was still standing, of course, jilted and sad in the dark blue overcast, and the few skyscrapers we had never toppled. But entire city blocks had vanished, burned down in the panic or pulled apart afterward to make room for gardens and livestock pens. The streets used to smell like rain and earthworms, with the occasional waft of coffee or donuts from a café. Now the aroma is more *Tombstone* than *Sleepless In Seattle* – dirt, manure and decay stamped out the clean rain smell.

This early in the morning – four o'clock, to be exact – Seattle wore an eerie cast of rising purple, like an embarrassed flush, and it was easy to see why. In the chaos, big cities fared the worst. So many people, so many things to destroy and burn – it was unavoidable that the aftermath here would be bleakest. From here, miles away from the waterfront, you could still see the *Golden Princess* cruise liner in the harbor, half sunk, like a miniature city descending gradually to its demise, a white-gold Atlantis. The rumor at the time was that everyone on board the cruise perished, and not only that, but someone on board was the carrier, the undead transmitter that spread The Outbreak to Seattle.

Looking at her now, all broken windows and crumbling stern, she seemed like a stand-in for a movie, a *Titanic* played out in small, modern scale.

At that hour the buses had started running but I hoofed it anyway. It was about a three-minute walk to the market by car, but nobody really drove. Any spare gasoline went straight to the buses. With the wind biting at me, I kept the folder and my sketches close in to the chest. They were precious – to me, at least – a blueprint, a project I'd been working at for months. I tucked the corner page with the ax down into the folder and turned up the woolly scarf around my neck, hunkering down for the mile or so walk to the market. By now the lines would be massive, but there was a hungry nephew waiting at the apartment, still asleep, if there was any justice left in the world. I couldn't be sure there was.

A few months ago, a casual walk through town to the market wouldn't have been possible. Back then, the terror of The Outbreak was still in full-swing. What was empty, stained pavement now was covered in moldering corpses, some just waiting to get up and have a second go. There were lots of strays, too, some bitten, but the virus seemed to affect animals differently. I guess their systems can't handle it the way ours can. A bitten dog would be a threat for a few short hours and then they would keel over. Some parts of town had looked like Cruella de Vil's Dumpster.

The walk to the market, unfortunately, left plenty of time to mull over Jason's chilly reception of my work. He was no stranger to me showing up at all hours with new sketches for him to peruse. Months ago, and what feels like forty million years ago, Jason was my boss, my editor. He was the only one left at the press and these days one of only three presses in the city. And when I mean press, I mean it literally – a nineteenth-century cast-iron book press. Everything he produced now was by hand, painstakingly inked and pressed, and every illustration was done by yours truly. Electricity was still unreliable so it was safer to just use the ancient press. Mostly we did what we always had – make quirky little books for kids about talking gophers and otters with adventure on the brain. There were still small kids around and they still needed entertainment.

But Jason had one rule, and it was the one rule I tried to break today: Nothing heavy.

It made sense – at least for a while – to focus on the uplifting. When your mom or dad or sister or brother had been eaten by a next-door neighbor or burned to death in a fire, it was nice to have an escapist tale about a wily, quick-thinking sea anemone outsmarting a shark. But I was hoping that Jason would be ready to try something new, something daring. So while my nephew, Shane, continued helping me think up cute stories to trade to parents for vegetables or clothes, I was leading a sort of double life, drawing what I *really* wanted to draw.

I felt a disappointed shiver, then a quiver in my lip. The panels had taken months of late nights to complete, with me bent over a row of candles, destroying what was left of my eyesight to sketch and ink a comic aimed at adults. I thought the story might give them hope in a different kind of way. But maybe Jason was right. It was too soon – too soon to be telling stories about fighting the undead, about the pain of loss and the greater pain of being betrayed by the living.

As I trooped down Boren the city came slowly to life. Lanterns behind windows sent up low, orange signal fires and men and women in Wellingtons and fingerless gloves emerged from their homes to tend community gardens. It was hard work, keeping a winter garden, and the kind of labor that got you out of bed at ungodly hours to rake mulch or repair raised beds for beets and cabbages. Too much carelessness, too much oversleeping meant someone went hungry.

Looming over the vegetable gardens, hooked to street lamps and windows, hung painted wooden signs and graffiti. THEY'RE NOT YOUR FAMILY IF THEY'RE INFECTED, read one. DO THE RIGHT THING: ALERT THE AUTHORITIES OR ANOTHER, OBSERVE THE CURFEW.

A street pamphlet careened up the street toward me, grabbing at my ankle. I paused and bent to retrieve it. The flyer, as usual, was garish – bright green paper, bold black font like a flyer for a topless bar. Impossible to miss. I read as I walked, perusing the latest news. There were radio shows and even a few television programs, but Shane and I weren't the types that could afford them. Most citizens relied on the street pamphlets to deliver their news, and the presses that provided them took an immense amount of pride in their work. It was old-school journalism. No celebrity birthdays or overdosing starlets, no CEOs fleecing their hardworking employees, just facts – weather tables for farming, locations where someone was giving away food or clothing . . .

And of course there was always at least one article about the population freaks. They preferred the term Repops or Repopulationists, a kind of religious or social group (some said cult) that feel a divine calling to repopulate the city and – I suppose in their warped minds – the world. The pamphlet was nice enough to refer to them as Repops, but everyone I knew just called them Rabbits, because all they seemed to want to do was shut themselves up in some hidey-hole and screw, screw, screw. And for months they had done just that, until the elected city council caved from public pressure and told them to cut it out. The Rabbits liked to brag about how many pregnant women they had. Then the city grew some balls and pointed out that those babies would be a major drain on city resources. Now the Rabbits didn't feel welcome and they were threatening to leave, taking with them a workforce the city – we – badly needed.

I was still perusing the pamphlet when I reached Pike Place. The hill sloping down to the fish market had become slick with misty rain and I nearly flew headlong into the line waiting for food. Not even five in the morning and already the line extended to 1st Avenue. But that was all right, I had expected that. With a hefty tote in one arm and my portfolio stuffed full of sketches in the other, I sidled up close to the stranger in front of me. Nobody was recognizable beneath their hooded sweatshirts and scarves. At this hour, even in April, a foul chill crawled up from the nearby waterfront. We might have been a horde of dock workers and clock makers and shoe shiners, a bleak Dickensian postcard of hungry people just trying to eke out a living. But it wasn't 1855, it was 2010. And we weren't recovering from an outbreak of cholera, but from The Outbreak.

But since The Outbreak things had stabilized. Stabilized. That's the word the street pamphlets liked to use – 'the situation has stabilized.' The fear was that the Rabbits leaving would upset the balance. If they stayed they would fuck things up and if they left they'd be a nuisance too. These people attracted hostility and vitriol like a corpse attracts maggots. I didn't quite get it. Couldn't they just slow down? There would be time to make babies and I couldn't see why anyone would be in such a hurry.

'Stabilized, my ass.'

The man that had gotten in line behind me had read the pamphlet over my shoulder. He had a strong Polish accent. I gave him a wan smile. 'Could be better,' I said with a shrug, 'Could be worse.'

That might've been true, at least in Seattle, which wasn't called Seattle much anymore. Back in September, when The Outbreak began, a group of firemen decided to take matters into their own hands. There was only one way to save the city, they thought, keep the living in and the undead firmly fucking out. They sealed off the city and enlisted as many volunteers as they could, and with an untold number of sandbags and cinder blocks, they had turned Seattle into what it is now, the Citadel. The waterway is still open, a meager fleet of boats still comes and goes, but there's one landroute into the city and one route out and it's guarded three-sixty-five, day and night. In December the sealing off of the city was completed and by early February the street pamphlets declared that the last of the undead had been cleared out of the city, hopefully for good. What anyone planned to do with the hideous no-man's-land just outside the city, nobody could say. All the same, Seattle – the Citadel – had become a haven, one sprawling, struggling refugee camp.

I looked at the man ahead of me – I assumed it was a man, but in the chunky sweater and hood he could've been a thickly padded mannequin – as he stamped his feet to keep the blood moving through his legs. I couldn't help but wonder where he had come from, where he lived now. He hacked a cough into the crook of his elbow. Everybody coughed. You got used to it.

The first Tuesday of every month, a caravan of trucks snaked into the one gated entrance to the city. They lumbered over to the old Pike Place Fish Market, now strictly a vegetable and food market, and dumped what ever produce they had managed to grow. The fruits and veg were sorted and carted to different stalls. The lines on Tuesdays started forming up at four or five in the morning, wending up and across the cobbled avenue leading down to the market – hundreds, thousands of people huddled together in the pink dawn glow, bags and baskets tucked under their arms.

There were fish to get as well – not the big, fatty beautiful fish we had eaten in better years but fish all the same. They came in brown paper packages, lightweight and smelling strongly of the sea – smelt and seaperch, salmon if we were lucky, cut and dried into leathery strips. A strip or two could flavor a big pot of cabbage soup and feed six or eight people. We made those packages of dried fish last all month long. The crowd was getting louder, rowdy, everyone in line shuffling anxiously, ready to get going and start their day.

'Fucking Rabbits. They haul ass out of the Citadel yet?'

I jumped, nearly dropping the street pamphlet. It was Carl, my boyfriend. He wrapped me up in a hug and I was grateful for the warmth. It's hard to hug back with so much stuff in your arms, but I managed. It was nice to see him. I felt just a little relieved to have company, a familiar face among a sea of coughing strangers. Carl, my boyfriend. Carl my boyfriend who was supposed to be watching Shane. I whirled on him.

'What are you doing here? Where's Shane?'

'Don't sweat it. Shane's with my friends.'

'*Which friends?*'

Carl shrugged, his lanky shoulders flying up around his ears like a pair of bony wings. 'Dave and Jill,' he said. 'They're cool. They work over in Queen Gardens.'

'I don't care where they work, Carl, I don't know them. You can't just leave Shane with strangers, he's not a Cuisinart!'

Shane is shy, bookish. He doesn't like strangers. He barely tolerates me, his own flesh and blood.

Carl heaved a dramatic sigh, his deep-set brown eyes rolling a complete three-sixty. I fold up the pamphlet and swatted him hard on the shoulder with it. On the back of the paper was a list of names, a lost and found of people. I was about to tear into Carl again when a fire truck rumbled by, three men in heavy rubber uniforms tucked along the ladder. They were going awfully fast for this part of town.

It was hard to stand still knowing that Shane was being watched by strangers. Trust is a commodity these days, and one I'm generally short on. I like Carl, but his parenting skills are about as sharp as a sea cucumber. I glanced back up the rising hill toward the distance, where the apartment was, the bottom floor of a stout apartment on Bell. Looking back at the market I saw the farmers had brought out the bins and the line was surging forward to push their ration papers into the farmers' hands. The front of the line disappeared into the shadow of the fish market, the coppery pig statue swarmed with hungry people with the distinctive PUBLIC MARKET CENTER crooked and straining at its hinges like an ox pushing into its yoke. I felt suddenly claustrophobic, short of breath.

'Here,' I said, shoving the market bag at Carl. 'You stay and get the food. I'll go back to Shane.'

'He'll be fine.'

'He better be.'

The ration papers were in my pocket. They stated in slanted handwriting that Shane and I, making up a family, were entitled to two bags of mixed vegetables, fruit and a packet of dried fish. These were in exchange for the beets and cabbages our family garden contributed to the city's food supply. My hand-drawn children's books don't officially rate of course, but they've helped to barter for medicine and blankets in a pinch.

'Use my papers and yours too,' I added. 'They'll be more than enough for the month.'

Shane and I didn't need much and with Carl's rations coming in too, we ate pretty well. I turned to go and Carl grabbed me by the forearm.

'I *said* they're my friends. What's the problem?'

'Just get the groceries, okay?'

I didn't feel like arguing with him, not just then, not when poor Shane was probably curled up in the fetal position, convinced that he'd been abandoned again. Shane is my sister Kat's eight-year-old. Kat and her husband were on a bus when The Outbreak hit downtown. They never made it home and voilà, just like winning a twisted game show, I became a mother to a quiet little nerd with sunshine curls and a gap-toothed, if rare, smile.

Even more people were out and about as I half-ran up 1st Avenue. Looming, burned out storefronts darkened either side of the road; a run-down strip club with greasy windows and sun-bleached posters looked as if a demolition team had gone nuts on its insides. The main

11

market still functioned as a grocer, but for basic things now – blankets and clothing and food and a few real gems, like booksellers and wine dealers. The Outbreak hit us in September. By early November, alcohol and books were at a premium. They still were, but at least now people like Jason and a few others produced new work, new books and comics.

I turned right, going more steeply up hill, away from the waterfront and toward the apartment. Most things change, but some things never did. The Olympic Mountains loomed over the Citadel, rising out of the fog, silent, stoic watchers that, on a daily basis, managed to remind me that enduring was possible. Other things, less majestic things, stayed the same too. Like the crappy all-night grocers in this part of town and the seedy bars. There was nothing to sell there now except sex with pock-marked flesh and the accompanying array of colorful diseases.

My whole body, sensing trouble, sped up. A nasty idea had occurred to me: Carl didn't have friends, Carl had customers. He dealt mainly in knives, self-defense junk, and he had a knack for finding army surplus all over town. Carl kept the knives elsewhere but the only people I'd ever seen him hang around with were in some way tied to his business. I didn't like his business, but it brought in extra food, a lot of it, and you just didn't complain about that sort of thing.

Belltown, now laughingly called Beet-town, housed entire city blocks stripped down and devoted to growing the knobby purple vegetables. It was a smart thing to grow when you had investment bankers and massage therapists tending the gardens; beets are hearty and hard to fuck up. There's another more alarming reason for the nickname: it's a rough area and Beet-town sounds a lot like its other specialty, beat downs.

Luckily, even with the dregs of the city up and stumbling out of their doorways, I was safe. People knew Carl in this part of town and so by extension they knew me. Nobody picked a fight with a man specializing in knives and they didn't bother his girlfriend either. Carl was better than a can of Mace and cheaper than a gun.

A prickly heat began rising out of the back of my scarf. I should've just waited to leave the apartment and dropped Shane off with Mrs Trieu downstairs. She didn't open her day care until after ten, giving her some time to tend her own expansive garden and do the cooking and washing for the day. Mrs Trieu charged exorbitant prices, even by post-Outbreak standards, but she was also a crack shot with a Luger and made the best Vietnamese food in ten blocks, so nobody minded. Her spotless record and tasty Pho spoke for her.

Our apartment took up the western half of one block, the eastern half reserved for the gardens. The redbrick façade was in bad shape, slender shadows falling down over the windows and front door from the ragged roof supports jutting out. Ivy had sprung up through the broken sidewalk, covering the front of the apartment with a gangrenous mossy film. Someone had taken an old Buick and turned it into modern art in the intersection, peeling open the roof and nailing lawn ornaments to it. A fat sleek crow perched on the curled car roof. Glossy black wings, slightly iridescent – crows are an illustrator's best friend; they're simple to sketch, beautiful and an instant dosage of gravitas to any frame.

Fumbling with the keys, I flung open the front door and

raced through the sand-colored empty lobby, down the hall
and up the back stairs. Our apartment sat right at the top,
around a bare two-by-four doorway, close enough to hear
the neighbors troop up and down day and night. The door
to our apartment was shut, a good sign, but the queasy
feeling in my stomach didn't ease. Inside it was dark.
The pink frills of early morning were just visible out the
windows, the sun appearing like a bright red egg yolk
behind the clouds.

I dropped my portfolio with a thud on the hardwood
floor.

'Shane?'

He never met me at the door. In fact, he was usually
hiding somewhere, either behind the mattress or in the
kitchen cupboards next to the rice. 'Shane? It's not a joke.
Come out here.'

There was a faint tinkling sound, like a distant jingle
bell. To the right, the apartment housed a cramped kitchen.
Even in the semidarkness I could see a cupboard door inch
open. I grabbed the edge and yanked.

'Shane! Oh God, Shane.' I pulled him out of the
cupboard, brushing the stray rice off his little shoulder,
and gathered him up in my arms. He didn't protest, which
was odd, and put his nose right into the crook of my neck.

'Are they coming back?' he asked in a tiny voice. He
was holding his favorite stuffed animal, Pink Bear. It was
actually a fluffy pig, but I didn't have the heart to explain
the discrepancy. Pink Bear was the star of many of our
illustrated adventures.

'Is who coming back?' I asked. 'Carl's friends?'

'They're not friends,' he whispered.

I pulled him back, smoothing the blond curls away from

his forehead, checking for bruises, signs of injury or abuse. He scrunched up his face and tried to dodge my frantic pawing.

'Did they hurt you?' I asked.

'They're not friends,' Shane said again.

A flicker of shadow passed over his face and I heard a quick intake of breath from behind us. But there was no time to react, not with a kid in my arms and my heart rate just starting to slow. Something hard and sharp hit the top of my head. I felt Shane slip and my body tip forward and the ground come for me like a swiftly rising tide. But it wasn't quite enough.

'Hit her again.'

It was Carl saying this. Carl speaking, my Carl, telling someone to knock me out. Shane's pale blond head flashed in front of me. I turned, stumbling out of the kitchen and pushing past the blurry stranger who had struck me. A black ink spill was falling over my eyes, dripping down like a liquid curtain. But I had enough of my wits to lash out with my arms, reach blindly for my nephew. He screamed. Shane never screamed – he protested from time to time quietly in his meek, middle-aged child manner, but never raised his voice above a thoughtful murmur. There was probably blood on me. Blood would make him scream.

Carl stood in the hallway, his tall, rangy body framed by the open doorway. I fumbled toward him, batting, my legs failing just in time to send me pitching forward. Carl and I tumbled out into the corridor.

'Hit her again. Jesus Christ. Hurry up!'

He slammed into the wall and grunted the air out of his lungs; my fists balled up and pressed against his chest. I grabbed him by the collar of his coat and shook and then pulled. But gravity and my aching head won, and I fell forward again, my weight sending us both toward the stairwell and the wide open arch of two-by-fours. Nothing stopped us. The stairs were suddenly there, plummeting downward, steeper than I remembered. Carl went down first, me on top, and I felt every hard crack against his spine as we toppled and rolled. I was getting nauseous, about to throw up. Everything spun as we finally found the bottom and Carl's neck, encouraged by my weight, crashed into the baseboard. The last thing I heard was a sound, an unmistakable, biological crunch as vertebrae met wood.

And then nothing and a deep tugging feeling in my chest, like I was being dragged down, like I was drowning.

TWO

The funny thing about being unconscious is that you don't notice you're passed out on top of a dead man. I didn't know that could happen. I couldn't have guessed. I slept, fitfully, not knowing how long I had been out. In the twilight sleep of pain, I heard words, terrible words that only began to make sense as I came slowly back to my senses. People came and went. Maybe they thought I was dead too. A pair of big, long-lashed green eyes stared down at me. Eyes I recognized, friendly eyes. Andrea.

'You're up,' she said.

I was laid out flat on my back, the pitted plaster ceiling with its familiar whorls and patterns overhead. Sitting on the mattress beside me, Andrea pushed a glass of water and a little blue pill into my hands. She must have moved me back up to the apartment, but I wasn't sure how. She's about my same size, petite and slight, one hundred and ten pounds soaking wet. In the back of my mind I wondered if Carl was still crumpled at the bottom of the stairs. She pointed at the pill.

'Take that. You'll feel better.'

'Shane!' I wailed. 'Is he okay?'

I knew he wasn't but I had to ask anyway. He was gone. I knew it, felt it and wondered if maybe some weak vestige of motherhood had actually begun to take root in me. That was a warm and fuzzy thought for another time. Andrea put her hand on my shoulder and squeezed.

'He's gone,' she said quietly. 'How's your head?'

'It hurts . . . it doesn't matter. He's gone. I have to find him.'

I tried to sit up but the rush of blood and feeling made me dizzy and I collapsed back down. Andrea reached over and pried my lips apart, shoving the blue pill between my teeth.

'Swallow,' she commanded, 'you'll feel better. There's not much time.'

'What are you talking about?'

With everything hurting, especially my head, Shane's loss seemed far away – blissfully distant. Eventually I would feel it clearly but right now the haziness was more than welcome to stay. She pushed at my shoulders, trying to help me into a sitting position. There was an uncharacteristic urgency in her movements.

'Up,' she said. 'We have to get you on your feet.'

'I can't. My head, it's . . . Am I okay?'

'Just a bad bruise,' she replied, pressing her fingers tenderly over the wound. I winced. 'There's a cut, too, but not deep. You've been asleep for a day.' Fidgeting, she glanced at the windows and then asked, 'Did you kill Carl?'

'No . . . I guess so,' I said, trying to remember. 'I pushed him and we fell down the stairs.'

'So that's a yes, then?'

I nodded. Andrea shrugged and popped a blue pill of her own. I had known her before The Outbreak, when she was in marketing, but now everyone in a ten-block radius knew her too. Chinese, Japanese, Russian, American – they called

18

her simply Lady Pharma, because she was more knowledge-able and better stocked than any of the functioning ration pharmacies. Pain killers, antidepressants and hallucinogens were her specialty – house calls only – but she could find virtually anything. Sometimes I was sure my surviving The Outbreak was pure luck, a fluke, but Andrea was resourceful; she didn't simply survive, she thrived.

'We have to get going,' she said. Her lips pursed with determination, she began gathering up her things, shoving orange pill bottles into a bottomless messenger bag. Outside a fire engine screamed by. Andrea pulled on a hat, a brown knit thing shaped like the best part of a muffin.

'Shane,' I said, sitting up with a grunt. 'I have to find him.'

'You won't,' Andrea replied. 'Whoever took him will be long gone.' That was Andrea – sensible, reasonable, and level-headed even when the sky was falling. 'I don't think your little tumble with Carl put a hitch in their step. They'll be out of the city by now. And pardon my fucking French, but the shit is really about to hit the fan.'

'Did you see them?' I asked.

'No, but it takes more than one person to wrangle a little kid.'

'Not Shane,' I said. Then quieter, 'Not Shane. I'm going after him.'

Andrea shrugged and leaned forward, her dark ponytail swinging as she yanked the curtains back. I gazed over her shoulder at the view down to the waterfront. I gasped. Luckily I was already sitting down. Déjà vu that potent could knock you flat on your ass. There was the city sloping down to the harbor and all of it alive with columns of smoke and fire, a picture that might've been painted straight

19

from my memory. The Outbreak. I shivered and covered my mouth, certain the retching would be soon to follow.

'How?'

'I'll explain on the way out,' Andrea said, standing. She ushered me to my feet, strapping the enormous messenger bag across her shoulder. How a person of her size managed to drag that thing around the city on foot was unimaginable. For her trouble, she had a gorgeous pair of leather all-weather boots and she could afford the kind of food Shane and I only dreamed of. Sometimes she shared. She always treated us well.

Us. Shane. I had to find him.

Andrea went to the shallow walk-in closet and pulled open the accordion-style doors. With a sharp eye she found the heaviest coats and sweaters I owned and tossed them into a garbage bag. Standing was difficult, but I managed it with a wincing sigh. There was more than just the painful wound on my head. The tumble down the stairs with Carl had left me as tender and soft as a bruised pear.

The room spun as I gained my feet and the reality of Shane's situation crashed down with sickening force. Kidnappings were not unheard of. Most things change, but some things never did, like humans just having to fuck up a damn decent thing. So even when the city was 'stabilized' and most people could eat and sleep safely, there were those, like the Repops, who had to tamper and tinker and have things their way.

These people didn't have a name but their shadowy presence lingered over children, like a boogey man or witch woman from a story your grandmother told. Thousands of newly childless parents meant there was a booming black market for children, especially cute, smart children like

Shane. There was no trail of crumbs through the forest, no promise of candy, just coldhearted thieves dealing in babies. If a loon spotted a child that reminded them of their own, the next week they might pay to have that very same kid for themselves. A replacement, a flesh and blood Barbie doll. This wasn't supposed to happen to us – having Carl around was supposed to *prevent* a kidnapping, not guarantee one.

Someone had paid dearly for this kidnapping and it was almost a relief to think of the price Carl himself had paid. *Almost* a relief. Relief didn't bring Shane back, nor did it change the fact that I had screwed up, royally screwed up and let down my sister, wherever she may be.

'Shane will be safe,' Andrea said, reading my mind and my crestfallen face. 'You don't go through the considerable trouble of kidnapping a kid to make his life miserable. He's probably safer than we are, so let's get a move on.'

'How?' I asked again, still stunned. Andrea tossed a coat over my shoulders. She had stripped me down to a long-sleeve T and thermal underwear when she moved me to the bed. Now it was time to get dressed, time to care. Andrea knelt and helped me pull on a pair of jeans and then an oversized wool sweater. She tossed the garbage bag full of clothes into my arms and made for the door. Her boots crunched. My portfolio. Months of work. My drawings.

'Stop,' I said, blindly reaching to gather up the sketches. I stuffed them into the torn folder and clutched it to my chest.

'Just the basics,' she said, clearly disapproving. 'Ya know – food? Clothing? Booze?'

'I can't leave them.'

'Fine. Jesus.'

21

Fussing like a mother hen, she shooed me out the door and down the hall, pointedly away from the back staircase and – logically – Carl. As if seeing his dead body would bother me. The smell might, but the rage was still a big, ugly knot in my chest and the thought of Carl rotting in a shitty apartment stairwell made me feel absolutely nothing.

I wasn't prepared for the panic outside. The streets were full, crowded with shoving, frightened strangers. I kept close to Andrea, following her dark ponytail through the turmoil in the streets. The drawings kept slipping out of the folder and so finally, frustrated, I pushed them into the garbage bag of clothing. Judging from the smell, Andrea had thrown some dried fish in there too.

Another fire engine shrieked by, red lights flashing like blood-soaked flashbulbs.

'The Rabbits,' Andrea said by way of explanation. I pulled up close to hear her. Even weighted down with her pill pack she moved at an amazing clip. 'They finally had enough. They broke through the Queen Anne barrier with a dump truck. Barrier's thin up in those parts,' she said, barreling over a man twice her size. 'The undead could smell them so they were congregated outside – waiting, I guess. You remember last time.' I did. 'Just takes one inside the city and boom, there goes your stabilization.'

There was that word again. I was really beginning to hate it.

'Not so easy to flee this time,' Andrea went on. 'With the barriers up, everyone is trapped. It's a goddamn buffet.'

That put a bounce in my step. In this case, being small had its advantages. We sliced through the panicking crowd quickly, squeezing into spaces bigger people couldn't manage. Nobody seemed to have any destination in mind, just milling and screaming. A few groups peeled off, heading toward the nearest bus stop. Others fled south, toward the Citadel gate. I realized with a jolt that we most definitely had a destination in mind – Andrea had a destination in mind; she was leading me down to the waterfront.

Water . . . Boats . . . Suddenly that bounce in my step was gone. Andrea was Portuguese. Her whole family was Portuguese and lifelong mariners. She was full of amusing stories about their rollicking maritime adventures, but those tales always had the comforting hallmark of fiction. But it was in their blood, Andrea said so herself whenever we ate fish, which was often, and so her intentions were suddenly, horribly, as clear as a funeral bell.

'No,' I said, shaking my head. 'I won't get on a boat, I won't. It's suicide.'

Andrea grabbed me by the scruff of my sweater and hauled me forward, apparently unmoved by my protests.

Ever since The Outbreak there was a general fear of going out on the water. Ironic, considering Seattle got its legs from being a port. But that changed when half the city tried to flee the first time across the water. One ferry managed to depart without any undead onboard. It never came back, staying across the sound, anchored at Bainbridge Island. The scourge reached Bainbridge eventually, through other means. The other ferry never left port. Its skeletal shell still floated at the ferry terminal, empty except for a few brave squatters. Even now, months after the initial panic, boats washed up against town, their poor owners starved to emaciated science projects or missing altogether. And sometimes – very rarely – a skiff landed with a crew of undead playing pirates in the hold. There was the *Golden Princess*, too, still upended in the harbor, a stark reminder of what might happen to those foolish enough to take their chances on a boat.

The terror those stories had instilled in me was not to be overlooked. How do you commit yourself to the waves knowing the terrible fate of so many others? A boat, the sea, the isolation and uncertainty – to me it meant only death.

'It's suicide,' I said again in a whisper. Not that it mattered. I had failed in my one simple task – protect Shane, give him a safe and healthy life. That wasn't the kind of failure you brushed off, like losing a wager or a favorite scarf. Maybe slow and inevitable starvation or death by zombie sailor was exactly what I deserved.

'Would you relax?' Andrea barked, dodging down an alley and then another. 'I know somebody.'

Of course she did. Uncle Arturo, Uncle Tiago, Uncle Whoever, every single one of them had salt in their blood and sand in their beards. They each owned a boat and lived and died by the whim of the waters.

I stumbled to a stop. I had to blink a few times just to make sure I was seeing what I *thought* I was seeing. Just down the hill, running horizontally across the road Andrea and I were sprinting down, was an achingly familiar head of blond curls, and they were bouncing and Shane was screaming, because two strangers were frittering him away to some gosh-darn *lucky* couple. They must have been holed up somewhere nearby before delivering Shane and now they were making a run for it because of this new Outbreak. There wasn't a lot of logic to it, the way I peeled off from Andrea and charged down the hill toward them, but in that instant logic ranked a distant second to desperation. Andrea spun, just out of reach to grab me and pull me back.

'Sadie! God*damn* it, Sadie!' But she was running after me; I heard her heavy footfalls just inches behind.

Shane must have seen me coming, because he started screaming harder, little mouth opening up like a sink drain to bellow out another round of terrified shrieks. I'd never in my life heard him make that sound. It's always the small, shy ones, the ones you least expect, who can really belt it out. Improvising, I stooped to pick up a tire iron abandoned next to some poor soul's crumpled body. They looked old and frail. They had been trampled by the crowd. That same crowd pushed against me, a tide rushing down to the riverfront, slowing down Shane's kidnappers but hindering me too. His arms reached out to me, his body slung over a slender man's shoulder like a sack of grain. There was a gap in the horde of people streaming down to the water and I had my chance. With Andrea pelting behind me, shouting at me to slow down and let her help, I broke into a sprint, catching up to the two kidnappers just as they reached the alley. Lungs burning, head pounding, I wound up over my left shoulder, still running as I took a golf swing with the tire iron. The bearded man carrying Shane glanced back at the same instant. Thank God for Andrea, who caught up in time to screech to a panting halt, throwing out her arms for Shane and scooping him up as I cracked the man's skull. He went headfirst into the pavement.

The bearded guy's partner whirled, a heavyset woman with a pale, round face and caramel-colored hair.

'Danny!' she screamed, watching her partner roll uselessly on the pavement, blood pooling beneath his head.

'You *bitch*! I'll kill you for that.' She pulled a switchblade, the sharp edge flashed, serrated and mean.

Andrea, more streetwise and ballsy than yours truly, grabbed the tire iron out of my hand and shifted Shane into my arms. I took a giant step backward, sheltering him from the squat little goblin woman and her partner. The bearded man flopped onto his side, as far as he could make it with his skull cracked. Laughing softly, Andrea pulled out a twelve-inch blade from the belt at her waistband. Apparently Carl was good for something. She held up both the tire iron and the knife, showing them to the woman as if this was *The Price Is Right* and these were her fabulous prizes.

'Start running,' Andrea muttered. 'I'll catch up.'

But there was no need. The woman took one last stuttering step and then turned on her heel, leaving her friend to wallow on the cold, wet pavement. He shouted after her, wild, inarticulate, and Andrea laughed again, shrugging as she tucked the knife back into her waistband. She threw one glance over her shoulder to make sure there were no undead bearing down on us yet. 'I should take your balls for what you did,' she muttered, spitting at his feet, 'but I've got a boat to catch and with that head injury you're zombie chow.'

Even so, she couldn't resist aiming a swift kick at his groin. He hardly seemed to feel it, stunned from the hard blow to his head.

Andrea led us back out onto the street, where the crowd had transformed into a headless mob. Shane swung onto my shoulder, piggyback, silent and trembling as we trotted down toward the waterfront. There would be time to explain everything to him later, but getting the hell out of dodge was priority one. We were getting closer, the slope down to the waterfront steeper by the second. A scream rang out like a gunshot from down the street. If this was the sequel to The Outbreak, then we were flaunting convention and getting to the harrowing climax in act one. It wasn't possible. It was too fast. If the undead were already at the harbor then escape, by any means, could be impossible. The Queen Anne barrier was not close by, which meant the undead were multiplying at alarming speed.

A fire engine and its whining sirens roared by, flattening a stop sign. Another scream and Andrea didn't need to tell me to hurry it along anymore. We turned north and then crossed Alaskan Way. The salt tang of the harbor and the squawking of seagulls announced the proximity of the water. As if that weren't enough to send my heart rate sky-rocketing, out of the corner of my eye I spotted something hunched and ragged lumbering toward us.

'Andrea!'

'I see it.'

Another creature appeared behind the first, his face collecting in an oozing pile around his jaw bones. Andrea broke into a run, brandishing Carl's knife but not moving to use it. I followed, the garbage bag over my shoulder knocking against my spine, Shane clutching my neck hard enough to choke.

I saw now that we were late to the party. Hundreds, maybe thousands of mismatched people converged on one tiny strip of land, like Ellis Island, if Ellis Island – at its peak – had been wreathed in flames. One woman ran by in a bathrobe and hiking boots, a tiny baby bouncing in her arms. Nobody was in charge. Here and there someone would bellow an order or try to conduct the flow of foot traffic, but the panic had set in. Months of carefully managed fears meant nothing now, not when a hoard of hungry flesh eaters had you surrounded.

Then someone seemed to get the idea to head for the ferry and suddenly *everyone* was heading for the ferry. I'd seen that kind of behavior before, in September, when a crowd of strangers all at once came to a conclusion together and nothing, not common sense or a rifle, could stop them. Andrea pushed against this current, leading me north up the sidewalk and away from the surging crowd. For a moment I questioned her sanity, noticing that going north also meant facing about three times as many undead stragglers. Empty fish-and-chips diners and seaside hotels broke out along our left like jagged teeth. We tore ourselves away from the main body of citizens and tumbled out onto an empty strip of pavement. It was easier to simply bat the undead aside with our heavy packs; stopping to actually decapitate them would take too long.

The thin masts of sailboats appeared, stabbing upward from the docks, limp sails fluttering on the boat decks like huge, white feathers. Gray morning gave way to silver as Andrea veered left, down a sloping cement embankment to a staircase and the docks themselves. The boards were slick. A cluster of people stood at the far end of the dock, their backs to us. Andrea sped up, clattering down the dock with her messenger bag bouncing and rattling. Close on our heels, dragging themselves down the embankment, came a handful of the undead, moaning as if to complain about our pesky ability to outrun them. That boat had better be ready to launch because, one way or another, Shane and I were getting on it. The choice between staying on the dock and shoving out onto the water was not much of a choice at all.

'There better be room,' I muttered, mentally taking a head count of the people on the dock. There were eight, not including us, and the boat in question didn't look big enough for that many passengers. Andrea grunted something under her breath. She elbowed to the front of the crowd, me close on her heels. Shane clasped his little arms around my neck more tightly, whimpering. A short, stocky man was piling up a stack of ration cards in his stubby hands. Bribes. Apparently Uncle Arturo was as enterprising as his drug-dealing niece. He glanced up from his counting and frowned.

'*Tio*,' Andrea said, slipping into Portuguese. She nodded to her bag full of drugs. His small black eyes twinkled in response. He reached up and scratched his scalp and adjusted his newsboy cap. Incredible. He didn't seem to notice or care that the zombies shambling down the dock were gaining ground. The old Portuguese sailor nodded and stuck his thumb over his shoulder.

'Sadie and Shane,' Andrea said, pointing at me. 'This is Uncle Arturo. Everything's kosher.'

Everything? That was one way to put it.

Stuck in the uncomfortable emotional wasteland between relief and terror, I sighed and followed Andrea onto the boat. Shane squirmed, sharing my unease about being out on the water. The boat was in remarkable condition, the wood still gleaming, the navy and white paint fresh and bright.

'Fifty-one-foot Formosa center cockpit Ketch,' Andrea announced, running her hand along the polished wood railing, admiring it like a piece of fine art. A Portuguese thing, I guessed. 'Isn't she beautiful?'

She was, but it seemed odd to be discussing this as if we were going out for a pleasure cruise, especially when the shouting started. Andrea, Shane and I had displaced passengers who had already bribed Arturo for a ride. What he planned to do with ration cards on a boat, I couldn't guess. It was the principle of the thing, I suppose. Arturo shoved the unlucky ones away, back toward the end of the dock. A pretty woman in bloody nurse's scrubs burst into tears. This seemed to make Arturo change his mind and he grumbled and nodded toward the boat. The nurse climbed aboard, still sobbing, as the other 'chosen ones' joined us.

Arturo scrambled up the plank resting against the edge of the boat and then kicked it over the side, stranding four poor souls at the end of the dock, their mouths falling open as they quickly realized the extent of their predicament. The outboard motor roared to life. I turned away, lurching back and forth as Arturo ran up the sails and the boat rocked. Screams followed us out onto the water, screams that died down to resigned groans. I grabbed Shane's ankles as he let go of my neck to cover his ears. He whimpered. A splash. Someone had jumped off the dock. They paddled toward us, gulping down seawater as they fell farther and farther behind. The water out in the bay had grown foggy, the color of dishwater.

Someone tugged on my sweater sleeve. Andrea was beside me, her messenger bag now resting on the deck, wedged between her knees. Arturo was shouting in Portuguese, to us or himself, I couldn't tell. Splashing . . . screaming . . . blood thundering in my ears as I tried to take in the panic and confusion. Back south, at the terminal, the ferry had drifted out into the bay, white and green and tiered, like an enormous rusted layer cake drifting into the fog. But this cake was on fire, pouring with smoke and going slower by the second. I couldn't imagine what was worse – jumping into the deep, freezing bay to escape the fire or burning to death while the ferry began to sink.

'Jesus Christ,' Andrea muttered, reaching for her floppy cap.

The ferry stopped in the middle of the bay, distant screams accompanying the shadows that flickered down over the side as desperate passengers jumped.

'Still wish you were on land?' Andrea asked.

'Thanks,' I said. 'We owe you one.'

'Sure.'

I looked at her, tired of looking at the ferry, at carnage. We had trusted each other the moment we met. It was at a bar years ago. We were both single, flirting with our thirties, both tipsy and trying to fend off the horny sharks circling the dance floor. Maybe I felt I could trust her because, in many ways, we're very similar, even physically. Both of us are petite, with dark, straight hair. She keeps hers in a long, no-nonsense ponytail and I cut mine in a messy, banged Louise Brooks bob. We both have pale, almost aqua-colored eyes. Her face is more severe and angular, like a fox's, with a pointed nose and mine is softer – more elfin, I suppose.

'It's not all bad,' Andrea said with a sly smile. I didn't see how that could be true. She nodded discreetly to the space over my right shoulder. Behind us, two men stood together, their hands on the railing of the deck as they watched the ferry go down in the middle of the harbor. One was young, just a teenager, the other was in his mid-thirties. I rolled my eyes and glanced over my shoulder at Shane, silently warning her. Luckily, Shane seemed to be slightly less anxious now that we had left the dock without sinking. I squeezed his hand and let him down like a monkey from my shoulders.

Andrea shrugged, staring stubbornly at her quarries. They were all hers. With Shane to worry about, I didn't have the energy to think about making a love connection.

'Please tell me you mean the grown-up,' I said to Andrea, hoping that would be the end of that.

'Don't be such a prude,' she said.

As we set out into the harbor there were seven of us onboard – myself, Andrea, Shane, Uncle Arturo, the nurse with the round, pretty face, the teenage boy Andrea had pointed out and the tall man in his thirties. The air was crisp and clammy with the fog. I had always had a fear of drowning and it took most of my energy to forget that the shore was becoming more of a shaggy line than a crisp silhouette. I nuzzled my nose down into the oversized neck of my sweater and watched my fellow passengers mill around. Only Andrea and her uncle seemed to know how to conduct themselves casually on the boat.

As Andrea and I watched, the tall man strode over to the main mast and introduced himself to Uncle Arturo as Moritz Kellerman. He pumped the old mariner's hand with exuberant gratitude. Mr Kellerman looked as if he'd just gotten off the boat at Ellis Island – not the one on fire behind us, but the actual historical one – dressed for a journey from another time. Of any of us, he seemed the most out of place, dressed in ponderously formal clothing, a brown tweed suit with a looped scarf and teal dress shirt. He wore loafers and carried a handkerchief where a pocket square would go. Stranger still, his hair was longish, caramel brown and swept behind his ears. I hadn't seen a man with hair longer than an inch or two in months. For hygiene's sake, most guys kept their hair very short, even buzzed. Bald-headed men with beards abounded. Kellerman's brown patchy coat was pushed up to his elbows, showing curiously hairy forearms and artistic hands. He walked away from Arturo to take a seat on a stack of life jackets and tripped on a loose piece of rigging. He swore under his breath in German.

Andrea followed my gaze. She chuckled. 'Nice,' she said, POV rooted firmly in the gutter. 'Very nice. I'd lick him on three sides.'

'Not me,' I said. I was off men. Maybe permanently. Fuck you very much, Carl. 'And keep your voice down,' I added, nodding toward little Shane, who didn't need to know about Andrea's sexual ethics, or lack thereof.

Shane leaned against the railing, peering down into the waves. Almost automatically, I pulled him back, a vision of him plummeting into the water below flashing in front of my eyes. He frowned in protest, the baby fat still clinging desperately to his cheeks settling down around his chin.

'Stay back,' I told him gently. 'Or hold my hand if you're going near the rails, okay?'

He nodded, took my hand and proceeded to sidle immediately up to the edge of the boat.

'Looks like he's got your number,' Andrea said smilingly.

I gave his hand a pinch. 'That true?'

With a shrug, Shane looked away and put his free hand on the rail. I was used to the silent treatment with him, but it made me nervous. There was nowhere on this stupid canoe to take him and have a private sit-down. I would just have to keep a close eye on his subtle mood shifts, which generally swung between broody and broodier.

Andrea elbowed me, apparently unconcerned by Shane's willful silence. She nodded toward Moritz. Fantastic. I was stuck there with not one but two children. Under different, more relaxing circumstances I could see where the German could be considered handsome. He was lean and long-faced with thick eyebrows and a prominent, crooked nose. On another man that nose would be hideous, but he wore it well. And there was that lingering sense of the old world, almost as if he were a ghost or a gentleman. Ha. Those didn't exist anymore. I don't mean that in the bitchy, girly magazine male-trashing way. I mean there simply wasn't room for chivalry anymore. Survival was everything and opening doors and pulling out chairs didn't mean much when you were starving or dying of pneumonia.

Mr Kellerman glanced up at us his with bright, frank eyes. I looked at my toes, embarrassed. Andrea danced her fingertips at him like a true born-and-bred minx.

After a while I couldn't stand to do nothing. I went to find Arturo, sure that I could at least pull on a rope or something. Shane came along. He seemed to perk up a bit at the thought of meeting the sailor again or at least being offered a distraction. It wasn't hard to guess why – Arturo did have a mythic sort of presence, weathered and lined, like a character out of a pirate story. Rigging, sails, that was about the extent of my seafaring knowledge. I'd paddled a canoe or two in my time, but that didn't exactly count. If it wasn't in *Master and Commander* I didn't know about it. We drifted north, hitting a strong current, and sailed by Queen Anne – with its dense atmosphere of smoke – and passed the Olympic Sculpture Park. A red spidery sculpture watched us from the hill top, abandoned and absurd in the rising fog.

Arturo split his time between dashing down into the covered cockpit of the Ketch and barking orders in broken English at the teenage boy. I learned that his name was Noah and that he also knew next to nothing about sailing. He did his best, his dark, curly head bobbing up and down as he tried to follow Arturo's directions, the old man's chosen assistant. It wasn't obvious whether the position was voluntary or not. I sidled up to the Portuguese sailor. He – or actually his bushy beard – smelled strongly of stale cigarettes and port wine. Shane hid behind me, peeking out around my arm to stare shyly up at Arturo.

'Anything I can do to help?' I asked.

'Don't worry. Not so hard for us. Straight,' Arturo said in his heavily accented English. He made a hatchet blade out of his hand and chopped it in a vaguely northern direction. 'Straightforward, very easy,' he said, and then again, 'don't worry. Very straightforward.'

Glancing at the maze of inlets and islands ahead of us, navigation looked about as straightforward as a bag of snakes. Peering down into the cockpit, I was temporarily cheered by the sight of fishing rods, wine bottles, tampons (Andrea's influence there, I hoped) and a stack of plastic-wrapped white bread. Arturo lit up a cigarette with a match.

'You go sit,' he said. 'Take care of boy.' He tried to smile, his square, pointed badger face breaking out into a series of wrinkly crags. 'You feel sick, you do your business over the side. Into the water.'

Well, gee thanks, Art, without your timeless wisdom I might have just barfed on my shoes instead.

When I ducked back out from behind the cockpit,

Andrea was already busy making conversation with the German man. His long legs were stretched out in front of him, his trouser legs hiking up to reveal woolly green socks bunched into his loafers. Nobody wanted to talk to the blood-covered nurse – for obvious reasons – who was still crying quietly in a lonely corner of the boat. She had a wild head of raspberry red hair, swept out of her face with a banana clip. For some reason, the sight of her reminded me of what we had lost – our apartment, our day to day, our offbeat little home . . . I felt my own tears coming on and fumbled for the deck railing.

Now wasn't the time to break down. The Citadel was becoming a vague pattern of grays and browns in the heavy cover of fog. It was disappearing behind us. The wind rushed in around us, ruffling coats, mussing hair, making Shane cuddle against me more fiercely. It should have been exhilarating, liberating, but the urge to cry persisted.

Wait for night, I thought. Don't cry in front of the kid. Wait until nobody's looking.

THREE

Finding privacy on a sailboat is like finding a Starbucks in the desert. You might desperately want it to happen, you might wish upon a star, but you're better off accepting that you're going to die, and not with a soy latte in your hand either.

The first afternoon on the sea I got sick. Tremendously sick. Green-faced, projectile vomit seasick. This was an excellent first impression. Somehow, the little boy with the picky appetite was just peachy, but I felt like I had swallowed a live eel. Not surprisingly, I wasn't alone in suffering from this affliction. The German, Moritz Kellerman, was seasick too.

I didn't expect to step onto the boat and become the designated tribe leader. Arturo, rightly, was in charge. His boat? His rules. But I know a thing or two about survival – not just because I was still alive and kicking despite zombies and food shortages and little-boy tantrums, but because my dad was the consummate outdoorsman. You can't live in the northwest and not catch the bug to hunt, fish, camp or hike at some point. My dad, Alan (but come on, who really calls their dad by his first name?) was your typical weekend warrior. Which is why it's more than a little surprising that he's . . . well, not still around. Sore subject? Yeah, you could say that. Because everyone just loves talking about their parents' untimely demise, right? And yes, I said *parents*, plural.

Pardon the sidebar, but it's now or never, or rather five empty pages while I collect myself and stop bawling like a tween outside Joe Jonas's dressing room. Dad – Alan – no, *Dad*, liked to hitch up the trailer to the SUV on weekends and head for the nearest patch of prime camping ground. He rarely, if ever, washed that stupid trailer. Mom would get on his ass about it, asking why he insisted on leaving a grubby, mud-splattered disaster zone in the garage. There was limited space in there, and she didn't want it taken up by what ultimately looked like an overflowing toilet. I was on my dad's side in this. I *liked* that the trailer was messy and rugged. I liked showing my grade school friends, swaggering into the garage under the pretext of getting a kickball and just *happening* to show them how totally outdoorsy and badass my dad was. And how cool was it that sometimes I got to go with him? Street cred. I had it.

He taught me about making fires, tying knots, all of the father-daughter bonding a former Boy Scout can stomach. Or are you a Boy Scout for life? Who knows? Anyway, Mom approved of this, to an extent, despite the fact that it meant putting up with a grungy trailer and more poison ivy rashes than you can shake a bottle of calamine lotion at. It was *our* time, and through mosquito invasions that made Normandy Beach look tame and collapsing tents and overcooked, cindered hot dogs, I learned to love it. It was misery as entertainment. Survival as badge of honor. Like one of Pavlov's dogs, the less I grumbled on these trips the more swag I got from Dad upon returning home. If I was quiet and uncomplaining there was Dick's Drive-In for me on the way back, and that's massive motivation for any little kid. Or anyone. Period.

But my dad was always better at the whole camping thing, more of a natural. He could put a stale Swedish Fish on the end of a line and haul in a ten-pound whopper. Me? I could bait that sucker with the highest quality lures, night crawlers and worms and fucking *diamond* earrings around and I wasn't going to get so much as a nibble. Thems the breaks, I guess, but it leaves a mark. I was never as in tune with nature as my father. He couldn't draw to save his life, which always amused me and was one tiny thing for me to gloat about, but damn it if he didn't seem like Paul Bunyan and Grizzly Adams and all those legendary woodsmen rolled into one. Mom accompanied us on these trips occasionally, but just like me, she didn't have that survivalist gene. It was Dad's area of expertise and he embraced it with the power of a thousand REI employees.

And Dad should have made it and Mom, too, but that's another story with another chance to send me into paroxysms of weepy regret.

More important than my seasickness or wishing my father was there to help, was making sure Shane wasn't one foot over the line of irreversible trauma. A quiet kid to begin with, it just didn't seem likely that he would take being kidnapped and seeing Andrea and me going berserk well. And really, the sort of person who *did* take that kind of thing well would probably grow up to become a serial killer. Lucky for me, he wasn't exactly hard to keep an eye on when trapped on a tiny boat. Well, that and the huge mess of curls on his head made him easy to spot from outer space. Or from an inch away, where he stood endearingly fused to my hip. Absence, however short, makes the heart grow even fonder, and in this case that meant fond to the point of paranoia. I was beginning to construct a giant papoose in my head, one big enough to put Shane in and strap him to my back for life.

Fighting the urge to stick my head in a paper sack and never emerge again, I knelt next to Shane, catching my balance and groaning from the rocking of the boat. 'So I'm not feeling great,' I said, putting my thumb over his cheek where, in better times, a dimple would go. 'But I want to make sure you're all sorted before I have a lie-down. Are you . . . Do you need a snack? We managed to save some stuff from the apartment.'

Shane shook his head, paused, shrugged. My heart broke a little. What kid turned down a snack? Wasn't there a rule somewhere in the parenting handbook that children, when presented with food, would always, always go for it?

'No? You sure? Maybe some water . . . It's good for you, bud. You need to stay hydrated.'

He knew what that meant. Hydration was part of the everyday vernacular now, even for eight-year-olds.

'Okay,' he whispered, quirking his tiny lips to the side.

'Good deal. Let's do it.'

Standing up proved a bit of a challenge. My stomach rolled, my eyes right along with it. Managing my own health and looking after Shane was not going to be easy.

Andrea, always the pragmatist, saw me teetering on my feet and intervened.

'I was getting him some water,' I mumbled, clutching my middle.

'You sure? You're looking about ten shades of green . . .'

'I've got it.'

I could handle this. I had to. Taking Shane's hand, I

stumbled forward, leading him toward the lowered cockpit and the supplies stacked up inside. The wind whipped at us, snapping the sails and ruffling Shane's curls. Just a few steps and we would be there. Shane clung to my hand, his fingernails digging into my palm like talons. Yeah. No. The kid needed to see things were okay, that his surrogate mom wasn't going to drop dead of seasickness any second. And maybe things weren't okay, but that wasn't the point. For now, he had to believe that we adults had our shit together. We *would* have our shit together and I would make that happen one way or another, no matter how bitchy and Momzilla I had to become.

'Here we are,' I chirped, putting on a strained smile. My guts seemed to be having a jolly good time settling down, tricking me into thinking I was all better before they tossed like a dingy in a gale. 'Water, food, blankets, stunning, brilliant artwork . . . all the fine amenities in life.'

Shane shrugged. Tough crowd. I could do better.

'Boats are pretty awesome,' I said conversationally, rummaging in Arturo's cooler for a cup. There were several, all with naked ladies on them. Class act, that guy. I settled for Styrofoam, not optimal but better than faded titties and plastic smiles. 'Maybe you can learn how to sail . . . I bet Arturo would teach you. And the other folks look nice, they can help out too.'

Shane nodded. One point. I could do this.

I rested against the edge of the cockpit while Shane drank his water. He gulped it down in one impressive go.

'Slow down, okay? Tummies can get a little messed up on boats.' No kidding. 'More?'

Another nod. At least it was communication.

Moritz Kellerman was getting a head start on the race to

see who could empty their stomach the fastest. Hearing the dulcet tones of his vomiting in the background reminded my gut that it was slacking on the painful convulsions.

'Are you all right?' Shane asked, blinking up at me and moving to the side, preemptively dodging whatever I horked up.

'I just . . . need to sit. You can come with, but it might be pretty . . .' My stomach gurgled audibly. '. . . gross.'

Shane finished his water and peered around me, his eyes shifting between Kellerman and me as if determining the likelihood that one of us would vomit on him if he came along. But he came with, the champ, taking my hand and leading me to the edge of the boat. I couldn't help but grin a little. It wasn't so bad to be looked after, even just for a brief moment. Shane joined the quarantined at the stern of the ship where the bouncing was felt less prominently and where a noticeable funk was beginning to settle.

Your personal bubble space quickly breaks down when you're confined to a four-by-four area with another human being. Instead of swapping stories or anecdotes, Mr Kellerman and I swapped guttural heaving noises and despairing groans as we fell back to the deck, temporarily relieved only to be nauseous again ten seconds later. Poor Shane put up with it, sitting cross-legged and staring up at the seagulls, maybe willing one to swoop down and carry him away from all the puking and complaining.

What do you think of when you think of boats? Romance? Adventure? Tasty fishes? None of the above for me, thanks. Just barfing and tons of it.

Moritz and I spent the night flat on our backs, me half-hysterical and him making pathetic whimpering noises whenever another harsh wave rocked the sailboat and, by extension, our queasy insides. Shane slept a safe distance away, the blanket pulled over his head, probably to protect from the unattractive sounds we were making.

Ah, the sea – the salt tang of the swift and freeing wind, the spray of the water, the chatter of playful otters and the incessant clutching of your stomach as you will that tiny bit of bread to stay down, please Jesus and all the holy saints, just stay down.

I didn't sleep much. In the morning it got a little easier and I dozed, flickering in and out of consciousness. My teeth were fuzzy, probably growing Christmas trees by now, and that unmistakable soup-smelling miasma of vomit hung around my face and neck. It was predawn when I woke for good, too disgusted with myself to fall back asleep. I glanced to see if Shane was up, but he was still dozing peacefully. Mr Kellerman was sitting up, his knees clasped to his chest. He watched the first hints of sunlight playing over the eastern fringes of the mountains.

'What a view,' I said, surely sounding more cheerful than I felt. He nodded.

'I was lost for a moment,' he replied. 'I thought I was nine years old again, waking up and seeing the Alps outside my window.'

'Where was home?' I asked. This was a usual question. Everyone had shifted around so much in The Outbreak that we were all transplants, orphans.

'Zurich,' he said softly. His voice was cultured, starched. I tried to imagine what he might have been before The Outbreak – a diplomat or perhaps a banker. He looked over at me, his dark hair swinging free of his ears. His eyes were startling up close, sparkling, as painfully earnest as a greyhound's. 'Yourself?'

'Portland,' I said, 'but I moved to Seattle a few years ago.'

He nodded, glancing back at the crackling light of first dawn. I wanted to appreciate it, but all I could think about was home, Seattle. How far had we gone? How many, what, *leagues*? Was it too late to turn back? Distracted by the seasickness, I hadn't had a chance to get that cry in. Now I was regretting it. I swallowed a thick lump and hoped Kellerman didn't hear it.

'Is he yours?' he asked suddenly.

'What?' My pulse froze.

'Shane.' Moritz nodded toward the crumpled form to my right. 'Is he your boy?'

We may have spent the night in a disturbingly intimate way, but I hadn't been given the chance to tell him much of my personal history. He seemed to read my startled expression and lowered his eyes. I stared at him, rigid. And fuck, did I really *look* like a mom? Was it bad if I did?

'He's my sister's,' I said brusquely. 'My nephew. I need some water.'

The German – or rather the Swiss – said nothing. As I stood and turned toward the cockpit, I saw him draw something out of his inner coat pocket. Maybe I'd ask him about it later, probe into his private life, poke around and make him uncomfortable. What was that in your coat? Did it belong to your son? Your girlfriend? I sighed and rubbed my forearms to get warm. He was just trying to be concerned, I decided. It wasn't his fault that I was still touchy about losing Kat and inheriting Shane, and it was logical to guess that a woman my age with a young boy would be his mother. Everyone in our neighborhood had known that Shane was my nephew and that talking about my sister was a surefire way to earn a tense silence.

I wasn't his real mom, I reminded myself for the umpteenth time, but I had to at least act like I was.

The big jug of clean water was in the cockpit, propped up beside the stack of white bread loaves. I tore off a piece of bread, softened it in a tin cup of water and ate. The sickness was abating and I hoped day two would be easier. This whole debacle was already reaching *Gilligan's Island* levels of absurdity and I was ready for a strong dose of *boring*.

Half-hidden in the cockpit, I could watch Mr Kellerman without being seen myself. His back was to me, but I could see that he was studying the object he had pulled from his coat. It was a little square of photographic paper, a Polaroid. Weird. I hadn't seen one of those in ages. Who even used a Polaroid camera anymore? Didn't they stop making those when they realized they were, ya know, completely fucking useless?

The photo was too far away for me to see clearly. He turned it this way and that, examining it from every angle and then returned it to his coat pocket. His first instinct had been to ask if I had a child, so maybe he had his . . . or a wife. I ate another piece of bread and decided to leave him alone.

We were all tender creatures now, wounded.

A pair of fluffy white seagulls floated along beside the boat, drifting up and down like paper airplanes coasting on the breeze. Drifting and coasting . . . Totally unaware that, somewhere behind us, Seattle was burning again. Did they know? Did they care? In my illustrations, animals talked. Maybe those two seagulls were carrying on a silent conversation or maybe they were just fucking seagulls, focused on fish and fish alone.

Uncle Arturo was soon up and moving about the boat. He ignored me, having his morning cigarette as he consulted a waterway map that looked like nothing but a series of loops and dots to me. The bloodstained nurse was where we left her the night before, curled up at the bow, her face pale and serious. It was too bad; she was a pretty woman and would probably break a few hearts if she learned how to smile . . . and ditched the blood-soaked uniform. Those tended to go over badly on a first date.

Andrea found me in the cockpit and we shared a hunk of bread as she yawned and rubbed the sleepiness out of her eyes. She glanced at the stern, her glittering blue eyes filled with mischief.

'What?' I asked, dreading the answer.

'So how was last night?'

'Superb. Moritz and I – he's Swiss by the way, I'm thinking of calling him my Swiss Mister – made mind-blowing love until dawn. Then he cradled me gently in his tweedy academic arms and I realized that, like the moon over the Alps, he was precious and perfect to me. And we didn't even mind that there was a *child two feet away, you moron, what the hell is wrong with you?*'

'You developed a sense of humor,' she observed, stone-faced. 'Should I be worried?'

'Not yet.'

She took a thoughtful sip of her water and chuckled to herself. That couldn't be good. 'Vomit sex, eh? I did that once. Does not bear repeating.'

'I don't know what befouled vent of hell birthed you, but I seriously hope we're sailing back there to drop you off ,' I said. 'For good.' She winked and finished her cup of water. 'I'm not joking.'

'Neither am I,' she said. 'Although that's not the worst of my transgressions.'

She was baiting me, and like a bunny staring down a hole full of carrots, I just had to leap and bite. I had no idea how apt that comparison really was. Luckily we were relatively alone, with Shane snoring softly a few yards in front of me, the blankets still pulled up over his head. 'What do you mean by that?'

'Once,' she said, lowering her voice, 'I screwed a Rabbit.'

I blinked. 'Once? Once *when*?'

'A few weeks ago.'

'And you thought this was a bright idea because . . . ?'

'Lighten up,' Andrea replied and refilled her water cup. She swirled it around like a brandy snifter. 'He was cute. Huge,' she said significantly. Then she stuck out her tongue. 'Covered in tattoos, though, weird ones.'

'Let me guess, there was a tally tattooed on him somewhere with how many women he managed to knock up.'

'Maybe,' she replied casually. 'It was dark. There was some Latin around his neck, a big rabbit on his shoulder that looked like it was on steroids.'

'So they've embraced their nickname?' I laughed. 'How forward-thinking of them. I don't suppose you used protection?'

Andrea threw back her head of long, dark hair and laughed. The floppy hat perched on her head nearly tumbled down her back. 'I'm on the pill. Big idiot thought he was getting the last laugh.'

'Well, when the syphilis develops I think he probably will.'

That was the most eventful conversation of the day. Thank God. The boat continued north, out into a broader

47

waterway, away from the tip of Discovery Park, and then farther north, north beyond beaches and coasts I had never seen and only glimpsed on a map. The rugged green outline of the shore remained more or less the same, dotted at random with buildings and homes. Shane was restless, contented only when I sat with him and said nothing as he watched the birds hovering over the water.

We needed to talk.

'What happened with Carl . . .' God, this sucked. It's always easier to self-flagellate in your mind. The shame is amplified a few hundred times when you have to say it aloud. To a kid. A kid that you let down in a big, big way. 'I made a rotten choice. I wasn't thinking straight, letting him hang around with us. Sometimes . . . adults are clumsy and make stupid decisions. We were sort of safe, I thought, and I got careless.'

Shane stared down at his hands, his fingertips red where he had picked at the nails. Just one of God knows how many neuroses brought on by my moronic behavior.

'I miss your mom and dad,' I said finally, hearing the catch in my voice. 'She wouldn't have done something so . . . so thoughtless.'

I just wanted something . . . one word . . . one indication that he didn't hate me to the core.

'It's not going to happen again.' I gestured to each compass point on the boat and lowered my voice. 'These people? We're with them, but it's really just you and me, right? They could turn out okay, but from now on I'm only going to worry about you.'

'You don't like them?' he asked, looking up at me finally.

'It's not that,' I said quickly. 'Like I said . . . they might be okay, but you matter most.'

And with that, he nodded, whispering a breathy, 'I guess that's okay,' before staring back down at his red fingers. Okay. One word. One indication. It would have to be enough for now.

It's amazing how quickly the options for diversion are exhausted on a boat. Uncle Arturo never spoke much but he was nice enough to lend Andrea and me a deck of ancient playing cards. Cross-legged on the deck, with the water swishing by and the clouds gathering overhead, Andrea and I played gin rummy when Shane decided to nap next to us. Arm's reach, I insisted – if he didn't want to play cards he would have to at least stay at arm's reach.

Sadly, there was no actual gin to accompany the rummy.

'What's the verdict on Scrubs McBloodstains?'

I glanced over my shoulder, following Andrea's eye line. The nurse – still in said scrubs, of course – sat huddled against the pointed apex of the bow. She held a patched carpet bag to her chest as if it was a buoy and we were going down. At different points during the afternoon, the young man, Noah, and Kellerman had tried talking to her. The attention only seemed to make her more withdrawn, though that didn't stop Noah from trying. It was surprising, actually. I didn't expect someone Noah's age to put that much effort into comforting the nurse. But he seemed genuinely concerned. Maybe teenagers weren't teenagers anymore, I mused, watching him crouch next to her and wait, patiently, for some kind of response. The one thing he could get out of her was a name, Cassandra. A tiny chain of islands shimmered into view and slid by behind the woman's profile.

'Something tells me we don't want to know,' I replied, looking back at my cards.

'Seems mean to just let her sit there shaking like a leaf.'

'Maybe that's what she needs.'

'We could ask if she wants to play cards,' Andrea suggested, still watching Cassandra.

'Leave her alone,' I said. 'She'll come to us if she wants to join.'

'Do *you* want to be left alone?'

I smiled down at my row of jacks. It was a good question, but I couldn't really decide. So I said, 'No, this is good' and we continued the game.

At nightfall we gathered around the cockpit and divvied up food. Andrea pulled out the cabbages and dried fish she had salvaged from my apartment. As she did, one of my sketches came out as well, stuck to the dried fish package. I grabbed it as quickly as I could and stuffed it back inside. Nobody seemed to care, but when I looked back at Arturo for a handful of almonds, Moritz Kellerman was watching me closely.

That was it, I thought, I can't hold onto these sketches. They weren't a liability, not at all; I just didn't want them anymore. It's not like they would be suddenly useful on a boat or on an island, or *anywhere*. If I couldn't say clearly to myself what they represented then there was no use lugging them around.

Kellerman's glance didn't mean much at the time, but it certainly explained things when I woke up that night to a rustling right next to my head. The garbage bag full of my sketches and clothes was open, two hairy forearms sticking out the end.

'What are you doing?'

He jumped, the flashlight wedged beneath his chin clattering onto the deck. He went for the flashlight but I was awake now, painfully awake, and faster.

When I shined the beam of light on him he froze, two pieces of paper pinched between his fingers. Busted.

'Those are mine,' I said lamely.

'I . . . I didn't mean to snoop.'

'Yes, you did.'

'Yes . . . all right, but only a very little.'

I sighed, too tired to start up a real argument. 'Here,' I said, handing him the flashlight, 'get a good long look. Tomorrow they're going overboard.'

He looked like a huge tweed grasshopper, perched over the garbage bag with his knees sticking out in opposite directions. His scarf hung down like a tongue blue with cold. Kellerman directed the flashlight's beam onto the sketches and frowned.

'Why would you ever think to destroy these?' he asked.

'Because they're total shit, that's why, and there are more important things to worry about.'

Kellerman didn't argue against that. Real encouraging. He was too busy scratching at his chin, mulling something over. It was too late for this. I wanted to curl up on my blanket again and revel in the fact that, blissfully, I was no longer seasick.

'Who is this woman?' he asked.

He had already seen everything there was to see, no use being coy. 'Allison Hewitt,' I said. 'She's um, a bit of an urban legend.'

Over the thin beam of the flashlight, Moritz stared at me unblinking. Right. Non-native English speaker – I had forgotten. 'It's like a myth, I guess, but a modern one.'

'I know what an urban legend is,' he said, curt but not irritated. He pointed at a panel with one of his long, knobby fingers. 'I know her. I've met her.'

'You've *met* Allison Hewitt?' Yeah right, buddy. 'How is that possible?'

'You've drawn her too short,' he said, ignoring the question. 'And Collin, her husband, he does not look so . . . so *fatigued*.'

'How did you meet her?' I asked, louder. He chuckled, and then glanced at the others asleep.

'They held a painting for me. So very many houses have been abandoned, and others ransacked. My colleague and I put out a general word of mouth about our services. Allison and Collin came across a Cassatt and kept it for me.'

'Cassatt? Hold on. You mean *Mary* Cassatt?'

'Yes,' he said. Then he smiled and it lit up his whole face. He pulled a Polaroid from his coat pocket and handed it to me. The flashlight beam fell on three people in front of an Impressionist portrait of a pale, lovely woman. 'Private collections have gone to ruin everywhere,' he explained, cradling the picture as if it were made out of butterfly wings. 'They were kind enough to protect this masterpiece.'

'And you have it?' I asked. Then I felt foolish, seeing plainly that he wasn't carrying around a gigantic oil canvas. But he nodded.

'In Seattle. It's at our safe house, in a bank vault on Seneca.'

I squinted down at the Polaroid. There was Kellerman – grinning like a child perched on Santa's lap – standing between a tall, vibrant man with dark hair and a young woman in a green hooded sweatshirt. Allison. She *was*

52

taller than I thought. And there was Collin Crane too. He had a salt and pepper beard. Had he always had one? I'd never considered a beard. It was like slipping downstairs early on Easter morning to find an actual giant, anthropomorphic rabbit in a pastel bowtie scattering eggs across your sofa.

'You're an illustrator,' he observed.

'*Was* an illustrator. Now I'm . . . I don't know, a castaway? First mate?'

He shook his head. 'You've rendered Miss Hewitt quite accurately,' Kellerman said. 'Have you seen images of her?'

'No,' I replied honestly. 'It was just a guess, and I had heard a few descriptions of her, rumors. I stopped following the blog after a while.'

'Why is that?' he asked.

'I had to focus on my own struggle,' I said. I don't know why I went on, maybe because finding someone who knew about Allison made us instant allies. 'It was just . . . depressing, realizing other cities weren't any better, that there was no greener pasture. I stopped caring what was happening in Philadelphia or Chicago when I was hardly eating. And then Shane dropped into my lap and I had to trade the laptop for vegetables.'

'Mm.'

That had been a bad day. I probably should've haggled harder and for more, but Shane and I were almost starving and suddenly that computer just didn't matter like it used to. Pen and paper would have to suffice.

I blinked, suppressing those cold, unfriendly memories.

'And what does a Cassatt go for these days?' I asked, changing the topic. 'Five hundred pounds of potatoes?'

'It was free, free with the understanding that I would take good care of it and see that it was safely stored until . . . Well, until it could be properly displayed again.'

A free Cassatt? This truly was a changed and frightening world. Carefully, I took the Polaroid from him. Allison beamed up at me, her hand around Kellerman's slim waist, her smile genuine and free. So it was true. Suddenly, throwing my sketches overboard in a defiant and dramatic act of purification seemed pathetic, unthinkable.

As if reading my mind he said, 'She would like to see these. Please don't destroy them.'

Maybe Jason was wrong, the pudgy jerk. There might be an audience for the comic after all.

'So is that what you do?' I asked. No one had woken up from our conversation. We were lucky to be traveling with heavy sleepers. 'You go around rescuing art? Captain Canvas?'

Kellerman began pulling more photos from his coat, handing them to me one at a time. A few of them I recognized, others were at least attention grabbing in that they were works of fine art. The water out around the boat squished against the hull, a rushing, breathing sound that made me simultaneously sleepy and energetic. For a moment, I wondered where we were going and whether or not Arturo had a destination in mind. Maybe we would drift forever. I frowned and tried to keep those thoughts at bay.

In the meantime, Polaroid photos of works by Julie Verhoeven and Piao Guangxie and others I couldn't name piled up in my hand. It was an illustrator's duty to know art, to steep in it, but it was impossible to know everything.

'I was a critic,' he said softly. That fit. 'But I don't do much criticizing anymore.'

He pointed to the photo lying at the top of a pile, a bizarre, modern canvas with very little paint and an excess of pretention. For once, I was glad I didn't know the artist. He laughed fondly under his breath.

'Oh goodness. I called that one fatuous and desperate in *L'Hebdo*,' Kellerman said. He gave a little breathy laugh and shrugged, 'But I nearly died getting it out of New York.'

I gave him a long look. 'Fatuous *and* desperate? I hadn't pegged you for a brainless leg-humper but even so, Moritz, that's really harsh. Why risk your life for something so . . . so . . .' I struggled for the word. '. . . average. I mean, if it doesn't qualify as art, why would you bother?'

Kellerman smiled, the same kind of smile he wore in his photo with Allison. I looked away, startled. 'I can't answer that. I'm not a critic anymore, I don't know what to make of any of this,' he said, 'and I think . . . I think all of the philosophers are dead.'

FOUR

'Does Uncle Arturo actually know where we're going?'

The shore, the water, the steel-bottomed clouds . . . it all looked suspiciously similar to the day before. It would be easy to lose track of the days out here and that's exactly what I became afraid of. Andrea wouldn't let me go near Arturo. She said I annoyed him and he wasn't fond of children either, which meant Shane couldn't do much but silently count shipwrecked boats along the shore. That was fine with me, in a way, because he could do that from any point on the deck and he didn't put up a fight when I insisted he stick to my side unless absolutely necessary.

Even I wasn't paranoid enough to make him use the bathroom while I hovered.

'Of course he knows where we're going,' Andrea replied, waving me away impatiently. Occasionally Shane would glance up at us, smiling wanly as if amused by the adult bickering. Before I could disturb her uncle, she cornered me against a railing where I kept one eye on her and one on Shane's still head of curls.

'Great – would he mind sharing that information with the rest of us?'

Uncle Arturo was quiet, Zen Master quiet. The man needed his boat, the water and a healthy swig of port and he was happy as a clam. Fitting, considering getting his mouth to form words was like trying to force open an oyster shell with a polite written request. His perfect paradise did not involve talking and neither did his day to day routine.

'Can't you just ask him for some details?'

Andrea was ignoring me.

'I trust him,' she said by way of explanation. 'And you should too.'

At that moment, Arturo had lowered the main sail and kicked the outboard motor to life. He was using the motor as little as possible, worried about gas consumption. He had a fuel canister in the cockpit, but using the sail was safer for us. I watched, my hands clinging to the rail, as he eased the Ketch toward a small, shadowy inlet. The sun hovered behind a gray wall of clouds, typical for the region, and just warm enough to make being out in the windy air bearable. Noah stood behind Arturo, watching him maneuver the vessel. He seemed to be the only one of us Arturo could stand, maybe because the boy seemed to be genuinely fascinated by the whole sailing thing. The two men couldn't be any more different. Noah was rail-thin, with white, peachy skin and a thick head of wavy hair. Arturo was stocky and paunchy and creased like a golden raisin.

'I was thinking . . .' I began, walking alongside Andrea as she went in search of soda. 'We've got a decent supply of food for now, but we could use more. If we did some fishing we could dry what we catch, you know, in case later times are leaner. We wouldn't have to land even . . . we could just, you know, float.' Lay anchor? Put in? Fuck it. Subway cars are more seaworthy than yours truly.

'That's not a bad idea,' Andrea said. She turned to her uncle, calling to him in Portuguese. I knew a bit of Spanish and it was similar enough in spots that I could make out her suggesting the fishing thing. Arturo considered the idea, chewing on the end of his cigarette with one brow in the air. Then he called something back, trundling down into the cockpit.

'He has to bait the line, but I think he's happy for an excuse to do something new.'

'It'll be a nice change of pace,' I said lightly. 'Instead of doing nothing on a slowly moving boat, we'll do nothing on a completely motionless boat.'

'Have a drink,' Andrea suggested, straightening her ponytail. 'Or is Auntie Flow paying Auntie Sadie a visit?'

'Language,' I hissed. Shane smiled, just a little, but enough to demonstrate the fact that he had clearly heard Andrea, and maybe even understood her. Damn it. The last thing I needed was those two making an unholy alliance.

I glanced at the water. It didn't look *inviting* exactly, but it did have a certain allure about it, exclusively because we were all beginning to smell. 'I could seriously use a bath,' I muttered, thinking aloud. 'It's not too choppy out there . . .'

'Go in,' Andrea said laughingly. 'There are no sharks around these parts. Scout's honor.'

'A fear of water is totally rational,' I said. She snorted. 'Well, it *is*. There could be anything down there . . . like . . . like . . .'

'Fish? Seaweed?' She gasped, covering her mouth with both hands. '*Algae?*'

'Now you're just trying to provoke me.' We would all have to wash up eventually, and who better to prove to

Shane that there was nothing down there to fear than someone who had a totally normal and rational fear of drowning?

'You really think it's safe?' I asked, peering over the edge of the boat at the water.

'Sure,' she replied, 'but you know it's going to be freezing cold, right? Just be fast. I'll watch Shane and stay close to the edge in case you start to seize up.'

At that, my skin broke out in gooseflesh preemptively. Just glancing at the cobalt blue surface of the water made my limbs try to shrivel up and recede inside my body. The placid surface resembled one unbroken, glassy film of ice. Heavy pine branches like green furry arms hung over us as the boat came to a stop a dozen or so yards from the shore. The pebbly bank was empty, as dark as pitch with the thickness of trees. Shane got up and stood against the rail, both pudgy arms over his head as he grasped the bar and stared out at the dark gloaming of the forest.

'I'll be quick,' I assured him. 'Just in and then back on the boat.'

'Can I come in too?'

'Not yet. Let me test it out first. You can keep watch and make sure I'm safe. Then maybe we can go closer to shore where it's shallow and you can have a try.'

I hated denying him, but I wasn't about to let him paddle around in water this deep. Even I wasn't perfectly comfortable with the idea of going in. 'It's going to be super cold too,' I added. 'And you don't want to get sick . . .'

'What if you get sick?'

'Well . . . I won't. I promise, how about that?'

'You can't promise that,' he said reasonably.

'I guess not. How about . . . I'll try really, really hard not

59

to get sick and I'll be in and out so fast the germs won't even have a chance to catch me!'

Shane frowned, arching one quizzical eyebrow. 'You don't get germs from the cold.'

I really shouldn't have let him read so many damn *books*.

'No, I suppose not, but it can weaken your immune system and then *other* germs can get you, right?' It was easier to argue with Andrea. She wasn't nearly so perceptive.

'I guess that's true. Okay. In and out.'

'Yup. You won't even miss me.'

Easy, right? Right.

Andrea walked to the ocean-side railing of the boat and waited for me to jump in. The others had congregated to watch Arturo bait a line and drop it into the water. Even Cassandra perked up, standing a few feet off to examine the process. Arturo gave directions to Noah, who followed the old sailor's lead and set up his own rig. I heard their lures splash over the side just as Andrea gave me a little nudge.

'Nobody's watching, you pansy,' she said. 'Go on, I've got your back. Shane is fine.'

I crouched down behind the cockpit and pulled off my sweater, T-shirt, jeans and thermal leggings. Those could use a good wash too. Since Arturo didn't plan on telling us our destination, I figured it would be easier to wait and do the washing up once we stopped for good. Wearing sopping wet clothing at night was not my idea of a good time and I had no intention of compounding seasickness with chills. I smiled to myself as I looked over the edge of the railing into the water; it was kind of exhilarating not to know where we were going. Maybe when we got there I'd ask Cassandra if she'd like me to rinse her scrubs. I'd even let her borrow a shirt if she promised not to cry all over it.

'Come on,' Andrea muttered, 'they won't fish forever.'

'Doesn't fishing take hours?'

'Get in!'

'I knew it. You just want to see me suffer,' I grunted, but she laughed and gave me a wolf whistle as I dropped into the ice-cold water.

A walk-in blast chiller on the polar fucking ice cap is probably more welcoming than Puget Sound before summer hits. The urge to panic was strong, but I remembered to breathe, to keep moving and make the blood pump hard through my legs and arms. At some point during my stalwart boycotting of the sea I had forgotten just how difficult it is to tread water. I held my breath and plunged beneath the surface for one second, half-terrified I wouldn't come back up. But the cool rush of water over my head was worth it. This wasn't grubby, industrial waste water just off the coast of a city; it was pure, refreshing and beautifully untouched. A silvery shape slipped by my side. A minnow, I thought, or something slightly bigger.

Odd, to think that there were still fish down there. Maybe the waterways were the last parts of the world to go on unchanged. Out of all the ways I could end up taking a swim in an unspoiled inlet in the middle of nowhere, international undead crisis was the least probable. But there I was. There was no denying it and no way to avoid the cliché. Something good and small was happening to me. And I didn't look panicked, which may just convince Shane that being on a boat wasn't so bad after all and that we might even return to some sense of normalcy.

Well, it was nice while it lasted anyway.

'Okay,' I said after less than a minute of splashing

around, 'I need to get out . . . preferably now, before the blood freezes in my veins.'

The railing above me was awfully quiet. I glanced up. Andrea was gone, nowhere to be found. She had taken Shane with her. 'Son of a bitch,' I shouted. 'This isn't funny! Andrea! Andrea? Shane?'

There was a commotion on the other side of the boat, shrieking and screaming and the sound of arms beating the water. My heart sank like a lead ball to my numb little toes.

Something was in the water.

Idiot. Idiot! I was about to prove that the water was absolutely something to fear. Just add yet another bad example set by Shane's poor excuse for a surrogate mum.

I turned a hasty circle. The side of the boat facing me was smooth, curved, with nothing to grab onto. A tiny rope ladder was curled against the railing, tied up and knotted. Theoretically I should have been on that ladder, joking with Andrea as she hauled me over the side, safely back onto the boat. The desire to panic rose again, too strong to fight this time. I scraped my hands against the side of the boat, trying to get purchase, my pulse coming as fast as my panicked breathing. There was nothing, not even a dent, and all the while I couldn't fight the idea, burrowing its way into my brain, that I needed to get out of the water for more than one reason. It wasn't just cold. It was suddenly very dangerous.

'Help! Help me!' I screamed. Finally, knowing it might be too late when somebody finally remembered to look for me, I began swimming around the stern of the boat to the other side. They would see me there. Where the hell had Shane gone? Why wasn't he listening for me? It was more than just dread, that sudden feeling that nobody gave a shit, that you were alone and drowning, cold and miserable in your final moment.

At least moving gave me something to think about. But when I rounded the edge of the boat I stopped, regretting it at once. Uncle Arturo was in the water – well, most of him was. Something bobbed on the surface next to him. I retched and flailed, coming up empty. It was his leg, severed raggedly at the knee. A fishing rod danced up and down in the swirling water and so did a pair of zombies – they must have pulled him in by the line. One of them had the fishing hook sticking out of its cheek like a gauche piercing.

Over the edge, Moritz saw me treading and freaking out. He loped over to my end of the boat, his arm dangling down uselessly toward me. It was too far.

'You have to get closer,' he called, out of breath.

Not an option. My sight seemed to be spinning, the world going topsy-turvy as I saw Arturo dip beneath the water. Noah was trying to fish him out but the old sailor was losing consciousness. We had to let him go. The water around me began to turn – cloudy at first but then swirling with scarlet. And like sharks scenting blood, the undead turned toward me.

'Leave him!' Andrea was shouting. She was sobbing, yanking back on Noah's shoulders. 'It's too late! Leave him!'

She was right. Leg or no leg, he had already been bitten, infected, and the change would come on soon. Having him in the boat with us would be guaranteed suicide. Noah heaved backward, trying to pull Arturo up by the arms while two bony creatures weighted him down into the water. I had a horrifying thought – that the water was too deep, that they couldn't have their feet on sand. They were swimming, or floating, though both were equally terrifying.

'The ladder!' I screamed, hoping Moritz understood. My teeth chattering like a pair of cocaine-addled macaws didn't make my speech very clear. 'O-On the other side. I'll swim there!'

This was purely hypothetical – my limbs were beginning to fail from the cold. Moritz nodded and disappeared for a moment as he ran to the other side of the boat. Losing sight of him made the panic more acute, and it felt as if the icy water were closing in around me, becoming something solid and sentient. It would strangle the life out of me. Shane's round face appeared under the railing. He stared down at me with a frozen expression of wide-eyed terror. Maybe he was preparing to lose me yet again.

But seeing his face was like a Taser zap to the ass. Survival wasn't an option, not with him peering down at me. It was an imperative, a duty that had little to do with me and everything to do with shielding him from another loss.

Here's one thing I'm now damn certain of: being chased by water zombies around a boat can turn a landlubber like me into Michael fucking Phelps on steroids. I didn't look back, knowing I might catch a glimpse of one of the undead coming for me. Then I remembered that they could be *under* the water. Each of my clumsy strokes was punctuated with a girlish squeak of hysteria. A thin rope ladder swung back and forth, just a few yards ahead. Moritz, bless his heart, was already over the edge of the ladder, waiting for me to get close. He was just in time. Something unnaturally strong tugged on my ankle, hard, nearly pulling me under.

Shane . . . I reminded myself sternly . . . I had to get back to him. No matter what, I had to make it back onto the boat. I was in deep, deep trouble, sure, but it was nothing, not when I thought about him being alone, surrounded by strangers and abandoned by every single family member he had.

I heard Andrea shout up on deck and realized she was screaming at me. Moritz clamped a hand over my wrist and yanked with enough power to pull the arm right out of its socket. With another jerk, he scampered back over the edge of the railing and we hit the deck with a cold, wet slap, like so many suffocating mackerels flopping out of a fisherman's net. Someone pulled the ladder up.

Distantly, very distantly, I heard the outboard motor start. It gave a roar like a meat grinder and Moritz cupped his hands over my ears, presumably to keep me from hearing the dulcet tones of Uncle Arturo and his new friends being sliced into chum. And dimly I realized that I was almost naked in the arms of a stranger. His tweedy jacket rasped against my skin.

'Cover her,' Noah was saying. Leave it to the teenage boy to be the first of us to have any sense. A blanket fell about my shoulders and Andrea rolled me a little, tucking the fleece around me and rubbing vigorously. The real aching cold was beginning to set in and I shook from toe to hairline. My vision wasn't cooperating, either from the water clouding up my eyes or the chills. As if gazing through a thick glass jar, I saw Shane standing a few yards away, his hands tightened into pale knots at his sides. He looked at me like I was a ghost. Stumbling forward, I pushed through the others and grabbed Shane, hugging him close, squeezing until he squeaked in protest.

'I was so . . . But we're okay.' My teeth chattered as I tried to talk. 'We're okay.'

Shane finally hugged me back. That was the signal I needed to stop gripping him so damn hard.

Moritz and Andrea waited until I had calmed a bit more to suggest I sit down. Shane came with me, not that he had a choice about it. His hand was icy in mine, though that might have been the lingering effects of the cold water. Moritz sat next to me, one hand on my back as he tried to rub some warmth back into my bones. The motor cut and Noah appeared again. His brows tented, his forefingers scraping up and down his temples. 'What do we do now?' he asked, looking between each of us. Nobody had an answer. 'What do we do now?'

Cassandra the nurse had started crying again. That was a given. Andrea gave her a look that could freeze lava.

'We should say something,' I managed between shivers. 'She's a wreck.'

'We're all a wreck,' Andrea replied shortly. 'And she didn't fall in the water.'

I turned briefly to look at Moritz, still too numb to properly overthink his proximity. His jacket smelled of dust and sweat. For some reason having him there, his hand on my back, made me feel better, or safer. It was all in the eyes, which were a color match for the crisp green-blue of the water surrounding us. And there was something in his gaze that reminded me of sugar-high toddlers, all enthusiasm and curiosity; and it was this feature of his that made me – almost against my will – relax.

Shane gave my knee an unexpected squeeze and even though I knew it would bug him, I leaned over and gave the top of his head a quick peck. We were alive, damn it, and I couldn't care less if it made little boys squishy and pouty to have their aunts show affection. But he didn't flinch away.

For a second, even half-drowned and freezing, my spirits actually lifted.

Gradually, it was dawning on us all that we were fucked, really and truly fucked. Uncle Arturo was the only person skilled enough to actually steer the boat and navigate the maze of inlets in which we now drifted, helpless and afraid. How long would the gas in the motor last? And how long until we needed more food and water? I wasn't going to be the one to say that fishing was out of the question.

Andrea had none of my reservations. 'We have to keep moving,' she said, a note of dread in her voice. She took off her hat and wrung it like a sponge. 'What if they can get onto the boat? We can't stop.'

She gave us a minute to let that sink in; the thought of underwater monsters crawling up onto the boat while we slept just about made me burst into tears. This was not a conversation I wanted to have in front of Shane, but there was no other choice. I wasn't letting him go and we needed to come to some sort of conclusion about our journey. I could feel a bruise forming on my heel where the zombie had nearly dragged me under. Emotions run high when your one and only navigator becomes a Jackson Pollock original splattered across the stern. I shuddered, thinking how close I had come to that exact same fate.

'Stay calm,' Moritz said – reasonably, I thought. 'There should be enough food to last for at least a week, if we're careful.'

'And then what?' Andrea asked, throwing up her hands.

'Then we land,' I said with reasonable confidence. 'We can't stay on this thing forever.'

'We could go back,' Noah said, throwing in his two

cents with a shrug. 'I'm sure I can figure out how to turn this thing around.'

'No,' I said, this time more boldly. 'We can't go back. The city's lost.'

'I agree,' Moritz said.

'So what do you suggest we do?' Andrea asked irritably. She hovered between the cockpit and the railing, pacing a trench into the deck.

'We might be near the San Juan Islands soon,' a helpful, squeaking voice spoke up. Each head turned together. Cassandra had finally opened her mouth, standing bloodied and wide-eyed at the bow, some feet beyond the cockpit. 'We could land there.'

Silence. Apparently no one else had a better idea or even a quick rebuttal. The afternoon, which had earlier seemed so promising and simple – swimming, fishing, card games – had taken a sharp turn for the worse.

And it was growing dark. I wanted to be alone.

'Can we have a minute?' I asked, nudging Moritz when he didn't respond. 'Alone?'

'Come on,' Andrea said, motioning to the cockpit. 'We can check the maps and see if anything makes sense.'

Shane relaxed when the others sidled away, his stubborn little fists easing apart. I gave him another one-armed hug, ruffling his hair with a mingled sense of relief and dread. No matter how hard I tried, I just couldn't manage to protect him from misery. He had seen Arturo die. He had almost watched me drown . . . I never expected our life together to be a day at the park, but this was getting pretty wretched. Someone had failed to protect Cassandra. She cried all the time. I didn't want that for Shane. He might always be quiet and serious, but he didn't have to be abandoned.

'I'm okay, bud,' I warbled unconvincingly, teetering from the cold.

'Okay,' Shane replied. 'That's good.'

'Your granddad taught me some stuff,' I continued, fighting through the tingling shivers in my limbs. 'I know it seems tough right now but we'll stick together and get through it. That's not just blowing smoke. Granddad taught me to fish, to camp . . . I can teach you those things too.'

Shane shrugged. He was so very good at ruining my little moments of inspiring speech.

'Are there lots of those things in the water?' he asked quietly.

Shit. I had hoped he wouldn't ask that. 'Some. I don't know how many. But we can learn to avoid them.'

'How? If they're right there in the water . . .'

'They can't climb up onto the boat. The sides are too smooth.' I had no intention of frightening him needlessly, but maybe a bit of honesty would actually help. 'I'm scared of them coming out of the water, too, we all are. We'll just have to be smarter. We can do that, can't we? I know you're smarter than a zombie.'

Shane nodded. 'Probably.'

I hadn't talked to him much about his grandfather. Surviving in the city was more about learning to readjust normal things – no electricity, different food, different ways to clothe and entertain yourself . . . But if we were headed for a prolonged stay in the wilderness, well, that was nothing like giving up fresh vegetables for canned or finding a renewed appreciation for books and knitting. It took a kind of rugged perseverance I'm not sure either of us possessed. I would just have to channel my dad and maybe some Allison Hewitt, and forget about the doubts creeping around in the back of my mind.

I wasn't the mothering type, not like my sister, Kat, but that was going to have to change.

'Maybe we'll hold off on fishing for a while,' I suggested, suffering flashes of Shane being yanked into the bay by the end of a fishing line. 'But there's some cool stuff we can do . . . building fires and shelters, making traps . . .'

'I guess.'

And that was *why* I wasn't the mothering type. For all your effort and care, a kid could just blow you off and make you feel two inches tall. But really . . . I couldn't blame Shane. Why *should* he get excited about fires or camping when every part of his life he had ever enjoyed had been ripped unceremoniously away? I was the only thing he had left. Put that way, I couldn't help but sympathize with his moods.

Kat was always better at this stuff. She didn't wind up with someone like Carl and his sicko friends. Some internal compass kept her on the straight and narrow at all times. She understood kids and they loved her right back. She knew how to glide through the awkward moments when a child looked at you like Shane was looking at me then. Like maybe this was all a mistake. Like maybe he had wished he had been on the train when his parents were killed and not stuck with me on a slow boat to nowhere.

'You'll see,' I promised, swallowing a knot of emotion I wasn't sure would ever go away. 'You'll see, big man. It's going to be an adventure.'

*

The bickering started as dusk fell, but I couldn't rouse enough energy to care. Someone would decide something. That was enough. The bare facts were impossible to ignore: we were on the boat and there were only two choices – keep going until we found a good place to stop or just keep drifting until we starved, were eaten, or went crazy.

I stayed put with my little boy sentry huddled there stiff and quiet. Andrea stopped over with my clothing. She seemed to hesitate, but left without a word. Dry enough, I pulled on my thermals and sweater and curled up in the soggy blanket, herding Shane into the spot in front of me.

A chill had crept into my bones, the iciness of the water driven inward. When the darkness came on, swift and foggy and damp, I was glad for the privacy of shadows. The boat felt emptier without Arturo, aimless. It was easy to start crying. I had been saving up. Shane fell asleep curled against me, wheezing with the quiet intensity of a child's deep rest. I thought of poor Arturo, dead and abandoned. I thought of those bastards who had tried to take Shane. And Carl . . . Carl. I pictured him in the water instead of Arturo, his leg bobbing up and down like a decoy duck. I couldn't remember the last time I had been so angry. This was worse than the initial outbreak, worse than losing family and friends and a home because it was just so damn *lonely*. Even with Shane there, or maybe especially *because* Shane was there. He was the only thing left, the last remnants of a family I could never get back again.

On rare occasions my even temperament keeled over like a flagpole in a gale, so sometimes it helped to release a valve and let out some steam. But there was nothing to punch, no pillow to abuse or solitary space to throw a screaming fit. So I shoved my hand into my face and sobbed into it, wondering what the hell I was doing on a boat in the first place and how to get off of it. I closed my eyes and saw the *Golden Princess* upended in Bell Harbor. Evil in the water. Terror in the water.

As if in coy response, the sound of the waves gathered up against the boat, pushing us toward our unknown destination with a lush rushing sound. Uncle Arturo, rest in peace, had gone to his death with our destination locked somewhere in his mind. Now we would never know.

Even as I sulked and tried to cry silently, I felt his eyes on me. Moritz watched me over the top of his tin cup, nodding his head and pressing his lips together in an awkward grin of apology whenever I caught him doing it, as if to say: I can't help but look at you and I'm sorry that I must.

It wasn't a comfort, it was an invasion. I'd known Andrea for years and trusted her, but that was it. I didn't know these other people. I hardly even knew Shane, so strange and aloof despite his young age. A bloodstained nurse, an eager teenage boy, and a deposed art critic playing superhero . . . I didn't know them. How could I? Two days on a boat? I shuddered and sank down into the warmth of the blanket; I didn't know them and there was nowhere to go, just the boat and the endless inexorable current of the sea.

FIVE

Shane and I woke up the next morning beneath a cavernous pile of blankets. I hadn't remembered falling asleep or being tucked in, but there was no mistaking the heap of blankets keeping me warm and snug. It was a small gesture, but one that might have kept me from growing weak from the cold. It was time to wake up, I thought, time to wriggle out of the sticky, safe cocoon and *do something*.

My newfound determination flagged a bit when I realized I was the only person awake. It proved difficult to rouse the troops when most of them were snoring peacefully. The others dozed at various intervals around the deck, curled up like shrimps on a roasting pan; Andrea had snuggled up to a pile of sweaters in the cockpit. She slept with furrowed eyebrows and I couldn't help but wonder if she missed her uncle, if they had been closer than I thought. It was always tough to tell; affection in one culture seemed like apathy in another. She was probably supposed to be maneuvering the boat. Lucky for us, we coasted through a broad bay, a safe distance away from the tangle of trees on the shore.

Shane never made much noise period, and he was mute in sleep, his little chest going up and down with the rhythm of the waves pushing us along.

Andrea started awake even as I watched. Realizing her mistake, she quickly stood up and surveyed our situation. I took one blanket for myself, left the rest for Shane, and shuffled over to the cockpit, sitting down on the shallow steps leading down toward her position at the helm. Only a scant few yards from Shane, I still felt nervous, jumpy from fear and the hungry hole in my gut, as if this brief period of safety was destined to be interrupted with tragedy. Accordingly, I kept one eye on him as I sidled up to Andrea.

'Morning,' I said, not knowing how else to start.

'Morning. You feel okay? Need a valium?' Even voice, eyes steady. She did me the favor of believing I could cope.

'I'm fine. Shaken, but fine. You know, the nice thing about being chased in the water is that there's easy clean up when you shit yourself,' I said. She laughed indulgently. 'But really, I'll be back to normal soon. You guys took good care of me.'

Andrea nodded and looked away, ponytail bouncing. I couldn't tell if she was proud or embarrassed. 'And you? How are you holding up?' I asked.

'I don't know,' she replied, letting out a sigh that deflated her whole chest. 'I'm worried.'

'Really?' I asked lightly. 'And here I thought things were going along without a hitch.'

She smirked and then quickly covered it up. 'Fuck you. Things could be worse.'

'I don't know, Andrea. Name me one thing worse than aquazombies. Go on, name one.'

She thought for a moment, her head quirked to the side. 'Zombies with wings?'

'Jesus. That *is* worse.' We were silent for a moment. She looked at Shane, her gaze a little unfocused and far away as

74

she tipped her head to the side, a silent question forming. I don't know what she was thinking, but personally I was trying hard to blot out the mental image of the undead descending from the sky.

'Were you two close?' I asked softly.

Andrea flinched, her jaw tightening as she looked away and muttered, 'Not really.'

'Still . . . doesn't make it any easier.'

'I'm *pissed*,' she said, shaking her head. 'I'm fucking pissed at that idiot for dying and leaving us on this fucking stupid-ass boat in this huge-ass bay. We're up a creek, Sadie. We are up a creek in the biggest way . . .'

'I get that,' I replied, keeping my voice down. 'But it's not his fault. He was trying to help us.'

'Yeah? Well fuck him for that too.' She blinked, hard, no doubt using every muscle in her face to keep the tears from dropping. This was her way. She probably loved the salty old bastard to death, but she'd be the last to say it.

'So where we headed?' I asked.

The sunrise was breathtaking. Long washed streaks of orange and pink glowed behind the tree line. Above the bright colors, the sky turned navy blue and then faded, up and up until it was white again with clouds. Nature went along cheerfully, oblivious to the world of humans falling apart like so many scattered and bloodied Jenga blocks. A cool, swirling mist disintegrated around us, replaced by a breeze that carried the heavy scent of pine from the forest. People came to these areas to fish and camp and get in touch with nature again. I could see why. My dad would have loved to come here. Besides us, this was what kept him going, what made his office life tolerable.

Then I remembered the watery marauders we had met

yesterday and looked harder at the shore. Maybe it wasn't so gorgeous after all. There were creatures in those woods, not just bears and mountain lions or whatever else, but things with a hunting instinct that defied reasonable thought. I shivered as Andrea turned and glanced at me.

'If I'm reading this chart properly, which there's about a fifty-fifty chance of, then Cassandra's right. We're getting close to the San Juan Islands. I don't know what the fuck, though. I mean, look.' She pointed out beyond the nose of the ship. 'Can you make heads or tails of this shit? What's on the map does not look like what's in front of my eyes.'

I consulted the chart and then gazed at the jagged lines of pebbly shore all around us. She was right. They looked nothing alike.

'Can Noah read it?' I asked. 'Your uncle kinda took him under his wing.'

'Maybe,' she replied, shrugging her slender shoulders. 'We can consult him, but it's one giant gamble. I think our best bet is to just go until we see a shore that looks open and safe. If we manage that without fucking it up we might have a fighting chance.'

A fighting chance? To do what exactly?

'And then what?' I grunted. 'We go bamboo?'

'Well, no,' she reasoned. 'It'll be temporary. If we wait a few months, things might get better and we could sail back down to Seattle, see what's what. If the harbor's cleaned up and it looks secure we'll land, pick up where we left off . . .'

It was as good a plan as any, if a bit naïve and delusional. I couldn't fault her for high hopes; I wanted to believe it too. She made it sound so easy. Shane and me back in our old haunt, or we could find a new one, start fresh. It was tempting to imagine. I nodded. 'Okay, then.'

'You're not so sure.' Andrea tossed me one of her hard, studying looks. Apparently I had to display Mickey Mouse Club levels of giddiness about this latest suggestion of hers. I smiled, faking it.

'No, I think you're right,' I said. 'I think that sounds solid.'

Andrea turned back to the chart, leaving me with my thoughts and my own lie hanging over my head. It didn't sound solid, it sounded ridiculous. After all, what were we? A drug dealer, an illustrator, an art critic, a child, a nurse and a teenager? It sounded like a setup for a bad joke, not a crack survival team. I knew a thing or two about the wilderness, but I wasn't confident that knowledge was extensive enough to keep us going.

'We should talk to everybody,' I said forcefully. Direction. We just needed direction. 'We'll round them up and let them know the plan.'

Noah had woken up by the time I left Andrea alone at the helm. She needed her space – that much was clear. She telegraphed her moods like a stop light; today she was flashing red and I'd let her be. I noticed the teenage boy stretching and pulling on another layer of sweatshirt. Moritz and Cassandra still slept, curled up at opposite ends of the boat. I envied their restfulness; yesterday had been exhausting, in more ways than one.

Shane only roused enough to sit up and glower out at the water, hands tucked into his lap.

Noah saw me sitting at the stern, swathed in blankets, my back resting against the railings and my body swaying with the rhythm of the waves. He came and sat beside me, swimming in his too-big sweaters. He had something tucked into his hand, half-hidden by his waist. For a while we were quiet, the sloshing of the water against the boat serving as a welcome distraction. Finally I looked at him. His face was so young, but he wore his struggles on his sleeve, too mature and calm for someone his age.

'Where are you from?' I asked. This was a natural post-Outbreak conversation starter and one I'd had lobbed at me hundreds of times in the last few months.

'BC,' he replied. 'Vancouver.'

British Columbia. Another transplant. He didn't mention family and as a rule, that meant they were probably out of the picture. I forced a smile. 'You're not too far from home, then.'

'Nope,' he said. 'And we're getting closer by the minute.'

I hadn't thought of that. We *were* headed in a generally northern direction.

'I just hope we stop before Alaska,' I murmured.

'What's in Alaska?' he asked.

'Exactly.'

We fell back into companionable silence. I don't know how long we sat there, perched like sunning seagulls at the end of the boat. After a while, Noah handed me a thin stack of worn paperbacks. He had obviously been secreting them away for just this moment. If I weren't so fucking bleary-eyed and afraid I might have actually jumped for joy. I had exhausted my patience with cards (and more specifically cards with Andrea, the damn dirty cheater) and the sight of so many ways to pass the time made me want to hug him forever.

I looked through the stack as he awaited my verdict and chewed his thumb nail. Dashiell Hammett, Raymond Chandler, Mickey Spillane . . .

'You're way too young to have taste this good.'

'They're my pop's,' he said shyly, but his cheeks reddened from the flattery. 'He used to read them to me over breaks, you know, Christmas and Easter and stuff. I took them from the house. I couldn't just leave them there.'

'How many times have you read them?' I asked. The yellow pages were beyond dog-eared.

He blew out a long breath. 'No idea, hundreds of times. Memorized by now. You borrow them for as long as you need.'

'That's generous,' I said. 'Thank you.'

My heart cracked a little at his bashful smile. He had a heartthrob's face hidden beneath a stubborn layer of baby fat and the torrent of dark curls falling over his forehead. In a few short years he would be a lady-killer. Looking at him made me want to throw something. Don't get me wrong, he was good company, but he didn't belong here. Noah should have been at the junior prom, picking out a corsage, buying his first car, chasing girls. Instead he was here with us, headed for nowhere on a boat with no captain. I snorted inside my head. That would be a good title for one of his hard-boiled detective novels – *On a Boat With No Captain*.

Noah pointed to *The Maltese Falcon* in my lap. 'Start with that one.'

'All right. And after that?'

'*The Big Sleep*.'

'You're the boss.'

Noah got up then, his job seemingly done, and stuck his hands into his pockets. He sidled away, leaving me to stare down at the stack of novels. He was bummed, lonely, trying to cope. It was tempting to call him back and ask if he was okay. He and Arturo had formed a bond. Nobody wanted to discuss it. I felt fortunate that I hadn't been there to see him get pulled down. Sure, I had seen his leg bobbing in the water, glimpsed the carnage, but Noah and the others had seen worse. So I let it lie and watched Noah go his own way, which – obviously – wasn't far.

I had never really gotten into the detective mystery thing, but the escapism certainly sounded tempting. There was no telling how much longer we'd be confined to the ship. We had islands, water, trees . . . but a direction? I suppose so. Not really. Vaguely.

In the meantime, dames and dicks and the thrill of the chase would have to be my life raft.

SIX

Rousing speech. Right. Nothing I couldn't handle. I turned down Andrea's generous offer of some pills to steady my nerves. If I was going to lead, it would be by example.

'It's no secret,' I started, looking from face to face, clinging to the cockpit railing to keep from tumbling over in the middle of my brilliant State of the Union. '...Look...It's no secret that we're in trouble, but Andrea and I have talked it over, and we think there's a solution that should please everybody and keep us safe for the time being.' Andrea nodded, lending her silent support. Cassandra sat curled up in a ball at Moritz's feet, her gaze settling somewhere on the middle distance. Little Shane was kind enough to hold eye contact when I looked at him. 'We're going to stop at the next beach that looks open or at the next sign of civilization. We can wait out the trouble in Seattle, and head back when everyone feels ready.'

'I can help navigate,' Noah put in shyly. 'I think I've got a handle on it.'

'And we'll ration the food carefully,' Andrea added.

That seemed to be all there was to say.

'We've got food and a boat,' I said in closing. 'That's more than enough if we're resourceful.'

Noah took me aside, or as aside as one could go on a

ship, when the group broke apart. Shane insisted on coming along, following me like a little blond shadow.

'Thanks for doing that,' Noah said, shaking my hand. He was a strange kid, but loveable, and I pumped his hand back with a wry smile.

'I don't really know what I'm doing,' I admitted with a shrug. 'But someone had to speak up.'

'It's a good plan.' He nodded and took back his hand, sticking it into his pocket. 'Arturo really did teach me some things . . . basic stuff, you know, but . . . I think we might really be able to do this.'

I glanced at Cassandra, who hadn't moved much since the speech's end. She never moved much, period. 'Do you think she's all right? I don't really know what to make of her.'

'She keeps to herself,' Noah agreed, scratching at the back of his neck as we both looked at her. 'I dunno . . . Every time I try to talk to her she just sorta stares at me and then clams up. I don't want to say she's *crazy*, but . . .'

'But you think she's crazy.'

'No . . . *no*.' He sighed, deflating. 'I dunno. I mean . . . would you wear bloody clothes for days on end?'

The boy had a point. 'No,' I replied, 'but I think we need to at least get her up on her feet. I've hardly seen her eat since we've been on this thing and we're going to need everyone's cooperation to make this plan work.'

Noah nodded again and bit down on his lip. 'I'll see if I can get her talking.' He paused, smirking as he asked, 'Did you get a chance to read the stuff I gave you?'

'Couldn't put it down if I wanted to.'

He blushed, lighting up like a tree on Christmas morning as he sidled away in Cassandra's direction. I hoped his disarming bashfulness might encourage the redheaded girl to open up a little.

Reading *The Maltese Falcon* got me thinking; not about fedoras and cigarette smoke and red, red lips (although it did definitely have all of those things) but about birds, falcons. Andrea unearthed a raggedy pencil and some legal paper in the cockpit and I spent the afternoon sketching, Shane at my side. He was talkative for once, telling me when something looked too silly or not silly enough. Like therapy or a stiff drink, it clears the mind. I drew falcons and sparrows, Pink Bear for Shane, seagulls and whatever appeared on shore. He asked for a few dinosaurs and I gave him Velociraptor vs. Decepticon. I know animals – and thanks to Shane, I also know robots. I've drawn creatures all my life, filled books and sketchbooks with their quasi-human hijinks.

Strangely enough, I never had pets growing up. My mother's tolerance for grime began and ended with Dad's grubby trailer. Dogs brought smells into the house and Kat was allergic to, ironically enough, cats. We tried fish. Kat and I weren't great about remembering to feed them and Mom got fed up with always being the one to clean the tank and scoop out the belly-uppers. On trips, Dad put up with me taking precious time out of hiking and fishing to bird-watch and sit extremely still in the hopes that a deer or two would glide by. In the city, pigeons and the occasional wayward mouse in the apartment were the only flesh and blood creatures I got to see up close. The zoo and sometimes a friend with a hamster or parakeet were my sole exposure to the animal world. It was a rare treat and I loved every second of it. I would pick an animal and sit on the bench in front of its habitat for hours, sketching the tigers or apes, wondering what would happen if I went inside the enclosure. On a school field trip I was left behind because I had hidden myself in the thick shadows of the nocturnal creatures building. They did a head count when they got back to the school and I came up missing. The teachers found me rooted to the floor in front of the Slow Loris exhibit.

My parents didn't have the heart to ground me, and instead took me back to the zoo. Dad gave me a tiny pen light so I could see my sketchpad in the darkened nocturnal house.

For me, it's hard *not* to think in animal terms – when you're living in a kind of apocalypse, you see people behave like wild beasts every day. And it helped me connect with Shane. It was the one game I could consistently get him to play – picking out what animals people looked like. He was good at it and sometimes – like on that day – it even brought him out of his shell. It made me consider that there might be a budding young artist living with me, but whenever I handed him the pencils he just drew spirals, dark ones, circling drains that wore the pencil leads down to soft nubs.

I didn't want to know what a child psychologist would say about that.

So I drew a sleek little fox for Andrea – that was as nobrainer – and a greyhound for Moritz. Cassandra and Noah were tougher to pinpoint, but eventually I drew a woodpecker for Cassandra and a penguin with a Maple leaf scarf for Noah. Shane, of course, got Pink Bear, but I also gave him a few companions, some cheerful squirrels and rabbits to frolic gingerly at the feet of Velociraptor and his mortal enemies, the Decepticons.

'Is that supposed to be me or something?' Andrea asked. She had snuck up to peer over my shoulder. The fox was carrying a floppy muffin hat in its jaws.

'Yes,' I said.

'Oh, what's that?'

Andrea and I looked up together. Cassandra was standing in front of us, her hands tucked demurely in front of her waist. It was a weird image to reconcile, her bloody blue scrubs and her sweet, pleasant smile. Cuter things dragged themselves around Silent Hill. I turned the legal pad around for her to see. Her face opened up into a beaming smile. Mother, I thought immediately. She had had kids at some point. Hmm. Perhaps my affinity for child-rearing was growing if I could notice that so easily.

'Those are adorable!'

Moms always respond to drawings like this. They instantly recognize the style, the intent. It's like reading *The Mitten* and *Never Smile at a Monkey* is encoded into their DNA. Cassandra flopped down next to me. She seemed young to be a mom, but maybe clean living had preserved her looks. Her eyes were as big as saucers as she gazed lovingly at the animals bounding across the page. She pointed at each character in turn and named who it matched on the boat.

She was, to put it mildly, a bit on the ripe side. I switched to breathing through my mouth.

'But where's yours?' Cassandra asked, crestfallen.

'I don't know,' I said, using the gentle, cautious voice I used with Shane. Maybe we'd find out more than just her name if we kept her going like this. 'What do you think fits?'

Cassandra glanced up from the drawings, studying me

closely, beady eyes all scrunched up with concentration. I blanched, sneaking furtive glances to Andrea for moral support. She was laughing silently.

'Maybe a crow,' she said. 'Or a panther . . . a baby one!'

'Or a weasel,' Andrea kindly supplied.

We compromised on a mink. Noah joined us, pleased with his penguin. Under his direction I sketched a few characters from *The Maltese Falcon*, humans this time. I tore off the drawing of the main character, Sam Spade, and gave it to Noah. Shane stared up at me and pointed to the sketch of Pink Bear. It was the most emotional communicating he'd done in days. I handed it to him and watched the tiniest of smiles tug at his lips.

Noticeably absent from our little powwow was Moritz.

He had withdrawn to the port side of the ship, silently watching the scenery go by. I brought him a piece of bread with some dried fish and an apple while Andrea looked after Shane. Moritz didn't seem to want to meet my eyes and concentrated all of his attention on the food in his hands. His scarf rippled in the faint breeze coming from the south.

'You almost died,' he said at last.

'It happens,' I said, not wanting to dwell. 'You saved my life.'

'That thing grabbed you. I thought . . . I don't know. I couldn't be responsible for that.'

'Well, you're not,' I replied. 'You saved a life. Think about that instead.'

My smile was shaky. I didn't like hearing just how close I'd been to death. In books people always say 'I'm no hero' but the difference is I mean that when I say it. Or think it. My heel still ached where the creature had pinched. I had the luxury of not knowing how that had looked and I could only imagine what Moritz had seen. I'm not even remotely a strong swimmer, so it must have been a photo finish from his perspective, with me just barely outrunning death.

'I keep seeing it in my head. I couldn't sleep or sit still. Andrea had to give me something or I would have been up all night,' he said. Then he mumbled something under his breath in German, a curse word maybe. 'Sometimes I think it would be better if I did not care for any of you. If we were to all remain strangers it would be so much easier.'

'Easier? You mean when we die?' Which was inevitable in his mind apparently.

'I'm aware of how callous that sounds,' he said, glancing away. 'However, that is how I feel.'

'Then don't worry,' I said coldly. 'I'll vanish.'

He laughed. 'I said it would be easier, not better.'

I couldn't help but see this all playing out somewhere else, in a smoke-filled train car or a seedy bar. Once you descend into the hard-boiled mind-set it's hard to climb your way back out. Everything is noir, or feels like it should be. With just a tiny squint I could place a cigarette between Moritz's lips and jaunty fedora on his head. He'd aim an ice-cold bullet of a look at me and I'd melt it with a smoldering gaze and a twitch of perfect red lips. He'd say something witty and ironic like, 'Come here often?' and we'd both laugh and call for paint thinner on the rocks.

I had drifted. He was staring.

'Sorry,' I said. 'Just thinking.'

'About?'

'About those ugly-looking clouds.'

Speaking of noir . . .

He looked above my head at the mass of clouds so gray they were almost black. They were moving in fast, dragging a curtain of slate-gray rain with them. At that moment I felt Arturo's loss like a smack to the face. There was a storm coming, chasing our tail with the kind of speed that made you want to curl up in bed under the covers. It would be a whopper – lightning, thunder, the works. That wouldn't be so bad in a cabin or even a tent, but out in the open water?

'Andrea!' I called. She and Noah had already begun scrambling around in the cockpit. The wind snapped, sail straining at the rigging. Shane shuffled around in the midst of all this chaos until I swooped in and snatched up his hand, deciding that if I went overboard then he was coming with me.

'Great,' I muttered, backing away from the railing with Shane. 'Maybe we'll get extra lucky and it'll rain zombies too.'

You know that feeling before a spelling bee or an important presentation? The one where you can't decide whether to diarrhea or vomit or both? We joined the others, huddling under the little cover made by the cockpit. My stomach began to ache in anticipation. My first taste of seasickness would probably be nothing compared to this. Not only that, but there was our safety to consider, and the fact that none of us knew what to do in the event of a bad storm. We couldn't exactly check someone's iPhone for a quick forecast or Google search: 'Oh, God, what the fuck do we do now?'

The rain pounded the deck without warning, rushing across the surface of the water like a cymbal roll. The clouds split open, unleashing a few blinding flashes of lightning to the south. I looked at the mast, trying to recall basic science and decide whether or not we were all shortly to become jalapeño poppers.

Noah was trying to shout over the downpour and deafening roars of thunder. Together, crammed into the cockpit, trying to hide from the lashing rain, I realized that no matter how much we wanted to go on and no matter how much we planned, Mother Nature would always have the final say. She was every bit as dangerous and threatening as the undead. Shane curled up, making himself as small as possible, a tiny humming noise coming from him as he whimpered in fear.

'It'll pass,' I assured him, hoping like hell it was true. 'Just a little longer.'

It was one of those indelible moments where you remember just how miniscule you are in comparison to the weather, how with one bad bout of PMS Ole Mama Nature can send the furies to terrorize you on the sea. Humans belong on land, I thought to myself, trying to become one with Shane and the rubber sheeting over the food supply. Someone was standing on my foot, it didn't matter. The cockpit was one mass of human limbs and sloshing rain. No one had volunteered to take the lead and try to sort out the mast or the rigging. We could only masquerade as sailors for so long. Even if Arturo had still been alive, I wasn't sure he could save us from this.

I managed to aim my first wave of nausea out of the cockpit, stumbling to the edge to heave it over onto the deck. Shane cringed and recoiled from me. I watched the vomit cascade in an orange blob straight down toward the edge and into the water. The boat had reared up, titled at a heart-pounding sixty-degree angle. I scampered back into the safety of the cockpit, clutching my stomach, letting Moritz have a turn.

Suddenly, day was night, darker than I could remember it being. The sky was no longer blue or even gray, but flat black that lit up with the oncoming spikes of lightning. Behind a glass pane it would have been beautiful, awe-inspiring, but jammed into a five-by-five cockpit with a tender tummy and five frightened compatriots made it unbearable. I shook and glued my eyes to my shoes, determined not to piss myself and to hold up with a modicum of dignity for Shane's sake.

'Soon now,' I told him in a pale-faced whisper. 'Soon it'll stop.'

The boat lurched, listing heavily to the left, portside, to the *water*. I couldn't muster the tiniest instinct. The sail wagged and then made a noise like a shotgun blast. I wanted to grab something, pull a rope or fix something, *anything*. I realized then that I should've found a life vest to grasp, but my legs were paralyzed and I didn't know where to look. Then the wind caught us and sent us reeling back the other way. Andrea screamed. I grabbed Shane, wrapping him in a bone-crushing embrace. He hugged me back as we held on for dear life, my tears mingling with the storm.

Whether we liked it or not, a destination had been chosen for us.

In a way, it was just like we planned. Find land. We found it, all right, forcefully.

I'd like to think we were fortunate. The storm had thrown us into a cove of sorts, with a curtain of green trees covering us overhead. Everything smelled piney and crisp. When the rain finally died down we poked our heads out to find that we weren't doomed to drown or wash up on shore. But the boat had taken a beating, the hull badly scraped and torn from being smashed against the rocky coast of the island. There was no beach, just a sheer rock face with fringes of mossy grass hanging over the edge at about our head height.

Shane trembled in my grasp, peering up with unblinking eyes as we both found ourselves in more or less one piece.

'See?' I said weakly. 'All over.'

He climbed out of the cockpit with me, shifting his grip to my left hand. Thank God he was all right – shaken, sure, wet and rumpled, but definitely not fish food. When I limped to the starboard side of the ship I could reach out and run my hand along the gleaming pale pink stones. The storm had appeared, tossed us around, and then left, leaving behind a creepy absence, birds singing happily as if nothing at all had happened.

'I can't believe it,' Andrea said, appearing at my side. She, too, reached out to touch the rocks, as if checking that they were real and not in a dream. 'We're alive.'

Miraculously, nobody was seriously injured. Noah had jammed his wrist pretty bad trying to steady the wheel in the cockpit, but other than that there was nothing to report but bruises and minor abrasions. We gathered at the railing, taking stock of our cuts and bumps and sneaking glances at the island itself. So close to the shore it was impossible to tell how big it truly was.

'Do you think we should explore a little?' Noah asked. He bounced on his heels. It was obvious he was eager to be on land again.

'I don't know,' Andrea said, 'Maybe we should wait and spend the night here, see what happens.'

'You mean see what comes crawling out after us?' I countered.

'We can't stay,' Moritz said, rubbing his jaw. He had the beginnings of a beard. 'We might drift back out with the tide.'

'The boat won't go anywhere if we tie it to the trees,' I said. 'We can't stay here. That was never the plan, right? We should get onto land while we have the chance.'

Andrea shot me a look. 'And when the tide goes out it'll beach.'

'Look, it was your idea to land anyway,' I replied. 'And now we've done it.'

Not very gracefully, I didn't add. Trying to navigate the boat back out would be touchy, especially with the hull wedged up onto a sandbar. You didn't need to be Vasco da Gama to see the problems inherent in trying to push a boat off of the sand *and* manage to scamper onto it in time. The sail was tangled, the outboard motor sticking up out of the water . . . Leaving didn't seem like much of an option.

'Fine,' Andrea said, throwing up her arms. Her hat had fallen off in the storm. She began searching the deck for it. 'But we need to find a beach. I'm not camping in the middle of a forest.'

We got down to the business of transferring what was salvageable off the boat. Personally, I was glad to feel firm earth under my feet again. Shane seemed to like it too. Even before The Outbreak he hadn't been a complainer, but living on short food stuffs, you'd think the kid would eventually gripe about eating rice for almost every meal. But he never uttered a peep of discontent. You had to look close, like now, to see that the barest hint of a smile was the only indicator that he liked this situation better.

Walking on stones and dirt felt natural, comforting. And the smells were different, as lush as a savage, prehistoric forest. The air was clean and filled with the wintry scent of wet trees. Feeling optimistic, I tracked down my garbage bag, which had snagged on a nail and managed to stay onboard. The things inside were more or less ruined. The sketches hadn't fared well, washed out by the water, and the food was soaked. We had Arturo's port, some old sodas from the hold under the cockpit and some random bits of food that had managed to stay dry. Shane puttered along behind me, collecting a shell, a broken pencil, Andrea's hat . . .

Noah's books had spent the storm in the cockpit and, while dampened, remained readable. Most importantly, Arturo's huge supply of matches for his cigarettes had weathered the storm, untouched. He kept them in a plastic zip bag. That decision could very well end up saving our lives.

There wasn't much to scavenge, so we boosted each other up onto the rocks and into the tree cover. Noah and Andrea took the tie-up ropes and looped them around the sturdiest pines. Shane scampered onto my back, hooking his arms around my neck and his heels alongside my ribs. I almost felt a pang of regret as we put the boat to our backs and headed into the forest. Almost.

We stayed near to the edge of the rock cliff, with the water on our right. From the compass Noah had taken, it showed us heading south, southwest. It was hard going. The trees were thick, wild and the terrain shifted constantly with the rocky ledge swerving in and out. Stumbling was inevitable. A few times I heard Shane grunt in protest as a low-hanging branch swiped at him. Guessing where the next good place to land a foot was touch and go. But the proximity to the water helped us find a beach with relative ease, and after half an hour of constant walking we followed the slope of the ledge down to a clearing and then a shallow beach.

'Not bad,' I said, trying to remain hopeful. 'We should mark high and low tide, just to make sure we set camp far enough up the hill.'

'Right,' Andrea said, momentarily surprised by my suggestion. I didn't like the idea that she wanted to be the only one rubbing two brain cells together. She adjusted her sweater and walked back up the hill, finding a pair of long, pointed sticks. Shane had given her the hat back and it sat crooked on her head. She broke off the extra twigs and marched down to us, then hammered one of the branches into the pebbly sand with the handle of Carl's knife.

'We still have one fishing rod,' I said. We stood in a half-circle, our backs to the water. 'And enough food survived to last us a few days. We've got the sail covers, and those could insulate a lean-to if we can set one up.'

'We'll need a fire,' Moritz added, 'and drinking water, and we'll have to take turns keeping watch at night.'

'Enough for a start,' Noah put in.

It was bolstering to know that once we finally got back onto land, our collective IQ rose by about two hundred points. Survival seemed manageable at this point, even probable. Beyond that, who could say? I glanced back northeast, in the direction of the cove and Arturo's boat. I doubted if she would ever sail again and our optimistic plan to wait out the panic in Seattle and return felt like a cute but flimsy notion. Behind us, other islands dotted the distance. The possibility finally dawned that they could be inhabited, and not just by animals or the undead.

'Why don't you and Shane go with Cassandra to gather firewood?' Andrea suggested. I whirled around, finding that she was talking to me. Firewood collector? Come on. I thought I had earned something better for my clever high tide suggestion.

'I'll try to get some kindling going,' she added, 'and Moritz and Noah can start on the lean-to.'

I looked at Moritz, who seemed utterly confounded by the idea of building anything so complex. His suit was now beyond bedraggled, and he looked more like a homeless man than a hoity-toity art critic and collector. He chewed down on his lower lip, his big, earnest blue eyes filled with sudden regret. I stifled a scoff. Yeah, I thought, let him build the lean-to, he's a regular Bear Grylls.

Andrea caught on to my private sneering and tossed me a stainless-steel glare. I grinned and headed off at a clip for the woods with Shane and Cassandra. Team spirit, I reminded myself, go – fight – win.

It wasn't as bad as I expected. Shane didn't bother to help gather wood, instead picking up whatever interesting tidbits he found on the ground. Traveling the perimeter of the beach gave me a chance to orient and to look for any bits of string or washed up detritus that could help us.

'Did you get banged up in the storm?' I asked Cassandra. We found a small deposit of dry-ish driftwood on the northeast side of the beach.

She looked back at me, one arm loaded down with wood. With her wild red curls in her face and her bloody scrubs it was difficult to judge whether or not she had actually sustained any wounds in the wreck.

'A bruise or two,' she murmured in response. 'I'll live. You?'

'Same.' I put down my growing stack of wood and wiped at my forehead. Even in the brisk weather I was breaking a sweat. 'Sorry we haven't . . . We haven't talked much yet.'

'You have your boy to look after,' Cassandra replied calmly.

'Well . . . yeah, my nephew.' I cringed. I really had to stop making the distinction.

'No difference,' she said. 'Little boys need lots of looking after.'

'Yeah.' I looked at Shane and felt something weird, a swelly feeling, like my heart was trying to beat too fast or there was too much blood in it. I had gotten us this far and that was something, right? Sure, I wasn't Supermom and I'd taken a few stupid risks and nearly gotten myself pulled down into oblivion, but I wasn't exactly going for style points. Shane turned at the waist, a sandy shell in his palm. He flicked the grains off, holding it up close to examine it.

'You have kids?' I asked casually.

'Little boys need lots of looking after . . .'

'Yeah, I heard that bit.'

Cassandra ducked down more quickly, the sticks in her arms jabbing her in the arm and throat. 'Lots of looking after,' she repeated, her gaze falling on Shane. 'Lots of looking after.'

SEVEN

Water would be a problem. Water was always a problem.

Honestly? It doesn't matter how many *Man vs. Wild* marathons you've embarked upon or how many times you were forced to watch *The Voyage of the Mimi*, and it certainly doesn't matter how often you tell yourself, 'Sure, I could do that! I know how to build a fire and whittle a weapon with a knife the size of a dill pickle. And hell, I could spear a fish and roast it over my own hard-won flames!'

Because when it counts, when that moment comes you'll forget everything. Wherever he was, I was letting my dad down. This was nothing new to me. I had camped, fished, roughed it in some pretty intimidating forests with my father, but that didn't mean I could magically make drinking water appear. He and I would either wind up near freshwater lakes and use a filter, or bring bottled water of our own. Arturo either hadn't owned a distiller or it had gotten lost in the wreck because now we had no way to get drinkable water of our own.

And unfortunately, Mother Nature, in her infinite wisdom, had not seen to it that we landed a stone's throw away from a freshwater spring. That first night, with a fire actually going (that one wasn't so bad with matches and my camping experience) and a lean-to fifty percent finished, I glared out at the endless sea surrounding us and scowled, really scowled.

'Water, water everywhere and not a drop to drink,' Andrea muttered.

'Thanks for the reminder.' I chewed through a piece of fish the size and texture of belt leather. I spat out a speck of grit that had stuck to the jerky. 'This salty fish sure does go down smooth.'

We had pooled the food, cutting off a square of sail tarp to make a waterproof satchel. Pro tip: Eating an entire meal of dried meat is a speedy way to turn your mouth into the Sahara. With darkness settling around us, there was no time to solve the water conundrum, but I would bet good money that every single one of us around that fire was trying to figure out a way how. Maybe dehydration was shrinking our brains, turning them to sawdust. If so, the zombies might actually leave us alone. Then I remembered something actually useful, something my resourceful father had taught me how to do. *Dew*.

'Dew,' I whispered, awestruck at the idea. 'We can set out some leaves to collect dew,' I said, louder. 'And in the morning we can walk around in the grass and wring out our pants.'

'That will not yield abundance,' Moritz said, reasonably. 'But it's a start.'

Eat your heart out, Les Stroud.

We picked straws for taking the watch. Selfishly, I'll admit, when it came my turn I was relieved to draw the longest one. Moritz had drawn the shortest straw (or blade of grass in this case). He now had the dubious honor of taking the last watch, but he offered to stay up and keep me company for a while. He wasn't sleepy and neither was I. In fact, being on land again had given me a buzz.

'Doing all right?' Moritz asked. We had moved to the edge of the clearing. Around the outer limits of the camp, Noah and I had rigged up a primitive twine trip wire connected to a pair of sardine cans. If we had unwanted visitors, be they bear or the undead, we would know. (That was Noah's idea so unfortunately I can't take credit.)

Meanwhile, Shane slept in the shelter of the lean-to, exhausted by a long day of collecting shells and asking me what animals lived in each one.

'Peachy,' I replied. 'I can't tell you how glad I am to be off that damn boat.'

'Agreed. But what will we become here?' he asked. 'We can't stay forever.'

'Give it a chance, Moritz. It hasn't even been twenty-four hours yet. Sure, it's not the Edgewater, but you could give it some time. Maybe it'll grow on you.'

I set down Carl's knife on the ground between my knees. That was the one weapon given to me for the watch. A few feet away, the gas canister and a matchbook waited, just in case things got seriously hairy. I had brought *The Maltese Falcon*, too, but the firelight didn't reach and I would need a flashlight.

Moritz and Noah had gotten enough of a shelter up to keep the tarp secured over a carpet of pine branches with blankets on top. Andrea stoked the fire, giving it one last prod before the job of keeping it up fell to me. That was part of taking the watch too. Under the sail cover, Noah and Cassandra slept at opposite ends of the shelter.

Shane had trouble falling asleep. I wondered if maybe so many days on a boat made it difficult for him to doze off without the motion of the waves. He came with me to the watch, lying on his side on a blanket. I combed through his hair with my fingers, something that usually helped him get to sleep, while Moritz – at my prodding – regaled us with stories about his treasure hunts for paintings, and more specifically, his time in Colorado with Allison and her pals.

'Liberty Village,' he began, fussing idly with the frayed end of his teal scarf, 'well, it reminded me of those American forts in old western films. Very . . . pointy. Many gates and walls, sort of . . . *blast* it, what's the word . . .'

'Frontier?' I asked, the first word that popped to mind.

'Yes! Exactly that. Frontier.'

'Did you see cowboys there?' Shane asked. I laughed and gently pinched his ear.

'Somebody is supposed to be getting to sleep.'

'I did not see any cowboys, no,' Moritz replied gently. 'Although they did have many guns. Just getting inside was quite an ordeal. One feels like a criminal, all of the gates and searches . . . But the town still stands, so such precautions must be working.'

Under my hand, Shane nodded.

'They had several paintings of interest, though some were not of professional quality. Some they used in the school and others they kept safe in a vault . . .'

'They have a school?' Shane asked, mystified.

'Yes, a large one. I'm afraid it's all very boring and normal there. Children must go to school and do their chores and help their brothers and sisters with homework.'

I smiled, knowing Moritz was teasing Shane. It worked.

'Hmph,' Shane mumbled. 'Boring doesn't sound so bad.'

'Well,' Moritz said, sighing, 'the children there don't

like their chores and sometimes they don't want to go to school at all. You might appreciate it, but they still want to fake ill and skip class and play football all day.'

'Shane doesn't like football,' I put in gently.

'Sure I do! I've just never gotten to play it right.'

And by right, he meant with other kids.

'It is scary there, too, sometimes.' Moritz frowned, a crease forming in his brow. 'Their parents go off to hunt or to recover supplies from other towns and they have to stay with a neighbor or in the community building. Not everything is school and football.'

Even I had to admit that what he was describing sounded heavenly by comparison.

'Anyway,' he said, hurrying on, 'I met Allison and Collin at the gates. They gave me a tour of the town, showed me the new buildings they were constructing and the new fences they were making for fields and gardens. I had supper in their home with a lovely fellow called Ned. He has boys around your age.'

'Do they go to school?' Shane asked.

'Almost every day, yes. They took me to the school-house. It's not very big, but they have teachers for different subjects, and they do what they can with limited resources.' He lowered his voice and listened, as I did, to the quiet wheeze emerging in Shane's breathing. Soon, he would be asleep.

'They had the Cassatt in the vault. She was beautiful; even damaged she was . . . radiant. You wouldn't believe the treasures in that room. I could have stayed for days just poring over them, looking for masterpieces. But the Cassatt was the focus and my reason for being there.' This time when he paused, Shane was snoring quietly.

'I think he's out,' I murmured, still combing his curls.

'I apologize. I think my story might have upset him.'

'It's not your fault. Some people have it better, he knows that.'

The fire crackled behind us, the light seeping to the fringes of the forest.

'Noah lent me some books,' I whispered, feeling charitable now that we were even more of a tribe. 'You should give them a read. Helps pass the time.'

'That would be lovely, yes.' Moritz smiled, leaning back and propping his hands on his knees. He was careful to keep his voice down for Shane's sake. 'I had quite a collection of books. Leaving them behind in Seattle was . . . unfortunate. Some were antiques. One,' he laughed, fondly, 'was a gift from your Allison upon leaving.'

'Really?' I perked up. 'What did she give you?'

He smirked, a lock of greasy hair falling in front of his eyes as he murmured, '*Twilight*.'

'*What?*' Yeah, that earned an incredulous guff aw. 'Talk about getting gipped . . .'

'Not so,' Moritz replied. 'She asked me to take it as a personal favor, citing an adversity to burning books. Collin accused her of snobbery. I was more than happy to take it off her hands. In doing so, I think I spared them a bit of domestic tension, or perhaps I'm attributing too much to my small gesture.' He glanced over his shoulder at the shelter. 'Perhaps young Noah would have enjoyed it.'

'Somehow I doubt that.'

'A romantic distraction might suit him . . . Might suit all of us.'

'Have you actually read that thing?' I asked, chuckling.

'No,' Moritz answered. 'The journey to Seattle left little time for relaxation.'

'Let's just say I don't generally approve of book-burning either, but in this case it might be justified . . .'

He frowned, shaking his head lightly. 'All books are to be treasured now, regardless of . . . well, regardless, yes? I have to side with Collin in this instance.'

'Says the art critic.'

'Says the snob.'

I laughed, remembering to keep my voice down at the last second. 'Pot calling the kettle, etcetera.'

Moritz shrugged. 'Perhaps.'

He stood, creeping to the fire to add another branch to the flames. My eyes swept the edge of the woods, looking for spare wood in case we ran out in the night. I couldn't help but remember earlier that afternoon – while we gathered firewood, Cassandra had acted strangely. At first she had insisted on repeating her little mantra about boys needing looking after, but then a switch got thrown and she wanted to chat my ear off. She blathered on and on, opening up to me as if we'd been friends for years catching up over a cappuccino and scones. And I was right – she was a mother. She had lost a son in The Outbreak. It had to be rough to see Shane, to be reminded constantly of the child she could no longer hug and kiss.

Moritz sat back down, wincing when a twig cracked under his foot and Shane stirred.

'You have kids?' I asked Moritz. It just slipped out. He didn't skip a beat.

'No,' he replied, 'and no wife. I kept myself busy and traveled. I traveled often. It was a solitary life, but peaceful. I think I was quite happy, comfortable, but perhaps I am remembering it wrong – rose-colored glasses and all that. Collecting garbage seems glamorous by today's standards.' He paused, and then looked over at me. The firelight danced amber in his eyes. 'What makes you ask?'

'Cassandra. She had kids. She told me all about them,' I said. It was getting colder. I looked over my shoulder at the fire longingly. 'Did you ever . . . I don't know, want a family?' Some of his snooping ways were rubbing off on me. He frowned.

'I *have* a family. Brothers, a mother and father . . . And no, I never felt compelled to start one my own. And that's good thing, too, wouldn't you say? I cannot imagine looking after children, not now. God. Especially not now.' He blanched, quickly adding, 'I didn't mean to . . . Not that Shane is . . .'

'He's my nephew, Moritz, but I'm all he's got. So he's mine. Not even technically. He's just mine.'

'And that makes him very lucky.'

I frowned, looking down at the blond curls slipping through my fingers. 'I don't know about that. We'll see.'

A quiet rustling in the trees at the edge of the beach followed my response. Moritz held up his hand, calling for silence. The fire snapped, sparked and then the leaves shook again. I felt a cold slithering crawl up my spine. I picked up the knife, shifting away from Shane. It was a long blade, but it felt totally inadequate given what might be coming through the trees. I actually held my breath and hoped for a zombie. The undead were slow, clumsy, I might be able to handle one or two, but if a fucking huge bear charged out of the darkness we would be torn to pieces.

Moritz grabbed my forearm and we stood, slowly, me dropping into a kung fu stance with the knife. I'm sure I looked preposterous, but the rustling was getting louder and any moment it would break through the branches and onto the beach. I stepped over Shane's sleeping form, putting myself between him and whatever lurked in the underbrush.

'Fuck,' I breathed, feeling my heartbeat reverberate throughout my entire body. It was close now, so close that I could actually see the bushes shake and shiver from the rim of the firelight. A black, furry form tumbled out of the undergrowth, pine needles and twigs matted to his back.

'Oh, Jesus Christ.' I nearly fell over with relief, grabbing Moritz's sleeve for balance. 'It's a fucking raccoon. *Fucker.*'

'Sneaky bugger,' he muttered. The raccoon righted himself and shook out his fur, giving Moritz an indignant sniff, as if he took the insult personally. Then he looked us over and slunk back into the darkness, a disappointed slump to his little shoulders. He had hoped to find a bunch of sleeping humans, not an armed guard.

Little did we know, he wouldn't be the last raccoon visitor to our camp, not by a long shot. We woke the next morning, to our horror, to find that we had been cleaned out. Fleeced. The raccoons had taken everything. Either we hadn't heard the sardine cans or they had figured out how to slide underneath.

Generously, they left one half-eaten apple, just to let us know that they weren't completely heartless. Also they had managed not to tip over our cupped leaves. The leaves had filled with drinkable water over night, so that was one pleasant thing.

Moritz stood pale and nervous to receive our combined judgment. He was the last person to take the watch.

'I fell asleep,' he admitted, scrunching his eyes up as if he stood in front of a firing squad. At the very least, I appreciated his honesty. 'I'm so sorry,' he said. 'I don't know how, I just . . .'

'It's okay,' I piped up before the blame game could start. There was no point in harping on it. 'We'll make the watches shorter, rotate more often.'

'That's just dandy,' Andrea replied, hands on hips for extra sass factor. 'But what about now? Right now? There's nothing to eat!'

'We can fish,' I said. Everyone fell silent. They – and especially Andrea – glared as if I had just suggested we get naked and sacrifice Noah to the gods in exchange for some miracle tacos. Shane especially looked put out by this suggestion. He took my hand, tugging on it urgently.

'The water is shallower,' I added, 'and we can appoint someone to keep an eye on the line.'

'She's right,' Moritz said. His support would've meant more if he hadn't just fucked up our whole food situation. Still, his agreement at least made the others stop scowling at me. 'Now that we know it can happen we'll just be more careful.'

'Like the raccoons,' I said. 'We're not going to get everything right the first day. Besides, there's other food. We're not on a boat, there's a whole forest out there.' I waved my hand at the woods sloping up to our left. There were no *oohs* or *aahs* of appreciation.

'Right, of course, silly me. I was just operating under the assumption that you forgot your hunting rifle – I mean, unless my eyes deceive me and those leggings of yours are actually a clown car,' Andrea said. I wouldn't take the bait. I had no interest in fighting for alpha female status. Moritz liked to take my side, which meant he was guilty by association.

'There are berries,' I said.

'That could be poisonous,' she quickly riposted.

'And there are insects.'

'That can have parasites.'

Tom Hanks was lucky; all he had to reach a consensus with was a goddamn volley ball.

'We can set some primitive snares,' I said, exasperated. 'I did it when I was twelve. I'm sure we can manage it now. And,' I hurried on before she could interrupt, 'standing around pissing and moaning about it isn't going to get food in our stomachs any faster. So either give me a better idea or start fishing.'

Andrea nodded, fidgeting with her ponytail as she always did when she was upset. I motioned for her to follow me and we separated ourselves from the group. We walked to the water's edge, just close enough for the surf to lap out our toes.

'What's going on with you?' I asked, lowering my voice.

'I don't . . . know.'

'Arturo?' I asked. She nodded. Her eyes were getting runny, overflowing with tears. Oh dear. She hadn't grieved yet, not properly. Everything was so rushed, so dire, there was never any time to let the feeling of loss really sink in. I wanted to tell her that I understood. But instead I said, 'You're strong. He was too. Make him proud, okay? And we'll look out for you, we all will.'

Not exactly an Oscar moment, but it worked. Andrea drew herself up, which wasn't to any great height, but she had the kind of face and eyes you paid attention to. People turned to look when she walked into a room and I looked to her now to keep it together.

'Okay?' I asked, looping an arm around her shoulder.

We walked back to the group like that, with her sniffling to cover up her brief breakdown.

'Here's what we're going to do,' I said, pulling focus. 'Noah and Moritz, you finish the shelter. We'll have to come up with a better system to keep the vermin out. Maybe we can line a pit and put the food in there and then weight down a cover. Cassandra, could you start on that?'

Cassandra nodded. There was no shovel, but there were a few good-sized pieces of driftwood around that might serve as a useful pick. I told her so in an undertone. She beamed up at me and nodded fast enough to scramble an egg.

'I'll fish,' Andrea stated. She was back to her old self.

'You need me to watch?' I asked.

'I'll manage.'

I hadn't volunteered for any of the tasks but I had an elaborate one in mind. Fishing would work but we would need more than that. I went to the fire and fed it. I showed Shane how to poke at the fire to keep it going and how to add smaller kindling to the bottom without scorching his fingers. He followed my movements closely with his eyes and then mimicked them, demonstrating he had listened. Without asking, he kept an eagle-eyed watch on the fire, tending to it whenever the flames gave the slightest dip. Having a straightforward job seemed to put him at ease, and he sat cross-legged a foot from the flames, shoulders straight and rigid, as if taking on *Mission: Impossible*. I wondered what was going on in that little golden head, and if maybe he really was acting out his part in a pretend drama.

Carl's knife stuck out of the sand, blade-side down. I picked it up. I hated holding it – every part of it reminded me of Carl and his ugly, mean face. Moritz walked by with a rotted log over his shoulder. He had stripped down to his shirtsleeves. With his free hand he squeezed my arm. I smiled, a little confused by the gesture.

I wandered up the beach toward the forest, mindful of our trip wire. What good was a knife? One weapon between five and a half people? And how could I hunt with this thing? I didn't exactly move with the speed and grace of a hawk. No, more like the speed and grace of a donkey. Fear I could deal with, the unknown could be met head on, but uselessness was a heavy burden. The image of those poor stragglers waiting on the pier as we sailed away flashed in front of my eyes. What if one of them had been a park ranger or passionate hunter? What if I screwed these people, and more importantly Shane, out of survival by elbowing my way onto the ship?

I sank down into the dirt, ignoring the itchy grass that stabbed through my leggings. Down on the beach, Moritz had wedged the log down into the ground and strung a line of twine from the shelter to the top of the log. He was securing something to the line, a row of papers. My drawings. They fluttered and bounced, faded and maybe ruined, but drying on the line all the same. Looking at Moritz and his little ingenious setup, inspiration hit and I smiled. What would Allison do?

There were no gun-toting rednecks or crazed religious cults here to contend with, but avoiding simple starvation presented a daunting challenge all its own. What had given me strength before – the knowledge that someone average, someone like me, was doing everything she could to overcome the undead and the new ways of the world – would give me inspiration again. How many times had I sat curled up in my barricaded apartment, peering at my computer in the darkness, reading about Allison and her friends, about just eking by without losing all hope? She had looked to her friends and colleagues for help, never losing sight of what mattered to her most – protecting the people she loved and searching for what remained of her family.

We might not be able to stay on this island forever, but it had to at least become a temporary home. Being transient didn't mean we had to suffer. Shane and I could be happy nomads if we chose to be and if I showed him how.

The pine branches scraped at my face as I pushed into the forest. I wouldn't go far, and even if I did, I had the knife. Keeping the campfire in sight, I searched the forest floor, picking up various pieces of wood and discarding them if they didn't meet my criteria. It took about thirty minutes to find the perfect specimens, but I felt triumphant – if a bit battered and scraped – when I marched back down to the beach.

As they finished the shelter, Moritz and Noah glanced my way every couple of minutes, curious. I hacked at the larger piece of wood. It was gently curved. I brought it to the water's edge and soaked it for a while, then went back to the campfire and carefully warmed it over the edge of the coals. Even Andrea was getting curious, peering over her shoulder at me as she fished off of a boulder to the east. This wasn't something I had ever attempted myself, but I knew the theory of it. I watched my father strip the wood and carefully mold it, wishing I had the skill and patience to mimic his efficient movements. He liked to show off and I always got the feeling that it made him feel like the best dad in the world to make a semi-functional bow right in front of his daughter's eyes.

This felt right. This felt like progress. I hacked at the smaller piece of wood, peeling back the bark. Occasionally I'd run down to the water to soak the larger piece again and warm it – soak, warm, soak, warm – until it was bending visibly in front of my eyes. Shane began paying less attention to the fire, peeking at my project beneath a brow furrowed with curiosity. It took the greater part of the morning, but by mid afternoon I had something that actually bore resemblance to a bow. When I was satisfied with the curve, I notched the top and stretched a piece of twine between the top and bottom arcs for a string. I tested the string, tightened the knots, and made adjustments until I could pull back the twine. The arrow was trickier and more time consuming, demanding a lot of careful peeling and whittling, and so for comfort's sake I moved the whittling under the shelter to get out of the sun.

'Holy cow, Sadie,' Noah said, admiring my work. He and Moritz had taken a break from helping Cassandra with the food pit. 'That thing actually gonna work?'

'I don't know,' I said honestly. 'But it's worth a shot.'

Oh, come on.

'Worth a shot? A *shot*? Get it?'

Noah laughed, sweet boy that he was, but Moritz only squeezed out a grin.

'Yeah that was bad,' I admitted. 'Seriously, it could work. Somehow I have to get these arrow points sharp enough.' I had started working on arrow number two, but I still didn't know what to use for feathers and said as much to the group. It might take days to gather up a significant amount from the woods.

'How about a bit of bark?' Moritz suggested.

'That could work,' I said, nodding.

He disappeared, blue scarf fluttering, and came back with a wide peel of dry bark. I cut triangles from it with the knife, praying that the whole contraption would work and not leave me looking like a complete boob. If the bow failed I would've wasted an entire morning on well-meaning incompetency.

I thought of leaving camp right then and there to try it out, but the afternoon was almost over and I wasn't about to head out into the forest just before nightfall. So far we had experienced nothing more sinister than a horde of thieving raccoons, but there was worse out there. I could feel it. We could all feel it. I wasn't about to go off into the darkness or take any unnecessary risks. This was already a chancy endeavor and I wanted it to succeed. I wanted Shane to look at me the way I had beamed at my dad. I wanted more than anything for him to believe that Aunt Sadie was a reliable guardian, even if she did make very pathetic puns.

To help the uneasy silence descending on the camp, I let Shane play with the bow, keeping the arrows safely out of his reach. He looked privately pleased as he handled the too-big handle, pulling back the string a little and grinning when it twanged.

It was stupid, but I felt proud, really fucking proud.

Instead of venturing off into the forest, I lounged in the shelter and read Noah's books, glancing up from time to time to make sure Shane hadn't wandered too far. The books were quick to read, engrossing, fun and hard to put down. And it was pure joy to imagine that world of nothing but liquor and fast times, indiscriminate sex and flagrant misogyny. Okay, maybe not the last part, but it was glamorous. Not even seven months of terror and death and limited hygiene could erase that memory. I had seen awful carnage, neighbors pulled to pieces right in front of my eyes, things that should've crushed my spirit, anyone's spirit, but didn't. If I tried, I could still remember what it felt like to wear lipstick, the decadent way it made you want to pout and the waxy taste when it accidentally touched your tongue.

I must have had a fool's expression on my face because Moritz was watching me. He did that a lot. He did it on the boat and the habit had carried right on over to this new camping thing.

'I believe the story's on the page,' he said with a chuckle. 'Not out there.' He waved lazily at the forest outside the shelter.

'Do you think we have enough water for tonight?'

'Don't change the subject.' This was a new tone of voice for him, a flirtatious one.

'I *want* to change the subject.' I stared down at the book but the mood was gone. Sadly, I couldn't slide back into *The Big Sleep* the way Vivian Rutledge slid in and out of a cream silk robe. He scooted closer. Right, as if that would help. 'Seriously, Moritz, just don't. No flirting, not now. *Verboten*, okay?'

With a sigh he got up, visibly hurt, and disappeared out of the shelter. Andrea turned up in time to read the frustration on my face. I didn't have time to try and cover up my shitty mood.

'Sadie? What's wrong?' she asked.

'Nothing,' I said, dropping my head down into the open book. I groaned. "Did that drug cache of yours survive the storm?'

'Yeah, why?'

'I think I might need a tranquilizer. A big one – if it can knock out a Clydesdale then we're headed in the right direction.'

Andrea laughed, her dark ponytail swinging from side to side. She pushed the bangs off my forehead, ostensibly checking my eyes to see if I was already on something. The touch of her fingers against my skin made me jolt. Human touch was a foreign thing now.

'Did you and Moritz fight?' she asked, sitting down beside me. Her hand rubbed up and down my back. So we were friends again. Maybe she really would give me that tranquilizer.

'It's Carl,' I said, cutting right to the chase. 'I can't get him out of my head. Every time I think he's gone for good he pops up again, staring at me, laughing. I don't know what he wants, but I just want him gone. That *bastard* . . . he tried to take Shane from me. That's all I can think about. Someone trying to take him away again.'

It was like some endless nightmare version of *Duck Hunt* but with Carl's twerp face popping up instead of a bird.

'Feeling guilty over losing him?'

'*Lose*? I didn't lose him. I didn't wager him in a game of keno, Andrea. I pushed him down the stairs and broke his neck. I killed him.' Getting it out, hearing the actual words, made the pain come again. There was Carl in my mind and right behind him, Shane, the little boy sitting a stone's throw away who knew that I was a killer. But I had to do it . . . It was awful, but I would've done much worse to protect Shane.

'Don't be so hard on yourself,' she said. 'It was a disaster, a really bad one. But you're miles away now. Remember?' It felt good to be helped, to be treated like a sister, a human being. I nodded. She went on. 'And there's nothing you can do. Listen, Sadie, without mistakes things would get really fucking boring. I know you know that. There'd be less poetry, no heartbreak . . .'

'No Vegas.'

She laughed quietly and then said, 'Carl's not here. Carl's dead. We took his knife. He can't get you. And you learned a lesson. I don't think you'll fall for another Carl anytime soon.'

'You're right,' I said. 'You're right. But I'd still like those drugs, please.'

'I'm afraid not,' Andrea said, patting my back. 'You're on your own for this one. Trust me, Sadie, it's better this way.'

'You're the worst drug dealer ever. But you're right. I'll get over it . . . not much of a choice, really. And I have to stay awake. You'll turn Shane against me if I let you spend any more time with him.'

Her glittering laughter trailed behind her as she stood and left the shelter. I propped myself up on my elbows and looked down at *The Big Sleep*. Sleep, especially the big kind, sounded good, but it was too early for that. There was the watch to think about and the high winds that were tugging at the shelter tarp and I couldn't let Shane wear out the string on the bow. I made a promise that I'd test the bow tomorrow and that no matter what, no matter how hard it was, I'd kill something for my fellow castaways. We were a tribe now, beholden to each other. Andrea had caught us fish, Cassandra had made a safe place for our food and Moritz and Noah had completed a fairly impressive shelter.

I ran my fingertips along the smooth curve of the bow. It was time for me to step up. Time to answer the question: What would Allison do?

EIGHT

There was no chance for me to test out my bow the next day. Winds gusted morning and afternoon, tearing at the shelter and sending cascading howls through the trees. The waves out around the shore became jagged, tall and peaked like whipped cream. There was a brief shower at mid-morning and we were grateful for that. Our trips out of the shelter were quick, only to collect rainwater in the tin cups we had taken from the ship. We lined them up just outside the shelter and the rain pinged against the rims, making quiet xylophone songs, pixie music.

Our food situation did not improve. With the high winds blowing all day it was impossible to fish or really do much of anything. Every twenty minutes or so Noah dove for the twine ties holding down the shelter. The wind tore them free. When it was my turn to collect the rainwater cups I was sure the gales would rip the flesh right off my skeleton.

Without the fire, my reading daylight was used up by five o'clock; out of light, out of luck, like a shattered mirror in a closet.

I'm sure we should've been making intricate survival schematics or digging some kind of bear-proof trench, but instead Noah and I held a contest to see who could come up with the most convincing finger puppets for Shane. Riveting stuff.

It was a miserable day, and worse than the winds was the brief glimpse of a figure looming in the trees up the hill. No one else saw it, just me. I would recognize that kind of slumped, lumbering silhouette anywhere. The undead. A chill descended into my bones, settling there like a damp mold. We were not alone on the island. I watched the creature hesitate on the seam dividing the forest and the hill running down to the beach. He seemed to be testing something, maybe the steepness of the hill or the rockiness of the terrain. We had found out in Seattle they were not completely without ingenuity – hundreds had died when one single creature found its way through a milelong stretch of ventilation pipe and into a warehouse. And now we knew they could handle themselves in the water. The thing vanished into the trees, its limp right leg trailing like a macabre little tail.

I said nothing.

What would it help, to spread panic like that? I couldn't even be sure of what I'd seen. And if it really was one of the undead, I wasn't equipped to take it out, not with an untried bow or Carl's knife. Not to mention, why didn't it just charge down the hill toward us? Sure, the terrain was rough, but just as a single zombie could find its way through an air vent, they could also be dumb as rocks. Animals were smarter. An animal might realize it couldn't make a safe path down the steep hill. What ever it was, I would stay up that night. If the eerie shadow made another appearance, or worse, actually ventured into camp, I'd share my suspicions with the others.

Right, because if a zombie tore through camp it would be time for reasoned discussion.

That night we got the flames burning again and I saw Andrea go to the first watch of the night. I joined her, claiming I couldn't sleep. Two of us would be better than one, and I could sit up and see if the visitor returned. No matter how sleepy I became, I didn't lie down, and when I started to doze the weight of my head falling jolted me back awake. I checked on Shane from time to time, and standing to do that helped keep me from abandoning the watch and giving in to sleep. The rest of the time, Andrea and I chatted softly or simply sat. She was the kind of person who didn't mind sitting in silence. I appreciated that about her.

Shane was sleeping fitfully whenever I wandered back to the shelter. After midnight, when Andrea's time was up, she went and roused Moritz to take his shift. Finally, when dawn came and went with no sign of another weird shadow, I joined Shane under the tarp, keeping Carl's knife close just in case. Half-asleep, I heard Moritz get Noah up for his time at the watch, though I was too tired to make out much of what they said.

We survived the night without an attack. I woke pinned to the tarp by half of Moritz, who had sprawled out like a parachutist with a serious deployment problem. Crawling out from under his sour armpit, I verified that we were all alive and still human. Noah dozed quietly on his side. Andrea was up and fussing with the fire. The winds were down. Outside, near to the water, Cassandra was building a sand castle. When I gave the okay, Shane bolted out of the shelter and ran down to the beach. He watched Cassandra from a cautious distance away. She crowned the top of the castle with a little piece of driftwood wrapped in seaweed. A flag.

Oookay.

'That's an impressive castle you've got there,' I said charitably, shuffling across the uneven ground. Her tower was lopsided and disintegrating into the sand. The flag was the only recognizable part.

'Thank you,' she chirped. 'I couldn't sleep, it was hot in there,' she said, using a voice that sounded remarkably like a child doing an imitation of a grown-up. The way she emphasized 'hot' made my skin tighten.

'I hope you didn't lose sleep,' I said. Then I turned and wandered away, motioning for Shane to accompany me, finding that Cassandra was too distracted to keep up the conversation. At the fire, Andrea was struggling to keep her eyes open. Shane went immediately to stoke the flames and tend the logs as I'd shown him. Poor Andrea. Her pretty face had gone puffy and there were dark violet bags beneath her eyes. I saw her throw a pill back and then blush when I caught her doing it.

'Hey,' I said.

'Hey.'

'What was that all about?' I asked.

'Just tired. Didn't get much sleep last night. I'm a drug dealer. I might as well use the drugs, right?'

'Again,' I said sharply, tipping my head toward Shane. 'Language.'

'Sorry,' Andrea muttered. She was glaring at Cassandra over my left shoulder. Andrea was the kind of woman who cleaned up into a knockout, but when she was pissed, she looked feral enough to bite your leg clean off.

'I thought that was the number one rule of, uh, pharmaceutical specialists,' I replied. Shane snorted, apparently unimpressed by my attempts to be sly around him. 'Don't get involved with the product.'

'Sadie, there are no rules. And if there are, well then fu— *eff* 'em.'

Her eyes wouldn't budge from Cassandra. I waved my fingers in front of Andrea's face. 'Something you wanna tell me?'

'No.'

'Oh God,' I said, finally putting two and two together. The pills, the excessive crankiness, the glaring . . . 'You're covering her watches, aren't you?'

Andrea leaned in close, dropping her voice. I could smell the fire on her hair. 'She can barely chew her own food. Do you think I'm going to trust her with my safety? Nuh-uh, no gracias.'

'I'll take one of them,' I said. 'We can split it.'

Andrea nodded, silent, but I could read the relief in the sag of her shoulders.

'No more pills,' I added, turning to return to the shelter. 'I need you sharp.'

She cocked her head to the side. I stuck my arms out and made a gargling groaning sound, rolling my eyes into the back of my head. 'You know,' I said, straightening up. 'In case we have company?'

Andrea chuckled and nodded, reaching up to tighten her ponytail. She had draped a blanket over her shoulders like a poncho and layered two pairs of thermal underwear. The wind and rain from the day before had left the beach drafty and foggy, unpleasant by anyone's standards.

'Sadie,' she said. I stopped. 'I know you just woke up and you probably don't want to hear this, but we have enough food for today,' she said. 'And today only. I can try to catch more fish but . . . they're not exactly jumping into my lap.'

'I'll take care of it,' I said.

'I beg your pardon?' She was laughing, watching me with her arms crossed over her poncho chest.

'I've got a plan.'

Boy did I ever. In the shelter, it took some creative limb arranging to shimmy the bow and arrows out from under the menfolk. Moritz started awake, his sparkly blue eyes flying open in alarm. I put my finger to my mouth and shushed him.

'Nothing's wrong,' I whispered, nodding in Noah's direction. 'He's still asleep.'

'What are you doing?' he asked. Well, he was awake now, no use lying.

'I'm going to go practice with this thing,' I said. *And get my motherfucking hunt on.* I didn't say that part aloud.

'Where?'

'Just up the beach,' I lied, 'I don't want to hit anyone by accident.' I tested the end of one of the arrows. I had whittled it down to razor sharpness. My fingertip welled with blood. 'These could shoot your eye out.'

Moritz swished his mouth to the side. He really did look like some kind of puppy. Those eyes could make a girl think twice about going off to war. Or to hunt. I smiled, gesturing breezily to the open air.

'I'll be fine,' I said. 'What's the worst that could happen?'

'Do you actually want me to tell you?'

'Good-bye, Moritz.'

He sighed and rolled onto his back.

'Please be careful,' he whispered. 'Don't do anything foolish.'

Thoughtful man. *Smart* man. He knew he wasn't going to win this one. Shane had stopped assaulting the fire with his makeshift poker, sitting next to the flames, watching from a distance as Andrea settled down to fish. So she was going to try and solve our food crisis, too, eh? A two-pronged approach. I liked it. I liked it even more when I remembered that I had never shot a bow in my life. What I didn't like was the thought of leaving Shane behind while I went off to play hunter in the woods.

There was a bit of dried fish left in my garbage bag. It was starting to go rancid, but I choked it down and chased it with a dented (probably also rancid) can of Shasta from the cockpit hold. Andrea had tried to experiment with smoking some of the fish she caught over the fire. It resulted in slightly mushy, smoke-flavored, undercooked fish. Couple that with the fact that I had no idea *what* kind of fish it was, and you've got yourself a tried and true Mystery Breakfast. Her deboning skills could also use some work. If the zombies or starvation didn't get us, then punctured tracheas might. My stomach growled. If I waited much longer I'd convince myself out of going. *WWAD?* I reminded myself. Allison would hunt. She wouldn't sit around waiting for hunger or zombies or rogue fish bones to show her the door to hell. Just before leaving, I grabbed our compass, Carl's knife, and a stale piece of white bread and wrapped it in a scrap of tarp. I'd need a break eventually and lunch too.

Shane was my last bit of business. He had started laying out his collection of shells and rocks next to the fire, waving his hands over his finds like some hypnotized, pint-sized shaman. I patted his curls, smiling wanly as I said, 'I'm going to go practice with the bow.'

He gazed up at me and then nodded toward the forest. 'Can I come?'

'No,' I replied. 'I have to go alone. Stay here and keep the others safe.'

That made him smile. Leaving him, even momentarily, was hard, but desperate times call for desperately stupid shenanigans. Even so . . . I crouched down next to him. 'I don't want you to worry, yeah? I'll be back as soon as I can. Are you going to worry?'

Shane's lower lip trembled. 'No . . .'

'You're a terrible liar.' I ruffled his hair again. 'Only I get to worry. Stick close to Andrea and I promise I won't do anything stupid. With any luck, we'll have something tasty for dinner to night.'

With that I stood and paused before turning to the forest. 'I love you, bud.'

'Yeah.'

'Yeah, what?'

'Yeah, you love me.'

'You could say it back.' I don't know why, but I couldn't justify leaving before hearing him say it.

He sighed, picking up one of the shells to use it as a pretend monocle as he mumbled, 'I love you too.'

'Thanks. Be good.'

I started up the hill toward the tree line with my heart heavy and my feet dragging. I must have glanced back at Shane twelve times, feeling like a depressed Robin Hood and his band of Merry Gastrointestinal Complications. Hunger, dehydration, malnutrition, Shasta gas . . .

'Be careful,' Andrea called after me. She wouldn't tell me to stay, wouldn't insist that I was foolhardy and suicidal. It was really that bad. And apparently she had more faith in

124

me than Moritz did. He didn't need to know that I was going into the trees. Small, furry and edible animals didn't generally hang out in the open on the beach, but art critics don't spend a lot of time thinking about these sorts of things I guess.

The sun spread across the water, blinding me as I paused to look back at Andrea.

'You'll shoot your eye out!' she cried.

'I already made that joke, loser!'

'You're the loser, loser!' she shouted.

I laughed and waved back at her. 'I'm taking the knife!'

'Fine,' she called. 'Just don't stay out too long.'

All variety of pants-pissing thoughts descended on me as I stared up at the fortress of trees marking the entrance to the forest. I remembered that we had no idea just how big the island was. It could be absolutely swarming with the undead or it could be some kind of killer bear sanctuary. Carl's knife was big but it wasn't *that* big. There was a bitter innuendo in there somewhere, but I was just too damn frightened to consider it.

Inside the tree cover it was about five degrees cooler. I took one of my arrows and aimed for a nearby tree. I would need some practice, and the trees were thinner here, with less brush. It would be a nightmare trying to find a stray arrow in the thicker parts of the forest. If I was going to blunder, I wanted to do it here, in the semi-open. With enough practice I might be able to make the trip short, and that meant getting back to Shane.

'Come on, Dad,' I whispered, testing the string. 'Show me what you got.'

This should be the part where I explain that I spent two hours trying to relocate one arrow, or that the bow fell apart like an Erector Set the minute I tried to pull back the string. But one thing was going my way. The bow worked like a dream – and better, I was a natural.

On my second try, I hit the tree I was aiming for and when I went to inspect the impact, found that the arrow had actually dug in about half an inch. Hell yes. I stifled the wild urge to raise my bow and trill like Xena: Warrior Princess. I had more dignity than that . . . I'd wait until I was at least out of earshot of the others.

Silently, I thanked whatever bow-hunting ancestry lingered in my mutt heritage and, more importantly, I thanked my dad for dragging me along on all those camping trips. I'd absorbed something and his enthusiasm and attention had paid off. And maybe I was part Viking or Cherokee or simply part badass and Dad had failed to mention it. Satisfied that I wasn't totally useless, and that a hunting trip might actually be worth the time and effort, I went a little deeper into the tress. If I could keep the camp due south, then finding my way back would be easy. Making liberal use of the knife would help, too, hacking a trail that would stand out against the untouched wildness of the forest. I would be back in a flash, I insisted, envisioning the look on Shane's face when I showed him that even a clumsy, goof ball aunt could put dinner on the table.

The density of the trees and shrubs swallowed up my footfall, muting birds and insects as if the vegetation and ground lay beneath a heavy blanket of snow. Here sounds simply died. I kept a close, careful eye out for infected animals. I'd seen my share of infected dogs in the city, and they tended to give themselves away quickly. They didn't act like normal animals. They rushed, desperate, unafraid. I was pretty confident I would at least notice a fawn charging out of the brush. I looked up, awed by the height of the trees. The pines were king and they held court in force. Their white scent touched everything. I felt alive, weirdly alive, like . . . I don't know. Like a person that wasn't me. Like a person who actually enjoyed the hunt and the idea of killing. Just the suggestion of hunting live animals used to give me kumquat-sized hives. But maybe there was something untapped in all of us.

Channeling Jack Handy would have to wait. There was a leafy rustling directly ahead to the north. Aha, yes! The prey, *my* prey, was near. It sounded perfect, just like it ought to, a deer maybe or a wild pig. Did those exist in this part of the world? I didn't know, but my blood was running high, going straight to my head, making me giddy. The oxygen here made a significant impact, too. It was rich, clear, and made your body run differently, the way high-performance fuel gives a sports car an edge, a spark.

I crouched, not because I could even see the damn thing, but because that's what my dad and people do in movies when they hunt. It made sense. Maybe if it were a deer it would spot me if I stayed standing. *Dumb ass, a deer would smell you from a mile away.* I pushed aside a tall ferny plant and tried to step over a thorny bush. The bush snagged my leggings and I cursed, stung by something that might have just been a nettle but felt more like a scorpion.

The rustling persisted. I hadn't scared the thing off with my goofus tracking.

I followed, trying to keep a safe distance away in case it was something big and hungry, promising right then that if it was anything larger than a doe I would retreat and hightail it back to camp. It was much farther away than I had originally thought. I wasn't going to lose it, not when I had this feeling. I could do this, I thought, and I even went so far as to picture myself returning to camp with a doe carcass slung over my shoulders like I was Kevin fucking Sorbo.

The forest emptied out into an oval-shaped clearing. The grass had been tamped down, flattened. There were deer droppings everywhere, sitting in clumpy land mines every few inches. I kept to the fringe of the clearing, trying to stay out of the den and still keep my eyes on the rustling. This was hard work. My arms were beginning to ache from holding the bow in its taught position, with the arrow carefully balanced. The forest had felt chilly and damp before, now it was just damp and I wouldn't have been surprised if I was the dampest thing in it. I honestly couldn't tell if I was hot, cold or just sweaty or maybe a generous heaping of all three.

Birds tittered down at me from the trees; I saw a few chipmunks and plenty of insects, but everything else fled before I came in glancing distance. Whatever I was tracking must have gotten wise to my game. It continued moving, carving a swerving path, pausing less and less. Still, I could see where the branches were broken and sagging – it was real, living, and sooner or later I would find it.

Finally, the animal stopped and I knew I had it. There was a flash of brown low beneath the branches, like fur, and I had a good line of sight. Now or never, I thought, you came to dance so get on the floor.

I pulled back the arrow, let out a long, calming breath and let fly.

Thunk.

The good kind of thunk. My arrow had flown true. The rustling of branches around the animal intensified and I heard a sad kind of grunt. That made me frown, but it was part of the experience, part of hunting. Circle of life, I reminded myself, you're going to save us all, my delicious furry friend.

I realized then that I had been hunting for hours, just trying to kill one stupid animal, and now I had done it and it was just about as easy as sawing through a steak with a gummy worm. All that remained was to collect my prize. I took out the knife, knowing the hard truth – that I might have to finish it off with a stab. I had to think of Shane, of the others, of food and not the gruesome reality of what *getting* that food actually meant.

'Where are you?' I whispered, pushing aside branches and ferns. It had fallen somewhere in the trees to the northwest. At least, that's where its dying noise had come from. I rounded the edge of a huge, snarled dead tree and just about dropped out of my own skin.

There was my prey. Oh, it was dead all right.

'Shit.'

I backed up, quickly, back through the ferns as fast as my little legs would carry me. I didn't want to turn. I was absolutely *not* about to put my back to that thing, not for a million cans of baked beans. It lurched after me, arms stretched out as if it wanted to give me a big, sloppy bear hug. There would be no hugging of any kind, I promised myself, aiming another arrow. If I could get it through the head I might have a chance of bringing it down. That whole aiming thing got a lot tougher when you were no longer predator and had become, unmistakably, prey.

The smell rolling off this thing was cataclysmic. Bad, overpowering, like a moose in a sweat lodge. It was a man, or had been, and my arrow stuck out of its shin at a straight-on angle. What I had mistaken for fur was brown corduroy.

He looked like a woodsy fellow, with a red flannel shirt and hiking boots. I had never been this close to a zombie before in my life, except maybe in the water. I was never much of a rubbernecker, which was good for me because the people who ran out into the streets during The Outbreak, determined to satisfy their curiosity, tended to die. I also don't have much of a stomach for gore; even tame horror movies make me queasy. The blood starts flowing and the limbs start flying and I'm seeking out the nearest toilet.

The creature slowed down, rasping at me through a jagged gap in his throat. The black hole of his mouth was ringed with fresh blood. Then he stopped altogether. I aimed. He made a strange sound, like a 'huh?' and, knowing I had to, I glanced over my shoulder. Oh, no. This was not a solo affair; it was a dinner date for two. His date looked hungry, or rather, her skull looked hungry. Most of her skin and the fleshy hollows of the cheeks and chin were gone, hanging in rubbery loops from her jawbone, as if she had stepped out of Madam Tussaud's and into a blast furnace.

I ran. Yes, I know I said I would never, ever turn my back on that zombie, but now there were two. Two is not nearly the same as one. I fled, right past the female with the melting face, and wove through the trees as best I could. Part of me wanted to drop the bow, to just say fuck it and get rid of the cumbersome thing. But they would keep chasing me, I knew that, and eventually I'd have to face the music. It was not a happy tune. There was one arrow left, unless I somehow found a way to get the other one back from Tim the Tool Man Flesh-Eater.

A different clearing opened wide in front of me, not a den this time but a glade where dead trees had fallen, rotted and left the ground squishy and dark. I stopped there, knowing that I might actually be able to get off a clear shot without so many trees in the way. My friends arrived, stumbling through the undergrowth, their faces thick with flies. Without breaking stride they came for me. I chose to aim for the man. He was bigger and if I had to face one of them with the knife, then I would rather take his companion.

Apollo or Paris or the spirit of Errol fucking Flynn was with me in that moment, because I hit him square in the face. The arrow stuck in so far I thought it might fly clean through. He paused, moaning again, and swayed. Then he crumpled to the ground, straight down, like a balloon deflating. This didn't even put a hitch in his girlfriend's step. I backed away and heard a new sound, an unexpected sound. Water. I must have run northwest and back toward the edge of the island. I might be near the wrecked boat or farther north. Too far north. Way, way too far from camp and Shane. What if there were more? What if they were heading to camp right now? I had to get back and sound the alarm.

These thoughts spurred me, and I crashed through the trees toward the sound of rushing waves. The bow was growing slick in my grasp and my hair and clothes were soaked with sweat. The zombie kept after me, giving chase, and she was gaining. Out of breath, with the beach visible through the trees, I whirled to face her head on. I dropped the bow and brandished the knife. Then I saw a fallen log and had a better idea.

Heaving and grunting, I shouldered the branch. It was wide, four inches around, and waterlogged, heavy as a motherfucker. I wound up and wound up some more. This Bud's for you, Bear Jew. I let the log go, swinging with every ounce of strength left in my sweaty little body. I'm sure I made a terrible shrieking noise.

Her head was as soft as a Christmas pudding. I had to drop down quickly to avoid the spray of blackish blood and fleshy goo that exploded up and out. That was enough of that. I didn't need to stay and examine my work. I took up my bow and knife and ran for the beach, lungs bursting, ignoring the stitch in my side as I thought desperately of a way to reorient and get back to camp. Breaking through the trees and feeling the salt air on my face was heavenly. There was nothing better, nothing sweeter, than knowing I had just faced death and kicked it squarely in the balls.

But I was crying. It was sweet and terrible. I looked at my hands. The log had chewed them to bits and they were raw from holding the bow for so long. I reached for my back pocket to take out the white bread. I would eat that delicious square of stale crap and love every bite. I would drop down on the pebbly beach, kick out my legs and just enjoy the sun on my face and live. Then I would head south and get back to Shane and next time I wouldn't head so deep into the forest.

The water here was shallow, with a rocky shore shielded from the wind, like a tide pool.

I pulled the bread free of the tarp scrap and looked out at the surf, ignoring the stinging in my hands. Time enough for a brief snack and then I would be on the move again. But I stopped with the bread halfway to my mouth. There was a sharp figure rising from the horizon. A man was in the water, the sun silhouetting him in black, and he didn't look dead. No, he looked very much alive and he was staring right at me.

NINE

I should qualify that last statement. He looked alive, but not for long. Suddenly his entire body jerked and his arms shuddered. In a flash he disappeared beneath the water. Something had pulled him under. I thought of the boat, of Arturo.

Well, shit.

It had to be the excess adrenaline freewheeling through my veins. I can't think of anything else that could explain my next act of heroism (read: Stupidity). In one motion I dropped the bread and bow (kept the knife), threw off my shoes and sweater, and waded into the water. Dry shoes and a warm sweater would seem inviting later because it was ice cold. I had forgotten that bit. There was another round of splashing on the horizon, water flinging up and spraying like Jaws was on the hunt.

It couldn't be that deep, right? Wrong. The water rose quickly to my waist and then my chest. My clothes were dragging me down but I was getting nearer the commotion. I saw a flicker of a hand appear above the water. There was still a chance I would get there in time.

It sounds awful, but I actually half-hoped it was a shark attack. A person could recover from a shark bite. Not so much with a zombie.

It's amazing how fast you move when motivated by fear. I had gotten close enough to feel the spray of the splashing water on my face. But then there was a shooting pain in my feet, a sensation like walking on hypodermic needles. I screamed, hopping up and down, which only made things worse. *Prick – prick – prick*. What *was* that? Limping forward, I kicked my feet up to swim a little and avoid the stabby hell-carpet underwater.

This was an even worse situation than I had initially thought. Now I was injured and returning to my friends would be an absolute nightmare. No food from the hunt and now this . . . what a waste of time and energy and, I thought with a gulp, potentially my life.

When I finally got to the flailing, struggling stranger I had gone up on tiptoes. The piercing needles along the rocky seafloor disappeared, but the pain lingered. My feet felt like ground chuck. I was in tears as I reached for the stranger's hand and yanked. I don't know what good I expected to do, but seeing someone in trouble, in agony . . . I couldn't just stand and do nothing, not when Arturo had been taken from us so swiftly. And I was riding on a high – I had just taken down two zombies by myself. I was Superwoman.

He started shrieking. It was awful, but there was no blood so I pulled harder, trying to bring him back toward the shore and shallower waters. He was dragging me beneath the water, his arm and torso too big for me to handle. The screaming changed pitch. I struggled to see his face, to determine just what exactly had hold of him. Whether it was the Kraken or just a cramp from swimming too soon after a meatball sub, he was going down fast. I was about to dive beneath the water to find out for myself, and

I had even tucked the knife into my mouth, when I noticed he was no longer screaming. He wasn't shrieking in pain, he was laughing. *Giggling*.

I reeled back, taking the knife out of my mouth to make room for gaping at him. He stood up, not in trouble at all. Perfectly fine. I glared up at him, and then up some more. He was tall, immense. With the sun blazing over his shoulder I couldn't make out his face. I glared at it anyway, frozen with rage.

'What?' he said, laughing. 'Is there something on my face?'

'Yes. Your eyeballs. I'm about two seconds away from stabbing them.'

'I wanted to see you up close,' he said. His voice was deep, booming. 'And here you are.'

He slicked the water off his face, some of it landing on mine. I slapped him, fast, with an open palm. He laughed again. The prickly, agonizing heat flickered through my feet and I winced. I bent at the waist, contorting from the pain. And that's when I saw it.

'What?' he asked. 'What is it?'

He was of course referring to my pain dance, but my eyes were widening in response to a hand, withered and white, just a few inches below the surface of the water. It rippled in the iridescent dance and play of the waves, but I knew what it was. I slashed at the hand with my knife, but the damn thing's other arm was already around the man's ankle.

He screamed. He screamed a real, genuine and panicky scream. I almost said: 'Serves you right, moron.' What I actually said was, 'Lean forward!'

The bloodless, severed hand floated to the surface. I

135

could see the zombie's face now and it was going for the stranger's ass. This was the third one in an hour. Christ, I thought, this was becoming a regular thing (zombies obviously, not asses). I crouched down into the water and stabbed at its face. That was enough of a distraction for me to take a chance, extend my arm and cut at its other hand. I saw the mouth, the broken, jagged teeth just centimeters from my wrist.

'Hold still!'

Even though it was rotting, the zombie's wrist bone was giving me trouble. I hacked for all I was worth and – with a final push – the hand finally came free, still grasping the man around his ankle.

Two hands locked around my arms and then I was sailing through the air before I could get a scream out. Water filled my nose and mouth. I landed a safe three or four feet away and immediately scrambled back to the light. My face broke the surface in time to see that the zombie had reared up, enraged and standing. But it was a fairer fight now. The stranger lunged for the zombie, grabbing it by the right arm with both hands. I tried to wade forward and give him the knife, but I realized it was gone. Somehow, it had slipped right out of my hand. But it didn't matter. With one wrenching jerk, the man had pulled the zombie's arm clean off at the shoulder.

And then, with almost nonchalant ease, he clubbed the zombie to death with its own arm.

I stood five yards away and watched, openmouthed, feet blazing with the fury of Satan and all his fiery minions. When he was done, the zombie didn't have much more than a meaty stump on its shoulders.

A burst of painfully obvious inspiration told me it

would be best to get out of the water. There could be more of those things. I waded back to the beach, cursing every step. Suddenly, I was exhausted. I wished with all my heart that I could magically transport back to our camp and lay next to the fire. Andrea would have painkillers – beautiful, beautiful painkillers. Just the thought of them made me swoon. I made the mistake of looking down at my feet. A trail of blood followed me up onto the rocky beach, my blood. I could see raw, angry pink flesh curving up around the outside of my toes. Jesus.

I would never make it back to camp on my own at this rate.

I'm not proud of it, but at the sight of my own blood I lost some time. I blacked out.

When I came to I was bouncing along in the air. Upon further and scrabling examination, I realized I was being carried. It wasn't a pleasant way to wake up. After all, I didn't exactly trust this man, whoever he was. He had nearly gotten us both killed, and for what? For all I knew he could've been a cannibal and I was the main course. The water bobbed along over his left shoulder. We were traveling down the beach.

'Put me down!'

He started at my outburst and then grinned. It was blinding.

'Welcome back,' he said. His voice was low and relaxed, amused. It rumbled against me where my arm touched his chest. For someone who had just beaten a zombie to re-death with its own arm he seemed remarkably calm.

'Put me down.' I wriggled and kicked.

'Are you sure?'

'Yes!' I started batting at his arms. If he was a cannibal then he was being awfully casual about his next meal.

'Are you *sure* you're sure?'

'For God's sake, yes!'

He swung out his left hand and I dropped down to the ground. As soon as my feet skimmed the pebbles I was jumping back into his arms.

'No!' I shouted. 'Okay, okay, pick me up!'

He did so without argument and smiled again. I was hoisted into the air like a sack of feathers. He had tied my shoes together and slung them over his shoulder. My sweater was wrapped tightly around my middle. Something clinked against his side, a big mesh bag filled with what looked like stones.

It was embarrassing to be carried like that. Husbands and wives did this on the threshold of their wedding night, and at that moment I couldn't imagine a scenario more inappropriate. There are, of course, worse things than being lofted around by a big strong man. But he was a stranger, I reminded myself, even if he was an obliging one. And it was his fault I could no longer walk. I thought about slapping him again, on behalf of my feet, but decided to save that for another time. If he dropped me I wasn't sure I could stand the pain.

Running back to camp and raising the alarm was the right thing to do – the *only* thing to do – but with my feet ripped to shreds I wasn't going anywhere without, well, being carried. Or crawling. Being carried was the slightly less repugnant option. An image of Shane frightened and alone nagged, vivid enough to make my cheeks flame with shame. I had abandoned him. That wouldn't stand.

'Stop! Just stop and let me think.' My head lolled back

on my shoulders as he came to a halt. 'Fuck! Goddamn it . . .'

'You'll walk again,' he said matter-of-factly.

'It's not that,' I said, although that was weighing heavily on my mind, too. 'My nephew . . . My friends will think I'm dead. I have to get back. You have to take me back.'

'There are more of you?'

The knife. Their only protection against zombies. It was gone. I didn't need to look to know that. Somewhere in the tidal pool the knife sat, forgotten and never to be found again. I noticed a taught string around his shoulder right next to my shoes. He had brought my bow.

'My friends are at the southern beach. I have to go back, tonight. You have to take me there.'

'So that's where you came from,' he said. 'I thought we might have riled the natives.'

'I know this is going to sound idiotic in every conceivable way,' I said, drawing a deep breath, 'but I will kill you with my bare hands if you don't turn around right now and take me back.'

'Sorry,' he said with a shrug. 'I've got to get back to my own camp.'

'Then put me down,' I said, sighing. I didn't like how sad and resigned my voice sounded. It was probably going to kill me, but it didn't matter. I wasn't going to leave Shane defenseless. Crawling might be the only option if he continued to refuse, but then I would just have to find some way to survive that. He gave me a studying look.

'I thought we established that was not a wise idea.'

'Says the boy who cried zombie.' I didn't exactly have the upper hand in the conversation, being luggage and all. I tried a different tactic. 'I know, and it sucks, but I can't leave them without a knife. They're expecting me back, and if I don't show up they'll really start to worry. Please . . . You don't know me, that's fine, you can leave me here. I just have to go back. Tonight.'

'Listen, Sacajawea, I'm not the kind of person to tell you your business, but I don't think you're going anywhere *tonight*,' he said tartly, nodding toward my feet. 'Not like that. If I let you hobble all the way back to your camp on those bloody stumps it's as good as killing you myself. And, hey, guess what? I'm not going to argue about it.'

He was right, but I felt cold all over. I had let my friends down, sure, but letting Shane down was worse. What if they went looking for me? Now that I knew the real truth of the island, of what lurked around every tree and sandbar, I could do things differently. But they didn't know because I hadn't told them.

My feet hurt like hell but I still had a bit of strength left in my arms. Do it for Shane, I thought, do what you have to.

I hit him on the cheek with my right elbow, fast and sudden enough that he swayed and dropped me. Ground. Ground bad. Ground hard and fucking *painful*. The pain could be ignored, I insisted, shrieking as I got to my feet and limped through the sand, huffing and puffing and paddling my arms. I fancied I could feel every particulate grain sticking to my bloodied feet. Crawling actually sounded more appealing in comparison to this . . .

'You are really, *really* stubborn, you know that?'

Apparently I hadn't hit him quite hard enough. He caught up before I could make it a few yards, scooping me back up into his arms as I flailed against him, sapped of coordination and energy by the pain radiating in my legs.

140

'Fuck you! No! Put me down!'

'Can you just – just hang on for one damn minute, okay? Jesus. Don't *hit* me again either.' He frowned, veering his head away preemptively. 'Can we talk about this? I think you could use some food and bandages before going on any long journeys, all right?'

'You don't get it.' I sighed, realizing that hitting him again probably wouldn't work. A bruise was starting to form along his cheekbone. 'My nephew is just a kid. They don't have any way to defend themselves at my camp. I can't *leave* them like that . . .'

'How long d'you figure it would take to get back on those things?' He nodded toward my feet.

'A few hours . . .'

'Try *many* hours, slugger, and come nightfall you'd be snapped up before you can say "appetizer". Either way, you wouldn't be making it back to camp tonight.'

'That's not the point, I—'

'I wasn't finished.' He sighed, hoisting me a little higher. 'In my scenario, you have a bite to eat and I take a look at your feet and then in the morning I take you back to your people. What's better about my way is that you make it back to them at all. Got it?'

'No, I don't. What if it's too late?'

'Then it's too late but at least you're alive.'

I hated it but he was right. That one taste of walking was enough to prove that I was in no condition to strike out on my own. The undead hadn't come the night before, but that didn't banish the anxiety that made me trembly all over. How many times did I have to promise to be a good protector for Shane and then fuck that up?

'Promise you'll take me back?'

'Yes.' He smirked, just a little. 'I promise.'

There was not much to do but grit my teeth and try to stay distracted. I got a clear look at his face. He was closer now and the sunshine fell on us equally. His soft dark hair had been swept back from his forehead, piling into a casually rakish coiffure. Spanish, I thought, or something like it, with a bladestraight nose and lips that wouldn't have been out of place on a woman. His eyes were blue, tucked under two thick smudges of eyebrows tented in perpetual amusement. The all-around effect was, I'm afraid to admit, dreamy.

It was hard to pin down his age. There were tiny flecks of gray in his hair, but he had the continuously sunburned good looks of a teenager. If you put a gun to my head and asked me to guess, I would've said late thirties or early forties. Early forties and as strong as an ox. I thought about him beating that zombie with its arm and wondered – for a brief, deeply shameful and adolescent instant – what he would look like with his tight wet T-shirt off.

Right. Time to look at something else. I stared out at the horizon, horrified: the day had come and gone and now a bright orange streak signaled sundown.

The beach angled right and we rounded a corner that opened up into a bay, a real honest-to-God harbor, with docks and squat cabins and several fires cheerfully burning away into the twilight. There was a huge sailboat floating off shore and a smaller canoe roped to one of the docks. It looked, quite frankly, like heaven.

'*This* is your camp?'

'Yeah,' he said. 'It's not much but it's getting better.'

Not much? I gaped. This wasn't roughing it by any-one's standards. I'd seen dirtier gas station bathrooms. I wondered how much food they had, how much water. A person could make a living in a place like this. A home.

He turned up a hill, passed the docks on our left, and into a wooded clearing. There was a row of five cabins set back from the water, and a fire pit in front of each building. Buckets were strewn here and there with plastic coverings. I glanced inside one as we walked by. It was filled with black, shiny mussels. They were practically living the high life. It didn't seem so strange now that Boy Who Cried Zombie was clean shaven – here they had the basic amenities of real, normal life. I wondered who 'they' were.

'We'll get you something to eat,' he said brusquely. 'And then I'll get to work on your feet.'

Food sounded good. The other thing? I could take or leave it. Then I thought maybe there was something seriously wrong with my feet and decided to keep my mouth shut. Getting back to Shane – that was the focus here, and having my feet bandaged was one step on the road back to him. As we approached the cabins, heads poked out to greet us. Boy Who Cried Zombie nodded to each one. A tall, slender black man came out of one cabin with a net in his hands. He was in the midst of mending it. He had a shaggy beard and large, round eyes. There was no suspicion in his expression; in fact, he grinned at us and belly laughed.

'You find a mermaid washed up on shore?'

'Not exactly, Nate,' BWCZ replied. He carried me around a fire pit and to the door of the middle cabin. 'Could you get the door for me?'

Nate rushed out in front of us and let us in. He gave me a friendly little wave. I tried to smile, but even the muscles in my face were beginning to feel tired and useless. The cabin was small, probably meant for one family or just two people. There was a simple cot in the back right corner, low to the ground, with a woolly brown blanket. I couldn't even remember what a bed felt like. In the opposite corner was a pottery basin with a jug. It was clearly a man's cabin. And BWCZ looked as if he had lived there all his life. He tossed things and left them where they landed – no intention of picking up after himself, no concern.

Nate followed us in and took a matchbook from his pocket. He lit a glass lantern with a red base and placed it next to the cot.

I hissed through my teeth to keep from screaming as BWCZ deposited me on the cot. He was careful, but even so, it was impossible not to bump my feet eventually. He dropped all of my things on the floor and then sprinted out the door with the mesh bag of stones. Nate poured me a tin cup of water from the earthenware jug. I must have looked like a real winner with my feet gashed and bleeding and my hair matted to my head with salt water. But Nate didn't say anything about that.

'What's your name?' he asked.

'Sadie.'

'I'm Nate.'

BWCZ rushed back inside during the introductions with another lantern (already lit) and a felt pouch. His mesh bag was gone. He went to the basin and rinsed his hands and face.

'Could you grab me a stool from outside?' he asked.

Nate ducked out and reappeared quickly with a rustic-looking stool, like the kind of thing you make at summer camp for your parents, the tree bark still rough around the outside.

'Her name is Sadie,' Nate supplied helpfully.

'Sadie? I'm Whelan,' he said. He smiled again and it touched his eyes. 'Pleased to meet you – I'd shake your hand but I need to keep them clean.' The implication being that I was filthy and covered in grit. I couldn't actually argue with that, I smelled like I had just come from a lifetime spent in the briny deep.

'Nate, could we have some privacy?'

Nate waved at me again and whistled as he shuffled back out the door. Whelan placed the lantern near my feet. It had the unexpected and pleasant side effect of warming my toes, which were getting chill in the fading daylight. He pulled a squeezy bottle of clear liquid out of the felt pouch and a slender black case. It was a first-aid kit. Inside was a pair of tweezers. Oh, lordy.

'I can get someone to hold your hand,' Whelan offered. He looked genuinely concerned for my comfort. 'It might help.'

'I'll be fine,' I said valiantly.

Whelan raised a thick eyebrow at me as if to say 'It's your funeral' and then shrugged and squirted some of the clear liquid onto my right foot. Hydrogen peroxide. He hadn't even picked up the tweezers yet. I yowled like an alley cat shoved into a bath tub.

'*By the horns of Satan.*' He pulled the bottle away. Talking became difficult with my teeth clamped together like a vice. 'You win. Please go get someone.'

'I'll get Banana,' he said, climbing to his feet. I didn't see how that could help.

'Sorry – did you say you'll get a banana?'

He chuckled, setting down his tools at the foot of the bed. 'Yes, Banana. She was a dancer.'

That was not nearly enough of an explanation, but Whelan left before I could ask what that had to do with being named after a fruit. When Banana joined us I felt something hot and wibbly in my stomach – jealousy or maybe lust. She was by far the most beautiful woman I had ever seen in my life. Men started wars over faces like this. She was tall and voluptuous, not MySpace voluptuous, but built like a long, sexy hourglass. The only resemblance she held to a banana was her shining blonde hair, which was pinned up away from her face and cascaded back down to her shoulders. Even dressed in sweats and makeup free, she was stunning. And intimidating. She had a bowl in her hands. Steam rose off of it in tiny white curlicues.

'Sadie?' she said. Well, that was one bubble burst. She wasn't perfect, and I suppose no woman is. Her voice was sharp, gruff, barbecue tangy like a trucker's. Maybe it was part of her dancing act or whatever she did. She strode over to the cot and pumped my hand. Man, what a grip. 'I'm Banana.'

'Hi . . . Banana.'

That's it, I thought with a sigh, I'm actually living in a Japanese game show. Banana dropped down next to me, kneeling. I accepted the bowl she offered. It was instant oatmeal, warm and perfectly cooked. There was even a swirl of maple syrup on top. I wolfed it down, abandoning what was left of my dignity. I was so hungry and nervous I could barely even taste the food. Whelan and Banana were thoughtful enough to hold a muted conversation while I ate. Meanwhile, I plotted, thinking that maybe I'd be able to sneak out after Whelan had cleaned my wounds. But contending with the darkness . . . he was right. Plunging out into the forest at night was suicidal.

When I was finished eating, Banana took hold of my right hand with both of hers. I looked at her nails. They were chipped, but had recently been manicured. She smelled faintly of salt water. I know I reeked of it.

'What exactly happened to my feet?' I asked, dreading the answer.

'Sea urchins,' Whelan stated. 'They graze on seaweed. You can see them better when the tide goes out. They've got nasty spines. Either they were generous enough to share them with you or you've been playing footsy with porcupines.'

'Yeah I really need to stop doing that,' I muttered.

Banana laughed, loud and throaty.

Whelan looked up from my feet – which were propped up on his forearm – and grinned crookedly. He had changed out of his wet T-shirt into a clean navy polo with an embroidered crest on the left chest. SPD. Seattle Police Department.

'These are most likely green sea urchins,' he added.

'So what were you doing out there?' I asked. It wasn't the time for twenty questions, but I was eager to prolong the procedure.

'Clamming.'

'I think there's a cream for that,' I said quietly.

Banana laughed again, tossing her hair. 'Whelan used to surf and snorkel,' she said, beaming down at him. Ugh. 'He knows where all the tastiest sea life hangs out.'

'Educational,' I muttered. 'Now please make the pain stop.'

'Here, sweetie pie,' Banana said. There was no patronizing in it. She called me that as casually as you might call a good friend your buddy. Her perfect rosebud lips split into a smile and she winked. 'You squeeze as hard as you want. I can take it.'

To Banana's credit, she really did let me do that. And I needed it. Whelan was careful, even artistic with those tweezers, but it didn't matter. It felt like every sea urchin pin had grafted to my skin, fusing to my feet in the time it took to walk from the beach to the cabin. They were holding on for dear life. I wanted to die. There was nothing stronger than a Tylenol for me to take and I felt every last searing jab of those tweezers. I screamed and groaned until I was hoarse and then just sort of grunted like a dying horse for the rest of it. The fact that neither Banana nor Whelan asked me to please shut the fuck up raised them both in my estimation.

Whelan wore a deeply pained expression through the whole ordeal, as if making me twitch and screech caused him actual physical discomfort, that or I was slowly making him deaf. By then I had half-forgiven him for the stunt he had pulled in the water. Sure, it had almost gotten us killed, but he was going about regaining my esteem with real pluck (pun intended). Between tweezes he would pat my ankle or the top of my foot and say things like, 'It's okay now' or 'You're doing great, babe.' In any other situation, being called 'babe' would have me fuming, but it made me feel better because – at that moment – any measure of comfort helped. I would do the same thing for Shane when he burned his tongue on a hot drink or got a splinter.

I could feel his warm breath on my toes and the tensing of his shoulders each time he yanked out another pin. It was a slow process and I passed out more than once.

'We're almost there,' Banana said. Her voice was dim,

distant. 'We'll get those little fuckers out of your feet.'

For a minute, when I regained consciousness again, I wondered why pain so often led to euphoria. I'm not a glutton for punishment, not at all, but after a while I began to feel giddy and hysterical and even *happy*. The whole debacle suddenly struck me as ludicrously funny, like some harebrained setup for a romantic comedy gag. Woman purposely trounces through sea urchin bed to get a gruff but handsome man to bend over her feet for two hours. It did seem vaguely romantic, actually, the fact that someone I had known for less than a day cared so deeply about what was – more or less – my own fucking problem. I was the moron who threw off my shoes before dashing into the water, even if it was with the best intentions. I couldn't remember the last time someone had done something so gross and unpleasant for me. Carl brought me a stale muffin once from a Dumpster. That was his idea of romantic.

Pick – ouch – pick – ow!

Luckily, my face was so red and the tears flowed so readily that neither of them noticed that I was blushing. Whelan's forehead was wet with perspiration, his face less than two inches away from my stinky, bloody feet. It was awkward and disgusting, but I couldn't picture being more comfortable given the situation. To show my gratitude, I shrieked and squirmed less and tried to catch Whelan's eye to give him a reassuring smile. He was too focused on my feet. No matter how many times I mentally commanded him to just take a minute and look at my face, it didn't happen. I closed my eyes and the missed connections ad flickered across my eyelids.

Under The Sea w/ PTSD w4m—29 (Some Island)
*You: Tan, blue eyes, nice shoulders, tall drink of Jack
Daniels.*
*Me: Dark hair, irritated, sea-urchined, blacking out with
pain.*
*You picked spines out of my toes after I saved you from a
zombie.*
Next time, let's do Uni.

I considered what the Ketch's wide-open deck might be
like if the world were a kinder, gentler place. Suddenly my
head was filled with the smell of coconut-scented tanning
oil and steamed mussels, and before I could stop myself I
was imagining Whelan on that boat, getting a perfect, line-
less tan. Either those spines were poisonous and I was
tripping balls, or the tingling all over my body was from
something different. Different, but equally troubling.

'Sadie?'

'Mm.'

'Sadie! Sadie? Damn it. Is she all right?'

'Hi. Yes. Yes?'

I was lucid again but the room was spinning. Poor
Banana's hand was turning blue from me squeezing it so
hard. I relaxed my grip, finding that the pain wasn't so bad
anymore.

'All finished,' Whelan said, holding up a palm-full of
spines, as proud as if he'd just won first place at the Science
Fair. White teeth, one deep dimple.

'Thanks!' I said, out of breath. 'Should my feet still
hurt?'

'It'll take a few days for the skin to heal. You should try
to stay off them as much as possible.' He slathered the soles

of my feet in antibacterial gel and began wrapping them up with strips of white fabric, T-shirt strips maybe.

'Don't be stupid. You promised,' I said. 'I have to get back to my camp and my friends. I've been gone too long already.'

Whelan and Banana exchanged a look. She sucked in a breath through her teeth and quickly excused herself. So much for sisterly solidarity. Whelan tossed the sea urchin spines into an empty tin cup and offered them to me. 'Souvenir?'

'Oh, I think I've got plenty,' I said, glancing at my feet.

He sat down on the cot next to me. I had to scoot over to make room.

'You can't leave tonight,' he said. He didn't sound sorry or mean, just firm. 'I know you're worried about your friends, but this is serious. I'm not going back on my promise. I'll take you back to them tomorrow morning, first thing. If you get an infection there's no one here who can treat that.' He grinned, showing me that dimple again. 'I'll chain you to the bed if I have to.'

'I'd like to see you try.'

'Don't give me a reason.'

Whelan stood, stretching his shoulders. He had been hunched over my feet for two straight hours without a break. I heard one of his vertebrae crack back into place. Looking at his face, at the hard set to his jaw, I knew he was dead serious. I could either start up a screaming match or wait patiently and nod along to everything he said and sneak out later with or without his blessing. Guess which one I chose?

'I'm exhausted,' I said, flopping back on the cot.

'I'll leave you to rest,' he said. 'Good night.'

''Night,' I said. 'Thanks.'

'Back atcha.'

The door closed and the cabin felt empty. I hadn't realized how much physical space Whelan took up until he left. He had provided me with one lantern and I would need it. The soles of my feet throbbed, but if I stayed on my tiptoes I might be able to walk long enough to reach the harbor. And that's all I needed to accomplish. Once I reached the docks there would be the canoe and the canoe would take me around the island without having to walk. I still had the compass on a string around my neck, and if I pointed the canoe due south then I'd be home free. My arms ached. It didn't matter; I couldn't abandon Shane and the others.

The sounds outside the cabin died down about an hour later. Staying awake proved challenging, but bumping my foot against the mattress was enough to keep me wired. I pushed myself out of the cot and limped to the door, alternately placing the pressure on my tiptoes and heels. The pain sizzled and forked up my ankles like a stab of lightning. But I had a plan and, more importantly, I had determination. Arturo was dead – Shane, Andrea, Mortiz, Noah and Cassandra would run out of water and food any minute and now I was missing in action. I didn't think, not really, but I sure as hell acted.

Outside it was pitch black. The clouds rolled in, obscuring the moon behind a veil of blurry gray. I turned the flame on the lantern down as low as I could, since they must keep a watch, too, and if they spotted my flame the plan would be foiled even before it began. Without the aid of moonlight or stars I'd be stranded, but once I rounded the corner and passed out of sight I could turn up the flame on the lantern to light the way. The fire pits continued to burn. I hobbled as fast as I could, swallowing the jabs of pain with each step.

I made decent time, even with my disfiguring injuries, and soon found myself at the bottom of a low hill, facing the canoe and its safety rope. Water lapped at the dock pilings, splashing and receding with a lazy rhythm. Freedom and home seemed close enough to taste. And I wanted to savor them, even if they sort of tasted like ass and old Shasta.

The knot wasn't too difficult to figure out but, of course, escape couldn't be that easy. The paddles were missing. Great. Time was running out – if I dashed back up the hill I would risk being seen and making a commotion as I searched for the paddles. But maneuvering the canoe with only my hands was out of the question. I needed those paddles.

I turned to limp back up the slope and stopped, finding myself face-to-face with a solid wall of blue polo shirt. Oh, hell. I tipped my head back to look up at Whelan. He didn't look happy, no sir. He ducked down and shot forward before I could utter one word of protest. I fell forward over his shoulder and he nonchalantly firemen-carried me back up toward the cabins.

'Going somewhere?'

'Just admiring the view.'

He laughed and shifted his hand closer to my ass. 'Me too.'

'Fuck you, dickhead.'

'Not going to ask me to put you down this time, are you?'

I couldn't answer that.

'Didn't think so.'

This was the second time I had ended up in his arms against my will. I promised myself it wouldn't happen a third time. Banana stood outside the central cabin, her arms crossed over her ample chest, her teeth worrying along her bottom lip. She gave me a sad little wave, as if she knew I was in for an earful.

Whelan was less careful about tossing me onto the cot this time around. I couldn't blame him. I had, after all, just tried and failed to steal their canoe after he took two hours to pick itty-bitty sea urchin spines out of my flesh. I'm sure I'd be mightily pissed off too.

'Stay here,' he said. His voice was flat and dull, heavy as an iron bar. Clearly, he was trying not to lose his temper.

I heard him talk to Banana just outside the door. Their voices rose and fell but I couldn't make out a single word. Whelan stomped into the cabin a minute or two later and came straight for me. I recoiled, backing up onto the bed. He dropped down suddenly, kneeling. Whatever anger filled his eyes before had softened to concern. He brought his face very close to mine, close enough to feel his breath on my face. There was a mole on the back of his jaw by his ear. I wanted to look away from his gaze but blue had never looked so blue before. He smelled the way an apple orchard feels at sunset.

For one wavering moment I was absolutely certain he was about to kiss me.

Then I felt a cold nip at my wrist and heard the sound of metal clinking against metal. My eyes flew to the left-hand corner of the cot. Whelan had secured me to the frame with a pair of purple fuzzy handcuffs.

'What the fuck do you think you're doing?' I shouted,

testing the strength of the cuffs. They didn't budge, Conan the Barbarian in a tutu. *Damn*. They bit too. Whelan grinned, pulling back. It was all a clever trick.

'You had better let me out of here,' I said, dropping my voice to a dangerous register. Whelan stood and shrugged, folding his arms up like a genie.

'Nope.'

'Let me out!' I tested the cuffs again. Useless.

'Sorry.'

'You let me go,' I seethed. 'You let me out or I will seriously get Madmartigan on your ass.'

His wide eyebrows jumped. 'Big words . . .' He made a pinching motion with his thumb and forefinger. '. . . Tiny woman.'

You know that expression, seeing red? Well I was doing it. Or maybe I was just seeing blood, his blood, the blood I was going to drench myself in after I cut him to pieces. I felt a surge like a tidal wave move through my veins, culminating in my fists.

'You'll thank me,' he said, interpreting my enraged silence. 'Might not seem like it now, but you will. There's no moon tonight. You'd never make it back. You'd be out to sea and up shit creek faster than you can say 'a three-hour tour.'

'You do that a lot,' I muttered, bitter.

'Do what?'

'"Faster than" whatever. Faster than you can say "appetizer". Faster than you can say "a three-hour tour".'

Whelan smiled crookedly. 'So you actually do listen then? Coulda fooled me.'

He returned to the cot, bringing his concerned expression with him. I had a mind to tell him just exactly where he could stuff that phony empathy. Whelan sat down next to me and I laughed, shaking my head hard from side to side.

'If you try to sleep in this bed I will chew your testicles off and that is a promise.'

Whelan nodded, sadly, and stood. His dark head nearly brushed the ceiling. 'You saved my life and I'm *trying* to pay you back,' he said quietly. 'I'm trying to keep you safe. It's called reciprocity, a concept that shouldn't be altogether alien to you.'

'One man's reciprocity is another man's kidnapping – which is a felony, by the way. You're a cop, right? You would know.'

'I'll see you in the morning,' he said. 'We'll take the canoe and I'll bring you back to your friends.'

This time, he took the lantern with him.

TEN

I dreamed about a drive-in movie theater. Sitting in a car I didn't recognize, I watched my life on the screen. My parents and Kat came and went, my childhood apartment scrolled by. I saw friends from high school and the art studio that had become my home away from home during college. Then there was seeing my illustrations in print for the first time and early adulthood with half-hearted bar hopping, drawing away from college friends I had never expected to lose and Jason, my editor, talking to me late at night on the phone. He would do that often, just to keep me company.

Everything came to a screeching halt just before The Outbreak. Apparently that was when my life stopped.

Now I had Shane and I was apparently doomed to fail him at least once a day.

In the morning I woke up alone. Overnight, the pain in my feet had subsided. I'd be able to walk carefully for short distances. Feeling drained and groggy, I rubbed my face with both hands. Both hands. The handcuff swung, limp and open, one half still attached to the cot's frame. Sometime in the night my hand had been released.

I opened the cabin door and walked out into pearly

morning sunlight. I'd head out on my own if Whelan reneged and tried to handcuff me again.

In this part of the world the clouds have a way of stretching into gauzy sheets, just thick enough to dampen the light and turn the sky silver. The camp bustled with activity, fires crackling cheerfully, makeshift spits balancing black pots over the flames. I spotted Nate down by the water, his dark head bent over a net contraption. A man I didn't recognize sat with him. He had spiky hair, olive skin and a thin build. Banana and a woman I hadn't met yet stood outside the cabin next to mine – *Whelan's* – talking. Something smelled delicious.

Banana hurried over, her friend coming with her. A polka-dotted handkerchief held Banana's hair off her forehead. She wore a too-big navy sweatshirt and gray leggings and looked like a pin-up girl just before makeup and wardrobe. I saw the tin camping kettle in her hand and felt the fog of waking up abate at once.

'Coffee?' Banana offered brightly.

At the sight and smell of instant coffee I just about broke down into tears of ecstasy. Even in the Citadel, coffee was notoriously hard to get. Once the pre-Outbreak supply ran out, finding a packet of even the cheapest instant stuff was like finding the Holy Grail, and it went for exorbitant prices.

'Oh, my God,' I said, momentarily forgetting that I had spent the night chained up to a cot in a stranger's cabin. '*Coffee.*' The way Banana handed me the cup and smiled sheepishly told me she was sorry about something. It all started to make a kind of sense – the cuffs were probably hers.

'Did you free me?' I asked. For a minute, I just stuck my

nose down into the coffee cup and breathed. Heaven. Pure, sweet, roasty heaven.

'A'course, hot cakes,' she said. 'Whelan's a brute,' she added, 'but he's a smart brute. What are you doing out here? You're supposed to be staying off your feet.'

'Can't. No time. Gotta get back.'

Banana's companion, I realized with a jolt, was glaring at me. It was a feat to cram that much disdain into one pair of eyes. Her hair was raven black and French braided down her back. Her tiny nose had the characteristic, too-pointed slope of rhinoplasty. She had the biggest, fakest tits I had ever seen outside of a porno. I hoped the surprise and shock weren't showing on my face. I glanced nervously at Banana. What was *her* name, I wondered with a mental smirk – Melons?

'Sadie, this is Danielle,' Banana said, following my gaze. I shook Danielle's slender hand, feeling the bite of long, sharp nails that belonged on a Bengal tiger. Banana had clearly lost the dancer name lottery. And by dancer, I was starting to think stripper. Maybe she had done something to anger the stripping gods and brought shame down upon her family. Although in a weird way the name Banana *did* suit her. Her huge smile and liquid eyes brought to mind sun-drenched beaches, cabana boys and piña coladas . . .

Danielle, on the other hand, reminded me of cheap, watered-down Tequila Sunrises and sweaty one-dollar bills. The Olive Garden of strippers. She wore a sunflower yellow, cutoff belly shirt and baggy sweatpants slung low on her narrow hips. I wouldn't have been surprised if, when she turned, JUICY – the international word for tasteless—would be splashed across her butt.

'Nice to meet you,' I said. Danielle rolled her dark eyes

and shrugged. Banana, maybe as an apology for her friend's manners, refilled my coffee cup. I was trying to piece together just what I had done to make Danielle instantly hate me when Whelan jogged up to us. He had brought the missing canoe paddles. Danielle's cold expression melted into a simpering smile.

My, my, my. That's a Bingo.

'You're up,' Whelan observed brightly. He thoroughly checked me over from head to toe, despite the fact that my injuries were confined to one quite specific area. 'How are you feeling? Did you, um, manage to get any sleep?'

That frigid expression of Danielle's returned and she puckered up her lips as if she'd just been punched in the face with a lemon.

'Yes,' I said, trying to keep my voice even. He had, after all, handcuffed me to a cot for the night. I glanced at Danielle and decided to test my theory. 'You know,' I said, smirking, 'next time you could at least buy me dinner before handcuffing me to the bed. It's only polite.'

I had crossed a line. At once, Danielle took a giant and awkward step toward Whelan and looped her arm through his. She may as well have dug a flag into the top of his head with her name on it. Banana coughed and shot me a look.

'Joke,' I said, sipping my coffee. 'It was a joke.'

Whelan glanced down at Danielle and I could imagine him wearing that same wide-eyed expression if an anaconda wrapped itself around his elbow. Several conflicting emotions crossed his face until he settled on total bafflement. I finished the coffee and handed Banana the cup.

'Thank you,' I said. 'I really appreciate your hospitality.'

'Any time, sweet pea,' Banana said with a smirk. Danielle

unwound herself from Whelan. Good timing – he had begun to squirm in place.

'We should get going,' Whelan announced. His voice came out a little too loud.

'You sure you have to go?' Banana asked. She held out her hand to me and I took it. With a little shake of her shoulders, she pouted, apparently sad to see me go. Danielle, by contrast, seemed positively candescent. She fluffed her hair and bounced her boobs around, for whose benefit I wasn't sure. Whelan certainly wasn't watching. He studied the horizon, flattening his hand over his eyes like a visor.

'Good wind today,' he said. 'Not too strong.'

Banana gave me a tight, squeezing hug. 'Later, dominator,' she said. 'Take care of Whelan.' At that, both of Whelan's eyebrows arched and a slow, crooked smile brightened his eyes.

'I guess I owe him one,' I added.

'No,' he said, starting down the slope toward the dock with the paddles tucked beneath his right arm. 'We're even.' He saluted Banana and Danielle and then nodded toward the water's edge. Time to go. Danielle blew him a kiss. I saw a fleeting look of panic cross his face. I gave him a wry smile that said: Yes, I saw that and no, I don't give a shit. Nate waved good-bye to us from his post down the beach.

'Your friends are cool,' I said. That was about all I could manage – just getting down the hill made my feet explode into pins and needles. Whelan offered his arm but I ignored it.

'Is it just the five of you?' I asked. Together, we untied the knot securing the canoe to the dock. It was a two-person canoe, durable plastic and in brand-new condition. The nose bobbed up and down in the rolling waves.

'No, seven,' he replied. 'The others are probably still sleeping.'

He seemed distracted as he held onto the edge of the canoe, keeping it steady while I winced and wheezed my way onto the front bench. At some point that morning, Whelan had already loaded my shoes and bow into the boat. Apparently it was a camp full of early-risers. He waded into the shallows and carefully lifted himself over the edge and onto the backseat. A paddle nudged my shoulder and I took it, trying to recall proper canoeing technique. Dad usually did most of the heavy paddling on our trips.

With Whelan doing most of the maneuvering and paddling, we floated out away from the shore and the camp. I watched the fire pits blazing, thin trails of smoke disappearing into the gray sky. Something like regret lodged in my throat. They had it good here, even if they did also have Danielle.

'I'm sorry about last night,' he said. We were riding the current, the camp disappearing behind the bend and the edge of the forest. 'I didn't want you to try escaping again.'

'It's okay,' I said, not at all meaning it. My feet had gotten wet and the salt water stung through my bandages. 'We're just straight south,' I said. Changing the topic away from last night felt like a winning idea. 'I suppose we must be on the opposite end of the island.'

Whelan either couldn't think of anything to say or he decided to plunge headlong into thoughtful silence. The only indication that he hadn't died was the swift, rhythmic sound of his paddle cutting through the water. I regretted not eating before we left. The coffee soured in my stomach, turning to acid. Whelan didn't comment on the fact that my half of the paddling was, decidedly, lame. I rested often, distracted by the sensation of hellfire bleeding up my ankles to my knees. Overnight the ache in my arms had intensified and now I felt like I had spent the day before power-lifting buffalos. A yoke of tension spread from shoulder to shoulder and down my spine.

The day grew hotter and we took an increasing number of breaks, letting the current carry us south. Spurts of wind were the only relief from the sun, which now sat bright and terrible directly overhead, bearing down on us and cutting directly through the chill air. At one point I heard Whelan rest his paddle on the edges of the canoe and pull off his sweater. It was around then that the silence became too much for me.

'Where'd you grow up?'

'California,' he said. He was quick on the draw, as if he'd been waiting all along for me to speak up. 'Glendale and then L.A. and then . . . well, all over the place until Seattle.'

'How did you meet the others?' I asked. 'Banana and Nate?'

'We all wanted a way out of the city,' he said. 'Nate had the boat and I knew the area. I'd been up this way before to camp and sail. This is a state preserve, a wildlife park.' I pictured him gesturing to the little island we now called home. 'We pooled our resources, invested in some camping equipment and left town. We timed it right, left just before the barrier came down.'

'Lucky,' I said. Very lucky. 'We got out the day of. There was no destination in mind – or, well, there might have been. Our captain died on the way. None of us knew much about sailing a ship and then there was this massive storm.'

'The weather started getting rough, the tiny ship was tossed?'

I heard him chuckle behind me and then hum the rest of the *Gilligan's Island* theme song. I quelled the urge to take my paddle and smack him upside the head.

'Sure,' I said, humoring him, 'but I wouldn't call us fearless *or* courageous. Mostly it was just dumb luck that we didn't all end up dead.'

'And now here you are.'

'Dumb luck,' I reiterated.

'Or fate,' he replied with a sinister cackle. 'Dun-dun-DUN.'

The water slicked by, shiny and rippled, close enough to touch with just the tiniest extension of my arm. It glistened invitingly but I knew better. It was ice cold and filled with unseen dangers. We were quiet again.

'My turn to ask questions?'

'Be my guest,' I said. 'Not much else to do.'

'You could try paddling.'

'Oh, no thank you. You're doing a fine job of it on your own.'

I felt a pinch on the back of my neck and the rough calluses of his fingertips.

'Let me see,' he said, puffing out a thoughtful sigh. 'Favorite drink?'

I had expected the usual questions: Where are you from? What did you do? Where's your family? Expectations are silly that way.

'Right now? Anything. But before . . . I don't know, vodka I guess . . . . Maybe a martini.'

'Zombie match-up?'

'That's easy,' I said, laughing. 'Hands down – it would have to be Jonas Brothers versus zombie Anthony Bourdain.'

'Ugh.' He made a gagging sound. 'Good God, what a bloodbath. You're merciless.'

'Yours?'

We were getting closer. On our left I saw a deep, rocky inlet and the top of a mast poking out of the trees like a pale, skinny finger. We drifted past the wreck of Arturo's boat. Whelan must have noticed it because he waited to answer my question until we were safely away from the depressing sight.

'Me,' he said calmly. The nose of the canoe dipped. 'Me versus any of them.'

The camp still stood. It stood but I didn't know for how much longer. Whelan made me stay in the canoe as he dragged it up onto the beach. The lean-to leaned a little *too* much in the distance. I felt embarrassed, as if I were bringing home a boyfriend to a messy, cheap little apartment. That anxiety would have to wait. First things first: make sure my colossal mistake hadn't resulted in anyone's death, especially Shane's. Whelan helped me out of the canoe, picking me up by the armpits and setting me down away from the water. My raggedy feet were in his debt . . . again.

Figures appeared one by one, coming fast down the beach toward us. I detected the thinnest trail of smoke, which meant the fire probably hadn't gone out. I hobbled up the beach to meet them, Whelan a few feet behind. Andrea crashed right into me, hug-choking until I begged for air. There were tears in her eyes. I expected Shane to

165

replace her, but he hung back, glaring at me. My heart fell.

Ignoring the others, I went quickly to Shane, as quickly as I could manage. I tried to hug him but he dodged, stumbling away.

'No!' he shouted, pushing at my shoulders as I tried for another hug.

'Shane . . . Shane, I'm sorry . . . Please don't be upset.' He struggled even as I managed to yank him into my arms. Grunting and whimpering, he wriggled, refusing to hug me back. 'I'm so sorry,' I whispered. 'I didn't mean to leave you like that, I didn't . . .'

'Again!' he screamed. 'You didn't mean to leave me again?'

'I hurt my feet . . . I couldn't walk back . . . I know you're angry, I know it. I tried to come back. I tried.'

'I don't care,' Shane grew still, panting. 'You said you would be back soon and you weren't.'

I kissed the top of his head, squeezing. He was being generous. I deserved so much more than his contempt. But it hurt. It stung that what had started out as something for us – something for *him* – had backfired so epically.

'I'll make it up to you,' I said. 'It was all . . . it was a mess. I'm sorry, Shane.'

'You're not supposed to go alone,' he whispered. 'Never alone.'

'And I won't, you're right. Will you forgive me? Please? I won't be a moron again . . .'

It felt like an empty promise. I'm sure it sounded like one to him, but I meant it. God, all I wanted was to do right by the kid and I kept fucking up. Was this how all parents felt? Scrambling to figure it out, to make things safe and perfect and finding it just wasn't possible?

'Okay,' he finally said, sagging.

Then he hugged my neck, just briefly, but it made all the difference to me.

I stood up, holding tightly to Shane's hand and bringing him with me. He stared at my bandaged feet as I hobbled back toward the group. Noah and Moritz stood next to each other, stalk-still, both of them wearing twin expressions, staring at me like I was a ghost. I felt like one. Whelan returned to the canoe and unpacked my shoes and bow.

'I lost the knife,' was all I could say.

'What happened to you?' Noah shouted, catching up to Moritz and Andrea. Cassandra lagged behind, eyeing us uncertainly. Andrea seemed to be at a loss for words.

'I got lost.' No explanation or excuse felt adequate. 'This is Whelan.'

He shook hands with everybody in turn, even Cassandra, who shrank back immediately after letting go of his hand. Seeing Whelan beside them put our camp's situation in sharp relief. He looked clean, well-fed, rested and strong, with just a ghost of stubble on his jaw. Moritz and Noah now had full beards. Our clothes were in a terrible state, ripped and stained and bloodied. Moritz, Noah and Andrea had developed dark bags under their eyes from lack of sleep and their cheeks were sunken from malnutrition. Shane looked slightly better, which made me think they had given the remaining food to him. Moritz appeared especially bedraggled, insisting on wearing his ridiculous tweed suit with the blue scarf, which was now more like a collection of blue strings.

To his credit, Whelan said nothing and smiled pleasantly, politely. At that moment I couldn't muster the slightest interest in his opinion of our little crew. Motley didn't even begin to describe it.

Suddenly, Andrea pushed me, hard, blue eyes blazing. 'I thought you were dead.'

Out of the corner of my eye Whelan bristled, drawing himself to his full height, which was – without a doubt – intimidating. He gave her a look that should've left her limp and bleeding. I put up a hand, exhausted, sore and ready for a nap.

'She's injured,' Whelan said. He placed a big, steadying hand on my shoulder.

That seemed to lessen some of Shane's irritation with me. He gave my hand a quick squeeze and then another, as if communicating his support in Morse code. Moritz shuffled forward, his sparkling eyes flicking nervously between Whelan's face and mine. Custer had gotten a warmer reception at Little Bighorn.

'I'm happy to see that you're safe,' Moritz said quietly. I had forgotten how lyrical his accent was. He trained his eyes closely on my face. 'How did you hurt your feet?'

'Saving me,' Whelan replied flatly.

'Actually, I asked Sadie,' Moritz countered.

'It's a long story.' I turned to Whelan, who was busy starting a staring contest with Moritz. Never in the history of man had two people reverted to adolescence with such unbelievable, single-minded speed. 'Are you going to piss on a tree now or can we proceed like adults?'

'My bad,' Whelan murmured. Good enough.

'Shane, Whelan,' I said, gesturing quickly between man and boy, though which was which was still up for debate. 'Whelan, Shane.'

'Hi there,' Whelan said, giving an awkward wave.

Shane waved back, just as awkward.

I began to walk up the beach toward the lean-to, refusing to relinquish Shane's clammy hand as I went. Andrea followed. She had gone suspiciously quiet since her little violent outburst. Whelan, Moritz and the others ambled after us at a relaxed, or maybe cautious, pace.

'Listen,' I said to Andrea. 'Yesterday sucked. I made a mistake. In the woods . . . I was ambushed. There are infected ones here, Andrea, but there's another camp too.'

Quickly, I related the previous night's events to her and Shane. They both listened closely, Andrea's face softening as I explained what had happened to my feet and the kindness shown to me by Whelan and Banana. She seemed to be emerging from a trance, her eyes growing clearer and more intelligent by the second. Then she began to nod and make sounds in response to my story. Whatever disappointment or rage she felt had subsided by the end of my explanation.

'We can make a go of it here,' I concluded, addressing primarily Shane. He nodded in response, his curls bouncing. 'But we'll need to figure out a better way to get water and make permanent housing.'

'Why don't you make a solar still?' Whelan had been eavesdropping on the latter half of our conversation. He was met with three very blank expressions.

'Here,' he said, motioning for us to follow. 'I'll show you.'

Even Moritz and Cassandra wandered over to listen to Whelan's instructions. Ignoring the others, I watched Andrea appraising him. Judging by her expression, she was warming to his presence. That was quick. Big, ocean blue eyes attached to six plus feet of tan brawn had a way of bringing people around, I suppose.

'You dig a hole in the wet ground,' Whelan was saying, 'and place a pot or a bowl at the bottom.' He pointed to the sail tarp draped over the lean-to. 'If you cover the hole with plastic and weight down the middle, the water in the ground will evaporate, stick to the tarp, trickle down and – automagically – you've got water.' Whelan punctuated his last point with a beaming smile and a flourish of his hands. He was a showman. Andrea grinned, under his spell.

'Hot,' she said, examining the back of his jeans.

'She means interesting,' I said quickly. 'Really interesting. The still. The solar one. Interesting.'

Frosty, blank looks all around. Damn it.

'We need the tarp for the shelter,' I said, changing tack, and Whelan frowned, deep lines appearing perpendicular to his eyebrows. His eyes lingered on Shane, pupils dragging back and forth between us as if silently making a connection. Yes, this was *that* nephew, the one that I kept talking about in my desperate and failed tempts to get back to camp.

'You need a lot of things,' Whelan finally muttered.

I didn't like it. I didn't like him delivering me back to my own camp like a bag of groceries. I didn't like that he knew more about survival than we did or that he had obviously picked up on the fact that we were in dire straits. I glanced at Andrea. She would be no help whatsoever. She was too busy making googly eyes at the back of Whelan's jeans.

'You could come back with me,' he said. Whelan directed this at me but I knew that he was implying the rest of the camp as well. 'We have water, plenty of it. We've got food, too, and cabins. It will be safer if we stick together.'

In that moment I hated him. He was undermining me, undermining all of us. At the mention of water and food, Noah had practically melted into a pile of goo. He was smiling so hard I thought his face might crack in half. I grabbed Whelan's forearm, which was too big for my hand to fit all the way round. He let me drag him away from the others. As soon as we were out of earshot, Andrea started to whisper and gesticulate wildly. They had to be discussing the possibility of leaving and, I had to admit, Whelan had put forward a solid case.

'What are you doing?' I asked. He took back his forearm and calmly stared at me. It was the first time I noticed his ears stuck out funny from his head and that his perfectly waved hair was probably kept long to keep his monkey ears hidden. The blue, blue eyes stuck between those ears stared back coolly, unmoved. He had expected this reaction. 'You were just supposed to drop me off. This is bullshit. Run along home, Whelan, we can take care of ourselves.'

'Really?' he asked, chuckling. Whelan glanced over his shoulder at the sad, crooked lean-to and our piddling fire. 'From where I'm standing it looks like you could use some help. No fire? No water? How long do you expect to last like this?'

'You could've asked me first,' I replied. I was losing ground and motivation. After all, they had oatmeal, beds, clams, *coffee* . . .

'All right. Sadie: Is it okay with you if I invite your friends to join my camp?'

'Not *now*,' I hissed, exasperated. 'Before!'

'Well sor-ry, *Mom*.'

171

The damage had already been done. I was whining. *He* was whining. It was like arguing with a brick wall with gorgeous eyes. No. I focused on the funny ears instead. Whelan squinted down at me and I threw back my shoulders to keep from wilting under his gaze. Andrea watched us, her gaze inscrutable across the span of pebbly dunes. Pathetic. Two grown adults posturing like mountain goats over *survival*.

'I'm not leaving,' he said. 'Not until you let me help you and your friends.'

'I'll *make* you go.'

'With what? Salty language? You don't even have a knife anymore. You've got a bow with no arrows.' He was right, of course, but his self-amused tone convinced me that he wasn't. I felt like pelting him with rocks. Sharp ones. 'You have to forget about your pride for a minute here and do what's best for your friends. They look hungry, Sadie. And – no offense – so do you. At least I think you are, hard to tell under all that belligerence.'

Calmly, he tried to reach out and touch my shoulder. I jerked away.

'You just have to be the fucking hero, eh?' I muttered.

'I know.' He rolled his eyes. 'The *audacity*, right?'

We had only barely managed to make it to this island alive. I just wanted a chance to prove that we weren't a complete accident. But maybe we *had* survived through sheer stupid luck, total chance. I didn't know whether to be grateful for that, deeply ashamed or afraid. If there was one thing I learned from The Outbreak, it was that luck was fickle and bound to run out. Fortune looked me square in the face, giving us another chance to grasp at life and hang on. The thought of living side by side with Danielle made my skin crawl but eking out a living on rotten rations and a dwindling spirit could be worse. I had made harder sacrifices.

Whelan fidgeted, impatient for my answer. For him it was simple. I don't know why I was so convinced I had something to prove.

'Let me talk to the others, okay?'

He nodded. When I turned to go he tried to follow.

'No,' I said. 'Alone.'

Andrea met me halfway. She made sure I saw the hungry expression on her face when she gazed over my shoulder at Whelan – and here I mean hungry as in desirous of man flesh, not hungry as in desirous of a bagel. What the hell? Didn't we have more important things to worry about?

'What do you think?' I asked her.

'Gorgeous. Is he single?'

'No, I mean his proposition. Could you just stop staring at him please? *Please?*'

'I get it,' she said, gritting her teeth. 'He's yours too, right? They're all yours. First Moritz and now this guy – you're on a serious winning streak.'

'What? No. Just . . . I don't care about that shit right now. I don't want either of them, okay? They're yours, got it? Done and done. I just want to figure this out.' I wanted to grab her by the neck and shake. But Andrea's face changed completely, like a bright curtain drawing across a stage, and she shrugged.

'You saw the camp,' she said. Her hat sat on her head at an angle, sliding back toward her ponytail. Her voice was clipped, efficient. It was good to know we were still comrades now that I had rescinded my claim on all the menfolk. Still, whatever her motivations, this was a major decision and I didn't want to make it on my own. 'Is it better?'

'Yes,' I said without hesitation. 'But I don't know how willing they'll be to share.'

'If you think we should go, we'll do it. I trust you.'

I seriously doubted whether or not I deserved that trust. Moritz and Noah waited nearby, halfheartedly trying to keep Shane entertained while they shamelessly eavesdropped. Cassandra wandered down to the water's edge. She peered at the canoe, fascinated. This was it, the turning point. I could say yes and possibly make enemies with Whelan's cohorts, or say no and subject my companions to more misery. Joining Whelan's camp felt like a commitment. We were here to stay. We would not return to Seattle, not for a long time.

Beneath his halo of curls, Shane gave me a small, sad smile of encouragement.

'Let's go,' I said, feeling like the wind had been knocked out of me. Why did it feel wrong? Why did it feel like a failure? 'Quickly,' I added. 'Before I can change my mind.'

ELEVEN

There was no flag-waving or confetti tossing when Whelan told his friends the news. In fact, the sight of me at Whelan's side made the atmosphere positively chilly.

We'd left Andrea with the compass and a hastily scrawled map. If they followed the beach north and kept the water close, they could walk to the camp in less than a day. I wasn't thrilled about the idea of leaving them to fend for themselves, but if they followed Whelan's directions and stuck together, they stood a good chance of making the trip safely. We learned during The Outbreak that larger numbers of humans drew zombies, but traveling in a group was always better than going it alone.

Whelan and I took Shane and made it back to the camp in the canoe by mid afternoon. Shane and I were both weak with hunger when we arrived and Whelan parked us in his cabin with two heaping bowls of oatmeal and a bottle of cranberry juice. Through the walls, I could hear the argument rage. From what I could glean, Nate and Banana were just fine with the merger but Danielle and someone called Stefano were not. Occasionally, Danielle and Stefano would break into rapid-fire Spanish and Whelan interjected sporadically until they switched back to English.

I finished eating and told Shane to stay in the cabin while

I limped out to listen in on the argument. I saw no reason to hide. Hell, I was the cause of all this upheaval and I might as well be present to defend my actions. Danielle gave me a poisonous look as I joined them around the central fire pit. She stuck close to Stefano, her monster tits trying to wrestle out of her low-cut top.

There they stood – Danielle standing next to Stefano, rangy and dark, with big, long-lashed brown eyes and a square face. He and Danielle were about the same height, standing so close together their hips just barely touched. Two young girls were with Stefano, sitting in the sand and playing what looked like marbles with seashells, their dark heads cocked to the side as they listened in on the adults. They looked tan enough and pretty enough to be related to Stefano, blessed with the same big, expressive eyes. Whelan stood flanked by Nate and Banana, the whole group forming an uneven circle.

The talking ceased abruptly as I showed up. They stared, glaring as if a leper had wandered into their midst, dripping flesh and pus.

'You don't have to listen to this,' Whelan said. He was going to shove me back into the cabin if I didn't stick up for myself right then and there.

'Listen up,' I said. My voice was hoarse, quavering. I kept my eyes on Banana, knowing she wouldn't give me the stink eye. 'I know you're not thrilled about us showing up like this and I can understand why. I just want you all to know that we're grateful for the help and we'll pull our weight. We didn't mean to end up here.' I swallowed, dreading the next bit. 'We don't know what we're doing. But we'll learn. I'll do whatever it takes.'

I swear I heard a cricket croak out its condolences a

few feet away. For a moment I expected the fighting to start up again. Danielle opened and closed her mouth a few times and I wondered if maybe she was overloading, like a fembot struck by lightning. It was that or a brain hemorrhage from having to process a concept more complex than paper or plastic. Then she threw up her hands and stomped away, leaving a faint trail of freesia perfume in her wake. Stefano dawdled. He seemed to be weighing Danielle's opinion and my little speech in his mind. Then he stuck out his hand and I took it. It was sufficiently awkward, but damn it if I didn't feel relieved. I imagine the pilgrims and the natives had brokered a similar kind of tentative peace.

We all know how that worked out.

'Isabella, Teresa,' Stefano said, gesturing to the young girls with him. He had a low, accented voice. 'Come and say hello, please.'

They were shy, blinky, reminiscent of Shane whenever he was introduced to a stranger.

'Tell me when my friends turn up,' I said, turning and going back toward Whelan's cabin and Shane. I was exhausted and ready to get off my feet. Somewhere along the way I had co-opted Whelan's house. If he wanted to dispute that, I was confident he'd bring it up.

Shane was inside, asleep. I curled up with him for a brief rest. There would be tons to do in preparation for the camp merger. Half an hour was enough to dull the stinging in my feet, and then I was up and out. Whelan put me to work on things that didn't involve a lot of standing or walking. I sorted through blankets they hadn't needed to use yet, picking out the ones with the least holes and folding them. He helped me set up a little assembly line where I could

177

make packets of rationed food, care packages for when they first arrived. And he uncomplainingly hauled me to my feet and carried me to the cabin every fifteen minutes or so to check on Shane. No offense against Whelan, but I wanted to make sure he was sleeping soundly with my own eyes.

Finished and beat, I was finally able to rest for good. The cabin resonated with cold, dark and relentless with silence. Shane napped on the cot. Banana followed me inside a moment later. I sat on the cot and swung my legs onto the thin mattress, putting one light hand on Shane's shoe. The pain had gotten to the point where I could no longer distinguish my feet from my ankles or knees. Banana came over to the bed and pulled up the little handmade stool. She had a glass bottle tucked beneath her arm. She still wore her cute polka-dotted handkerchief.

'Here,' she said, handing me the bottle. 'To your health.'

There was no label but one sniff told me it was rum. I took a swig, coughing into the crook of my elbow. It burned. We traded the bottle back and forth. First she held my hand through surgery and now she was bringing me rum. This woman could do no wrong.

'Who's this little trooper?'

'Shane,' I replied in a whisper. The boy didn't stir, though I had a feeling he might be faking it to eavesdrop. He was crafty that way. 'He's my nephew. I look after him now.'

'Stefano's girls play nice, I promise. Trust me, they'll like having a new bud. Can you imagine just having your sister around all the time?' Banana asked, giving me a firm smile.

I thought of Kat and just how much I wished I could

have her back. With her alive, Shane wouldn't have to put up with me. 'I can imagine it, actually.'

'Sorry.' Banana winced. 'Didn't mean it like that . . .'

'It's fine, I get it.' I nodded toward Shane. 'He's pretty shy around other people. He doesn't talk much at first.'

'Those two girls talk plenty for the whole camp.' She paused, sipping from the rum. 'Are you worried about them?' she asked.

Banana's eyes are lovely. Most peoples' eyes are at least slightly tapered but hers are perfectly round. Her presence is warm and lively and wraps around you like a fuzzy winter scarf. I considered her question; Andrea was one of the most competent people I'd ever met. Noah was young and strong.

'They'll make it,' I said, nodding to show my certainty. 'I just hope they show before nightfall.'

'Whelan will go out looking for them if they don't.'

'That's nice of him,' I said lightly.

'Yes, it is.'

I was tired but not *that* tired. I could see where this was heading.

'Whelan told me you used to, uh, dance,' I said, cutting her off. Banana smiled and I wondered if it was possible for her to not look flirtatious. She lowered her thick lashes; unlike us mortals, this woman didn't need the help of mascara.

'Burlesque, sweetie, not stripping. Well, not the kind you're thinking of anyway.'

'Oh.' My face felt hot. 'I guess I don't know the difference.'

Banana shifted her light brown eyes from side to side and then shrugged. I left it at that. It was hard to say whether the subject of dancing made her homesick or uncomfortable. Changing the subject felt like the best course of action.

'Do you plan on staying here?' I asked.

'How do you mean?'

'You know, permanently. Do you think you'll ever go back to Seattle?'

Her eyes bugged. I was speaking sacrilege.

'*Go back?*' From her voice, the idea was about as appealing as swallowing razors. 'Why would we go back?'

'For one? It's my home. That's why I want to go back. For another, we can't stay here forever, right? I mean, it's just temporary. I want Shane to grow up with other kids. Not just Isabella and Teresa, I'm sure they're sweet girls . . . I just want to give him what he deserves.'

It sounded like I was insulting their camp. Banana snorted softly.

'That came out wrong,' I muttered, sighing. 'I just . . . this is okay for now, but what about when he grows up? How is he going to learn about, I don't know, *life*? What teenager grows up without girls and cars and turns out okay?'

'Good question,' Banana replied, smirking. 'I certainly can't imagine mine without either of those.'

'And won't we run out of food eventually?' This sounded reasonable to me but Banana didn't appear ruffled in the least.

'There's plenty to eat,' she said. 'Fish and clams if you know how to get 'em. We can plant gardens and hunt for meat. I don't see any reason to leave. We've got everything we need here.'

'Right, except that whole civilization thing,' I replied.

'Which I'm fond of.' We were putting a dent in the rum.

'Give me a stage and I'll put on a show,' Banana said. Tempting offer – then I realized Danielle might get in on the action too and thought better of it. 'How's that for civilization?'

'So,' I started, 'how'd you get your name?'

She giggled softly. The rum was hitting us both. Her laughter bounced around in my head for a minute, making me giddy.

'When I was first starting out at Annie's,' she said, licking booze from her lower lip and lowering her voice even further, 'I did my act in a yellow gown. My boss joked that the way I peeled off my clothes made me look like a banana. It stuck.'

'No actual fruit in the act?'

'No, not unless you count the piano player.' She laughed. 'No, no fruit. I'm not that kind of girl,' she said, teasing. Her apple-round cheeks flushed a pretty crimson. Then her face became deadly serious. 'You should stay, and not just you, but your friends too. You'll see. Things aren't so bad here. It'll grow on you.'

'Eventually,' I said in a whisper, 'we'll run out of booze.'

'If we get real desperate we can always try our hand at moonshine.'

She did have a point there. With Banana's help, I was tipsy by the time Andrea, Moritz, Noah and Cassandra arrived. They showed up tired and scratched and hungry but undeniably human. I felt like an empress on a silk bed of pillows when they trooped into the cabin to say hello. And furthermore, I felt like an asshole for being a bit drunk. Shane roused long enough to say hello and welcome them back. I might've at least tried to look as miserable as they felt, but the blankets and food prepared for them did take the sting off. They seemed appropriately awed by the accommodations of the camp and gratefully ate the food provided. Whelan brought a lantern and left us alone, taking Banana and her rum with him. They bid us good night.

All of us slept in the same cabin that night. Andrea crawled into the cot beside me and Shane without complaint. Noah tried to turn out the lantern but I kept it burning long into the night. Exhausted as I was, I couldn't sleep. While the others collapsed into snores and dreams, I slipped *The Big Sleep* out of Noah's bag and read until my eyelids simply refused to stay open another second. My friends were safe and sound. Things were looking up. It didn't even bother me that Noah had scribbled all over the margins of *The Big Sleep*. Notes and sentences under- lined . . . but I didn't let it distract me. I finished the book, but instead of feeling satisfied I felt afraid. When I closed my eyes I saw the faces of the creatures that had chased me through the forest, I saw the fate they had forced me to choose.

The island loomed dark and full, and when I thought too hard about what might be out there, watching us, I knew I'd never sleep soundly again.

I woke to the sound of gunfire and the sinking feeling that I was the last to hear it.

The cabin was empty. Blankets and pillows had been abandoned in a hurry. I hobbled out the door, grateful to find that my feet were hurting less and less. The fringes of a hangover clung to my brain, turning the sunshine into a knife aimed right for my eyes.

Nobody stood near the fire pits or down by the dock and so I followed the gunshots to the back of the cabins, closer to the edge of the forest. A line of people spread out in front of me, their faces turned toward the thicket of trees and the white shadows creeping out of it. Whelan stood in the center of the line with Nate and Banana at his sides. They each held a rifle and peppered the advancing zombies with several rounds. Andrea watched, fascinated, and Moritz and Noah hung together to the side. I noticed Cassandra hanging back from the others, both hands covering her ears. Her body jerked after each round of fire. Shane stood beside her, his fists frozen at his sides as he stared resolutely at the tree line.

I hurried up to Andrea, leaning on her shoulder to take some of the pressure off my feet.

'Morning,' she said. I could barely hear her voice over the sound of the rifles. She didn't seem to think anything of the earblistering racket. Andrea sipped from a tin cup. I smelled the warm, bitter scent of coffee.

'What a way to wake up,' I replied.

'They just keep coming,' Andrea said. She shivered. 'Whelan thinks they followed us up from the southern part of the island.'

'Does he now?'

'It's not a comforting thought,' she added with a frown. I had to agree. The sight of so many undead shambling toward us made my empty stomach twist. The island didn't feel very big and that was a lot of zombies for such a small parcel of land. Then I remembered the boat and nearly being dragged under the water by one of those things . . .

'Where do they all come from?' I asked her.

Whelan answered instead in a yell. 'No way to tell. We've dealt with them ever since we got here. Seems like there's an endless supply.'

'Sorry,' I said to Andrea. 'I know this isn't the most cheerful housewarming.'

'They've got coffee,' she said simply. 'And that's pretty damn cheerful.'

While she and Moritz and Noah were taking the appearance of the undead in stride, Cassandra looked ready to crumble. I went to talk to her but she jerked away. She smelled terrible. The bloodstains on her scrubs had turned rust brown and her red hair was matted down to her head.

The sight of her shrinking away from me made me wonder if joining Whelan's tribe was such a hot idea. I glanced over my shoulder as the gunfire stopped and the last undead straggler fell forward into the dirt. We couldn't have held off an onslaught like that. No, I'd made the right call.

Isabella and Teresa stood at the very end of the line next to Stefano. They were tucked into his sides and they turned to look at me with matching brown eyes. Not twins, as I had initially thought, but siblings, close together in age. Stefano saw them watching me and leaned over to whisper something in their ears. The two girls sidled up to me, Teresa tugging shyly at her braid.

'Good morning,' the girl on the left murmured. They wore matching T-shirts for something called 'Stardusters.' Judging from the logo and explosion of pink and glittery stars it was some kind of dance studio or tap class.

'Morning,' I said. I tried to dredge up the meager amount of Spanish I'd learned in college. '¿Como estas?'

'Not bad. How is your little boy?' the one on the right, Teresa, asked.

'He's doing okay. You're not . . . afraid of them?' I gestured to toward the tree line.

Isabella shrugged. She was taller, with less little kid chub on her face. 'Sometimes they come,' she said. A flicker of fear darkened her eyes. 'But we always kill them.'

'Whelan kills them,' Teresa corrected, poking out her tongue.

'Whatever. *Estupida*.' Isabella rolled her eyes, adding, 'There's breakfast ready, okay? Help yourself.'

Their duty done, they fled back to Stefano. He seemed more like an uncle or guardian, too young to have girls their age. Giggling and chatting, the girls glanced at Shane, alternately hiding behind Stefano's legs and peeking out to glance at my nephew. Shane seemed oblivious to their gawking, choosing instead to amble up to Whelan and stare at his rifle. That wasn't what I had in mind for this early. I ran to Shane, herding him back to the campfire so we could eat, safely out of stray bullet range.

Now that the immediate threat of the zombies had been put down, nobody seemed to have any idea what to do or where to go. Whelan turned away from the thicket and stalked back to the fire pits. I watched, swallowing a mouthful of oatmeal. His jaw worked as he slopped a can of baked beans into a cast-iron pot. He slid the pot onto a spit and jabbed at the dwindling fire before pushing both hands through his floppy hair. I was finally getting used to the idea that from now on I'd either smell like a campfire or fish.

'Shouldn't we arrange some kind of . . . ice-cream social or something?' I asked.

'Be my guest.'

Banana and Nate drifted past, tossing a casual greeting to me as they continued on their way to the docks. Nate had acquired a fishing rod and some buckets. I had a feeling someone would soon be put to work clearing the dead bodies from the thicket, and us being the newcomers, I could see the task falling to us. For the moment I'd wait and hope that someone else volunteered.

'Maybe not ice cream,' I said, shifting around on a fat log rolled up snug to the fire pit. Shane had already finished his food, eyeing the pot of oatmeal. I didn't feel comfortable yet telling him he could go for seconds. 'How about a clam bake?'

He shrugged, his back to me as he hunched over the fire. 'Sure,' and then even more curtly, 'if you want.'

Caveman poke fire. Man grunt. Caveman no like pushy woman with prickly feet and too many questions.

'Right, sorry for that.'

I took Shane's empty bowl, stacked it on top of mine and stood.

'There's a lot on my mind,' he said. I guess that was maybe the start of an apology, or an apology wearing the dastardly guise of an excuse. 'That's the most I've ever seen. Here, I mean, on the island.'

'Isabella and Teresa didn't seem concerned.'

'They're *kids*.'

Shane frowned.

'How many?' I asked.

'How many what?'

'I was half-asleep. How many did you take out?'

'Fifteen,' he said, rubbing his darkened jaw. He needed a shave. 'Maybe more.'

'But the rifles . . .' I slowly pointed out. 'It didn't seem like they posed much of a threat. Are you low on ammunition?'

'No,' Whelan replied, then, 'not yet. We'll run out a hell of a lot faster if that many keep turning up.'

Well, this was a cheerful way to start the day.

'Besides,' he continued, 'we were fine because we were awake, Sadie, ready. But there's no predicting when they'll turn up. If we're swarmed at the wrong time . . .' He paused, fixing his gaze on the flames at his feet. Shane made a soft sound of confusion or maybe fear. I put my hand on his head, hoping it was enough to ease his anxieties, at least until I could come up with something encouraging to say.

'I get it,' I said. 'Crap. I thought we'd left all this behind in Seattle.'

'Wherever you go . . .'

'There they are.'

Whelan nodded. He had changed out of his blue polo and into an oversized fisherman's cardigan, gray and speckled like a wren's egg. I caught a glimpse of something dark at the collar, a tattoo maybe. The baked beans began to bubble, drawing my attention, their scent and sound making my mouth water. Baked beans weren't a natural follow-up to oatmeal, but when you haven't been eating well . . .

'Still hungry?' he asked, chuckling. I wondered if maybe my stomach had yowled and I hadn't heard it.

'You bet.'

When Whelan handed me my bowl, I saw that he gave me a slightly bigger portion. Ludicrous, considering our respective sizes, but I accepted the small gesture with a grateful smile. After Shane received his portion, I discreetly leaned over and shoveled most of my extras into his bowl.

Whelan ate with his eyes in his beans. Over his shoulder I watched Noah and Moritz chatting in front of one of the cabins. Moritz watched us, his mouth moving, responding to Noah and all the while his gaze lingered on me, or Whelan, I couldn't tell. I shivered.

'We need to make more arrows for that bow of yours,' Whelan said. Isabella and Teresa had found their way down to the beach. Cassandra tagged along at a distance, laughing and skipping, putting her feet into the divots their shoes had left in the sand. The girls soon began sword fighting with driftwood. Cassandra watched, her toes in the surf, just close enough to the water to make me nervous. Maybe the little girls would help bring Cassandra out of her shell. Stefano wasn't down there with the girls, which struck me as remarkably laissez-faire. But this was their camp. They knew best.

It was shaping up to be a bright, mild day with just the softest cool breeze rolling in from the water.

'You can have it,' I said. 'The bow, I mean. I'm not any good with it.'

'Then where'd the arrows go, hm?' He smiled. That motherfucking dimple was back. It was a start.

'One's in a lumberjack's leg and the other's in his face.'

'You shot some zombies?' Shane's eyes went wide.

I blushed.

'I was lucky. Really lucky.'

'So let me get this straight,' Whelan said. His spoon plopped down into his bowl, splattering his hand with bean

188

juice. 'You went into the woods, alone, armed with a homemade bow and a handful of arrows?'

'I had a knife too.'

'Sadie . . .'

'Yeah okay, it wasn't the brightest idea I've ever had. But desperation makes you do funny things,' I said. I shrugged over my beans, feeling sheepish at his implication that I was, for lack of a better description, fucking insane. 'I wanted to get food for us. It didn't turn out like I expected.'

'Sounds to me like that bow's in good hands,' he said, softening. 'You hang on to it. And kill us a deer or two if it's not too much trouble.' He held up a spoonful of beans. 'Red meat could make you a lot of friends around here.'

I smiled back at him, wondering if I should feel this relaxed after a wave of zombies came for us at the camp. The two girls down on the beach began laughing, and then one of them burst into tears, holding her arm. She had lost the sword fight. They were still awfully close to the edge of the water. Cassandra rushed forward, kneeling to help Teresa, who was the smaller of the two sisters and had fallen to her sister's blows.

'You know they could be coming from the mainland,' I said quietly.

'Who? The undead? You're kidding, right?'

'No, I wish I was. That's how we lost our captain. He was fishing off the boat and one of those things yanked him into the water. They almost got me too,' I said. My ankle throbbed right on cue. The bruise lingered, just about to fade. I put my hand on Shane's shoulder, hoping the mention of the event wouldn't upset him.

'Your ankle,' he said. So he had seen more than just the spines in my feet. Observant. 'How deep was the water?'

'Well . . . too deep.'

'*Shit*.' Whelan coughed. 'I mean, *shoot*.'

Whelan stared at me, unflinchingly. A tendon worked like a piston below his ear. He was afraid. I couldn't help but share in his renewed dread. His eyes narrowed, and he squinted, sizing me up maybe or rethinking some estimation he had made previously. This was new information, important information. I hated being the bearer of bad news, but – to be honest – I didn't mind the feeling that I was now someone to be trusted and looked to for advice.

'The one that tried to drag you down in the tide pool . . . He wasn't a fluke. They can handle themselves in the water.' I glanced over my shoulder at Isabella and Teresa again, just in case. Whelan seemed to pick up on my concern.

'No,' he murmured, 'that's north. They'd come from the east. If they're crossing the water they'd come from the east.'

'Mainland?'

He nodded. A piece of dark hair fell over his forehead and he shook it away impatiently. I tried to swallow another spoonful of beans but they had gone lukewarm and tasted too sugary sweet.

'It doesn't make sense,' he said after a long stretch of silence. 'I mean, supposing they *are* filtering over from the mainland. Why us? We're so few here. Unless everyone on the mainland . . .'

'Is dead?' I laughed. 'No way. We're probably just closer. Or maybe they have refined tastes.' Neither of us could rustle up a chuckle. Near the cabins, Noah and

Moritz stopped talking. Moritz ducked inside, taking one last glance at me as he did so.

'Whatever the reason,' Whelan said, standing, 'I'll add a watch on the docks and to the east and hope that that's enough.'

I nodded, thinking what a stupid word that was. Enough? Looking down at my lukewarm beans I shifted, anxious in my own skin, anxious under a sudden weight. Your defenses were always enough, until they weren't.

TWELVE

'Clams! Clams! A love affair begins.' Andrea dipped her head down into the wooden bowl filled with steaming, fragrant shellfish. 'I could die right now and be happy.'

'Please don't say that.'

I was on edge. I realized I hadn't drawn anything in days. That energy stored up inside can make me jumpy and out of sorts. And besides that, my discussion with Whelan over baked beans had helped a cold suspicion settle in my chest.

I had half-hoped Whelan would brush off my suggestion that the undead were coming over from the mainland. But he hadn't brushed it off, not at all. He was spooked. Together, he and I were the only dash of ill temper at an otherwise rousing success. The clams, and also Banana's rum, had given us southerners a good excuse to mingle with the northerners.

No Mason-Dixon bitterness here. So far introductions were going swimmingly.

To my surprise, Cassandra took a shine to – of all people – Danielle. The presence of little Isabella and Teresa seemed to make the nurse more lighthearted too. The little girls flitted around the fire playing tag with their dark hair turned burnished gold from the flames, while

Shane looked on with a disdainful little scowl on his chubby face. Danielle had managed to coax Cassandra out of her disgusting scrubs and into a candy pink T-shirt and white denim shorts. The change in Cassandra's mood was startling.

Even Moritz, like the chosen cuisine of the evening, was coming out of his shell. And despite a bad mood flickering on the horizon, at least I could see that Andrea was looking healthier. With food and water in abundance, her face was looking less gaunt and desperate. She smiled more. She looked pretty. Everyone did, the raging fires giving us a healthy glow, the weather holding out to bless us with a perfect, mild evening. The clams and booze didn't hurt, either.

But Whelan and I, like fidgety, sober parents overseeing a prom party, hovered on the fringes of the celebration. I didn't enjoy casting my crotchety shadow over the festivities, and the clams really were excellent and fresh, but some worries you just can't shake off.

'Something up?'

I nearly dropped my bowl of clams. Banana stood right next to my shoulder. I should've smelled the Aquanet. At least if the undead ambushed us Banana would have a badass supply of flame-throwing materials at the ready. I wouldn't light a match in her presence.

'Just a little distracted,' I said. 'And tipsy!' I made a flailing stab at lighthearted. Banana wasn't impressed. In the firelight, the silk handkerchief bundling up her hair sparkled; so did her eyes.

'You look like someone pissed in your drink.'

I looked down at my half-empty cup. 'What a delightful figure of speech.'

'You can be coy or you can come clean,' she said. 'I'm only offering a service.'

'I didn't think the transition would go this smoothly,' I said, gesturing to the others. That was true, even if it wasn't really what was weighing heavily on my mind.

'The sky ain't always falling.'

I should have grabbed onto that sentiment and clutched it for dear life. But instead I went on sulking and let Banana wander over to Moritz and Noah, who seemed happy to have her company. I felt like making a speech or at least giving everyone a warning, but every time I worked up the courage to open my mouth, I saw Whelan brooding over his drink. I didn't want to encourage panic and, selfishly, I didn't want to be the one spoiling the party. But I couldn't keep quiet. Not this time.

'Would everyone mind gathering around for a minute?' I called, clearing my throat and waiting for the chatter and laughter to die down. Whelan shot me a look, but I ignored it. With so many happy faces staring at me, it was hard to find the right words. 'It's been great getting to know you all and I'm glad we're all having a good time, but there's something I wanted to say. It's going to be a downer, so I apologize for that.'

'Boo,' Andrea heckled, chuckling.

'I know, sue me.' With a shrug I continued, 'I'm sure we're all aware that it's important to be safe and cautious but . . .' I hoped Andrea wouldn't hate me too much for bringing it up. 'We suffered a tragedy on the way here because we didn't know any better. It's scary to think about and it sucks, but we realized that the water is just as dangerous as land.'

'What Sadie is trying to say,' Whelan cut in abruptly, 'is

that they could attack us from the water. We have to adjust accordingly.'

'What?' Banana asked with a gasp. 'The water? I can't believe it.'

'Believe it,' I replied. 'We saw it happen.'

'Life of the party, these two,' Andrea muttered. But she nodded when I looked at her, agreeing with the decision to tell the others. Danielle joined Banana in voicing her outrage and surprise. I sidled back toward Andrea, wishing I could disappear for being the doomsayer. But Shane gave me a nod too, and his acceptance made the bitter pill go down easier.

Later, the night took a turn for the pleasant, for all of us. Banana gathered us together, teasing good-naturedly until we all agreed to sit in a lopsided circle. She stood in the middle, clearing her throat and sipping her drink for courage before announcing the night's entertainment.

'We're all going to sing,' she said, pointing significantly at each of us in turn. 'And I don't want to hear any complaining. And if you don't sing loud enough well then you'll just have to do a solo, got it?'

Shane shifted nervously, looking to me for help.

'It's okay,' I said in a conspiratorial whisper. 'I'll sing extra loud for both of us.'

He smiled, his shoulders lifting a little as he turned his attention back to Banana.

First came 'I've Got a Lovely Bunch of Coconuts.' It turned out the kids didn't know that one so well – which was probably a positive, considering the slightly bawdy lyrics – and it fell to the adults to pick up the slack. Poor Moritz struggled, baffled by the lyrics, joining in only when we reached the memorable chorus. Isabella and Teresa laughed along, drumming first Stefano and then Danielle on the shoulders.

'Hakuna Matata' proved a much easier choice for the kidlets, although Moritz found himself similarly stymied and Banana mercilessly chose him to sing a solo of about half the song. Teresa, taking pity on the man, got up and helped him, swinging his hand in time to the rhythm and singing louder to drown out the times he blundered the words.

'One more song,' Whelan cautioned as Moritz was allowed to sit down again. 'Since I think we've already alerted every walker from here to Addis Ababa.'

He stalked the perimeter of the circle, turning on a flashlight to sweep the sand and the area surrounding the campfire for any unwelcome guests. Isabella and Teresa were quick to pull him back, one falling on his ankle, the other launching onto his shoulders. Whelan put up a valiant fight against their giggling, slogging back to the song circle with Teresa clinging like a barnacle to his ankle. He pretended to go down, grunting dramatically as they pushed him down into the sand.

Whelan's punishment for leaving was a song of his own. The group came to the conclusion that 'YMCA' was suitably humiliating, but the girls were kind enough to act as his backup dancers, twirling, forgetting half the time to make the usual letters with their arms.

Looking around, listening to the laughter, seeing that even Cassandra was getting into the spirit of things and that Danielle, for once, wasn't seething at me, it made me think that maybe Banana was right. Things could be permanent here. Maybe Shane wouldn't get to go to school like other kids and sure, a place like Liberty Village would afford more opportunities for a 'normal' upbringing, but there could be fuzzy, good things happening here too. And even if it wasn't permanent, Shane might take away memories that weren't all about struggling to eke out an existence or just get by.

So when, the next morning, I woke up to screaming, I wasn't only surprised but also deeply disappointed. We had been so close to . . . *something*. Something that made the fright of fleeing Seattle and the danger of the boat seem worth it.

Suddenly, I wondered if I'd open the cabin door to see the beach flooded with zombies. But the campsite was exactly as we'd left it the night before, a little dirty and scattered with dishes, but otherwise familiar. The only noticeable difference was the screaming.

Andrea and I woke at the same time and together we stumbled out of the cabin, bleary-eyed and half-dressed. Shane tumbled out after us, both fists buried in his eyes as he tried to wake up. We fit right in with the others, who stood in a semicircle around Stefano and Danielle's cabin. They, too, were in their pajamas, barefoot and staring.

'They're gone! Fuck, *fuck*, how could this happen? They know not to wander off!'

'Who's gone?' I whispered, silently slipping into the half-circle next to Whelan.

'The girls,' he murmured. His voice was hoarse. 'Isabella and Teresa.'

'Gone as in dead, or gone as in—'

'Vanished,' Whelan finished, shooting me a black look. 'Disappeared.'

Oh, no. At least we had warned about water zombies, but that wasn't enough. Stefano broke down into tears, hiding his face in Danielle's shoulder. She stroked his spiky forest of bleached hair, giving Andrea, and especially me, a stabby glare. Right. Just by virtue of being new, we were somehow responsible for two little kids wandering off in the night. I couldn't help it; I crossed my arms over my chest defensively.

'So where are they?' Danielle asked. Her voice was high-pitched and whining, like hot pink manicured nails on a chalkboard. If she were one of those weird, acid-spitting dinosaurs her rainbow-colored lizard collar would be flaring up around her pointy face. I wasn't actually certain I could take Danielle if we came to blows – I'd probably ricochet right off of her bouncy-castle chest.

'Really? You want to start this?'

'Calm down,' Whelan said, addressing both of us. He turned to Stefano. 'Kids are curious. Sometimes they get frightened by dreams or maybe a sound and they wander and get lost.'

'Not Isabella,' Stefano wailed, 'and not Teresa!'

'He's right,' Danielle said, turning up her nose. 'They're smart girls. They know better.'

Another pointed look in my direction. Oh, Danielle was a smooth operator, all right – she knew just how to push my buttons. One more snotty glance and I'd be pleased as punch to wring her neck.

'As much as I'd love for this to turn into *Mad Max Beyond Thunderdome*, we should make up search parties,' I said. '*Quickly*.'

Whelan nodded. Banana and Nate had come to investigate the trouble, the others bringing up the rear behind them. Poor Noah looked like he was still asleep, shuffling forward with his eyes almost completely closed, his dark hair mussed and sticking up in every direction. Cassandra still wore the pink T and white shorts from the night before. She went to stand next to Danielle.

'Good, you're all up,' Whelan said. 'We've got work to do.'

I was asked to join the group going, presumably, into the most dangerous part of the island. Whelan would be going in this group, along with Moritz and Andrea. Nate was the other team leader, since each group would need someone who was handy with a rifle. Banana volunteered to stay behind at the camp and guard Shane. Unsurprisingly, Cassandra refused to go with anyone but Danielle. I had no complaints about that. I wasn't the only person to notice their budding friendship.

'Looks like our girl Cassandra's fitting in,' Andrea muttered. Danielle and Cassandra joined Nate in the search party going southwest along the beach. Andrea and I stuck close behind Whelan, letting him go first into the dense wall of trees. He did, after all, have the rifle. Moritz had been given Nate's knife and helped cut a path through the bushes clustered around the trees.

'I'm gonna go ahead and say that's a good thing,' I replied. I was all nerves, chattering aimlessly to keep from dwelling too much on the missing girls. 'I was starting to worry about her. Building sand castles? Those nasty-ass scrubs? I sort of expected to return to camp and find her prancing around naked in the surf, wearing your guts as a fascinator.'

'That Danielle chick's got a way with her, I guess.'

'The lord works in damn near confounding ways.'

Whelan shushed us over his shoulder. From the rigid line of his shoulders, arms and back I could tell that he was nervous too. He had volunteered to take us straight to the heart of the island and I was absolutely certain that was no coincidence. Still, there was no time to plumb his motivations. As I had discovered during my Will Scarlet phase, the forest had a way of eating up certain sounds and intensifying others. Birds shrieked and it sounded like they had swooped down right next to your ear. But footfalls disappeared, softer than they had any right to be. It made me feel tiny, at the mercy of so many cloaking leaves and clever hiding places.

But there was no sign of the girls, no crumb trail of shoes or ponytail binders. I hadn't spotted one snagged piece of cloth or any of that other exciting bullshit that makes you think you're on the right path. As we cut deeper into the forest, I felt a clammy sweat spring up around my neck and ears. It was hard work navigating the trees, fallen stumps and uneven, shifting ground. Nobody spoke. Our shoes trampled down the brittle grasses and Moritz's knife slashed at branches here and there, but otherwise we said nothing and let Whelan lead the way.

I felt a small seed of insecurity in my brain, a seed that didn't take long to sprout and flower. How well did I really know Whelan and his cohorts? Hadn't he faked a zombie attack to get me in the water? Hadn't that led to my feet being torn to pieces? And now those two girls were missing, but there was no trace of them at the camp. We had split up, going into the wild with Whelan and Nate, both of whom carried serious weaponry. What had begun as a search party, I realized with a jolt, could easily turn into a cold-blooded execution.

'They're not out here,' I said, shuffling to a stop. Inside my boots, my feet were beginning to throb. Whelan turned at the waist, shooting me a look that said plainly: Keep moving.

'This doesn't look good, Whelan,' I added, glancing around helplessly. 'Shouldn't we have found something by now? A shoe? Something? Maybe we're going the wrong way, or . . . I don't know. It'd be better if we fanned out but we shouldn't get separated . . .'

'There's something up ahead,' he said, drawing a damp hand across his forehead. His dark brown hair shined with sweat. 'Something through the trees. If we don't find anything there we'll try a different direction.'

Andrea lifted her right foot to go on but I grabbed her hand and squeezed. When Whelan had his back to us again I slowly shifted my head from side to side. We hung back, Moritz and Whelan forging ahead while Andrea and I did our best to trail without being too obvious.

'What are you thinking?' she whispered. Her hand grew slick in my grasp.

'Split us up? Take us into the woods? What does that remind you of?' I asked in an undertone.

'Should we run?'

'No, not yet. Let's wait it out.'

I hoped desperately that those wouldn't be my last words. I had seen with my own eyes Whelan's cop-trained skill with that gun. That SPD polo clearly wasn't a hand-me-down. If he decided to turn on us we'd be dead in a heartbeat. Speaking of, my pulse had risen to the point where I was sure everyone, Whelan included, could hear the drumming. The forest, which moments ago had simply felt strange and vast, now felt oppressive. I nearly collapsed with fright as gunfire erupted in front of us. But Whelan was firing at something through the trees, a lone zombie.

Our pace quickened. I could see now that there really was something beyond the trees, a clearing. I heard rushing water, like a fast-moving stream or waterfall. We four came to a stop just before breaking through the tree line.

'I don't like it,' Moritz said firmly.

I couldn't agree more.

Just beyond the branches and bushes lay a house, a blue clapboard house propped up on pilings. Underneath the deck, a stream rolled by and then bubbled and roiled into a waterfall. It was no Angel Falls, just a trickling by comparison, but a waterfall nonetheless. The house itself looked like something out of a fairy story, poised over the stream like a hunched beetle with a dulled blue shell. The windows were dark inside, some were boarded up. It didn't look like anyone had lived in the house for ages. The white banisters around the porch sagged, threatening to snap and fall right into the brook at the next strong wind.

'I don't like it,' Moritz said again, this time in a quieter voice with more conviction.

It did look incredibly like the perfect place for a bunch of zombies to congregate. Whoever had lived in that house might have been attacked and now their flesh-hungry legacy waited inside. I knew it would take more than a polite suggestion to get me to go through the rotting door. The cheerful blue paint did absolutely nothing to convince me; the darkened windows and cold, cold quiet of the place filled me with dread.

'I don't care how brave or stupid kids are,' Whelan muttered, 'they wouldn't go in a place like that.'

'You feel it too, then?' I whispered.

'Of course,' he said, scratching at the back of his neck.

'But I think for Stefano's sake, we have to look anyway. Goddamn it.'

I wondered if he was right. Maybe when Hansel and Gretel looked at that gingerbread house they could only see the gumdrop doorbell and not the evil behind the icing. Still, try as I might, I couldn't imagine two sweet little girls, even after escalating dares, working up the courage to peek inside.

'If they were lost they might have needed shelter,' Whelan went on. 'It got cold last night.'

'Fine,' I said, pushing through into the clearing, 'Then let's get it over with.'

A hand clamped over my wrist, shaking me back. I looked up into Moritz's face. I had never seen him looking so panicked or so sick. Even two horrific bouts of seasickness had been kinder to his expression. The frank, canine sparkle in his blue eyes had vanished.

'Don't go in there,' he said.

'We have to.'

I didn't add that, were it Shane and not Isabella and Teresa, I would have charged into that house without a moment's hesitation. If their places were reversed, I would want my friends doing everything they could to find him. That thought gave me courage.

'Sadie!' It was Whelan. 'Sadie, duck!'

I trusted. I ducked. The bullets flew close over my head. I could hear the unmistakable squishing pop of meat imploding. I scuttled forward onto my knees, crawling back toward the tree line. When I flipped onto my back I found that there were more of them, way more of them than I had thought. This wasn't just one errant creature trying to snag me for a meal – there were dozens of them emerging now from the trees. It was almost, I thought with a gurgle in my stomach, like the undead were protecting the house. They wandered into the clearing, their heads turning in unsettling unison toward the sound of Whelan's rifle.

'Run,' Whelan said in a quiet, steely voice. 'Leave now before I run out of bullets.'

There went that theory. I felt like a grade-A idiot for mistrusting him. An executioner wouldn't stay to provide cover for his victims. I had now mentally accused him of being a cannibal and a murderer. I really had to work on being more charitable.

Andrea and Moritz disappeared into the forest but I hesitated, staying behind.

'You're coming too,' I said, grabbing Whelan by the sleeve.

'They'll follow us.'

'So fucking what? Come on!'

He relented and turned to follow, but not before taking the time to shoot up a few of the closest zombies. Their moist rotting smell choked the clearing. Andrea and Moritz were already far ahead, flat-out sprinting.

'Taking us straight to hell,' I muttered as he ran and I hobbled to keep up. 'What's wrong with you?'

'Balls. I know. I should have been more clear last night.' He was out of breath and getting impatient with my pace. My feet had gone completely numb. The pins-and-needles feeling seeped up toward my knees. The groaning filtering through the trees behind us forced me to ignore the throbbing pain.

'Whatever,' I said. Whelan might have been out of breath but I was wheezing like an asthmatic at a cat show. 'It's too late for that now.'

Whelan slowed down, turning a circle in place as he waited for me to catch up. When I finally did, he swept me up into his arms and swung me over onto his back. I didn't appreciate being the C-3PO to his Chewbacca but my feet wouldn't have lasted much longer. He started running again, using the side of the rifle to bat stray branches out of the way. The smaller branches *thwap-thwapp*ed at my face as we threaded through the trees.

'I could have chimed in,' I added in a murmur.

'You had a chance to undermine my authority' – pant – pant – 'and make me look like an asshole in front of everyone and you didn't take it?'

I pinched his ear. He growled something, but it helped him swerve just in time to avoid a low-hanging pine bough.

'Every nice thing I've ever thought or said about you? I take it back. Do that again and so help me, I will drag you back to camp by your pinky toe.'

'What was that house?' I asked. It was easy to ignore his threats – which were only playful, I hoped – when I didn't have to look at his face. I ducked my head down close to his shoulder, wary of the scraping needles on the branches that dipped down from above. The leaves rushed by in my ears, punctuated now and then with a particularly loud moan from behind us.

'I don't know,' Whelan said. 'I've never gone that far into the woods. It looked old, maybe a smuggler's den.'

'Why did I feel like it was something out of *The Twilight Zone*?'

We were nearing the camp. I could make out Andrea and Moritz not far ahead of us and hear the distant rushing of the waves on shore.

'Because there's something inside it,' he said, gasping for breath, 'and I don't think it's those two little girls.'

'But you can't actually *feel* evil.'

'When you've been around death as much as we have, I wouldn't be surprised if you could.'

Whelan let his run turn into a jog and then a fast walk. We broke through the thicket and onto the beach. The familiar sight of the cabins and fires sent a tingling shudder of relief through my spine. Whelan helped me down and both of us turned quickly in opposite directions. I wasn't going to dwell on the feeling of being wrapped around his back or the sensation of sliding down over his taut backside. Not that I noticed.

The other parties had already returned. They met us with solemn, searching faces . . . except for Danielle, who clearly didn't believe I was draped all over Whelan's bodacious bod due to my feet and not for more nefarious reasons. Stefano's cheeks were streaked with fresh tears.

'Nothing,' Whelan said. He glanced my way and I shrugged. Did they really need to know about the creepy house? 'We didn't find anything.'

'Nothing?' Andrea cried. She pointed to the south. 'Yeah, we didn't find a single thing – oh wait, we found a whole fuckload of zombies!'

'What?' Nate asked. He shouldered his way through to the front of the crowd. A few dry leaves had stuck in his tightly coiled hair.

'Reload,' Whelan said. 'They'll make the beach soon.'

Danielle and Cassandra swept Stefano away, bringing him to sit down on one of the logs in front of the fire pit. I wasn't surprised to see that Cassandra was still glued to Danielle's side, but it was a bit unusual to see Cassandra acting like such a grown up. Her days of making sand castles were, apparently, behind her.

Since those of us without weapons were more or less useless, I took Andrea by the hand again and pulled her into our cabin. Shane was still with Banana, sitting with her on the logs outside by the fire pit. I didn't want to see the carnage and I didn't want to have my ears assaulted by the rifle fire. Despite the fact that we shared the cabin, nobody was inside. I shut the door and immediately felt my pulse relax. I needed to think. I needed her help.

'Something is fucked up here,' I said. Brilliant. That was pretty much the long and short of the rousing speech I'd thought up.

'What tipped you off? The missing girls, the horde of undead, or the fucking death shack in the middle of the island?'

'Christ,' I muttered. Andrea slid down onto the cot. She pushed aside Noah's copy of *The Big Sleep* and I almost snapped at her to be careful with it. But snapping wouldn't help. My hands shook. Pacing felt like the right thing to do so I went about stomping a trench into the floor. 'I actually thought for a minute there that Whelan was going to kill us. Whelan! What is *wrong* with me?'

'Nothing's wrong with you,' she said. She was straining to keep her voice down. I had forgotten that the walls were thin. 'Remember, Sadie? We don't know these people. You're the only one here I really trust. We've been through some shit together – real life, The Outbreak, Carl.'

'Please don't—'

'My point is that we have no reason to trust these shitbirds.'

'I think Whelan is all right,' I said. Andrea rolled her

eyes. Earlier she had taken off her floppy hat and stuffed it into her hoodie pocket. She took the hat out now and pinched and pulled it between her fingers, working it like a slab of dough.

'Don't give me that look. He stayed behind, Andrea. He was prepared to sacrifice his life for us.' If she couldn't see the significance of that then I wasn't sure I wanted her as an ally. She finally nodded, her long brown hair swishing over her shoulder.

'Okay,' she said. 'So Whelan we trust. Who else? Moritz?'

'I don't know,' I said. I stopped suddenly, wondering why the response had come so quickly and without my meaning it to. 'I mean . . . He was looking at me weird yesterday. I don't know if that actually means anything . . .'

'But it gave you the creeps?' Andrea asked.

'Yeah,' I said. I had the good grace to at least sound reluctant. I felt disgusting, like a betrayer. 'And today when we found that cabin . . . He just seemed really . . . intense, you know? His eyes . . . Ugh.' I shivered.

'Right. Then Moritz is out. Noah?'

'This is ridiculous,' I muttered. 'There's no way to know these things. It seems so unfair.'

'So what? Survival, remember? You're not a cutesy illustrator anymore, you're a survivor. Hoppy bunnies aren't your business now, being ruthless is,' she said. 'Whatever we have to do to stay alive, we're going to do it. If that means using our instincts *and* our brains then I say so be it.'

She was right, but I couldn't help but wish that Pink Bear and his fuzzy friends still *were* my business.

'I like Noah,' I said, getting back on track. 'He seems

like a good kid. And I trust Banana. She held my hand for two excruciating hours and didn't complain once. She shared booze with me. I think we can rely on her.'

'I agree,' Andrea said, 'and I like Nate.' She blushed. 'He read my palm last night. He said I have a great life line.'

'I'll bet he did. So you like Nate? Or you love him long time?'

'Shut up. He's just . . . He's goddamn reliable. It's in the eyes. Count him in.'

'That leaves Tits McGee, Cassandra and Stefano. I wouldn't trust any of them.'

'You really do hate Danielle,' Andrea said with a chuckle. 'Can I ask why?'

'Really? I need reasons? Her poisonous personality isn't enough?'

'Cassandra's actually turning into a person because of Danielle and – no offense, doll – she obviously had or *has* something going with Whelan. So she can't be all bad, am I right?'

'Look, you can cover a shit sandwich with caviar all you want, but guess what? It's still a shit sandwich.' Andrea rolled her eyes. Twice. Once to the right and then back again the left. 'Why do I feel eight years old again, getting sent to time-out for bullying someone on the playground?' I hated that Andrea might be right. And the thought of Whelan going anywhere near that plastic swamp donkey and her hateful little eyes made me furious . . . made me hateful. I winced. That was strong medicine. I'd make an effort to be kinder to Danielle in the future, assuming she hadn't chopped up Isabella and Teresa and put them in a soup.

Neither of us pointed out that, though we trusted almost

everyone, we still felt besieged. I decided to return to that thought later, when I could be alone. And I needed to talk to Shane, let him know what we were up against and to be vigilant. Maybe the zombies were making us paranoid. Maybe they were our only true enemy.

'So say Isabella and Teresa are gone – that takes care of everyone,' I said, breezing over our small disagreement. Whether or not Danielle was going to be my future bestest friend didn't matter; even if I detested her, I couldn't imagine she'd do anything to Isabella or Teresa. As a matter of fact, I couldn't picture *any* of the people on the island hurting those girls.

'I wouldn't count them out,' Andrea whispered. She was worrying a hole in her hat. 'It's a small island. They'll turn up. One way or another, they'll turn up.'

THIRTEEN

Give her a turban and call her a swami – Andrea was proven right the next morning. Well, half right.

Isabella turned up, but not Teresa.

Everybody was up early, Stefano going from cabin to cabin, rousing us to make up more search parties. Shane and I were just stumbling out of the cabin together, he lamenting the early wake-up and me mumbling about coffee, when Whelan rushed up to us.

'Down on the beach. Just one,' he said.

I knelt next to Shane, wondering how exactly to approach something like this. Losing an adult was horrible, but this was a kid . . . a kid like Shane. They had played together, started a friendship, and now she would be gone forever.

'I don't think you should see this,' I told him, touching his cheek. 'It's okay if you want to stay at the campfire.'

'Why do *you* want to go see it?' Shane asked, frowning.

'I don't *want* to, but . . . we need to figure out what happened to her and how she disappeared.'

'Can I come with?'

I hesitated.

'Let him,' Whelan said. 'We won't let him get too close.'

I ignored him, looking back to Shane. 'It's your choice,'

I said, mourning that I couldn't keep things like this from him forever. He was going to grow up whether I liked it or not. 'But you can change your mind if you want to.'

'I'm coming with.'

Isabella had washed up on shore, her clothes ragged, a hole chewed into her neck. It didn't take a PhD in zoology to see that the teeth marks weren't made by any animal. They were human and – God help us – small. Shane stared at her for a long time. I didn't allow him to get close enough to see just how bad it looked.

It took three people to hold Stefano back while Noah and Whelan fished her out of the water. Stefano collapsed into a heap at our feet when they took little Isabella into the cover of the forest. We couldn't bury her like that, not with her head still attached to her body. I don't know how they managed it. When Whelan and Noah returned, a rolled tarp swinging between them, Whelan looked shaken to his core.

Helpless, aimless, I took Shane away, down the beach toward the docks. In the distance, I heard the sound of shovels digging into the sand. They might bury her clothes or a keepsake, but nothing of the real Isabella would go in that grave. I hadn't known her, not at all, but the thought of that empty pink tap-dancing shirt going into the ground made the tears come anyway. Shane nestled down into the sand, immediately tangling his fingers in the lanky strands of seaweed that had washed up on shore. The waves lapped nearby, the tide still relatively low at midmorning. I looked at Shane, at the familiar curls and doughy cheeks and the not-so-familiar adult tilt of his head as he studied the seaweed sliding through his grasp. He always had a strange knack for appearing completely out of place. Here, in a park, in the apartment back in Seattle . . . It was almost like watching an alien life form study a foreign planet. When his big curious eyes took me in it was as if he were thinking, 'Do I know you? Will I ever know you?'

'Hey,' I said, sitting down across from him and removing my shoes. The bandages were starting to itch like crazy. 'Those girls . . . I don't want you to worry, okay?'

Shane nodded. At least he was listening.

I glanced over his head. Nobody had come looking for us – well, not really. Moritz watched from the log benches at the fire pit, his head resting in his hands and his elbows on his knees. He didn't so much gaze at us as *through* us. I knew the feeling.

'It's just a reminder, you know? It's dangerous everywhere. But at least here we have friends and some food and weapons. That's pretty good and I'm sure it will get better.' Shane nodded again, but now he was staring at the seaweed again. 'I know it's sad and scary, but we're all going to get through this. And Teresa hasn't come back. She could still be alive.'

I didn't mention that, in the unlikely event Teresa *was* still alive, she had apparently taken up a troublesome habit of chewing on her relatives. Whether she was crazy, a zombie, dead or gone didn't matter. Shane mattered. At a loss for what else to say, I picked up my own piece of seaweed and shuddered from its gooey, stringy tendrils unraveling against my fingers. The shovel noises up the hill and behind the huts continued, slower now as the diggers grew tired, but drumming out that heavy, hollow beat. Scratching idly at my feet and the fire ant sensation building on the soles of my feet I wondered again why Teresa and Isabella had wandered off. Maybe they were sick of beans . . . or sick of Danielle. Or maybe they didn't like the arrival of so many strangers.

'She's not alive.'

At first I thought I'd imagined the voice. But no, Shane had definitely spoken. It had been so long I had forgotten the sound. He frowned, studiously not with emotion, and continued striping the seaweed into even green ribbons.

'She's one of those things probably,' Shane added matter-of-factly.

Stop gaping, he's going to think you're a mental patient.

'You're right,' I said slowly. Treating this moment with too much overenthusiasm might put him off the whole vocal communication thing again. 'But I still don't want you to worry.'

'I don't,' he said with a tiny shrug. He needed to eat more. His little sweatshirt was swallowing him whole. 'Are you going to marry Whelan?'

'What?' My voice came out in one ridiculous squeak. 'What? No.'

I almost added that it was none of his business and that nobody got married anymore and that if they did it was like spitting in luck's face and just asking for star-crossed tragedy, but he didn't really need to hear those things. Shit, if he talked less like an adult I'd actually remember to treat him like a kid. 'I've got you, little man. That's all I need.'

Apparently satisfied, or perhaps unimpressed, Shane shook out his hands and watched the strings of sandy green float to the ground. Then he turned and stared out at the water and acted like I wasn't there at all.

When I used to imagine what my kids would be like, way back when, before my life turned into an endless loop of *28 Days Later*, when I still thought I might have a chance at a normal adult life with a normal adult relationship, my imagination never conjured anything like Shane. It was tempting to think that all kids growing up through The Outbreak turned out like him – curiously overgrown, adults confined to pudgy little kid bodies. But Shane was a special case. I don't know if it was the loss of his parents or being unceremoniously transferred to my custody or what, but something had shut down the thing that made him young. I couldn't remember the last time he laughed and in the midst of death and change and uncertainty, I began to feel like a truly miserable parent. No, guardian.

But I hadn't completely failed yet. Keeping him alive, making sure he didn't end up like Arturo or Teresa or Isabella might give him the time and space to sort everything out. There would be years and years for him to loosen up, I decided, as long as I made sure those years happened.

Growling stomachs drew us from the beach, and Shane accompanied me in his grave, serious way back to the fire. Moritz was still there, bent over his knees and staring alternately at the bay and the waves. He smiled as Shane arrived, straightening up and grinning just a second too late.

'They done?' I asked, nodding over his shoulder and toward the mourners.

'I believe so, yes.' Moritz glanced nervously at Shane, as if we could somehow fuck up the weird little kid any more than he already was. 'Nate has taken Danielle and Stefano out for another search. They want to try the beach to the north again since that's . . . well . . . ostensibly the current would . . . she might have drifted . . .'

'I get the picture.' I squeezed Shane's hand. 'You hungry?'

Nod.

'Beans okay with you?'

Shrug.

'How about we settle on beans but I'll draw you something too?'

That at least garnered a moderately more excited response.

Andrea appeared from our designated cabin, the state of her hair suggesting she had taken a nap. She pulled her muffin cap down onto her head and arranged her ponytail into a sloppy bun below it. 'Shane, my man,' she said with a sleepy grin. 'What is up?'

Another shrug. Andrea volunteered to help with the beans, showing Shane again how to stoke up the flames and leaving him with that task while we searched out spoons and bowls. A sort of cache or crate made of sturdy wooden slats had been wedged down into the sand beside the log benches. Most of the utensils and eating accoutrement stayed in there and a bucket was kept nearby with rain water for rinsing and washing. The food was secured in a wooden shack Whelan and Nate had built out of driftwood when they first arrived. The food hut was set well away from the water and ringed with can traps and bags of soap to keep raccoons and other furry sniffers away. It was a mighty fancy setup, or it looked like one to me, considering we had gone from Motel 6 levels of seedy desperation to what felt like the fucking Hilton.

Fuzzy bathrobes and free shower swag were just about the only things missing.

The bean operation successfully underway, I took a deliberately slow walk around the cabins to the stretch of more or less cleared land between the huts and the forest.

Only Banana and Whelan lingered, both of them resting their arms on the handles of shovels. Despite the slight morning chill that was now advancing into an honest-to-God cold front, Whelan wiped at his forehead, depositing the sweaty strands of his hair back behind his ears.

'Goddamn reckless to let them go off again,' Whelan was saying. Sweat stains darkened the collar of his sweater and hung in spreading circles below his armpits. He turned at the waist at the sound of footsteps on the sand. My feet tingled at the sight of him, as if remembering all over again the agony of being riddled with pins.

'What's wrong now?' he asked.

'Nothing,' I said carefully. Banana retied the bandana around her hair. 'I was wondering if you had any paper or chalk or anything. I wanted to draw something for Shane . . . to cheer him up.'

'Yeah, sure, of course! It just so happens we keep a whole trunk full of art supplies for just such a purpose. In fact, before we left Seattle I was thinking to myself, hey, what if I need to draw some pretty pictures to keep morale up? I better trade these fucking *indispensable* and *lifesaving* cans of food for some fucking *Cray-pas* and smelly markers.'

'Christ on a cracker, Whelan! Keep it together,' Banana whispered sharply.

'I get it,' I said. 'Being a sarcastic douche bag is how you grieve. Forget I asked.'

I turned on my heel and left, a sharp pain cramping my feet, as if I'd been dancing a jig on a bed of nails. Banana followed. Whelan didn't. She caught up to me around the huts, Whelan's dismissive grunt still fogging up my ears and my better judgment.

'No fun allowed,' I muttered as I reached the fire. 'So says the lord high crusher of gaiety and song.'

'He's just messed up,' Banana said. 'Fuck, you know, we all are.'

'Don't apologize for him. He's a grown-up,' I replied hotly. 'At least, I thought he was . . .'

My wizened greeting card of a father always liked to say, 'There's a big difference between aging and growing up.' But he only said that when I was being a shithead. Hey! Sorta like . . .

'He feels responsible,' Banana raced on. She reached for her bandana again, taking it off to fuss with in her hands. 'He's . . . he calls the shots around here. He thinks those girls . . . He thinks it's his fault.'

'Any idiot with eyes and a brain can see he didn't do it,' Andrea mumbled, stirring the beans. Man, it felt good to have someone on my side.

'Exactly,' I said. 'If anything we should all share the blame. They're just kids. We should've been more careful.'

'Just . . .' Banana glanced over her shoulder at Whelan's distant silhouette and then down at her hands. 'I've got some pencils and a notebook in my bag. Will that help?'

Banana's the sort of woman you want to hug all the time. All the damn time.

'Is there something I can do in return?' I asked.

She turned to retrieve the supplies. The smell of cooking beans wafted up, smoky and rich and mixing with the tang of the burning kindling. Salt rolled in from the sea, pine pushing against it as the forest's fragrance swept down from the tree line.

'Yes,' Banana said, with a toss of her hair, 'I think I know just the thing.'

*

'Just the thing' turned out to be waiting around well after dark in the glow of the fire pit, sitting there while everyone else slept, except maybe Banana, who I'm sure was spying for kicks. Repaying her was pretty much compulsory after she diffused the situation so expertly *and* came through with pencil and paper, but that didn't mean I was jazzed about her plan.

She didn't seem to care that this whole thing was about as subtle as a dump truck to the cerebellum. Whelan grieved by lashing out. Banana grieved by turning into burlesque yenta.

'It'll be fun, babe,' she said, 'and your feet hurt anyway.'

'Sure,' I had replied. 'It'll be fun! Fun like tongue-kissing a puffer fish.'

A quiet, mingling symphony of snores drifted from the cabin behind me. Moritz and Noah had recently become loud sleepers, which made nocturnal dealings with them extremely frustrating. I'm a light sleeper – car alarm, heavy breathing, you name it and I'm starting awake. Even just listening to their snoring while wide awake was starting to give me that twitchy, irritable feeling. Instead I tried to listen to the crackle of the fire, burning high now to keep zombies at bay. Some believe the fires draw them, a literal beacon for TASTY HUMANS HERE, but I'm of the school that thinks it's the opposite. Zombies and flames do not mix . . . well, not happily in their case, and it's as much a warning for them as it is a source of warmth and security for us. And of course that's assuming they have any actual thoughts going on in those drippy, holy skulls of theirs . . . which is a stretch.

Snuggling down into the giant sweatshirt Banana had

lent me, one clearly salvaged from her former place of work – the words I GOT CAUGHT IN THE ACT . . . were splashed across the front and AT BENNY'S BURLESQUE! delivered the punch line on the back – I decided that fire was indeed friend not foe and that my spot might actually be the safest in camp.

Out on the water, small boats danced, cupped leaves filled with bits of cheerfully burning tinder. It was Banana's idea, to send out little ships of fire to celebrate the girls' – well, *girl's* technically, but we pretty much all knew Teresa was a lost cause, too, poor thing – spirits, like miniature Viking pyres bouncing out onto the waves. They looked hypnotic there, burning down, almost out, a dozen flickering eyes disappearing out to sea.

A crunch of sand, a low, masculine snigger in the dark and then Whelan was there, standing at the edge of the circle of light described by the flames. He stepped into the bright orange glow and took a seat on the log next to me, bringing along a spicy scent that wasn't terribly different from the fire smoke.

'It was a setup,' Whelan remarked softly, chuckling.

'You don't seem terribly broken up about that.'

'I'm not.'

'Banana gave me paper and pencil so . . . she asked that I hear you out.' He'd been told that my feet were still in bad shape and needed to be looked at. And yes, I'm adult enough to admit that it was a silly lie and pretty flimsy to begin with, but apparently he believed it or wanted to show up. Secretly, I hoped for the latter. In preparation for perpetuating the story I sucked it up and unwrapped the bandages and peeked, nervously, at the undersides of my feet. Just then I held them up for inspection and Whelan pulled in a breath through his teeth.

'Remember when I said you should stay off these as much as possible?'

'I'm not a very good listener,' I said with a shrug. I had to turn, canting my hips slightly to the side and lifting my feet. Whelan grabbed for my ankles and gingerly settled my heels onto his thighs. It was warm there. He forced a smile, which was kind of him considering my feet looked raw and shredded enough to fit in behind a deli counter.

Now would not be a good time to point out that Whelan's lips, which some might call girly, were, in fact, what laymen refer to as 'fucking hot' – as in 'holy shit, your lips are fucking hot and I want to kiss them.' The whole puffer fish comparison was almost apt, but a little vulgar and mean, really, and something a more mature person would take back.

And now would not be a good time to also point out that puffer fish are delicious on the inside, a delicacy, but incredibly poisonous on the outside. Their skin causes vomiting, paralysis and usually death within twenty-four hours. What? I eat a lot of sushi. *Ate*. With that cheering thought in mind, I stared at his funny ears.

'I didn't know you were an artist,' Whelan said. He pulled a packet of cotton balls and a tube of medicated gel from the pocket on his work shirt.

'*Am* an artist,' I corrected gently. The gel stung. Yowzers. 'Shane and I don't connect on much, but he likes my pictures.'

'Can I see them?'

'I'll think about it.'

Another smile, another reason to gaze stonily at his ears. 'I don't know the first damn thing about art, so I won't know what to criticize.'

221

'Assuming that would be the natural response,' I said with a snorty laugh. 'Criticism.'

'Hey, whoa, I can praise, praise, praise if that's what you want.'

The gel had almost numbed the feeling of the cotton balls dabbing at the torn skin. Still, the pain was there, dulled, but there. I hadn't been noticing it, thanks to his distracting conversation.

'Shane doesn't talk much, does he?'

'No,' I admitted softly. The glow of fire caught on the cotton in Whelan's fingers, making them look like cloud-soft puffs of flame . . . they burned like 'em too. 'He's always been a quiet kid. Serious. I never have any idea what's going on in his head.'

'He seems pretty well-adjusted to me. I mean, by comparison. I saw a lot of sad kids after The Outbreak. A buddy of mine at the precinct had a boy about Shane's age. He stopped talking altogether . . . just stopped. Nothing. Mute.' Whelan frowned, the thick dashes of his brows tugging down simultaneously.

'What happened to him?' I asked. You never wanted to know the endings to these stories, but curiosity compelled that you ask anyway.

'I lost track of them. Queen Anne exploded . . . almost . . . It was a nightmare. Fires everywhere, people everywhere . . . death everywhere.' He paused, the latest clean cotton ball still touched to the big toe on my right foot. 'I had a nervous breakdown . . . Stayed in my apartment for a week with the doors and windows barred.'

'The first time or the second time?' I asked.

'Hm?'

'Was that during The Outbreak or this last time?'

Whelan frowned, sitting up and fixing me with a dark, uneasy look. 'The Outbreak. I told you, we left before the Citadel fell.'

'Right,' I replied. 'I forgot for a second there.'

His expression eased, his smile returning as he hunched over my feet and went back to work. 'Christ, you have the ugliest pinky toes I have ever seen, Sadie.'

'I blame the sea urchins.'

'I would too.'

Scrambling for an appropriately juvenile comeback, I settled triumphantly on, 'Well, your ears are stupid.'

Smirking, Whelan sat up again, bringing that one incorrigible dimple with him. He dropped a dirtied cotton puff onto the ground. It landed among its brethren and rolled to a stop just before the stones marking the fire pit. 'I'm glad I survived measles, ten years on the force and a zombie outbreak to have you remind me of what a special hell fifth grade was.' He laughed, bitterly, shaking back the dark strands of his hair. At some point he had shaved, his jaw gleaming tan and smooth in the flames. 'Curious George,' Whelan added, shuddering.

A loud, spontaneous burst of laughter probably wasn't the sympathetic response he was hoping for, but that's what he got. 'I wield the cotton balls, you heartless bully,' he said, pretending to jab at my raw toes. 'I could easily slip and *oops* and—'

'All right, all right,' I said, breathless with laughter, 'I get the idea. I'll be good! I'm sorry I made fun of your monkey ears . . . I mean, they're not monkey ears – they're regular ears, just a bit sticky-outy, I mean . . .'

'You know,' Whelan began, smiling lazily and threatening me with that cotton ball again, 'you and your ilk are the reason I almost paid through the nose for ear-pinning surgery.'

'When was this?' I asked, relaxing when his next swipe with the cotton was gentle and forgiving.

'In the dreaded bowl-cut phase of seventy-nine, a bleak time for many. That was before I realized the magical powers of a good haircut. Ugh, I looked like a *chalice*.'

'You looked like a chalice and I wore sandals on the playground and wondered why everyone pointed and laughed.' Either from the gel or the flames or the cotton balls, my feet no longer burned so badly.

'And childhood is supposed to be the happiest years of your life . . .'

'So . . . did you ever find the Man With the Yellow Hat to your Curious George?'

Yeah, that netted the blank stare it deserved.

'That . . . sounded so much wittier in my head,' I mumbled, waving the offending question away as if it were a physical vapor hanging around us.

Whelan gathered up the cotton balls and pitched them into the fire. I pulled my feet away, reluctantly, knowing there was no reason to keep them there, especially with my gangle toes freaking him out. 'Amber hat . . . orange hat . . . close . . . but no, no yellow hat.'

'Danielle's not the yellow hat, then?'

'Uh, no. No, she isn't.' Whelan smiled, tipping his head to the side as that smile eased into a far more nefarious, devious sort of half-grin. Even his dimple looked ominous. 'You really don't like her, do you? It's the boobs, right? Makes you uncomfortable?'

'No, no, it has nothing to do with the fucking Hindenburgs hanging off her chest and everything to do with her . . . glaring. She's like a Shih Tzu, all beady eyes and crazy little snappy teeth.'

'Danielle danced at a nice place,' Whelan replied, lowering his voice. I could tell a sad, sad story was coming on. 'Or so she said. The point is, she was the only one to make it out of there. One girl out of, what, thirty? I know it's tempting to laugh at the mental image of all those sweaty-fisted businessmen being decimated by a horde of ravenous undead, but she came out of it really . . . jumpy. She doesn't trust anyone but Stefano . . . and maybe the girls, but . . . you know.'

'Yeah, I know.'

Fuck.

'I should probably be nicer to her,' I said. This was sounding like déjà vu. 'I should be a lot nicer in general.'

'You're doing all right,' Whelan assured me lightly. 'Danielle's just like the rest of us, coping as best she can – which, granted, might mean she's turned into a Shih Tzu, but it might also mean she's seen a lot of bad shit and doesn't quite know what to make of it. She's like you and me, Hindenburgs or no.'

'Are you calling me flat-chested?'

'There's no correct way to answer that and you know it.'

He was right, but I wanted him to try and dig his way out anyway.

'I should get some sleep,' I said. 'Sounds like the snore chorus have died down a little.'

'Banana and I have room,' he replied so casually that it was not casual at all. The firelight was playing tricks, making him even tanner than usual, smoothing out the slight wrinkles at his eyes, emphasizing the pronounced

225

curve of that dimple. Tricks. Shenanigans. Inconveniently torn, I glanced at the water. The little boat lights had gone out.

'I should stick with my people,' I said. 'And you stick with yours.'

FOURTEEN

Two nights later I slept like the dead – the truly dead, not the living dead – exhausted from an embarrassing fancy. Spending the day shooting arrows into the water, trying to kill fish that way is . . . not to be repeated. I don't recommend it unless you have actual hand-eye coordination or a bag full of Jedi mind tricks.

With calluses the size of donut holes forming on my fingertips and palms, I listened to the dulcet tones of Andrea sniping in my ear, hissing at me for being a prude and not enslaving Whelan with my womanly wiles. No amount of reminding her that survival and not *procreation* was our number one priority would get her to shut up. The last thing I heard before drifting to sleep was Andrea's voice buzzing in my ear as she muttered, 'Flash forward, Sadie, here's your life in ten years: You, a sad, hunched spinster blitzed on vodka gimlets at a karaoke bar singing 'Do You Really Want to Hurt Me?' to a room of like-minded, sawdust repositories.'

'I don't think we'll have karaoke machines on the island,' I sleepily replied. 'Not even in ten years.'

I wouldn't have gone to sleep smiling if I had known I'd wake up to flames.

This time I was up at the first call of alarm, stumbling

over Andrea and Shane on the cot and tossing on Banana's burlesque sweatshirt, backward, over a pair of thermal leggings and somebody's work boots. In this fetching ensemble, I stumbled out into the wan sunshine, finding at once that the air on the beach choked with smoke and the faint burning smell I had detected inside the cabin was not, in fact, the result of someone cooking breakfast.

'Holy shit,' I mumbled, drifting numbly toward the food hut. It was all but blackened, crisp and ashen, pieces of it crumbling inward from the smallest, gentlest hint of a breeze. I couldn't talk, couldn't breathe, staring at what had once been a sturdy if crooked monument to our survival. Fish had been stored in there after drying, and cans of food, bags of cookies, chips, all of the salvaged goods Whelan and his folks had brought from the mainland. Noah and Andrea came up behind me, their gasps joining the sound of Nate and Whelan furiously throwing seawater on the smoldering ruins. Stefano and Danielle stood apart, huddling together in matching pink sweatshirts. Noticeably absent was Cassandra, and for a shameful moment, I almost hoped she was the culprit. She certainly did act unbalanced enough to have gone pyro. Through the tears, I saw Danielle glaring at us, an accusation no doubt forming on her lips as she looked at us, the outsiders, the obvious suspects.

All the blanket dampening and seawater in the world wasn't going to reverse the damage, and as soon as the rest of us came in speaking distance, the accusations started to fly.

'Way to go, Whelan,' Danielle burst out, shoving Stefano away as she stalked toward us. 'Bring a bunch of outsiders here and this is what happens!' She whirled, aiming her bile at Whelan this time. 'They're not like us!

They're . . . whatever they are! The girls and now this . . .'

'Hey!' I yelled, feeling a little less than purely authoritative in my harebrained outfit. 'Hey, we didn't do anything to those girls. That's not on us.'

'Oh, but the fire is?' she shrilled back.

'Why would we burn our own food?' Moritz asked, carefully modulating his voice. 'That does not make any sense. We were nearly starving before. Why would we come here only to destroy your food?'

'Yeah!' Noah added, punctuating his yell with a finger pointed at Danielle. 'We all sleep in one place. Do you have any idea how hard it is to move an inch in that cabin without stepping on someone's face?'

'Everybody shut the fuck up,' Whelan thundered. We obeyed. You obey a tone like that. 'There's something in there,' he added in a much more subdued, uneasy voice.

'What kind of something?' Stefano asked, cuddling up next to Danielle and holding onto her arm like an anchor. His voice shivered around the words. 'Can . . . Can you tell?'

'Oh, my good Jesus,' Nate muttered. He and Whelan were the closest, standing just inches from the shed. They clapped their hands over their mouths in almost perfect unison.

'It's too small,' Whelan said, just loud enough for the rest of us to make out. Nate nodded. 'It can't be Teresa.'

'Can't be . . .' Danielle marched up in between Whelan and Nate, leaning over and squinting into the charred wreckage. 'Is that . . . oh, God. Oh, God, it's Cassie.'

'Cassie?' Andrea repeated, a little tartly. I elbowed her.

'*Cassandra*,' Danielle hissed. 'Ya know, the one you all ignored because you thought she was crazy.'

229

'Does that mean she set the fire?' Moritz asked.

'Hard to say,' Whelan replied. He stood back, hands on hips, and swore under his breath. 'If she used a lighter it might still be in there, melted. If she used a torch . . . it would've burned up with the rest of the wood.'

Right. Cop. I was hoping those skills of his would never come in handy. Wishing thinking, as usual.

'I don't mean to get all Benson and Stabler on you here, but wouldn't we have heard her screaming?' I should've just kept my mouth shut, but Whelan turned, frowning.

'Damn it. I didn't think of that,' he said quietly, thoughtfully.

'That is fucking creepy as shit,' Andrea whispered, inching closer to me. 'She just . . . sat in there? Silently? And burned to death?'

'Unless someone killed her, put her in the shed and lit it on fire,' Whelan replied.

'Yeah okay, creepy as it is, I prefer Andrea's theory.' And I did. But I couldn't help but glance around, thinking suddenly that there might actually be a murderer in our midst. It wasn't impossible – the girls go missing and then Cassandra. But why?

Mmhmm. As if unrepentant psychopaths need a reason.

Craning my neck, I peered into the bowels of the shed and caught a glimpse of rough black skull. Chills. Chills, I tell you. I wish I were being flip.

I felt a tiny hand slip into mine. Shane. I knelt and pulled him up into my arms, ignoring the strain in my biceps that reminded me I wasn't exactly in shape for hefting a young child around. He curled into my neck, his breath warm and almost comforting.

'It might be Cassandra,' I told him in a whisper. 'But we're not sure.'

He nodded, his curls brushing against my ear.

'Nate and I will pull her out of there, somebody start digging a grave for her. We need to restock. Anybody good with a rod should hit the docks and see what they can fish up.' Whelan delegated with a slight hunch to his shoulders, a heaviness that told me he felt responsible for this loss too.

Stefano and Noah volunteered to dig while Moritz hung around in his shirtsleeves to help Nate and Whelan dismantle the shed without it destroying the burned body inside. That left Andrea, Shane and – goody – Danielle to do the fishing. Andrea dawdled at the fire pit making coffee for us. She hated fishing, calling it 'the favored pastime of narcoleptics and hoboes,' but I got the impression she preferred it to pulling charred bone matter out of a charred maze of oozing bean cans and ashen fish carcasses.

Danielle, still pink and bottle-tan and smelling strongly of freesia even at the fucking crack of dawn, sat an insultingly safe distance away on the dock, dangling her legs over the edge. Familiar with the sensation of having a zombie tug on my feet, I kept my legs crossed and instructed Shane to do the same. Ah hell, Whelan was right. Danielle might have made questionable choices when it came to her plastic surgeons, but she didn't deserve my disdain or my suspicion. Not yet.

And, after all, she wasn't the yellow hat. There wasn't even a reason to be catty.

'You might want to pull your legs up,' I ventured, clearing my throat when it came out all froggy. 'They can come up out of the water.'

There. Now do I get my fucking gold star for maturity?

'Oh, duh,' she said, mimicking a little punch to the side of her head. Sighing, she rearranged her legs, sitting with them slightly to the side. 'I guess I blocked that.'

'S'okay.'

'I shouldn't have blown up at you like a tard. I'm sorry.'

'Yeah, me too. We're all . . . feeling it.'

'Cassie really liked you and Shane,' Danielle said after a brief silence. I heard the soft *bloop* of Shane dropping his line into the water. I watched closely for any unwanted faces lurking beneath the surface. 'She said he was the perfect little boy.'

'I should have tried harder with her,' I said. Shane listened, silently, not even looking up as his name was mentioned. 'I thought giving her space was the right thing but . . . fuck me, dude, I didn't know how to handle her. She just . . . seemed like a time bomb.'

'The shelter I fled to after The Outbreak had a lot of girls like her. I was kinda like her once – shut up, clammed up, all crazy and paranoid and still hating everything. I guess I got used to it or maybe I just give off some weird vibe.' Danielle shifted, her sweats scraping quietly across the untreated wood. She must have flipped her hair, because another little waft of freesia rolled over us. 'Cassie said she lost kids. That must have . . . God, that must have really fucking *sucked*.'

Indeed.

'Maybe it's not her,' I said, trying to lighten the dour mood. Disturbingly enough, that was happening with troubling frequency recently. 'Maybe some zombie wandered through the camp pit, set herself on fire and then tumbled into the shed and . . . stayed there.'

Danielle giggled. 'You're funny.'

'It wasn't a joke.'

Nope, just wishful thinking. Again.

'Whelan said you were funny,' Danielle replied, a hitch in her voice. 'And I thought he was stupid or making fun of me, I don't know, I got fucked up over the girls. We were all a little cray-cray.'

Mm, yes. Real cray-cray.

Even footsteps echoed down the planks, a rich coffee perfume preceding Andrea's late but most welcome arrival. My stomach greeted her, trumpeting my hunger and my resounding love of the roasty, bitter morning juice cradled in her hands.

'Enjoy it,' Andrea said, setting down the tin kettle between Danielle and me. 'Only one canister survived and that's because I was a forgetful moron and left it outside in the sand.'

'Thank God for your lazy ass,' I mumbled, diving into the coffee. And then later, when the initial joy wore off and the chatter simmered to nothing but a few quiet sighs over our cups, I asked, 'So were the girls Stefano's or . . . ?'

'No,' Danielle said, her little girl voice dropping down to a restive whisper. 'His cousins. Like, Shane isn't your boy, right? I mean he's yours, but he's not like, your son . . .'

'He's my nephew.'

'Yeah. Like that.'

'Teresa could still be out there,' I said. Andrea nudged my back and gave one of those frosty looks that were meant to scorn you into ashamed silence. It wasn't worth fighting over and I wasn't trying to reopen old wounds. She really could be alive, or worse, she was undead and wandering around like that. The right thing to do was to find her, rescue her or take her down. Even just one less zombie was one less body hunting us down.

'I've got something,' Danielle said, the water splashing below her as she tugged and reeled. Look, first I should just say that you would be distracted too if you were having heaven-sent coffee and trying to enjoy the company of your friends after a scary, unsettling morning. That's my excuse for why I didn't see it earlier. But then Danielle screamed and all of us leaped to our feet, the rod clutched in both her hands as she leaned far back. Surprisingly, the insane weight of her tits didn't wrench the zombie clear up and out of the water – which was extremely lucky, because I didn't like the idea of some big, wet undead *thing* soaring up out of the surf and wriggling around like a brain-starved orca on the dock.

The hook had caught on the zombie's eyehole, and I'm sure there's a scientific, less vulgar way to say that, but I'm not sure what it is. So we're going with eyehole. Andrea shrieked, pushing Shane back toward the land. He got the idea, fleeing down the dock as fast as his little feet would carry him.

'Let go!' Andrea was screaming. 'Let go of the fucking rod!'

But Danielle must have been really damn attached to that rod or paralyzed with shock, because she held on tight. One hand and then two appeared on the boards at her feet, gnarled, white, slivers of bone peeking through the decaying flesh. I stomped. While Andrea tried to pry Danielle away from the fishing rod and the edge of the dock, I went for the knuckles, yelping every time the heavy work boot came down and the bottom of my foot banged against the unforgiving sole.

If it wasn't fucking zombies in the woods or zombies in the water it was zombies on the dock. *I have had it with these motherfucking zombies on this motherfucking island.* Despicable reference aside, I think I'd rather actually deal with snakes on a plane than a zombie, period.

It became a sort of morbid dance – Danielle jumping up and down frantically, squealing while Andrea ripped at the rod and I switched from the scrabbling, bony hands to the now emerging skull, more or less curb stomping the thing while trying not to die from the pain shooting up my leg. Fear and pain mixed, firing up my heart rate until *that* was painful too. And the hook dislodged, helpfully, allowing Danielle and Andrea to reel back, nearly toppling off the other side of the dock as they were suddenly let free. All in all it involved an embarrassing amount of shrieking and ended with the work boot splattered in goo, shards of skull imbedded in the all-terrain treads.

Breathless, in agony, still doing internal somersaults from sheer shock, I hardly registered when Whelan and Nate came thundering up the dock together to see what all the commotion was about. I'm told they found me sitting on the ground, shaking, staring blankly at the destroyed head still on the dock and the arms and legs of the zombie twitching as its gray matter dripped down off my boot.

'I think I ruined these boots,' is the first thing I remember saying. Spilled coffee seeped into the wood near my hand.

'Aaand up we go,' Whelan mumbled, pulling me up by the armpits. 'If I didn't know better,' he said in a private undertone, slinging an arm under my shoulders and helping me hobble down the planks toward shore, 'I'd say you were *trying* to keep those feet mangled just to have a reason to shove them in my face.'

'There will be no shoving, sir,' I whimpered, 'no shoving of any kind.'

'Tender feets?'

'Mildly put, yes.'

'Thank you for helping Danielle,' he said. The hand against my right side squeezed in a sort of hug. The volcanic level of heat radiating off of his body was number three on my list of priorities, right after *ouch* and *yeesh*.

'It was my pleasure,' I wheezed.

'Yeah, I know it wasn't. You didn't have to do that.' His arm slid lower, to my hip, squeezing me there too.

'Yes,' I said, losing sensation in my right foot. 'I did.'

FIFTEEN

Submitting to bed rest must be what a decorative throw-pillow feels like.

People start to treat you like vaguely amusing scenery. Oh look, the settee is talking again! Which summarizes most of the next day – I wasn't allowed to move much, my right foot banished of all footwear except for Whelan's expertly applied bandages. I had at least one victory to gloat about – I had sworn not to end up carried in his arms again and had returned to the cabin on my own two feet. Hobbling on them, sure, but upright, which is the important part. (I maintain that the piggyback ride he gave me through the woods was spent on his *shoulders* and therefore does not technically qualify as being carried.)

Andrea helped me move from the cabin to the dreary, overcast clearing to stand with the others while they put what was left of Cassandra into a shallow grave. Whelan had been saddled with the unpleasant task of removing her head from her skeleton, a paranoid but thoughtful measure to make sure Cassandra didn't rise again. Danielle assured us it was Cassie – she recognized a few scraps of pink T-shirt and insisted this was evidence enough. It was good enough for the rest of us, who didn't want to admit that there was too little left to make an accurate identification.

Danielle did most of the talking, telling us that Cassandra was shy and troubled, but loved children. Nothing was said about the grisly way in which she had gone or her possible motivations for going all Human Torch on the food bin. I suggested we bury her carpet bag and old bloody scrubs with her but Whelan wasn't thrilled about the idea of letting anything, even dirty old clothes, go to waste.

Everyone threw a bit of sand onto her corpse and waited while Nate and Whelan refilled the grave. Shane clung to my hand, giving a short pull. When I glanced down he was staring fixedly at the tree line. Then he pointed, indicating a moving shape in the canopy of trees. It was too dark to make out, but the lumbering stance made me think our watchers were already dead. Why they didn't leave the safety of the woods and come for us left me shifty and nervous. It wasn't like a zombie to pass up a chance at a meal. We were armed and could've easily defended ourselves, but still . . . why wait like that?

Whelan seemed to shrink when I explained later what I'd seen. 'I'll take a second watch,' he said, 'I'm not sure what else we can do.'

The rest of that cruddy day was devoted to restocking the fish and clam supply. But we were having bad luck – first with Danielle's unfortunate catch and then with a general lack of fish altogether. Whelan made assurances that it would get better and that if it didn't he would take the rifle into the forest and rustle up some game. It was odd, I decided, to be taken care of. I wasn't used to that. When it was just me out on my own I looked after myself, and then after The Outbreak it was me looking after Shane until Carl came along. It made all those organizations, all those whacko clubs and factions that sprung up more understandable. The Repops were crazy town, but I'm sure the feeling of a shared purpose made surviving each day easier. The few churches left standing in Seattle were flooded every Sunday, and other denominations not lucky enough to have a physical building would congregate in empty lots and pray over a shabby wooden cross or simply stand in a circle holding hands and praying. Having some-one reliable and capable there to take charge and declare that everything would be all right made it seem, improbably, like it really would be. And quite possibly Shane thought of me that way. Oh lordy – no pressure.

Staring at the mounding sand and dirt, sand and dirt that soon turned into a legitimate grave site, I remembered that first instance of not-giving-a-fuckitis. It's a common condition these days, the morose but ultimately numb sensation of just not caring. You know you should, you know that the mound in front of you holds a dead human body and that tears should be screaming down your face like coaster cars down Wild Thing, but they're not. And you don't know why. And it's jarring and then flat-out scary. I didn't know Cassandra. Pretending I did, pretending I knew more beyond 'she was a nurse and she liked kids and had a thousand-yard stare' would be a lie. Everyone there, except Danielle, was feeling it too. Shane was the next closest to showing some raw empathy, but I suspect that's only because of his uncanny ability to look severe and reflective at even the most lighthearted of moments.

Shiff, sheef, shiff . . . Sand and dirt, then the thump of the shovels flattening and compacting the earth. Nothing. Not a single tear, and this coming from the person that still, as an adult woman, cried every single time she watched *Homeward Bound*. I swear I'm not callow, none of us are, but we've all seen so many strangers and brief acquaintances go to their doom that it just doesn't strike anymore. Heart strings that were once catgut are now hardened iron and you begin to wonder just what it will take to make you human and emotional again.

Survival 101: If the random schlub beside you bites it, don't stop to weep, just keep running.

In the end, I just hope nothing *does* happen to trigger those long-lost real, hot tears. Seeing those figures hovering on the fringes of the forest renewed something, revitalized a part of me that forgot the fight was twenty-four/seven. With Shane in hand I turned, left the others, and stalked back to the huts on throbbing feet. I needed to make more arrows for the bow. Shit, I needed to learn to actually get *good* with it. I needed to teach Shane to survive, really survive, not learn by watching some bumbling nincompoop take advantage of luck and chance. So I plopped us down in front of the fire and showed him how to make arrows. Yes, logically I understand that teaching an eight-year-old to make projectiles probably violates some innate rule of parenting, and that he shouldn't be handling knives or crossing the street alone or fucking *breathing* without supervision, but too much complacency, too much inactivity bred the sort of unprepared meatbags that were bound to end up zombie fodder.

I explained as much to Shane, in politer terms, of course.

'Survival, Shane,' I said in closing. 'That's what we're here for. It's not a game, it's not a vacation.' Oh God, I was beginning to sound like all those annoying reality TV bobbleheads I had heard shriek 'I'm not here to make friends!!!' over and over again, as if that were a good thing.

'And we can make friends,' I said, just in case. 'Friends

are fine. But you and I getting through this? That's the most important thing. Survival. Say it back to me.'

He nodded. Fair enough.

'You sure that's all?'

Long, imposing shadow. Shit-eating, self-amused tone. Whelan. The sky was just bright enough to make squinting up at him painful. He crossed his arms over his SPD polo, a fresh one and this one white, sweat ringing the crumpled collar from digging and filling Cassandra's grave. Somebody explain to me why those over the chest gun holster things are so damn attractive. I don't get it, but I don't have to to feel the effects. I hadn't seen Whelan with it before, but maybe three disappearances and/or deaths had planted a seed of paranoia.

'Please,' I said, lifting a skeptical brow, 'regale us with your folksy cop wisdom.'

'No, hey, don't let me interrupt.' He turned, idling with one toe digging into the sand. 'Though I could teach you to shoot . . . Maybe show Shane too.'

'I am *not* letting you teach an eight-year-old to handle a firearm.'

But Shane had already hopped to his feet, scattering the half-finished arrows in his lap and sending them tumbling into the fire. Ouch.

'Shane!' Gah. I hate scoldy voice, but apparently even legal guardians develop it. 'Watch what you're doing!'

Shane frowned, taking one tiny, irritating step toward Whelan. Fine. Great. Throw your hat in with Officer Jackass and make me look like a fussy killjoy. Carefully – deliberately – I put my bundle of arrows on the ground, making a big show of it to . . . I don't know, make a belabored point or something. Already Whelan was leading

241

Shane away, adding another layer to the betrayal, acting as if he didn't need my permission or supervision to hang out with my – my *sister's* – kid.

'I'm coming,' I said, trundling along with all the grace off a three-legged elephant.

'Of course you are.'

Smug! Smug, smug, smug. And for what? For knowing how to shoot a gun? Of course he could shoot a gun. What else is a fucking cop good for? That's what they do. The recriminations went on and on in my head, building speed and bitterness there because giving voice to them would prove just how deep Whelan's talent for pushing my buttons went.

Whelan took us back to the clearing, my mangled feet and stuttering gait meaning I had the very bad luck of falling behind, putting me at the perfect vantage to get a glimpse of Whelan's backside in khaki pants that were, in my opinion, much too fitted for island wear. Just seeing him show Shane how to position himself twisted a bundle of nerves in my stomach. And then when he handed him a gun . . . It just looked huge, comically so, and terrifying, as if the recoil would rip Shane's little arm right out of its socket.

'He's going to be fine,' Whelan said, kneeling behind Shane and steadying him.

'I didn't say anything.'

'Yeah, but you were thinking it.'

'What do you want me to do? He's eight. Jesus Christ, my sister would disembowel me with her bare hands if she could see this . . .'

Shane glanced over his shoulder and Whelan's, too, giving me one of those long, menacing stares, one that was way too cold for his age. It all looked disturbingly out of whack, Whelan's huge hands on Shane's shoulders, the gun that looked heavy enough to make Shane tip right over onto his side. I found myself bunching up, twisting inward, bracing for the first shot. But Whelan went on and on, explaining every single part on the gun, its purpose, how to handle it, what to expect. And when the firing finally started, Whelan stayed there the entire time, his finger over Shane's, his arms still supporting the brunt of the weight and taking most of the recoil.

And after the first loud pop, Shane exploded with giddy, nervous laughter. He looked up at me and *smiled*. Smiled! That made it not so hard to ignore the stinging in my feet, to stand when I wanted to sit, to stay quiet while Whelan did his thing and showed his expertise and took Shane under his wing with the kind of male influence I knew I was never very good at giving. I could show Shane comic books and even knew the basics of throwing a football or explaining checkers, but that didn't seem to replace the missing ingredient that had been his father. Maybe if he hadn't known his parents at all filling both roles would have been easier for me. But here it was, like the last piece of a puzzle, discovered under a shoe on the carpet, missing but not really gone.

Heaven help me, I was going to get emotional.

'Any questions?' Whelan asked, taking the gun from Shane and standing. The smell of gunpowder and sweat hung around us like a fog.

'Ever fired your gun whilst jumping through the air?' I asked.

'That's a joke, right?'

Shane giggled. Oh, God, this was like a real *thing* now, Shane could actually laugh! Display merriment! *Let go*. It was almost too good to believe. And yes, showing *Hot Fuzz* to a child is probably negligent parenting and could get him booted over to child services or something – if it still existed – but he asked to see it, repeatedly, and not many DVDs survived the carnage. He'd only ever seen it on a little handheld video screen, but at least it was something.

'What's so funny?' Whelan asked, watching as Shane and I dissolved into a fit of laughter together.

'A cop who doesn't watch cop movies?'

'I hate cop movies,' Whelan muttered, holstering the pistol Shane had been using. And again with the chest holster. I looked at the sand. 'They never get any of it right.'

'So that's a no, then? To the firing a gun whilst jumping through the air?'

Shane stared up at Whelan, teetering on his heels, his lower lip tucked under his teeth. The poor kid's life was practically hinging on the answer.

Smiling, Whelan shrugged and patted the gun locked safely in its cradle. 'I never said that, did I?'

Whether I liked it or not, I was going to be seeing a lot more of Shane and Whelan together. With that one little clever response, the man had become Shane's hero. Mine, too, to be honest, if he was telling the truth. And even if he wasn't, Shane was enamored.

Before I could explain to Shane that Whelan was probably just being silly and that it was nothing to get worked up over, Andrea was banging away on a pot, signaling lunch. Shane scampered off, a cloud of sand kicking up in his wake. I hadn't seen him that excited since before The Outbreak . . . when he still had parents . . . when he didn't need me.

'I'm going to say two things right now,' Whelan began. I

turned at the waist, waiting for him to go on. He had entertained Shane for a solid hour and lifted his spirits. He at least deserved my attention. 'One is that I have a bad, bad feeling and I need you to keep your eyes open.'

'For what?'

'For anything weird . . . anything . . . that doesn't fit.'

'And the second thing?'

'I want to see you tonight.'

'I . . . Oh.' I think I maybe choked a little on my own voice.

'Alone,' he added in an undertone.

'Yeah . . . I sort of worked that out for myself.'

'So?'

'Wouldn't that qualify as weird?' I asked, stalling because I didn't have an answer for him and the one I did have that was jumping to get out was . . . not welcome. 'I mean . . . would that *fit*?'

'Oh. I see what you mean. Ha. I suppose so. If you're not comfortable being alone with me that's understandable.' He flinched. 'Maybe not understandable, but . . . It's tense . . . everything is. If you'd rather not then I get it. Or, you know, we could always ask Banana to chaperone. I'm sure she'd be delighted.'

You know that feeling where you suddenly know that someone or someones are staring at you? Like their eyes are actually little laser beams cutting into your head? Well we had a bit of an audience now. Everybody gathered around the fire pit for lunch was staring, bowls and plates abandoned in favor of watching our little drama play out. With burning cheeks I forced myself to ignore it, to look away and up into Whelan's bright blue eyes.

Big mistake.

'No . . . let's.'

'So that's a yes?'

'That's a yes.'

'I have a confession to make,' he said, catching my arm before I could leave.

Oh, dear. Those were never good.

'I've never actually discharged my weapon while jumping through the air.' Sheepishly, he scratched the back of his neck, a pretty pink suffusing his cheeks as he glanced away. 'There were several times where I jumped and then fired or fired and then jumped, but never simultaneously.'

'I don't know what's worse, Whelan. That you lied to Shane or that you lied to me.'

The blush faded, his dimple curving around a crooked smirk as he murmured, 'I'm contrite.'

'*How* contrite?' Oh, God. This is not me. I am not the person who says things like that. No more pulp novels for this classy little dame. Now I was making *myself* blush.

'Hell, if you don't show up tonight then you'll never find out.'

SIXTEEN

'You're a lifesaver.'

Noah blushed, looking up from the little figurine he was whittling. I had seen him futzing with wood and a knife before, but this was the first opportunity I'd had to see his work up close.

'Don't worry about it,' he said, shrugging. 'Shane's a good kid. It's no trouble watching him.'

'Are you sure? I feel bad asking.'

'You shouldn't.' Noah turned the figurine in his hands, brushing off a few stray curls of shavings. 'I like hanging out with him. Reminds me of my brothers.'

'Two, or?'

'Three,' he smiled sadly. 'One older, two younger. Matty and Tad. They were real rambunctious, though. Not like Shane.'

'Sometimes I wish he was a little *more* rambunctious,' I said, sitting down on the bench next to Noah.

'No, trust me, you don't.'

'That's really good.' His figurine was shaping up to be an owl. The tiny knife cuts on the feathers were delicate, soft.

'Heh. I get plenty of practice.'

I could imagine that yes, he did. There wasn't much for a teenager to do. Well, there were chores, of course, but no girls to chase and no movies to go see. He had his books, but you could only re-read the same story so many times. I blinked, shivering, seeing Shane's future right in front of me. In many ways, Noah was a full adult now, but in others . . . he was still just a kid. The old rites of passage were gone. He wouldn't have prom. He wouldn't get to sneak out and break his curfew. He was expected to act like one of us, cut off from the rebellions that made growing up so damn fun. I hoped his being cooped up wouldn't drive him too crazy.

'I could do one for Shane,' Noah mused, turning the carved owl this way and that. 'Maybe a bear. Pink Bear, right? He talks about that thing all the time.'

'Actually,' I said, smirking, 'Pink Bear is a pig. He, um, well, he thought it was a bear that just happened to be pink and the name stuck.'

Noah tossed the owl, flipping it idly as he looked beyond me to the coast.

'Sounds like Gigi.'

'Gigi?'

'My older brother, Gabe. I guess I had trouble with his name when I was little . . . kept calling him that 'til I could finally say it right. My parents thought it was hilarious. He was Gabe "Gigi" Newerth in the yearbook.'

'He didn't . . . ?'

'Nope.'

'My sister . . . We were like that too.'

Noah fiddled with the owl, making small adjustments with the knife, making feathers more particulate and smoothing out the head.

'I'm sure I was incredibly obnoxious, intolerable, probably, but she put up with it,' I continued. 'Gigi is a

pretty cute name, all told. I called her much worse.'
Although I also called her Meow-Meow, Kitty-Kat, Meow
Mix . . . 'Her name was Kat and she was allergic to them.
She wanted a kitten so damn bad and would beg to go to
the pound. She'd come back swollen up like a heavyweight
boxer, grinning from ear to ear.'

'Did she get the cat?'

'No,' I said, 'never. Mom didn't want to deal with the
doctor visits. Shots . . . antihistamines . . . In hindsight it
seems like such a small thing. She should've just gotten her
the stupid cat.'

'Do you let Shane do whatever he wants?' Noah asked,
chuckling.

'No. Well, yeah. I guess I see what you're getting at.'

'Your sister would have been miserable all the time,'
Noah continued. 'I lost my . . . my parents, right? And I
don't remember what they wouldn't let me do. It's
pointless.'

'You think about Gigi,' I said, nodding. 'That your silly
name for Gabe stuck.'

'They were pretty all right. Not perfect, ya know? But
they were good to us.' Noah shrugged, carving deeper welts
into the spaces between the owl's talons. 'Pop taught me to
like books. Mom taught me to stand up for myself . . . I
guess Gigi did, too, but that involved a lot of bruises.' Noah
paused, both his words and his work, and shifted to look
down at his feet. 'We used to play this game . . . We'd all
gang up on Gabe. He was big, ya know? A brute. He'd beat
on us all the time. Sometimes I'd get my younger brothers
and we'd all pin 'im down and try to shove a dirty sock in
his mouth.'

'Ew!'

'Yeah . . . It wasn't, er, fun? Well, hell, it *was*. It was crazy fun.' Noah laughed, tossing back his head. His hair had grown out and the waves were not as curly, more crimpled, like lasagna. 'He hated it, I mean, obviously he hated it, but he always let us win, just once, then he'd chase us off and throw our G.I. Joes up in the trees.'

'You light up when you talk about them.'

He shrugged. ''Course I do.'

Noah began to whittle again, the knife squeaking quietly across the wood. 'Think Shane would like a pig?'

'Don't put yourself out,' I said, standing to collect the little boy in question.

He smiled, glancing up at me as I went. 'It's no trouble. I've never tried a pig before.'

At some point that whole *survive, survive, survive!* mantra disintegrated. It was somewhere between hearing Shane giggle for the first time in months and sitting on a blanket under the stars with Whelan. It was somewhere in there. I'm not exactly clear on the subtleties.

Before this becomes a rousing rendition of *How Sadie Got Her Groove Back*, there's something I've been meaning to explain.

It's not that I have trouble with men, all right? It's that I have trouble with *me*. Carl, may he absolutely not rest in peace, is the perfect example of what I mean. Unfortunately, I can't entirely blame my being with him on The Outbreak. I can, however, blame it on what I like to call The Poker Problem. I cannot play poker. I mean, technically I *know* how to play it, but I should never be allowed within twenty yards of a casino, or now, post-Outbreak, back alley games. I have the antigut, the anti-instinct. As soon as I have a decent hand I'm all in. I can't help it. I get one whiff of success, however unlikely, and throw myself in one hundred percent. Idiotic? Yes. Pathological? Also yes. And The Poker Problem applies almost letter for letter to men. One good moment, one iota of chemistry and I'm pushing that pile of chips across the table like I've got a full house. It's more probable that I have two pair, but that doesn't matter. I'm all in, baby, committed, before I really think it through.

So that's why Carl happened. And that's why Whelan was terrifying. No seriously. Petrifying. He *looked* like a straight flush but maybe he was just a lousy pair of jacks. Either way, I was stupidly giddy around him. The thought *I want to grope his hair* actually occurred to me at one point during the evening, proving that I'm not only horny to the point of atrophied intelligence, but that I was also becoming a creepy, creepy little fuck.

So here's the romcom montage for your convenience: slightly romantic meal of overcooked fish on a ratty blanket under the clear, night sky. Brief moment of panic when I realized a fish bone was wedged between my two front teeth and I had to do the duck down dance of shame to shimmy it out with my napkin. Another, even briefer moment of panic when I thought that maybe he had lured me out away from the others to hack me into little pieces. Then a long, long moment of blushing and indignity while I realized that he was just being nice. And then the post-dinner, first-date awkward conversation that started with chummy, mutual explorations regarding past careers, family and 'dreams'.

'Can I ask you something?' I was going for it. I had to. I couldn't stand to sit there, huddling under my sweatshirt, pretending like I wasn't freezing my fucking ass off.

'You can.'

'I need to either go get a blanket or press up against you. And I thought I'd ask first because . . .' Oh, right, now I needed to come up with actual reason. 'Because I didn't want to just invade your space and hope for the best.'

'We could go inside.' It wasn't a sexy suggestion. There would have to be empty cabins for that to be a come on.

'Maybe some other time,' I replied. 'With the rate people are dropping dead around here one will be free by the end of the week.'

He didn't laugh. Neither did I.

'Sorry. It's not funny. I'm just scared. And nervous. Very nervous.' *And I say shit-brained things.*

'No, you're right,' he said firmly. Then he was closer and I was getting a lot warmer. 'I was thinking . . . that house we saw? I feel like we should go back and look inside.'

'I . . . do *not* want to do that.'

He chuckled and the rumbling heat of it scorched a path against my side. I rested back against his shoulder, finding it was easier to sit that way and have an excuse to stare up at the sky and not at his dizzying smile.

'I haven't said anything to the others. I don't want to cause a panic . . . I just can't see the girls and Cassandra being a coincidence. Something is wrong and just waiting for another casualty doesn't seem right. It's not in my nature. It's not in yours.'

'And how do you know that, sir? You haven't known me for very long.'

Whelan laughed again, and this time it came with a

bonus hand nestled up against my hip. If we squeezed any tighter together we'd have to share a last name.

'I know that you dove after a stranger to try and save them.'

'Yeah . . . he turned out to be a real twat, though.'

'Well, that's a given. But the fact remains – you saved him.' Either I was imagining things or his lips were brushing against the back of my head. Goodness gracious, staving off the cold wasn't much of an issue anymore. 'And I know you were so desperate to get back to your nephew and your friends that you tried to steal a canoe in the middle of the night with two busted feet.'

'I'm . . . not actually sure what that says about my nature, but I don't think it's anything good.'

'To me it says you're brave. Look at what you did for me, for Danielle . . .'

Son of a bitch. He had a point. But most of those things just felt like recklessness and tragedy narrowly averted by sheer luck. 'I don't feel brave. I just feel less afraid than I did the day before.'

'That's a start.'

Again, the details are fuzzy, but I know a hand came up and tucked under my chin. Then I was staring down those unbelievable blue eyes and realizing his ears weren't so funny that I couldn't get over them and we kissed. If I had been listening, and I really wasn't, I might have heard the tiniest of excited shrieks from the direction of the camp. Somebody was up past their bedtime. Andrea, probably, or maybe Banana . . . or possibly both.

The cold disappeared, the outside world and its noises and danger reduced to the warm lips on mine and the hand holding me snugly around the waist. When he pulled back

I couldn't help but smile dreamily. But then I jerked back, hard, noticing something dangling near the corner of my right eye. It was a strand of hair with a gray thing the size of a chickpea. I shrieked and batted it away. A little slug bounced harmlessly onto Whelan's thigh. He laughed and flicked it away into the night.

Oh, jeebus. Strike me dead, just do it right now before I have to look him in the eye. My face was on fire, my throat so tight I couldn't do anything but cough out a relieved, mortified laugh. It could have been worse. It could've been a spider. Sadie Walker is Scheherazade, performing one night only the Dance of a Thousand Fails.

'That was . . . Yeah.' I stared resolutely at the sand. 'If you want to get up right now and never speak to me again I totally understand.'

'Forget it. Those things get in everything. I woke up with one hanging out of my nostril once.'

'*What?*' When I looked up, Whelan was smiling so hard at my expense it made his eyes close. 'No. Oh. That's gross. Even for a joke that's too gross.'

'Oh, come on. Everyone loves brain slugs.'

'I swear, I will mark this down in my diary: "Romantic evening or *the most* romantic evening? To be determined".'

We kissed again. This time when we pulled away there were no rogue slugs to destroy the moment. I fought the urge to look away, because I had done that before and because I was done with that, with hiding. And when you stop to look closely you notice things – freckles you hadn't seen before, creases around the eyes from laughing, scars, *details* . . .

'Since September, things have gone from bad to worse,' Whelan said gently, embarking on what, at first, sounded like a bad country song. 'But the one nice thing so far is having a night like this. Just talking like this.'

'The kissing isn't so bad either,' I ventured.

'Sort of freeing, don't you think?'

I nodded.

'I don't have to ask you on some painful first date at an overpriced dump,' he continued. 'I don't have to silently judge you for ordering a salad instead of a steak. We can cut right to what matters – brain-slug jokes.'

'Okay, first of all,' I said, turning toward him, 'If you can't laugh at a brain-slug joke, then what *can* you laugh at? Second, I would never order a salad on a first date. That's just false advertising. And third, is it wrong if I sort of miss that? Do you realize that this is the best I'll probably ever look? Just once it'd be nice to get dressed up. I wish you could see me in a dress, with a bit of makeup and something besides slugs in my hair.'

It was a good thing there were no mirrors around. I couldn't even imagine the state of my hair. Whelan used a reflective belt buckle to shave. I'm not sure I would ever have the balls to drag a straight razor over my skin with only an inch-by-two-inch square to show me the way.

Whelan's shoulder shook with silent laughter. 'Your hair is fine. The slug was a fluke.'

'Once upon a time, it wasn't just an indecipherable mess. It was cute. It had character. It was *me*. Now it's just a . . . I don't know . . . A stupid brown mop.'

'A *charming* brown mop.'

Gosh. The blush from the slug incident had faded, replaced by a different kind of rosy glow. As we hovered there in silence, I started to get why so many songs are written about eyes.

'If I kiss you again, do you promise that absolutely no brain slugs will wriggle out of your nose?'

'You bet.'

'Oh Lord Jesus, what did you do to the man?'

'I beg your pardon?'

Cornered. Cornered by a pretty girl with a bright bandana and even brighter eyes. And the irony of Banana drinking her morning coffee out of a chipped mug that read I KISS AND TELL while pinning me down like a cheetah pins a gazelle was almost too ridiculous to handle.

'Bright-eyed and bushy-tailed is an understatement, sweetie,' Banana went on, batting her lashes and mincing around the fire pit toward me. 'He's a whole new man this morning.'

'Yes, I am truly amazing,' I said, rolling my eyes as hard as I could without causing permanent damage. 'Illustrator by day, killer vixen by night!'

'Is this what he puts up with to earn your womanly wiles? You deflecting everything with a bad joke?'

'More or less, yeah.'

Banana smiled, or rather beamed, literally, the supernatural charm of her grin actually making me feel uncomfortably warm. She slithered up to me, wrapping one arm around my waist while she chugged down her coffee like it was Powerade. 'Sweetie pie, what ever you did, please do it some more.'.

Now that was advice I could actually follow.

But not before I earned another slow and mellow night with Whelan by doing some actual work. He was fixated on the idea of returning to the cabin we had found. I wasn't thrilled about it, but I knew I was a logical choice to accompany him – I had seen it before and might be able to help retrace the route. Andrea, Moritz and Noah would stay behind with Shane, while Nate, Whelan, Banana and I suited up to go into the woods. Stefano and Danielle had overslept, apparently, but would be expected to spend the day fishing. The slugs and ticks were bad, hanging on despite the chilly weather, so we bundled up for the cold and for protection.

'What're you expecting to find?' Nate asked as we slowly approached the tree line. It was like passing beyond a wall, a gate, leaving the safety of the known and the light and giving ourselves over to the dark uncertainty of the forest. It was blustery, leaves and sand whirling across the beach, dissipating as the gusts hit the trees and dispersed, winds breaking on the trunks like waves on the shore.

The crisp leaves above us rattled as branches creaked and groaned, protesting the wind.

'I don't know,' Whelan replied, readjusting the rifle at his shoulder. A sweatshirt hood obscured the soft waves of his hair. 'I'll know it when I find it.'

'Like porn,' Banana mused softly.

'What?' Whelan didn't sound amused, or in the mood to be lighthearted.

'Nothing.'

Behind us, just as the trees and shrubbery swallowed up our view of the beach, I heard Stefano calling to the others, his voice raised to a shout.

Progress was slow, hindered by unruly branches and my thickly wrapped feet. Even bandaged and protected by weathered boots they still ached. It was tempting to use the pain as an excuse to stay behind, but curiosity compelled me and so did the feeling that I wanted to know what was in that house. What if they saw something but didn't tell us when they came back? I wanted to know. I wanted to be part of the inner circle.

After ten minutes or so of crunching through the unwieldy growth and piles of shifting leaves, we began to find broken branches, twigs, evidence of others traveling through the forest. Then blood, drips of it here and there, on leaf beds, on soil, on the cracked sticks that poked out from the tree trunks. Whelan slowed, his shoulders bunching up tensely as they always did when he sensed danger.

'*Fuck*,' I heard Nate breathe. He came up beside me and stared down at the droplets of blood marking a distinct trail.

'Drag marks,' Whelan said, keeping his voice low in case any undead were lurking nearby. 'Do you see them?'

'Yes,' I whispered, watching as the blood marks on the ground became swipes, wide and uneven, like brush-strokes.

'We're close,' Whelan added. Somehow, that didn't make me feel any better about the blood.

'Someone's living in the house,' I said suddenly, the idea so clear, so obvious that I felt like a dumb ass for not saying it earlier.

'That's my guess,' Whelan muttered.

Our footsteps slowed yet further, caution and fear silencing even our breathing. Through the heavy branches up ahead I could see a peek of blue. The house. No amount of thermal underwear, sweatshirts or jackets could keep the cold from descending right into my marrow. The wind whistled above us, careening over the tops of the trees, creating a shrill, dry music that came and went at unpredictable intervals. The blood underfoot continued, spread, and I gasped, breaking our silence, when I saw it come up with my boot.

Wet. Fresh.

We never made it to the house.

SEVENTEEN

'What am I looking at?' Nate mumbled. We gathered in a circle, all of us staring down in horrified awe at the greatest concentration of blood and . . . *stuff* yet. It was mostly confined to one particular spot, a messy circle just on the edge of the clearing and quiet brook where the blue house waited. It was impossible to escape the feeling of the place watching us, *studying* us.

'Blood,' Whelan replied flatly. 'And some other shit— what the . . .'

He toed aside a few clumps of blood-matted leaves.

'. . . Christ.'

Two misshapen silvery lumps lay in the dirt, blood smeared over the sides. I gagged, turning away to heave, realizing what exactly I was looking at. Silicone sacks. Implants. Big ones. Apparently the zombies hadn't cared for that bit.

Banana stifled a cry. 'Oh, my sainted aunt.'

'You didn't see her this morning?' Whelan demanded, grabbing Banana by the shoulder and shaking.

'No! They . . . they overslept. I thought she was just hungover. Oh, God.'

Banana turned to me and dove for my arms. She began sobbing, huge, full-bodied cries that shook us both.

'This is some serious *Ten Little Indians* bullshit,' Nate said as I pulled Banana away.

'I have no idea what that means,' Whelan muttered.

'That's probably for the best, man.'

When Banana had calmed, her sobs diminishing to throat snorts as she tried to breathe without weeping, Whelan whipped off his top layer, a nylon jacket, and gathered up what was left of Danielle. I had never really considered that zombies would distinguish flesh from fake but . . . of course they would.

Whelan stomped by me at a clip and the rest of us hurried to keep up. Nobody was eager to be left behind in that cursed place.

'What the *fuck*! What the fuck was she doing out here?' Whelan trounced across the underbrush, batting leaves and twigs out of his way haphazardly. I could feel the temper rolling off of him from two yards back. 'She . . . It doesn't make any sense. It doesn't make any *goddamn sense!*'

'We know she was dragged.' I was trying to be reasonable, trying to work through the scenario without sounding disrespectful or crass. 'Those blood drops start close to the camp. Have you ever seen that before? Do zombies even *do* that?'

'No,' Whelan hissed. 'They don't.'

Stefano was, understandably, a wreck. He wouldn't accept consolations from anybody. He didn't want to hear it, didn't want to see us. He took the wrapped up jacket from Whelan and stumbled down toward the water, his head bobbing like the top of a buoy as he sank down in front of the waterline. For a long while he stayed there on his knees, the rest of us waiting by the huts while Whelan paced and swore.

It was different now. This was more than just the undead. We were fighting something we couldn't see. I had never believed in ghosts or demons, but the coincidences were now too coincidental to ignore. Nobody wanted to accept that people could be the greater threat. I'd seen it in Seattle, with the way people climbed over each other to eat and drink and then with the Rabbits. I'd heard about it from Allison's blog – mothers driven to horrifying extremes, their sanity savaged by losing their children and their stability; militia that looked out only for themselves, resorting to violence when it suited them. We had to start thinking that way. Allison had outsmarted them, confronted them, and now we would have to do the same. Damn it. I just wanted to be Shane's surrogate mom, but that wasn't enough now. I would have to be a hell of a lot more.

Something was hunting us. Something *worse* than zombies.

I couldn't shake the feeling that my instincts were right – they were human. It would take human strength, human dexterity, to drag a body through the forest like that. But then the remains were gone . . . skull and all, decimated, which pointed to zombies. Whelan was right. It didn't make any goddamn sense.

'I'm so fucking sick of funerals,' Andrea grunted. She collapsed down beside me on the cot inside our hut. I was busy trying to forget what I had seen, hoping Noah's books would be adequate brain bleach. 'And then there were nine.'

'Why would you say shit like that?' I let the book drop out of my hands, twisting around to glare at her. She finished tying off her hair in a tail, smashing down her floppy hat with a disconsolate little sigh.

'Sorry, I'm sorry. It was a stupid thing to say.'

'You're damn right it was.'

'Just . . . hear me out, okay?' She drew her knees up onto the bed, boring the dark blue of her eyes into the far wall. We hadn't been alone in a while, her time split between the chores we were all saddled with and spending time with Nate. 'What kidnaps little girls, turns them into zombies, then burns a human in a food storage bin, and then kills a stripper but leaves her fun bags for us to find?'

'Is this an actual riddle? Like, do you have an answer in mind or are we brainstorming?'

'The answer is: not a zombie.' I rolled onto my back, relieved that – for once – my feet weren't pounding like tiny spikes were still being driven into them.

'Christ, I need a valium,' Andrea murmured, rolling her eyes and flopping down onto the bed beside me. 'Anyway, what's the plan, toots?'

'We need to get in that house,' I replied.

'Wouldn't it be hilarious if you finally got inside and it was, like, empty and covered in cobwebs? Oooh, spooky!'

'No, actually, that would be a fucking nightmare because we'd be no closer to figuring out what the hell is going on.'

'So when are you going back?' She rolled onto her side, propping her chin up on her palm as she gazed down at me. Fidgeting, she picked a piece of lint from my sweater.

'I don't know. I don't know if I want to go back.'

'But you just said it's the only thing to do . . .'

'I'm just . . . afraid of what we'll find.' I just wanted to read . . . forget . . . sleep. It wasn't just the increasing cold that was making us all irritable, but the dread that came along with the casualties. If Cassandra hadn't been one of them then I wouldn't blame Whelan for running us out of camp. But there were no consistencies, which made it worse . . . There was no way to plan for what you couldn't even understand.

'Is it just me or are we both ignoring the enormous elephant in the room?'

'Which would be?'

'They have a boat, Sadie. And it's nice. We could go. Why don't we just pack up, leave, and find an island that isn't hell-bent on killing us?'

That was, in a way, an elegant solution, but what was the guarantee the next place we landed would be any better? And it was getting colder by the day, real winter weather, nothing to play with. The security of actually having sturdy shelters wasn't one I could easily ignore.

'That's a legit idea,' I said, taking hold of her hand and squeezing. 'I knew we kept you around for a reason.'

'Just don't sit on this, okay? We should go. This place gives me the fucking creeps.'

That valium was sounding pretty damn tempting right about now. 'Why do I feel like everything is going to hell?'

'Probably because it is.'

Just then I started to understand why those idiots in horror movies *don't* get out of the house. Part of you wants to know – *has* to know – and various other parts of you are screaming for vengeance, resolution, nagging at you to fight back. Just leave the island. Get out of the house. But even if we did go, and I agreed with Andrea that it was most likely the safest solution, some piece of me would always stay here. I could just imagine laying awake nights, trying to figure out what went wrong, what was out to get us, and the not knowing might be worse than the staying. Then again, I had Shane to think about.

Survival.

As if to slam home that I was being selfish by letting my curiosity get the better of me, Shane tiptoed into the cabin. Wordlessly, he crept up onto the cot with us and curled up to go to sleep. Danielle's passing hadn't seemed to affect him much. I hated guessing, entertaining the thought that maybe he was deeply torn up about it but didn't know what to say or who to turn to. Andrea left us alone, begging off to find Nate and fuck the fear away. Good for her.

Shane declined my offer of a story, half-asleep even as I asked.

Reading it was. By now I was well into *The Big Sleep*, putting up with horrible lighting, innumerable distractions and Noah's notes scribbled all over the margins to stay with Philip Marlowe Vivian Sternwood. We could use a little Philip Marlowe ourselves. Maybe the disappearances and deaths wouldn't look like a jumbled, disjointed mess to him. Maybe I was missing something right in front of my eyes.

The girls, the fire, Cassandra, Danielle . . . If someone was living in that blue house and stalking us, then perhaps they were just crazy. Dangerous. At first they might have been trying to make everything look like it could be blamed on zombies. Dangerous and at least passably smart. But then how did they survive in that house? Wouldn't we have heard gunfire as they tried to defend themselves? There were zombies everywhere there and the forest was the perfect place for them to hunt and hide. I was missing something. I could feel it, and like a joke you just don't get or a rumor whispered out of earshot, it needled and jabbed.

Sighing, I slammed the book shut a little harder then I meant to. It fell, splaying open on the floor, the spine crooked and awkward. I grabbed it, feeling ridiculous for letting my temper take over. Reading would clear my head, calm me down.

So I cracked the book again and maybe because I was tired or maybe for some other, luckier reason, my eyes roved and caught, snagging on words scribbled in red ink in the margins.

They Burn

And then beneath it, underlined so hard it had almost ripped the page:

They All Burn.

EIGHTEEN

'Faced with this I'd probably be defensive too.'

I felt wrong. Dirty. He was just a kid. But I couldn't find something like that in his book and not say anything. In all honesty, I just couldn't imagine Noah doing such evil things. He was sweet, always helpful, always willing to look after Shane. *Oh, God*.

'You don't . . . you don't get it!' Noah was flailing, his arms sailing above his head as he tried to articulate just what exactly he had meant by *They All Burn*. It was looking pretty bad for him. 'I like to look for patterns. It soothes me. It's like . . . it's like a mental game I play with myself when I'm reading something. I just . . . connect words, letters . . .'

Those heartthrob good looks I had predicted were emerging, the chubbiness in his cheeks whittled away by a spare diet and too much manual labor. Now that handsomeness only lent a sinister bent to his face, one that I'm sure he was regretting at that moment. Still, I couldn't reconcile the nice kid who had lent me those books on the boat to cheer me up and the young man in front of me . . . Could he have done it? It just seemed odd.

'Noah . . . you have to admit, it looks really creepy.'

'Why would I show you those books in the first place if

I . . . if I . . . if I was going to do those things? I wouldn't! I *couldn't*.'

A good point. I could concede that one.

'Maybe   you . . . You're   not . . . schizophrenic   or something, are you?'

'No! What the hell, Sadie? Look . . . look, I know how this seems, but I didn't do it. You have to believe me!'

And I did, God, I did, but how could I just breeze by the Redrum shit in his books? There were more, other weird, unsettling phrases I had found. None of it really coalesced yet, but maybe those were future plans, crimes Noah had yet to commit. He was strong enough to drag a body through the woods. He was smart enough to try and make everything look like a simple zombie attack. The girls would have trusted him, with that nice face and unassuming air . . . If kids would get into a windowless van with a creepy mustachioed pedophile for a few sweaty Werther's Originals then a nice-looking guy like Noah would have no trouble luring them at all.

'I haven't said anything to the others.' Like that was some kind of fucking comfort. 'I wanted to give you a chance to explain.'

'I *am* explaining!' He flailed his arms again, sighing and tossing his head. His boots wore deep ruts into the sand. His watery eyes shifted past me as he gazed down the shoreline toward the huts. I had asked him to come for a walk, deciding to confront him in an open, neutral place, one where a brutal murder would be noticed but also private enough that we could have a quiet word.

'What do you want me to say?' he murmured, deflating.

'I want you to give me a good reason for your serial killer doodles, Noah. And not just, oh I like to look for random patterns! Can you see how that's just . . . that's just not good enough? People are *dying*.'

'And you really think I did that? You think I killed little girls?' His voice rose, growing frantic and squeaky as he took a step toward me. I backed up accordingly.

'Not . . . you, necessarily. But somebody got them away from the camp. Maybe you didn't mean to kill them . . .'

'I can't believe what I'm hearing! I can't believe you would think of me like that.'

Suddenly I wanted Whelan there. He was a cop, for God's sake, I was sure he'd be better at this whole interrogation thing. I was only antagonizing Noah and now, if he really was the one responsible for the deaths, I would be his number one target. And if he hadn't done anything wrong then I had just alienated a good friend. God. Damn it.

'I'm sorry, Noah.'

'What now? Are you going to tell them?'

I didn't appreciate his looming or the way his spit was splattering across my forehead.

'Yes, but you'll be with me. Tell them what you told me.'

I know, extremely lame given the stakes, but what else was I supposed to do? I had no proof other than a few weird notes in a margin, notes that Noah had known I would see. It was all just a little too flimsy. The others had to know, but not without Noah there to defend himself.

'I promise, Sadie. It wasn't me.' His eyes were pleading, his hands were clasped and knuckles white as he repeated it over and over again until his voice rasped. 'It wasn't me . . .'

Too young. Too young to be mixed up in this shit.

'I'm sorry,' I repeated, knowing he would never forgive me. 'I really am.'

It wasn't fair, but what was I supposed to do? Not jump to conclusions, asshole, that's what. Still, this was too big to keep secret. The walk back to the cabins went by with my eyes flicking from the ground to the trees. I was growing seriously sick of the word *dread*, but a dreary, pervasive sickness had settled in my stomach, a constant jumpiness. They could come from all sides and at any moment, in droves or one at a time, but that was only one half of my unease. We had all caught it, like a plague, the tightness in your gut that tells you to be alert, be on your guard, the tension that doesn't let you eat without wanting to vomit, that doesn't let you sleep without jolting you awake every few hours.

The commotion from camp drifted toward me on a salt-scented wind. Noah followed at a distance, taking his time, but I heard his footsteps quicken as the voices carried. At first I thought maybe someone else had died, but no, it was Stefano, very much alive, and storming toward us with something tucked against his side. A book. Noah's book.

Heart, meet toes.

'What is this?' Stefano demanded. His delicate features weren't made for scowling, and he looked positively possessed as he threw *The Big Sleep* down in the sand at my feet. Then his arms were crossed and his gaze shifted over my shoulder to Noah.

'I'm taking care of it,' I said.

More bodies and faces, Whelan's prominent among them as he shouldered by to join us.

'Good,' Stefano said, nodding once. 'So how do we do it? It can be fast. I'm not barbaric.'

'What?' I crouched, gathering up the book and brushing the sand from its bent cover. 'No, I mean, I talked to Noah. He didn't do anything wrong. At least listen to what he has to say.'

Noah stood silently aloof, watching us with his mouth clamped shut, his arms mimicking Stefano's defensive posture.

'Sadie . . .' Whelan stepped forward and took the book out of my hands, pulling hard until I relinquished it. How? How had Stefano found it? 'Honestly . . . It doesn't look good.'

'Good? Yeah, it looks very, very bad.' Stefano didn't seem keen on letting Noah out of his sight. 'His pretty-boy looks can't help him now.'

'Noah deserves a voice here too,' I cut in. 'The book thing is suspicious, I admit, but there's nothing else. We should look at his clothes. There's no way he could drag Danielle through the forest without getting some of her blood on his sleeves.'

'He could wash them, no?' Stefano replied.

'Or destroy them.' Damn it, Whelan, be on my side.

'We have to believe each other. If we start throwing accusations around without actually listening to one another then we're already screwed.' Whelan tore his eyes away to search the sand. At least he was a little bit ashamed for ganging up on Noah like this. 'You're a cop, Whelan. Doesn't someone need means, opportunity *and* motive? What's Noah's motive?'

'He doesn't need one!' Stefano grabbed the book and opened it, shoving the water-stained pages in my face. 'He's fucking bat shit. He did it.'

'You're not making a real strong case for yourself by

staying silent, Noah,' Whelan murmured.

'He said he didn't do it.' I was starting to feel like a broken record. 'And I believe him.'

'Whelan, do something.' Stefano drew himself up. Oh, nice, so he wouldn't actually take responsibility for punishing Noah, just ask that someone else do it. Pathetic. 'Maybe she's in on it. We can't be sure.'

Hold the fucking phone.

'Me? Are you kidding? I'm the one who confronted him!'

'Which would make you look real innocent, no?' Stefano smiled but there was absolutely no joy in it. The urge to punch him in the throat or toss him down onto the sand reared almost too fast for me to curb. 'Just sayin'.'

'You're a real class act, Stefano,' I muttered, shaking my head in disbelief. 'Why don't you just point the finger at everyone to be sure? Cover all your bases, man. Don't be shy.'

'Enough.' Whelan didn't need to shout, not when a whisper like that did twice the work with half the volume. 'You're both out of line. I'll talk to Noah; the two of you cool off. We're on the same side here.'

Stefano marched away with his nose in the air and a little huff that quite clearly said: this isn't over.

Meanwhile I felt like a dirtbag, hovering there trying to think of the right thing to say to both Whelan and Noah. He just couldn't have done it, and the more I thought about it the surer I became and the worse I felt for bringing it up at all. I had only wanted to do the right thing and now I had started a shit storm that could easily build into a shit hurricane.

'How did Stefano find out?' I asked, grabbing Whelan's elbow before he could walk away with Noah. His blue eyes looked duller, muted, as if the weight of dealing with this intertribal bullshit was sapping the energy right out of his body. I sympathized. 'He didn't just randomly go through Noah's stuff . . .'

'We should talk about this later,' Whelan whispered.

'Tell me now, Whelan.'

He sighed, that heaviness in his eyes seeping out to his shoulders, dragging them down into a hunch. 'Shane showed us.'

'*What?*'

'I'm sorry, Sadie.'

'Shane . . . but he . . .' Had been right there in the bed with me when I read Noah's book. He must not have been asleep. 'This isn't what I wanted to happen.'

'Go easy on Shane. I think he just wanted to help.' Whelan left then, walking back down the beach with Noah. Why wouldn't Noah fight? Speak up? Maintaining that stubborn silence would only make him look guiltier than he already did. Clearly, in Stefano's eyes, he was the culprit and of any of us, Stefano had lost the most – first his cousins and then his closest friend. He was out for blood and I couldn't blame him.

And Shane . . . He just *had* to pick today to come out of his shell.

I found the little tattletale sitting at the fire picking apart a blackened piece of fish. He ate in tiny, precise bites, wiping his char-stained fingers off on his pants after every mouthful. Moritz and Andrea fell silent at my approach, giving me the classic big-eyed, straight-mouthed, deer-in-headlights expression, the one that meant they knew Shane was in for a tonguelashing.

'Come with me please, Shane.'

He shook his head no. Did he actually want me to turn into Momzilla?

'You're not in trouble.' Okay, maybe not entirely true. 'I just want to talk.'

It was like coaxing a rabbit out of its warren. Eventually Shane stood, setting down his plate on the log bench and taking my hand, casting a forlorn, helpless look over his shoulder at Andrea and Moritz. I had seen that look many, many times. It no longer fooled me.

Shane dug his feet in stubbornly as I led him away, halting us every few seconds as he tried to drag to a stop. Discipline really isn't my strong suit, but something like this had to be addressed. It was time to put on the mommy pants, whether I enjoyed it or not.

We stopped near the edge of the water, out of earshot of both the fire pit and the huts. I spied Banana on the docks fishing with Nate. Whelan and Noah were having their little heart-to-heart farther down the beach. Stefano stewed by the tied up canoe. Maybe he was thinking of leaving, I don't know. Good riddance. Andrea and Moritz sat eating at the fire. That meant everyone was accounted for. I found myself doing that a lot now, taking a quick head-check every once in a while just to make sure dinner wouldn't be interrupted with screams as another of us met an untimely end.

The tide, still low, had deposited a number of new shells and blobs of seaweed on the sand. A wet stripe ran along the beach, darker than the rest, marking where the water would creep up as the tide came in. Another windy day. The waves chopped, rising in jagged peaks as they rushed toward us, stopping just shy of already damp shoes. And for once Shane looked up at me, facing me squarely, not studying the myriad marine treasures still slick and foamy on the ground.

'I'm not upset, Shane,' I said. Also a half-truth, but I didn't want to frighten the poor kid. Scared straight wasn't really my style. 'I'm just confused. Why didn't you talk to me before going to the others?'

He shrugged.

'Not good enough, little man. Gonna need some words. So out with it.'

Shane regarded me quietly for a moment, canting his head this way and that, reminding me of a bird that's sure you want to communicate, but can't understand you or know how to talk back.

'This is serious, Shane. I'm not mad, okay? I just want you to explain yourself.'

'I didn't know what to do,' he said.

Not much, but we could build on that.

'Noah stays in our cabin. I thought I . . . should show someone.'

'But I thought . . . He carved you that Pink Bear. Don't you think he's too nice to hurt someone?'

'I . . . guess.' Shane toed the ground. 'It's just a pig.'

'Were you *afraid* of him?' Oh, great. The damage had been done. Now, no matter what, Noah would carry the taint of that book and its fucking scribbles for the rest of his life. Even if he was guilty of nothing but poor judgment, he would be treated like a psycho.

'Yes,' Shane answered. 'I thought I could show Whelan because he's a policeman.'

That . . . was actually pretty logical.

'Next time come to me first, because now Noah is in

trouble with everyone and that makes it much more complicated.' *Clusterfuck* probably wasn't the right sort of language to use around him. 'Do you get what I'm saying?'

'Yes. Show you first when I find weird things.'

'Right. I know Whelan is a policeman and that's nice, but I'll pass something on to him if I think it's important, okay?'

Shane nodded.

'Go finish your food.'

I thought of making him apologize. But for what? For finding something that frightened him and showing a cop? That was positive behavior. That was the sort of thing you wanted to enforce, not chastise. It was almost heartening to think that, even if he was sort of strange and mute, Shane had his head screwed on right. I watched him trundle back to the fire, almost completely spherical in the number of coats Andrea had piled onto him. A cheerful cry went up from the docks – Banana and Nate had caught something. We might actually eat, then. Shane probably didn't know it, but food was becoming scarce. Without the canned goods and cache of the food storage, we were almost entirely reliant on the food we caught each day. Scavenging for clams and mussels was becoming less and less viable as the temperature dropped and the water became icy. Whelan could no longer safely stay out in the sea for long periods of time. Fishing off the dock still yielded decent amounts of edibles, but we would need to diversify our diet. Plant life in the forest was a possibility, and insects, but foraging was dangerous, even just inside the tree line.

But whatever we had was divvied up and the first round of it went to Shane. The rest of us ate what we could, though my appetite was apparently inversely proportional to my fear level. Everything turned my stomach, even water. My guts were lined in razor wire and I couldn't rightly say when the slicing would stop.

NINETEEN

'Shane is a good boy.'

I *wanted* to trust everybody, really I did, but ever since finding Noah's margin notes, I'd become a suspicious, twitchy wreck. The good boy in question had just left, toddling into the cabin under his usual superhuman weight of coats and blankets. I'd swear the kid was cold-blooded.

'Thanks, Moritz.' Fish for dinner again. What kind of fish, you ask? It didn't matter. It all tasted the same once it'd been in our cast-iron pan, a cooking implement that really should no longer have been called a pan but an instrument of destruction. It actively de-flavored things. All you could taste when you bit into fish that'd been in that pan were all the burned fishy brethren that came before. Once upon a time I liked food. I had what over-bearing type-A soccer moms in Crocs called 'a passion.' You couldn't live in the Northwest and not be some type of foodie. Sometimes I thought I still had that passion, but since I hadn't eaten anything that qualified as food in weeks, it was hard to say.

'I feel like we never talk,' I said. The others had split off, pairing off for cards or sleeping or battling horrific indigestion.

'We don't,' Moritz replied simply. 'You and Officer Cabral have grown quite close.'

I wasn't sure if that was an observation or a question. Why he couldn't call Whelan by his first name, I couldn't guess. Well, I could, but I didn't.

'Officer . . . ? Right, Whelan. You don't have to call him that.'

Moritz's greyhound face sharpened in the firelight, the darkness around us and the hot glow of the flames igniting the raised edges of his nose and cheekbones. He smiled, shrugging, the haggard remains of his tweed suit clinging to him like flayed strips of tree bark to a trunk.

'Do you think Noah is innocent?' I asked. Of all of us, Moritz probably knew Noah best. They spent a lot of time together, though I couldn't imagine what a rustic Canadian teenager and a former art critic had in common. His expression softened again, almost melting like wax from the heat, his mouth drifting down into a ponderous frown.

'Art informs us that we all have monsters inside . . . hidden evils. A civilized man, a family man, can paint his demons and shock the world.'

Huh.

'So . . . that's a no? You think he's guilty?'

I thought of the little pig Noah had carved for Shane. It just didn't seem right that he could do something so thoughtful and then . . . well, you know.

Moritz chuckled softly, brushing crumbs from his pants and depositing his plate on the ground. He rested his elbows on his knees and leaned forward, pursing his lips in a way that made me feel stupid and patronized.

'No, I do not believe he is capable of such crimes. Whoever or whatever hunts us is not smart but determined.

There is savagery there, not planning. Noah is a bright boy. Were he our enemy I would perhaps feel better about it. At least then there might be a pattern, some sense of what's to come.' Moritz redirected his gaze to the fire and the jumping sparks illuminated the dark reaches of his pupils.

'Hold on – whoever or *whatever*? You . . . think it might not be human?'

'Is that so hard to believe? Just a few months ago I did not believe that the dead could walk and kill, but I was proven wrong. I could be proven wrong in other fundamental ways.'

'You're not making me feel any better here, Moritz.'

'My apologies. I didn't know that was the goal.'

'It's not. I just . . .' Suddenly the food on my plate was even less appetizing. I shoved it away, feeling guilty for being wasteful and then feeling stupid for feeling guilty because it was my damn stomach.

Silence and the flames. I wondered what Whelan might be up to. I wondered if Shane wanted a bedtime story. I wondered about the quiet, shuffling footsteps and the whispers that sounded oddly heavy and strained and why there were so damn many of them emerging out of the water-washed peace of the night.

'Whelan,' I muttered, jumping to my feet, leaving Moritz staring after me with his mouth hanging open. 'Run,' I called back. 'Come with me!'

And then the beach was filled with them. It was like someone had banged on a dinner triangle, summoning the local undead to rise up and hop on down to the buffet. Whelan and Banana were in their cabin, losing badly to Nate and Andrea at charades. At least that's as much as I could glean while huffing and puffing and shrieking at them to get the guns.

Andrea rushed out by me, bee-lining for the cabin where Shane was napping.

The hard, metallic slide and lock chorus of faith-instilling badassery began, and Moritz and I were politely shoved out of the way as first Nate, then Banana and finally Whelan emerged from the cabin. Their arsenal never failed to impress.

'Stay near the fire,' Whelan instructed, tightening the buckles on his chest holster. 'If anything gets too close, holler.'

Word to your fucking mother. Moritz and I clamored back toward the warmth of the fire. Stefano soon joined us and Andrea wasn't far behind, tumbling out of the cabin with Shane on her back. Improvising, I grabbed a protruding branch from the fire, deciding that I could Jane of the Jungle it if anything broke through the gunfire.

'It's okay,' I told Shane with a smile that stayed put only as long as I faced him. 'Just stay close.'

That was most definitely the plan, as all of us huddled near the fire pit, standing as close as we could without actually bursting into flames. The darkness exploded, rifle fire illuminating the mayhem in yellow-white bursts of color and noise. Smoke drifted, gunpowder singeing my nostrils as our protectors fanned out, creating a tight triangle. Whelan shouted orders to them as they lit up in turn, glimpses of pale, gaunt faces appearing when the silence split again with a pulse of gunfire. It was like a disco club nightmare, the starless night swallowing up the coherent pictures of just what we were facing. How many? From what direction? It was impossible to tell, the only images quick, flashing there, too fast to be seen, surreal and violent.

But soon the undead had something to say about, groaning and wheezing, their voices undercutting the pop, bark, rattle of the rifles. Shane's whimpers became cries as he clung to Andrea's neck, his wide eyes visible just above her shoulder, giving him the appearance of some terrified bush baby holding on to a branch for dear life. We circled the fire, panicked, every single one of us panting as we watched the perimeter, eyes peeled for any stragglers heading for us. One made it, shuffling toward us, naked, her arm left blown apart at the shoulder. You had to admire that kind of determination – limb torn off by bullets and still coming for us. She only had one hand to grab with, her mouth a perpetual snarl, the lower part of her jaw missing, torn away, leaving only a hollow scowl and lazily unhinged tongue.

I don't think even humid, rancid garbage smells that fucking bad.

I dipped the burning branch into the flames again, swinging the torch at her with all the coordinated grace of someone trying to dance a bee out of their bra. But my spazzy swinging worked, pushing her back, giving Whelan the time to see the flame in my hand soaring back and forth. I saw his face in the sudden brightness thundering out of the rifle's barrel. It didn't make me feel any better, not when I could see an entire legion of those things behind him, coming from the water. It was just a flash, a millisecond of strobing lights where I saw his grimace, his furrowed brow, and then the wet, slimy faces creeping up behind him.

We were surrounded. There were way, way too many,

and the thought of Whelan being dragged down into the surf with them paralyzed me. Moritz grabbed my elbow, guiding me back into the safety of the fire's glow.

'Noah,' I mumbled. 'He's not here.'

'I fucking told you it was him!' Stefano shrieked. 'What did I tell you?'

'Shut up and concentrate,' Andrea said, shoving him.

Impossible. It couldn't have been Noah . . . but Stefano was right. He wasn't with us. There was no time to consider the possibilities – that maybe he got caught off guard by the first wave of undead and had been killed before we even noticed. Or maybe he was orchestrating the whole thing. Maybe he had figured out some way to lure the dead to the camp, deciding that we were too close to the truth, too close to figuring out he was the killer . . .

Footsteps pelted toward us, heavy, fast footfall that couldn't belong to a zombie. Noah careened into the light, stopping just inches from the flames themselves. He was flushed, out of breath, and before Stefano could chime in with some smart-ass accusation, Noah had torn the torch out of my hands.

'Hey!' I shouted, scrambling for it. 'What are you doing? Where the hell have you been?'

'There's too many.' His eyes were wild, huge, dirt streaked down his face and sand clotting his curls. 'What'll it take, Sadie, for you to believe me?'

I wanted to answer. 'Nothing. I already do,' was ready on my lips. But Noah left us, sprinting out into the roiling war zone outside the circle of light. Dimly, as if I had lost all control of my body, I watched my arms go for him, my hands reach, but it was like he simply disappeared, there one minute, dissolved by darkness the next.

We watched the arc of the torch, the fire flickering, threatening to go out as Noah raced toward the water. He started shouting, jeering, raising holy hell. Whelan called back.

'Get back to the others!' Whelan roared, another burst of gunfire nearly drowning out his voice. 'What the fuck? Noah! Noah?'

'Come get me, you fuckers,' Noah was shouting, taunting and dancing the fire back and forth. 'Here – you want some blood? Have some fucking blood!'

I didn't have to see to know what he was doing. And the blankness around us began to move, the horde enticed by Noah and whatever blood he had spilled. The moaning intensified, hungry and constant, a hum that became a drone that became a chorus. The torch moved, bouncing away toward the dock. Now Banana and Nate had joined in, trying to call Noah back. The torch lowered and a wavering, orange pool of light spread at Noah's feet. He was being followed, not just by two or three undead, but by dozens. Their feet shuffled into the light, then hands. His taunting stopped, overtaken by panicked screams.

'Oh, my God,' Andrea whispered. 'He can't be serious.'

'Still think he's guilty?' I hissed.

Stefano sniffed.

Our gunmen picked off what members of the horde they could, but not fast enough. Noah would be devoured if he didn't move. But there was nowhere to go. He was trapped, pinned by the undead before him and the water below. Still, we watched, dumbstruck, as the torch danced down the dock.

'What is he—' Andrea began, siding up next to me. Shane grabbed onto my shirt, squeezing.

284

'Whelan!' I could see it. I could see it all unfolding. It would be an accident, just an error in judgment, a well-meant gesture that might only make us worse off. 'Whelan, you have to stop him!' I rushed out of the safety of the circle, jogging down toward the water.

'Go back,' Whelan said as I collided into his side. The smell of gunpowder was overpowering, ashen and bright. 'Get out of here. Now, Sadie.'

'We have to stop him!' I pointed. Whelan followed the trajectory of my finger. Then he was darting off toward the dock, leaving behind the imprint of his warmth, a shadow, and that lingering smell of gunpowder.

Down on the dock, Norah's torch flared. Banana took my hand, her clips empty, her skin clammy and too-warm. I heard Whelan's heavy tread on the dock planks and then heard Noah's scream. The torch overbalanced, falling in a slow arc that would have been beautiful were it not so foreboding. He had tripped, or been pushed or maybe tackled, but not into the water. The effect was instantaneous. Clothes caught fire, undead screaming their unnatural cries as the flames spread and jumped, feeding. Noah's voice dimmed, overwhelmed, the undead consuming him even as the fire consumed them all.

More disturbingly still, none of the zombies attempted to put themselves out. They had found one meal and would destroy it. That was their one purpose. They made no effort to peel off and dive into the water. They simply burned – burned as they ate, screaming in protest of the flames even as they did nothing to stop them.

And then everything could be seen perfectly as the flames found new paths, leaping up as the whole tangled, burning mess of Noah and the slavering mob tumbled into the boat. It was bigger than Arturo's Ketch but still a sailboat. Whatever additive was in the wood spurred the fire and the greedy flames were soon searing a path straight up the mainmast.

'Back up!' Whelan had turned, fleeing down the dock toward us. 'Fuck, fuck, fuck . . . *Get back!*'

Banana dragged me toward the cabins, both of us walking backward as we watched, horrified and transfixed, as our best hope to leave the island went up in flames, and Noah with it. The tuffs of fire on the dock went out, sputtering, as the boat became one blazing cone of heat and light. Whelan caught up to us, pushing insistently, gasping for breath as he shouldered us back toward the others.

It was obvious why. The flames covered the deck of the sailboat and touched, inevitably, the outboard motor's gas compartment. One collective gasp went up as the back of the boat seemed to rear up, exploding, shards of flaming wood streaming out in every direction, arcing like a Fourth of July display. The smell of char and gasoline filled in the space around us as the fireball became one mass, undead indistinguishable from wreckage.

A single moan trickled over from my left, silenced a second later by Whelan's rifle barking back. I couldn't move. The surface of the water seemed to be igniting, the boat burning down, its cast off pieces in flames until they too dwindled, spent. The bulk of the sailboat would take a while to flame out, but when it did . . .

Unless we could all fit into Whelan's canoe or fix Anton's boat, we were stuck. We were stranded.

TWENTY

We had come to a point where even articulating the losses was too difficult. Condolences were given with looks, touches on the shoulder or back, and the silence was more comforting than any longwinded speech.

Every time I opened my mouth to say something, even something as mundane and little as 'good morning,' I found my throat closing up. It was easier to say nothing and avoid the threat of tears.

Losing Noah and the boat did something to Whelan. He took every loss hard, but this one was different. He helped me bury all but one of Noah's books. I wanted one to keep around, foolishly, to sort of remember him by, or maybe to keep it as a reminder of why sometimes keeping your damned mouth shut is a good idea. He had saved us, given us another day, destroyed a massive number of zombies, but also – accidentally – destroyed our safest chance at relocating. That realization was slowly settling over everyone, blanketing us in a quiet melancholia that made eating breakfast together a reflective affair.

But Whelan fought against the tide of despair, eating his breakfast quickly before striding away, quick and determined.

He decided that without the boat the next best thing

would be a raft. I know it sounds foolish, but we all grieve in different ways, and it obviously gave him a comforting sense of purpose. The raft began taking visible shape by midmorning. I appreciated that he was doing his best to get us a way off the island, but it also did strike me as, well, a little misguided. His energy, I thought, would be better spent fishing with us, finding Anton's boat, making provisions for the advancing winter and trying to figure out what exactly was in that creepy blue house.

Shane helped me sort blankets and clothing that needed to be washed. Everything smelled like the smoke from the burning boat. We would have to wash things in batches, since the cold was too dangerous now to risk wearing damp clothing.

We sat together at the campfire with the sound of Whelan's ax thinking an even, sharp staccato. Shane's fingers trembled as he pulled up a blanket and shook it out.

'Do you want to talk about Noah?'

I didn't want the silence to hurt Shane. There was no way I was going to let him absorb the carnage from last night without at least making a go at conversation.

'He didn't do anything,' Shane said, hiding his face from me with the outstretched blanket. I knew the carved pig was among the contents in his pockets. He had been taking it out from time to time and turning it over in his hands.

'Sometimes it's not easy, you know? It's nice when you know what's bad and what's good,' I said. 'It's hardest when we have to fear each other.'

An icy wind traced across the beach, ruffling the blanket in his grasp.

'And it's not your fault – what happened with Noah.

Everyone was scared and mixed up. I don't want you to think you did something wrong.'

'But I *did* do something wrong. I shouldn't have said anything to Whelan. I didn't know what . . . I didn't know.' The blanket came down. He looked at me, right in the eyes, scowling as if determined to take the blame.

'You couldn't have known, bud,' I said gently. 'And it's okay that you showed Whelan too. You saw something that made you scared and you did something about it.'

'But it was the *wrong* something,' Shane insisted.

'Look, I've done lots of wrong somethings . . .' I didn't even like saying the asshole's name in front of Shane, but I considered that owning up to my own lapses in judgment might help him understand what I meant. 'Carl was a wrong something. Letting him get near us is one of the biggest regrets of my life. Going into the forest alone was a wrong something. I know that might not make you feel any better, but you're not alone. In fact, if there's one thing that makes us all similar, it's that we all screw up from time to time.'

'You're right,' Shane mumbled, shaking his head. 'It doesn't make me feel any better.'

'It's fine to feel upset about this, but . . . this isn't your fault. Whoever is trying to hurt us – it's *their* fault.'

'Then why do I still feel so angry?'

I knew what to say now. It wasn't easy, necessarily, but natural, and it made me hope that I was getting the hang of looking out for him, or at least fixing things when they went horribly awry.

'Because you're a good kid,' I said. 'And it makes you angry when things don't turn out for the best.'

This wasn't a one-time patch job. We would need to

talk about it again, later, when he had time to process his confusion. But it was a start.

Shane and I finished sorting through the blankets as Andrea appeared from the far end of the cabins. She offered to make lunch and I left them together to check on Whelan. He probably didn't need me snooping around and God knew there was plenty to keep us busy, but it didn't seem right to let him go on beating himself up all alone.

'The raft is looking good, Officer.'

There wasn't a single hitch in his rhythmic hammering. I wasn't even offended that my greeting went unanswered. He was somewhere else, on a different plane of thought entirely. Sweat rolled down his neck, and yours truly had the pleasure of imagining those enterprising little droplets picking up speed as they hit the gunnels on either side of his spine before racing down toward the waistband of his jeans.

'Don't call me that,' he grunted a moment later.

Bang – bang – bang.

'Why not?'

'Because I've chosen' – a slight pause as he pulled a nail out of the corner of his mouth – 'to work out my frustration this way instead of fucking your brains out. Please respect my decision.'

Calling him . . . ah. Yes. Well, then. I really dislike the word *flabbergasted*, but sometimes you just have to embrace it.

'Well?'

Oh. He wanted a response to that. Funny, I was just thinking about how I had completely lost the power of speech.

'Hang on. I'm trying to think of a pithy response. Geez, pushy, pushy.'

That actually made him stop what he was doing. He plucked the rest of the nails out of his mouth and dropped them onto the sand before I could consider how incredibly unsanitary it was. Then he twisted at the waist, resting his palms on his bent knees as he pulled a smile out of his back pocket and grinned up at me, cheeky dimple and all.

dis • arm
[dis-**ahrm**]
—*verb (used with object)*
1. *to deprive of a weapon or weapons.*
2. *to remove the fuse or other actuating device from:* to disarm a bomb.
3. *to divest or relieve of hostility, suspicion, etc.; win the affection or approval of; charm:* His smile disarmed us.
4. *to completely wipe Sadie's brain cells of all useful thought or argument; to moisten panties:* His disarming smile should legally be considered a weapon of mass destruction.

'I've pissed you off,' Whelan commented dryly, one eyebrow going skyward.

'Uh, no, on the contrary, you have not. In fact, I do not know of this "pissed off" you speak of.' *Look, libido, we need to have a sit down, one where I explain that it's unacceptable to take over my brain like a Centaurian slug and turn me into a gibbering, sweating dullard.*

Whelan stood and the angels rejoiced on high as the salt air and that sweat-that-isn't-quite-smelly-sweat-but-like-tigermusk came along with him. His T had gone partially transparent from perspiration, showing a bit of the tattoo on his pectoral, the design that I had caught only a partial glimpse of from the collars of his shirts. It was still impossible to make out what it actually was, but knowing it was there was motivation enough to fund an expedition.

One is unfortunately reminded of those sex-crazed maniacs who, immediately after The Outbreak hit, were so desperate to go down doing it that they screwed it in the middle of the streets. I bet they were disappointed when they didn't actually end up getting eaten and had to live out their days with their neighbors knowing the location of every mole, dimple and freckle pattern on their bodies.

That doesn't mean I was convinced we were all going to die and soon. But danger has a way of making those bits of unfinished business an imperative rather than a choice. Luckily, this imperative was pretty damn appealing.

'That thing you said . . .' *Really, brain? That's what we're going with?* 'We should do that.'

'The part about fucking?' Eyebrows that dastardly should really have their own mustachios to twirl.

'Yes.'

'Hmm.' *Hello, tenterhooks, pleased to be releasing your Shaolin grip on my heart.* 'Now?'

'No, not now."

'Then . . . later?'

'*Definitely.*'

'Okay, then. I'll find a sitter.' Another smile, another little piece of my soul floated up to the clouds to frolic with unicorns and baby Jesus.

'Sweet.'

Sweet? What was this, *Sweet Valley High?* Christ, at least I didn't say *rad.* The eloquence astounds, I know, but I dare you to do better with eyes that blue and shiny staring like your mouth is an all you can eat sushi platter.

'I should go,' I said, inching away. Almost at once the guilt hit. We had just buried Noah. Was this what people did at funerals? Did it matter? The initial terror of dealing with the undead meant that the usual ethics went out the window. But now we were a little removed, or at least, used to it, and behaving rashly wasn't as justifiable. Maybe this wasn't so rash. Maybe we had been arriving at this point for a long time and the threat of more loss, more death, pushed that deadline up. Comfort isn't always where you expect it to be.

He knelt again, pushing a dirt-stained hand through his dark hair, working a crick out of his neck as he hefted his hammer.

'Yeah, you probably should. Now I'm only feeling more frustrated, and you absolutely do not want to get sand in the places I'm thinking about.'

And the things *I* was thinking about were not legal in most states.

'Then I suppose it's a date,' I said, turning to go with a crooked smile of my own. 'Officer.'

We move in circles. Success, happiness, love – we move toward these things, graze them, maybe touch them, but something inevitably pushes us away. Maybe it's a weird drive to feel, I don't know, *bereft*. If we have the thing we want it's suddenly not the peak – if we can hold it, feel it or own it, then it's no longer amazing. Suddenly the intangible is tangible and the magic goes out of it and you're left moving in that circle again, edging toward the next great person, the next job or whatever else it is you want that's doomed to become yours and then, by its very nature, unsatisfying.

We kill good things. We do it all the time.

The cabins didn't let in much light. The rough muslin curtains looked like something a bored campground employee put up long ago to get the tourists to shut up about privacy. Burnt orange stripes ran through the fabric, reminding one not of rustic sunsets – which I was sure was the hope – but of the runs. With the curtains drawn at night, the cabins became little voids, boxes where no light penetrates. That was both good and bad – good because there was no denying the excitement of the darkness. Bathed in shadow, there was mystery and the unknown, there was the chance to explore with senses forgotten in the daylight. There was Whelan, impossibly warm, all of him firm, and the lack of light provided the opportunity to find the variations in that firmness – the callused roughness of fingers that had shot and hewn and protected, the rise of shoulders made iron from a lifetime of physical rigor, a stomach that was neither completely hard nor soft, rigid but forgiving and dusted in coarse hair.

The bad was that darkness meant surprises in the morning. Hopefully happy surprises, but one never knew.

And there were words whispered in the darkness, sometimes incoherent with delight and other times ringing with a strange clarity. Bodies bent more naturally in the dark, unimpeded by self-consciousness or anxiety, moving where they wanted to go and doing what they wanted to do. Desires were communicated subtly, in breaths or sighs, nervousness manifesting as giggles, gasps, and then resolved with another, more certain touch.

I woke up, sore in places I forgot about, feeling the savage, deep thoughtfulness of a mind reawaken to its physical counterpart, and I stretched and smiled and made those contented, muzzy morning sounds. Then with the light there I turned to survey my conquest, reacquaint myself with the being that gave me so much unexpected joy, and found that the sunshine ruined everything.

Everything. Not happy surprises then.

It was there, on his chest, the design I thought I saw through damp cloth, a design that once thrilled but now, when I could see just what it was, it made the world spin. And it was on his arm, too, not as big, but there just the same. A conversation weeks old lashed out, like a snake you've stepped on, accidentally, and provoked – Andrea, making her usual crass conversation, bragging about bedding a Repopulationist, a Rabbit, and his tattoos.

'Oh my God.' It slipped out and I covered my mouth to stifle the scream that wanted to follow.

It was something you just knew. The aggressive slant on the cartoon rabbit's mouth, its ludicrously oversized musculature . . . No wonder they got out before Seattle fell. They knew what was coming.

In the next instant I was sliding out of bed, gathering my things, dressing clumsily with fingers numbed by rage. He couldn't have said something? He couldn't have mentioned this when my hand was touching that tattoo the night before? Whelan woke up when the door shut. I heard my name, a confused murmuring, but I was already outside in the cold, storming across the sand and back to my cabin. I was *right*. I should've stuck to my people and let him stick to his.

'Sadie? Is everything okay?'

He sounded so earnestly hurt and confused I almost feel bad.

But not *that* bad.

'Don't play the innocent, Whelan. You know damn well it's not *okay*.'

Turning to look at him would swing the argument in his favor, so I didn't, focusing straight ahead, staring at the fire pit. I had to get there, had to get back to Shane and Andrea. Had to get away from—

'Stop. Stop it, just hold on, would you?'

He caught up and a gentle hand closed around my elbow.

It wasn't like I could avoid him. That raft of his looked about as seaworthy as a sieve and he was, unfortunately, who Banana and Nate looked to for guidance. And I liked Banana and Nate. But maybe they were Rabbits too. Maybe they were just as sneaky and deceptive as Whelan. The beach was empty and we were alone as I slammed to a stop and spun, yanking my arm out of his grasp.

'You make me ill,' I whispered. Before his eyes could get any bigger with confusion I jabbed, hard, right in his left pectoral. He hardly seemed to feel it, but his eyes shifted to where I'd poked him.

'Why do you think I left, Sadie?' It was the too-soft, too-calm voice of a man who knows he's been busted.

'I don't care.' Blaming him, not just for the way I felt right then, but for everything, seemed perfectly logical. 'How many chicks did you knock up, then? I mean, that's what you all do, right? That's your thing.'

The blood drained from his face, from his chest, leaving him ghostly pale.

'I didn't . . . Nobody. Look, there are a lot of misconceptions—'

'Fascinating. You'll have to tell me about it sometime, like when I'm done vomiting on myself.'

'You're not being fair, Sadie. I never . . . Would you just listen? Christ, I'm trying to explain – isn't that what you want?'

'It's all of you, right? You're all Rabbits, aren't you?'

Shifting from foot to foot, he wet his lips and glanced around. Ha. Nervous to out his pals. Fucking unbelievable. I turned for the cabin again, eager to be out of his sight, to have an epic cry and let the emotions explode before I actually thought of what to do. I really should have burned the eyeballs out of his head for lying, for *somehow* managing not to tell me about his membership in a fanatical, disgusting cult. They had destroyed the city with their bullshit antics, divided an already divided population, and set in motion the events that nearly took Shane from me. As far as I was concerned, his current status with the group meant nothing. Irrational? Maybe, but you would have to have been in the city, experienced the rising paranoia and discontent, to know what we felt. And Whelan had been part of it.

'They had guns.'

'How nice for them.'

Why was I even listening? He could concoct whatever story he wanted now and I would have had no way to prove him right or wrong.

'I met the others there, inside. None of us wanted to stay. It's the truth, Sadie. We thought it was crazy. Guns and food only go so far. It was a nuthouse. We left.'

'Right, but not before getting inked.'

Whelan's sharp, bitter laughter stopped me just before the cabin door.

'I can't exactly get it taken off,' he said wryly. 'I would if I could. It's not something I'm proud of.'

No more. The only place I wanted to be was somewhere he wasn't. He didn't try to stop me again.

'Don't do this. You're making a mistake, Sadie.'

'I already have.'

I didn't turn to look back at him, not when I knew I'd see those hideous tattoos on him. He had lied to us. They had all lied. Now we weren't just stranded on an island riddled with the undead and harboring some sort of psychotic murderer, but our fellow survivors were Rabbits. Maybe they had come here trying to establish another colony, their own little paradise they could flood with children they couldn't control or feed or care for. So what if they had left the Citadel? That didn't mean they had changed.

And I had just slept with one.

I was back outside, around the cabin and vomiting against the side of it in about ten seconds flat.

Andrea found me outside in the midst of rinsing my mouth out with seawater. Not the smartest move, but I wasn't going to waste our drinking water on what I planned to spit out anyway. She wore an uneasy frown that told me just about everything I needed to know. Her mouth was broadcasting loud and clear.

'No,' she said, shaking her head. 'Don't make a sad, make a happy!'

'You *knew*,' I said. Nate. Of course she would know. 'Does he have them too?'

'Just one,' Andrea replied.

'Oh, well, then that makes it all better.'

She sighed, fussing with the rat's nest on her head. Her floppy hat had been left behind in the cabin. 'I should have said something. It just . . . didn't seem like a big deal.'

'It is, Andrea. It is to me.'

'But you still like him, right? I mean, before you knew . . . It's not like it magically changes his personality.'

'I don't know what the fuck is going on around here, but I'm thinking I should just take my chances and *swim* to get away from it.' Of course that would involve Shane swimming too. Maybe he could hitch a ride on my back. I could steal the canoe . . .

Lightbulb! Torch . . . *whatever*. I could steal the canoe. I had flubbed it the first time, but now my feet were a bit better and I knew my way around the camp. Nobody would look twice at me wandering around at night. No . . . it was crazy. I had no idea how far the next island might be. We could see several in the distance, but you couldn't trust your eyes with that sort of thing. They might be a mile or two away, they might be much, much farther.

'I know that look,' Andrea muttered. 'What are you thinking?'

'I'm thinking you should leave me alone.'

'I'm fucking *sorry*, Sadie. You don't think you might be overreacting here?'

'Shut up, Andrea. I'm done being naïve.' I stripped, tossing my things onto the sand with the kind of impotent fury of a child throwing a tantrum. The water would be freezing, but I needed to get Whelan off of me. 'You can all just fuck right off as far as I'm concerned.'

'That's real compassionate of you,' she mumbled, shoving a binder around her hair. She flounced her hair and turned to go, marking her exit with a dramatic huff.

'Don't talk to me about compassion, you flake.'

'I hope you freeze to death!'

Half-starved people with emotions running high,

zombies closing in and a murderer on the loose just shouldn't talk to each other. They shouldn't do it. Right away I regretted provoking her, but the wound was raw.

It was foolishness to go in the water alone. I barely felt the cold, my temper running so hot it filled my veins with fire. With my back to the camp I scrubbed, hard, wishing I could get rid of Whelan altogether and knowing that I couldn't. But I could get away from him. I could escape. I could get away from them all.

TWENTY-ONE

'But where are we going?'

Winter. It was coming, unmistakable on the air now with its crisp, sharp forewarning. It would be on us any second. Shane shivered outside the cabin, flinching as I shoved yet another jacket over his head, shimmying it down around his shoulders until his arms popped out of the sleeve holes.

'You have to be quiet,' I whispered. The great escape was taking place in the middle of the night. I'm not proud of the fact that I may have stolen a few of Andrea's sleeping pills and crushed them into the baked beans. Nobody would be up for hours and they would doze right through our departure. They wouldn't know we had gone until they woke and found us missing, a few cans of food, paper-wrapped packets of fish and blankets gone too.

Saying goodbye wasn't an option, and I would miss Banana and Moritz. They really did seem like good people. The others . . . the others I couldn't accurately say, not anymore. How could I trust these people with my life, with Shane's life, when they were just as shifty as Carl? He had seemed nice, too, but he was also a liar. He had tried to murder me and take Shane, and I wasn't about to sit around and wait for something awful to happen. Nate and Andrea had been sleeping together for weeks – maybe that was all just part of the plan. Whelan had seduced me . . . I could be part of the plan too.

Creepy. It was way too creepy and not something I was willing to let Shane witness.

'We're not safe here,' I said, shouldering the bag with our things. I had taken Cassandra's bag, shoved our food, cantina, blankets and my drawings inside, and hoped to God the strap wouldn't bust. Just in case, I grabbed the bow, knowing it was too risky to creep into one of the other cabins and take a gun.

'I don't want to go,' Shane whispered, frowning. Little creases formed over his eyebrows.

'I know, sweetie, but it's time . . .'

He followed me down to the water. The paddles were easy to find, and though my hands shook with the cold, I knew there was no going back. Shane scrambled into the canoe while I unhooked it from the pilings. I tossed the bag in beside him and carefully scooted off the dock and into the rocking canoe. A pang started, doubts collecting and punishing me for being so rash, so selfish . . . No, not selfish, cautious. With just Shane to look after we might be able to scavenge enough food or maybe meet up with another band of survivors that didn't hail from the Land of Misfit fucking Toys. And we would be escaping the killer. We'd have to contend with zombies and finding food, but those things seemed manageable by comparison.

Sitting in the back position, I dipped the paddle carefully into the water. Nobody came running. Nothing in the camp stirred at all as I pushed us away from the dock. The canoe drifted out into deeper water, away from the shore and the pilings. Still in the shallows, the bottom of the boat scraped some rocks, making Shane jump.

'Everything's going to be fine,' I said quietly. 'It's our time to go.'

'What about Andrea?'

'She's smart, okay? She can look after herself.'

We both started to sniffle, the jacket pulled up under my nose becoming damp with snot and tears that came from the bite of the wintry wind. I started off on an alien route, traveling opposite the way Whelan had taken me to the southern camp. The tide was unexpectedly insistent, and paddling against it slowed us down considerably. I had tried to plan it so that we would have enough time to drift out of sight before dawn came and the camp awoke. So far, I hadn't seen the other side of the island and I decided it would be best to aim us toward other island chains, away from familiar sights that would make it more tempting to stay.

Shane picked silently at his mittens and looking at him there, his curls covered by a heavy knit cap with a yarn tassel, another prickle of guilt started in my gut. Almost everything we were wearing had been taken from Whelan's supply of winter clothes. The food and cantina were all his. The boat was his. Not the smoothest way to forget him – like there was enough vodka in the world for that – but if we found another pocket of civilization we could trade for new supplies and clothing. We could do this.

Paddling became the only way to stay warm. More doubts swirled and surfaced. What if we ran out of water before we could find another supply? What if the canoe was light enough for zombies to tip over from below? What if I fell asleep paddling? Was that even possible?

As the hours crawled by, Shane finally fell asleep, his chin tucked down against his chest as his breathing deepened. Fear or adrenaline kept me wide awake, and dawn arrived with a brilliant surge of purple across the horizon. We had made it around the first hump of the island, a geographical feature not mimicked on the other side. Traveling this route took longer than the way Whelan had showed me. There were more outcroppings to navigate, and more than once I heard the scrape of rocks along the underside of the canoe. A few birds started up their calls in the forest and with more light to see by I began to feel more confident. I stopped paddling, resting my arms and my sore hands. Shane mumbled something softly in his sleep. Tired but exhilarated, I watched the sun peek above the waterline, pink and orange bleeding in around the purple and lightening the scattered clouds.

I had never drawn or painted many landscapes, but that was one I wouldn't mind capturing on paper forever.

Now I paddled sporadically, keeping us on a course to follow the layout of the island's shore but still stay in deep enough waters. Every now and then I looked closely at the surface of the water, checking for any gruesome faces hovering below. But we were alone in the humbling quiet of the world waking up. I pulled the cantina out of Cassandra's bag, unscrewing the cap with my half-numb fingers and taking a frugal sip. There were still a few bloodstains on the carpet bag, unsettling but unavoidable. I'd have to remember to wash it when we had a chance.

We drifted in toward the shore and I dipped the paddle back in to keep us a safe distance away. As morning advanced we found ourselves near the middle of the island lengthwise. Mentally, I could imagine Arturo's boat on about the opposite side of the island from us. A slight curve inward marked a cove, water trickling down from what looked to be a stout waterfall. Above it, a little bridge hung over it, a fraying rope the only sign of any handrail. I went digging in the bag for the pencil and pad Banana had given me. We were floating along slowly enough that I could keep us idling. I wanted to draw it, I wanted, sentimentality be damned, to have one good memory of the island before we left it altogether.

In the bag, my glove caught on something, a piece of rope or ribbon. When I yanked it out I found a sort of key chain, a badge, with a nylon string to loop around the neck. It was a hospital badge, an old one, judging from the faded quality of the laminated paper. You know that feeling when, pre-Outbreak, you would walk down a street and a lamp overhead would suddenly go out? You feel like you're being watched, like something bigger and badder is happening around you than just a coincidence of you being there and the timer on the lamp engaging. Logically you know it's nothing but dread comes anyway, sliding around your neck like a cold, clammy hand.

The badge was stained with blood. I remembered seeing Cassandra for the first time, seeing those nurse's scrubs and wondering how someone trained to deal with gore and death had come to fall apart so completely. It began to come together, all of it, not quite a clear picture but more like a steamed shower curtain. Seattle Mental Health Coalition. The badge ID photo looked nothing like Cassandra. The woman in the picture was at least fifty, with graying, close-cropped pixie hair . . . and blood stained all over her badge.

And her scrubs.

I dug back into the carpetbag. A torn page had been folded up tightly at the bottom. The handwritten script had once been neat, done in sprawling cursive, but after water damage it took a lot of squinting and sounding out to make out the message.

Heart failure, stroke, lack of oxygen to the brain resulting in abnormal behavior . . .

Karen Garner had signed the bottom of the note. My mind raced ahead, passing go, jumping straight to terror. No . . . It was just my paranoia. Maybe Cassandra had the badge because Karen Garner, nurse practitioner, was a close friend she wanted to remember. I found the pencil and the pad. Sketching would help that cold, itchy feeling go away . . . because it was nothing, a coincidence, and dwelling on it would only make me feel even guiltier for leaving the others and striking out with Shane . . .

When I looked back up at the picturesque bridge and waterfall, I found a figure perched there on the bridge, watching me. At that distance, I wouldn't have recognized her but for her size and the bright pink T, torn but still recognizable. Little Teresa. Very much not alive and very much not alone. Other figures moved among the trees, walking too noisily to be animals. I waited, looked closer, demanded that my heart stop trying so hard to shatter my rib cage. Beyond the bridge, up a ways, hunched over the disappearing line of the waterfall's source, was that fucking blue house. A light flickered in the back window.

After sketching for too long I used to get these hard cramps in my fingers. Sometimes they wouldn't go away for minutes at a time, and I would sit there, thinking of what might happen if my fingers never stopped hurting, if they were twisted into a weird little claw for the rest of my life. But the pain always eased and I'd shake out my hand and go back to work. But this creeping feeling wasn't going away. In fact it spread outward, a cramp that paralyzed my entire body. And so horrified, I watched Teresa turn, losing interest in what she could not immediately reach or eat. She lurched across the bridge, north, toward the camp, and as more undead appeared on the bridge, they followed in generally the same direction.

I turned us around with much cursing and splashing. If I paddled hard I could reach the camp before the horde. But my plan to travel this route had been genius in one way, idiotic in another. If we had continued on our way south then the tide would have buoyed us right along. Now the current was stronger, pushing at us, nosing the boat back toward the south. But I couldn't just let Andrea and the others die. They would still be asleep . . . asleep and hard to wake up because of my fucking sleeping pills.

Fuck.

Shane woke soon after, probably roused by the furious thrashing of my paddle against the waves.

'We have to go back,' I said furiously, sweating in the chill. 'Help me paddle, Shane.'

God love 'im, he did, at once and without question.

'Eyes straight ahead,' I whispered. If he looked at the shore he would see the trees shaking, branches breaking and twisting as the undead moved through the forest. They were outpacing us, not by much, but enough that my hopes began to fade. I had fucked them over. Maybe Whelan, Banana and Nate were all Rabbits, maybe they were somehow responsible for all the shit that happened on the island, but somehow I just couldn't see it. I had been wrong about

Cassandra, wrong about Noah, and now I was sure I was wrong about this too.

I had overreacted, fled, and now they were all going to suffer because of me.

With my heart sinking, I watched the horde move ahead, leaving us behind. We didn't stop, didn't pause, but as the minutes became an hour and then two, I knew we had lost the race.

The beach looked deserted, almost peaceful, when we finally returned.

A weird popping had started in my elbow from all the paddling, but I ignored it, pushing us hard and fast up onto the sand, beaching us and hopping out even as the canoe came to a stop. I told Shane to follow, to keep up. At first I thought we had managed to beat the undead somehow, but no, blood, just hints of it at first, splattered on the sand near the fire pit, then more of it. I checked the cabins. They were empty and the guns were gone. That made me think that maybe the group had held the zombies off and then gave pursuit in the forest, but then I heard the moaning. It was faint but growing louder.

'Stay back,' I told Shane.

'But you just said . . .'

'I know what I said. Just stay here in the open where I can see you.'

There was nothing for defense so I grabbed one of the shovels leaning against our former cabin. I headed toward the tree line, glimpsing a figure not far from the edge of the forest. It was a man, tall, bloodied, still dressed in tweed. Moritz.

'What happened?' His injuries looked manageable until I noticed the amazing amount of blood pooled around the end of his right sleeve. Not a glancing blow, that. And then there was the mark – known now to all – that had torn open his slender neck. Teeth.

A line of blood raced down from the edge his mouth. He coughed and more of it came up.

'You're turning.'

He nodded, a milky haze obscuring the sparkle in his eyes. Oh, God, I promised myself I didn't care about these people. I promised. He looked so helpless, flailing there, half eaten, his mortality sinking away to the dark place where it would become unnatural rebirth.

'The others?'

'Forest.' Another fountain of blood gushed over the side of his mouth. His left hand began to move and I backed up, instinctively, thinking he had already fully changed. But no, he dug into his trouser pocket, pressing a key, slippery with blood, into my hands.

'What is it?' I asked, staring down at it in bewilderment.

'Vault,' he grunted. He blinked. When his eyelids slid back up his pupils seemed to have spread like a broken yolk. 'Paintings.'

'I'll take care of them.'

If I ever get off this godforsaken island.

Moritz nodded. I don't know why, but I reached into his coat. The pocket inside was lightly padded and when I slid my fingers along the edge I felt what I was searching for. I took it out, showed it to him. He seemed to smile. Then his eyes slid to the shovel. A plea. If I didn't . . . But I would have to. Friends don't let friends suffer.

'Shane,' I said, standing. 'Turn around and cover your ears.'

I waited until he had, seconds inexorably slowing to

agonizing minutes. Looking back at Moritz, his one hand had begun to convulse, as if he were physically fighting the urge to lash out for my ankle. I'd never done this before, send off a neighbor, someone with a face I knew and liked. I had seen my friends taken, we all had, watched them disappear into a sea of snarling, snapping faces . . . but Moritz was still smiling calmly, as if waiting for a bus and daydreaming, as if catching sight of an old friend.

The shovel went up, the shovel went down. It was easier than I expected – not the feeling of course, but the act itself. You can't trust your hands after that. You have to just let them shake for a second. I looked away as soon as it was done, sickened and heartbroken. I glanced at the picture – there was Moritz, in a better time, his arms around a petite woman with crazy, cropped hair and a hooded sweatshirt, a tall, bearded man on the other side. They were all smiling, warm.

What would she do? I wondered. What would Allison do?

I tucked the Polaroid into my back pocket. She wouldn't stand still. She wouldn't turn her back on the people she had already left once.

'Shane,' I called, shouldering the shovel. 'Come with me.'

TWENTY-TWO

It was the last time, I promised myself, that I would go into that horrible forest with its grabby bushes and whistling branches and birds that watched you like they were all in on a grand plan. I hated being there, hated taking Shane there, but running was not an option now. Trying to be his protector, stumbling through parenthood, meant setting an example. We wouldn't run. We wouldn't leave our friends behind when we had a chance to save them. Either I would come back out and stay out, or it would snatch me and hold onto me forever. The fact that Shane would be with me when that happened . . . But what could I do?

The forest was, unsurprisingly, free of the undead. They were where the action was and Shane and I discovered the unlucky hot spot almost immediately. I hardly felt the brambles tugging at my legs or the scratchy branches swiping for my face. I heard the gunfire up ahead and kept a steady, determined pace.

When the shots stopped I hurried us along. It's unsettling in the worst way, when gunfire becomes something you actually want to hear. Andrea, Banana, Nate, Stefano, Whelan . . . I had to prepare myself. There was no telling what I would find once I reached the house and no way to predict how best to shield Shane. The others could be like

Moritz, or they might be beyond even the point of draining humanity.

'Shane,' I whispered, squeezing his hand. 'You have to do exactly what I tell you.'

'Okay. What happened to Moritz? Why was his head all funny?'

'He was going to turn into one of them, Shane.' I swallowed, hard, feeling it catch like a thistle in my throat. 'That's what you have to do for friends when they're bitten.'

'Will you do that to me, Sadie?'

'No, sweetheart,' I said. 'That won't happen because I won't let them near you.'

I wanted it to be true. I wanted it to be true so badly I even believed it.

Gunpowder and a vaporous fog lingered in the air when we stepped out into the house's clearing. It was a war zone. A few undead corpses littered the ground, all of them unfamiliar bodies and faces. I heard voices from inside the house, angry ones raised to the point of arguing. At least there was a back and forth. *Someone* was still alive. The footprints in the dirt were too scattered and random to read. Not that I was some amazing tracker, but there wasn't even a clear indication of direction. Just mayhem. Lots and lots of mayhem.

Now I was stuck. Taking Shane inside was dangerous, but I couldn't risk leaving him alone, either. For better or worse I wanted to keep him in my sights.

'We're going into that house, Shane. I know it's scary but we have to stick together.'

He nodded, holding tighter to my hand.

I kicked the bodies and limbs out of the way for him and together we shuffled across the bloodstained clearing to the porch. It was rickety, creaking with even the gentlest footsteps. We may as well have rung the doorbell. The voices inside quieted. Maybe I was taking us directly into a trap. Decision time. Yes or no. Forward or backward. We could still turn back . . . but no, Moritz had said 'forest.' This was the end of the line.

With one nudge, the door flew open and Shane and I tumbled inside. The hinges had almost rotted away completely. I raised the shovel, but the front room was empty, messy, smelling like ass, but empty. The house stood in complete disarray, the beachy wood floors dirtied with a spray of sand, mud and stains that looked suspiciously like blood. Worse, some of the stains had a pattern, form. Drawings. I could make out stick figures all in a jumbled row, their rudimentary line and circle bodies drawn in blood. A light, uneven and flickering, like a lantern, glowed from the open doorway to our left. This was insane, I didn't even have a gun – we could be jumped the second we stepped through that portal. Then I heard a low, pained voice and my heart shuddered, expanding so rapidly it squeezed the air out of my lungs.

'Banana?' It was Whelan. He sounded awful.

'Be quiet.'

Oh, fuck me. I knew that voice. Part of me knew it was coming and had since the canoe, but hearing and knowing just weren't the same. A prickle of fear started at the back of my neck, skipping down over my spine a second later.

Motioning for Shane to stay behind me, I inched slowly, carefully into the doorway, the shovel raised high over my head.

'Banana?' Whelan called again, just before I made it into the room.

'It's me,' I said, darting inside. 'It's Sadie.'

His face, bruised, battered, but still lovely, fell.

'Oh, God, Sadie, no! Get out of here, now.'

I wish I had words.

Whelan was there, stripped to his jeans, rope wound several times tightly around his chest and arms, keeping him secured to a rusted metal chair. A bright bruise purpled his right eye, a cut there congealing. The rabbit tattoo on his left upper arm was missing, a raw, skinned patch still slowly trickling blood down over the ropes and onto the floor.

My confidence turned quickly to despair and then horror as I saw the creature chained to the wall not far from Whelan. Teresa, her hair hanging on in stringy chunks, an iron chain looped around her neck like a leash. She was chewing on something. Either I was seeing things and the fear was fucking with my mind, or she was chewing on a decorated piece of human flesh.

And close by . . .

'Cassandra.' My voice shook.

The room reeked of death. It made you want to choke on your own breath.

'You came back,' Cassandra said brightly. A knife dangled from her left hand, no doubt the same one used to skin Whelan's arm. She wasn't wearing Danielle's hot pink top. Instead, Whelan's T hung loose and boxy on her bony shoulders. Whelan was shaking his head, his mouth tightly grimaced with pain. He was right. I should go, take Shane as far away from there as I could, but I wasn't about to let her skin the rest of him and feed it to Teresa.

Behind me, Shane let out a tiny whimper.

'Heart failure,' I whispered. 'Your heart stopped, didn't it?'

Cassandra tilted her head to the side, her red curls rippling down onto her shoulder. I could barely look at her wild eyes, terrified she would hypnotize me with her crazy.

'How'd you know that?'

'It's not important, Cassandra. For how long?'

'I was legally dead for two minutes.'

I looked at Whelan, seeing the exact moment when it hit him too.

'She's already died once,' I told him in a whisper. 'They can't sense her.'

As if to illustrate, Cassandra reached out and brushed her fingers down Teresa's cheek affectionately. The undead little girl had no reaction beyond a curious groan.

'She likes pictures,' Cassandra murmured fondly, giggling. 'So I gave her one of Whelan's.'

My stomach lurched.

I had to get her away from Whelan. That knife was too close to his neck for my liking, well within striking distance. Cutting a throat didn't take much skill or accuracy. If I tried to bash her brains in now she would have his neck opened before I made it halfway across the room. 'Where are the others, Cassandra?'

'Stefano and Danielle are out back,' Cassandra replied with a shrug. 'I'm sure Moritz will be along soon.'

'I— *What?*'

'It's too bad about Noah and Isabella. They can't be part of our family now.'

Family? Good Lord.

'Cassandra . . .' What exactly does one say to someone so mind-bendingly insane? Noises from outside. Commotion. She had only mentioned Stefano and Danielle, maybe that meant Banana, Nate and Andrea were still safely out of her clutches. It wasn't over. I just had to remember that. 'You can stop this now. No one else has to get hurt.'

Like that *ever* worked in the movies. Cassandra laughed. Hell, it was worth a try.

'What do you want, Cassandra?'

'We can be a *family*, Sadie, all of us. All of us forever.' She heaved a tragic sighed. 'I tried to explain it to Teresa and Isabella but they just wouldn't listen.'

Whelan was trying to signal me, tell me something. His eyes flicked to Shane over and over again.

'So what?' I asked, stalling, trying to kick the gears in my head into overdrive. We needed a way out, a diversion, anything at all to give us time. 'You imprinted on us like a baby duck?'

'I had a family once,' Cassandra replied sadly. 'I'm going to have one again.'

'Shane,' I whispered, nudging him with my boot. '*Run*. Run outside and find Andrea.'

'Don't do that, Shane,' Cassandra shouted, waving the knife in the air. But Shane ignored her, taking off like a shot, surprisingly agile in his puffy layered jackets. Cassandra darted forward, hooking the knife around Whelan's head and holding it in front of his neck. He flinched, a thin trickle of blood racing down the column of his throat.

'Who's first?' Cassandra asked. She made a soft, thoughtful sound, twisting her head to look at Teresa. The little girl had completely devoured Whelan's tattoo.

'Sadie,' Whelan said hoarsely. More noise from the outside, most of it coming from the window behind me, but nothing I could make out. The gallons of blood thundering in my ears didn't help. Whelan's Adam's apple dipped perilously behind the knife. 'They're soft . . . soft around the neck . . .'

The neck? I wasn't exactly armed for a headshot and, hello, had he forgotten about the knife under his chin?

'You first, I think.' Cassandra said, clamping a hand down on Whelan's shoulder. 'You'll be better company once you stop talking. You'll be the daddy. Teresa needs a daddy.'

She pulled the knife away, showing it to me as she shuffled toward the end of Teresa's chain, never putting her back to us. A shovel . . . I just *had* to bring a fucking shovel to a knife fight.

'Now,' Whelan said, risking one last try. 'Now. The *neck*.'

Frantic, I did the first thing that came to mind. I wound up, hoping my sweaty hand would keep a decent grip, and let 'er rip. I think hurl is the right word, though there was really no technique to it. The shovel flew out of my hand like a javelin, nailing poor little Teresa in the throat. It didn't quite sever her head, but it was enough to send Cassandra into a panicked flurry. She shrieked and whirled on Whelan, slashing at him with the knife. He threw his body weight to the side, hitting the ground with his injured arm and a short grunt of pain. But he was quick to toss his weight back the other way, rolling onto his and the chair's back. He Van Damme kicked with both legs, catching Cassandra square in the stomach. She coughed, sputtered, clutching her gut as she reeled back against the far wall.

I saw the knife fall as if time had stopped altogether, watching it drop down toward Whelan's face.

He dodged to the side at the last second, the blade twanging as it stuck in the floorboards beside his cheek.

Gunfire from outside, shouts, screams . . . Cassandra recovered from Whelan's kick, spinning and disappearing out the doorway to her left. I darted forward, reaching the shovel first and the knife second.

'Go after her,' Whelan grunted, struggling with his bonds.

'Not without you.'

'Nice toss, by the way.'

'*Lucky* toss. I think you mean lucky . . .'

The house was suddenly filled with dragging footfalls and the droning song of the undead. I heard the back door bang on its hinges, the smell of decay preceding the zombies that Cassandra had let in through the back.

'Faster,' Whelan whispered as I sawed at the ropes. '*Much* faster . . .'

Even with the ropes off they were on us too quickly. The first one in the door almost made me forget to breathe. It was Danielle, her upper body little more than a ragged, oozing cavity. Someone had tried to put her shirt back on but it was only hanging on halfway, looped over her neck like a cowl.

'Holy shit,' Whelan hissed, backing up on the floor like a crab.

I stayed in a defensive crouch, jabbing at her with the shovel. Whelan had no useful range with the knife, and more flooded in behind Danielle. Teresa thrashed against the wall, her head hanging on by a few stringy sinews, her chain keeping her from joining the action. The smell of death, of rot, was overpowering as more and more creatures poured into the room. The shovel wasn't enough, only long enough to keep them temporarily at bay.

'I'm sorry, Whelan,' I murmured behind a sudden sob.

'Don't cry, babe. Not yet.'

'I can't . . . h-help it . . . the *smell*.'

He laughed. It was sort of sweet, I thought, that we'd at least go down giggling madly. Not sweet, however, was the thought of leaving Shane to fend for himself. This wasn't over. Not nearly.

I felt his breath on my neck and then a kiss beneath my jaw. 'Friends?'

'Friends.'

The glass window above and behind us imploded from gunfire, glass raining down in sparkling shards. I tossed myself over Whelan, shielding his face from the glass. Most of it fell harmlessly onto my thick jacket; my leg wasn't quite so lucky. The pain was intense and sudden, spearing up from my ankle. One of the bigger shards had fallen there and stuck. Blood brightened in a lobed flower from where the glass stuck out of my leg at a ninety-degree angle. I peered out from behind my arm, watching as Danielle rocked backward, rifle fire hitting her skull, shattering the bone and zipping through to the creature behind her.

'Get your asses out of there!' Banana yelled.

'My leg,' I muttered. 'I don't know how bad . . .'

Whelan leapt to his feet, bending down and scooping me into his arms before sprinting for the front door. 'Oh, walk it off,' he mumbled, and I laughed, sniffling. Banana held the zombies back while we dashed out onto the porch. Shane had crouched down at Banana's feet, covering his ears and scowling as she fired into the house.

'Andrea and Nate?' I asked, breathless.

I heard Whelan make a little grunt in his throat and then my leg erupted with another burst of pain. He had pulled the shard out of my leg.

'They're looking for a way off this fucking place,'

Banana yelled back. She had pulled down her bandana over her ears to muffle the noise.

Whelan set me down, but only briefly, ripping off a strip of the thermal shirt below my jacket. He looped it around my leg and pulled, making a quick tourniquet.

'Too tight,' I murmured dizzily.

'That's the point.'

'You know the way back to your old boat?' Banana stopped firing, yanking Shane to his feet.

'Arturo's? It's beached,' I replied. Whelan tossed me back up into the cradle of his arms. 'It'll never get us out of here.'

'You got a better idea, baby cakes?' Banana replied.

Good point.

'I think I can get us there.'

'Show us the way,' Whelan added, shifting me into a more comfortable position.

'Shane,' I said, peering down at him as he sidled up to Whelan's shin. 'Stay close. You've got to stay close. Hold onto us, okay?'

He nodded. His chin quivered but he was trying to be strong. He was a fighter, and I was confident he had learned *that* from me.

We were no longer alone in the clearing. The trees seemed to come alive, the branches shivering and dancing as the undead dragged themselves out from behind the house and the surrounding woods. Those that Banana hadn't managed to pick off in the house filtered out from the front door.

'I'll cover us,' she said, waving. 'Haul ass.'

'Shane, can you keep up?' Whelan asked, turning and striding toward the opposite side of the clearing.

'Yes.'

'Okay. You holler if we're going too fast, understand?'

'Yes.'

Shane grabbed onto Whelan's belt loops. Banana kept pace with us, popping off a few rounds every few feet to stop the closest zombies. Their stench and their howling followed. One voice was loudest, a human voice, screeching and wailing as we reached the other side of the clearing and ducked into the cover of trees.

'I swore,' I said softly, 'to never end up in your arms like this again.'

Whelan laughed, pressing his nose into my temple. 'Admit it – you don't mind.'

'Not really, no.'

That's one small step for feminism . . .

Fuck it. I really *didn't* mind, not when we were struggling to outrun our deaths.

We wove through the trees, mindful of the poky under-brush and swooping branches. This was much less traveled than the sort of path between the camp and the blue house.

'What about Cassandra?' Banana asked. A *rat-cla-tac* of rifle fire came close on the heels of her question. Shane ran as hard as his legs would carry him, clutching Whelan's belt loops.

'She's ill,' I said. 'Let her have her zombie paradise.'

'You serious? After everything she did?' Banana stopped, though Whelan didn't seem to notice.

'We can't go back, not now. Let's just get out of here.'

'Sadie . . .'

'Listen, Banana.' I dug around in my back pocket, risking an uncomfortable fall to find the crusty key I had been given. I held it up until Banana began to walk again, trotting to catch up and see it. Shane gazed up from where he held onto Whelan's belt. 'Moritz gave me this. It's the key to his vault in Seattle. I want to see what's in it. I don't want to die here.'

'Fuck,' Banana murmured, whirling to watch our retreat. A spray of glossy blond curls fell free of her bandana. 'I liked that mousy little dude.'

'So did I.'

'I hate to break up the Kodak moment,' Whelan mumbled, 'but we've got company up ahead.'

Banana breezed by, the shoulder of her sweatshirt slipping down as she lifted a low-hanging bough to survey the way forward. The leaves rattled; moaning that was almost certainly not Andrea and Nate drifting toward us from the direction of the water.

'Unless those two stopped for some afternoon delight . . .'

'No, Whelan,' I pointed. Wind and tide had pushed the ketch off the sand bar. So that was one thing going our way. There was the boat, its mast bobbing as it idled in the cove – a flash of blue, the water, and a shifting along the sand. Then gunfire – not ours, but Nate's. 'We're almost there,' I added softly, sadly.

'Almost there,' Banana said, 'and surrounded.'

Whelan pushed forward, through the trees, his arms squeezing around me more tightly as if in preparation for the trouble ahead. We burst through the edge of the forest, stumbling out into an embankment of pebbly sand that led down a steep hill to the shore. The tide was high enough to cover most of the sand at the bottom of the embankment, allowing Arturo's Ketch to find water. I shielded my eyes from the sun, staring at the Ketch, at Nate and Andrea on board and the ring of undead closing in on them. A few had peeled off, trying to climb up the embankment toward us. They clamored at roots and rocks, but none had actually managed to find their way up the hill.

'What now?' Banana asked, firing into the trees behind us. The groaning from that direction was growing disconcertingly near. My leg throbbed, numb now from the knee down.

'Go!' Whelan shouted, waving one hand when Nate and Andrea looked up at us. 'Start out!'

'What are you doing? There are too many of them in the water.' Not that I had a better plan.

Even more undead crept up out of the water, foam streaming down off of their pale flesh and gleaming skulls as they alternately turned toward the boat in the shallows or us.

'Go!'

The Ketch teetered, the hull looking scratched and battered in places. The outboard motor sputtered, caught. Fuck. If they couldn't get the motor going then there would be no possible way to get out of the cove – the mast was crooked, and might not fly a sail. The motor whirred again, clicking like an empty gun.

'Come on,' Whelan mumbled, glancing nervously over his shoulder. 'We only get one chance at this . . .'

'They're here,' Banana warned, firing into the trees again.

The motor purred to life, a cheer going up on the boat and on the embankment.

Whelan began gesturing to the north. On board, Nate and Andrea seemed to conference, then she went to steer the motor, guiding them down the beach while Nate continued firing at the undead from the deck.

'Here we go,' Whelan said, veering right and down the embankment. 'Hold them off as best you can, Nan.' He knelt carefully, turning his back to Shane. 'Hop on, bud.'

The way down was almost too quick to be nauseating, which was fortunate, because if Whelan had given me even the tiniest hint of what he was about to do, I probably would have choked him out rather than endure it.

He sprinted against the tree line and then toward the water, careening down the hill to the shore. It wasn't as steep as the embankment, but it was steep enough to give me a heart attack. We gathered speed, Banana behind us, her gun silenced for the moment as she and Whelan concentrated on not plummeting straight into a zombie.

Which isn't an exaggeration. We hit the bottom of the hill, and a zombie. Whelan kicked it in the jaw as it tried to scamper up out of the surf. Banana finished it off with a spray of bullets to the face. I listened to her change out the clip behind us as Whelan jogged down the beach, following the Ketch as it slowly slid south.

'We're going to swim, aren't we?' I asked.

'It's going to sting your leg like hell,' he warned.

'I can do it.'

The undead that had followed us from the house reached the embankment. They slid willy-nilly down the hill, some of them losing their footing and tumbling like bike wheels down into the water. A few were so mangled by the fall that they simply stayed put, twitching and groaning. The others were luckier, joining their brethren down on the beach.

'Start swimming,' Banana grunted, slamming a fresh clip

home. 'I'll give you a head start.'

'You're coming with us,' Whelan replied curtly, wading out into the water.

'I know that, dummy. Don't you think I know that?'

Wet, floating, I started to paddle, ignoring the persistent throb in my leg and the burning of the saltwater as it soaked the bandage and the fresh wound below. Whelan couldn't have felt any better, his throat nicked and his arm slashed. I said nothing, fighting the little squeaks of agony that died in my throat on each stroke. Whelan swam closer, Shane on his back, and brushed a kiss across my cheekbone.

'Could be worse,' he said breathlessly. 'Could be sea urchins.'

The boat drifted, less than half a mile from shore. It looked like an ungodly mess, that boat, but it was *our* ungodly mess and, more importantly, our one shot at escaping. Nate seemed to be watching us through the scope of the rifle, Andrea poised at the aft beside the motor.

Behind us, the rifle fire came in a constant, deafening stream. Banana taunted the undead as she mowed them down, laughing like some crazed Amazonian war goddess as she poured bullets into them. Each stroke began to hurt, the canoe paddling catching up to me, the lack of food catching up to me . . . Shit, damn near everything catching up to me. Whelan broke out ahead of me, a stronger swimmer even with Shane on his back.

'We're almost there, Sadie,' Shane called.

'Thanks, little man.'

But I was falling behind. And Banana wasn't swimming yet. I made the mistake of looking back over my shoulder. She was swarmed. I could see the glint of her hair and the bright fabric of her bandana, but the zombies in the water were outflanking her, and the horde closed in around her, an unbroken ring.

'Whelan,' I sputtered, splashing harder as I tried to keep up. My arms were failing, my leg felt like it had been doused in kerosene and thrust into a fire.

'Look at the boat,' he said. 'Think of Shane. That's all you can do.'

Banana's cries grew sharper, different, and then the gunfire halted abruptly. I didn't have to look over my shoulder again to know they were coming for us now.

No matter how hard I pushed myself, I just kept falling farther and farther behind. Whelan circled back, swimming up beside me, his face bright red and his hair salt-plastered to his face as he looped an arm around my waist. He began swimming with one arm, dragging us through the water in quick bursts.

'I can hear them,' I whispered, trying to find that last store of energy. I had to have something left . . . I only had to make it to the boat and we were getting closer, closer . . .

Andrea screamed, 'Come on, come on!' I swam to the rhythm of it. Just a few more strokes, just a dozen or so kicks and all three of us would make it. Banana had gone down for us. Moritz had gone down. Everyone was gone, but the island wasn't going to take me too.

Something was around my ankle, pulling and jerking. I slipped right out of Whelan's grasp, yanked backward and then down. I felt the bite of too-hard fingers, *bones*, and kicked with my other leg. Water rushed in, filling my mouth, the sudden agitation turning the space around me all to tiny, bright bubbles. I kicked, felt flesh beneath my heel, kicked again. But I was tired, exhausted and sore and in pain, the swim had sapped me to the bone, and it didn't seem to matter that I was kicking the thing over and over again in the head, it just wouldn't let go.

And I was going down with it, sinking, and everything was turning to blue.

TWENTY-THREE

In the swirling black you hear a sound, a zip. It's hope and a promise and it's coming for you.

The zip breaks the hold death has on you. It's quiet and you almost don't hear it . . . but there it is again and suddenly, inexplicably, you're free. And you'd fight back if you could, if there was anything left, but you're tired and you don't know why. Then you're floating, flying almost, and things that were blue and then black are white, too bright, *painful*.

You think of all the things you didn't do, all the times you told Shane no, you cannot go down to the shore to collect shells. And you regret it. You regret not showing him more, teaching him more, making him smile as much as humanly possible.

Then you're flat on your back, choking on what feels like a gallon of seawater and four sad faces are staring down at you. No, it's not your funeral, but it is fucking embarrassing.

'Oh, my God, she's alive.'

'Surprise.' *Ow*. It did not feel good to talk. Or think.

When I blinked, Nate was there, grinning, a rifle braced in his hand. I could hear the hum of a motor and the quiet splashing of the water as the blades whipped it into a frenzy. Shane rocketed into my arms, there and warm and *wonderful*. We had made it, maybe not to the end, but we were free of the island and still together.

'You're okay,' he whispered, squeezing my neck.

'Couldn't leave you, bud.'

Nate peered over Shane's shoulder, smirking.

'Nice shot, by the way,' I said to him, shutting my eyes against the sunlight.

'*Lucky* shot,' Whelan corrected gently. 'I think you mean lucky shot.'

I grinned. 'That too.'

It took a few minutes before I was ready to let go of Shane, but then Andrea helped me gradually into the cockpit. She pulled off my soaked clothes and used her own sweater to dry me off.

'You should've seen it, man,' she said as she patted my shoulders. 'You guys are, like, two feet away and then wham, you're gone! I almost shit my fucking pants. Whelan dove down about five times and then Nate was just all, "Get outta there! I'm gonna shoot!" Truly epic.'

'Sad I missed it.'

She went quiet then, letting me redress in one of Nate's discarded layers and a men's pair of thermal underwear. It all smelled like campfire smoke. Andrea laid out my wet clothes on the deck to dry, turning back with a thundercloud frown and her arms snapped rigidly over her chest.

'You left us,' she said. 'You *drugged* us. With *my* drugs.'

'I know. I'm sorry about that. I just . . . lost it. Everything was closing in. I didn't know what else to do.'

Andrea nodded satisfied. 'See what I did there? I forgave you. You should try it sometime – it's a neat feeling.'

'I know. I should've listened to you.'

'Naturally.'

'And I'm not mad about the Rabbit thing. I wish you had told me but . . . it doesn't matter now. It probably shouldn't have mattered then.'

Andrea nodded. In the fray she had lost her hat and her messy brown waves tumbled around her face as she looked me up and down, satisfied with her work, and turned to go.

'That magical pill bag of yours didn't happen to survive, did it?'

'Afraid not, sailor.'

'Figures.'

Laughing, she had one last pat for my shoulder and then she was hopping out of the cockpit, whistling merrily across the deck to where Nate was keeping a careful eye on the motor. Shane sat beside him, listening raptly while Nate described the finer points of boat mechanics. I'm not sure I could have felt luckier at that moment – if I were Shane's age and had just narrowly escaped about five different ways of dying, I certainly wouldn't be calmly listening to a lecture on boat propellers. I'd be a sobbing mess, inconsolable. Shane glanced in my direction and waved, looking like an ant hill with a head in one of Nate's huge, dry sweaters.

'Hey.' Whelan dropped down beside me. He had changed, too, wearing a pair of thermals that looked a lot like mine, though they fit him considerably better, and a ratty T-shirt with one sleeve. The missing sleeve had been appropriated for a new bandage, one that was tied tightly around his wound.

'So are we even or do I owe you a rescue now?' I asked.

He smiled. It had only been a day but I had seriously missed that dimple.

'We're square, but you might owe Nate one.'

I nodded. It wasn't awkward, just . . . frightening. I felt like there were a million different apologies I needed to make. Then I remembered that moment in the house, zombies coming at us, overtaking us, and the weird half-peace that had descended. Maybe apologies weren't what he wanted. I know I was sick of hearing them.

'Whelan . . . how did she capture you?' A big fella like Whelan didn't seem like the type to be taken down by one person with a knife.

'I woke up, saw you were gone and just . . . took off like an idiot into the woods.'

He leaned against the edge of the cockpit, staring out over my head toward the water. A deep, bright blush crept over his cheeks as I asked, 'You didn't notice the canoe?'

'For your information I wasn't exactly in my right mind. You two were gone and my first thought was: house. So I went. The others tried to follow but there were tons of 'em in the trees. Moritz went down, then Stef. When I finally made it to the house I saw Cassandra there . . . I just didn't put it together. I thought she had survived somehow . . .'

'I figured it out on the canoe,' I said. 'I took her bag to store my stuff and . . . I found some crazy shit in it. Her nurse's note, a badge . . . I think she must have killed her nurse, stolen her identity and escaped from a hospital. She was dead for two minutes . . . that can't be good for your brain. Or maybe it was something else. Maybe The Outbreak was too much for her.'

'And you thought I was cuckoo for Cocoa Puffs.'

'So what then?' I asked, reaching for his hand. He lifted it, kissed my knuckles. Hm. Maybe I was cuckoo for Cocoa Puffs . . . or just him.

'She got me on the head with a rock.' He pointed to the bruise on his eye with his free hand. Chuckling, he murmured, 'I don't know how she manhandled me into that chair, but given how sore my ass feels, I'd say it involved a lot of dragging. She woke me up with another nice thump on the melon and started rambling about this family she wanted us to be . . . I couldn't believe you could actually pack that much nuts into one person.'

'This is . . .' The salt on my cheeks was about to be refreshed. 'If I hadn't left . . .'

'I can't blame you. I didn't. I don't.' Whelan wiped at the trails burning down my cheeks. 'I mean, yes,' he went on, relentless, 'I was pissed, but I get it. I shouldn't have lied to you.' We kissed, just a short one, but it made the tears slow a bit. 'And hey, look on the bright side, cuckoo Cassandra took care of one of my tats.'

'Too bad she didn't get 'em both.'

Whelan winced. 'Ooh, *ouchies*. No, it's good she didn't. I have plans for that one.'

'What sort of plans?'

'Well, you being an artist and all, I thought maybe you could come up with something to cover it. We get back to civilization and make it into something new. How does that sound?'

Do I need to write down the definition of *disarming* again? No. Didn't think so.

'I approve of this idea.'

'Yeah?' O dimple of ultimate destruction, you will be the death of me.

'Yeah.'

'Maybe a spiky little sea urchin,' he mused, bumping his hip against mine.

'I was thinking more along the lines of Curious George. He could be beating the tar outta that bunny.'

Whelan laughed and it would've hurt my ears except it made me feel good all over. All the chuckling drew looks from the others. Shane watched us, not smiling, not frowning, just his usual observant self. I didn't believe in heaven – it's hard to when you pretty much live in a physical hell – but if it was real and my sister was watching me, I wanted to think she would be proud. Shane was going to be a lucky kid, not one or two parents, but four. I wasn't sure where we were going, but wherever it was, we were going to look out for each other. Back to Seattle or to somewhere else to wait out the storm, he was going to get a better childhood. I promised that to him silently, and maybe later I would make it official and say it aloud. We would need to rustle up a jump rope for him, Pop Rocks, a bicycle, a puppy – all the good stuff that made the fear worth surviving.

'So where to?' Whelan asked, looking out again at the blue, blue water surrounding us.

'That's a good question.' I started up the short stairs to the deck, intent on asking Andrea and Nate where they thought we should go. A big, warm hand wrapped around my wrist, tugging. I looked back, felt a tiny internal gasp, like a sigh or a hiccup but nicer. I had a feeling that would be happening just about every time Whelan gave me that look.

'Yellow hat,' he said.

'Sorry?'

'You're my yellow hat.'

'Thanks,' I said, starting back up the stairs. 'I love you too.'

It had been almost a year since receiving the key. Maybe the vault would already be empty, looted or moved. But I had to know. *We* had to know.

'What are you waiting for?'

Beneath a wild mop of curling hair, Shane stared up at me, fidgeting.

'I just don't want you to get your hopes up too high,' I said. The key felt inordinately heavy in my hand. I brushed at the thick layer of dust that had settled over the door. It looked like nobody had entered the lower levels of the bank for months, maybe not since Moritz had been there. Like an ancient, undisturbed tomb, the narrow halls lay under an almost snowy coating of grime. Finding the place untouched lit a warm hope in my chest. Nobody had been down here in a long, long time, and I had the cobwebs in my hair to prove it.

'It might not even be the right bank,' I added softly.

'Only one way to find out.'

Behind me, Whelan waited, tapping his boot toe impatiently on the linoleum. Shane mimicked him, and the combined force of their anticipation pushed me forward, toward the door. The key fit into the lock with a low, rusty squeak. It was a regular door, retro, not the round, max security ones you always see in comic book movies. With electricity spotty at best, it would have been too risky to use one of the electronically sealed vaults. Nobody wanted to sit around twiddling their thumbs, waiting for a generator, or worse – until the grid came up – to check on their cache.

'Holy shit,' I murmured, my breath ruffling the streaky cobwebs swinging in front of the door. 'I feel like Indiana Jones.'

'Indiana Jones would open the damn door,' Whelan whispered.

'Yeah,' Shane added haughtily.

'Do I have to separate you two?' The key turned, grinding, but it fit. Finally. We drew in a loud, collective breath, months of searching hinging on this moment. Treasure hunting was glamorous until it was boring, frustrating and time consuming. Treasure hunting in a burned out city that was now the gaping asshole of civilization was also dangerous, but I was getting handy with a pistol. I felt like a regular Lara Croft but, you know, without the massive knockers and sexy accent. Recently Whelan, with that beloved chest holster and khakis, was starting to look much more Malcolm Reynolds than Indiana. Not that I was complaining.

'Any day now, Doctor Jones,' Whelan said with a nervous chuckle.

Those moments of disappointment would be worth it.

'Here we go,' I said, pulling. The door wouldn't budge. Drat. It took all three of us to haul the thing open, the hinges screaming in protest as we forced it back. You always imagine these rooms to be vast, cavernous, glittering with jewels and riches, coins and necklaces and genies overflowing from chests stuffed too full to close. It was a narrow space, with the walls on either side lined in safety deposit boxes. It wasn't filled with chests belching out strands of pearls, but there were paintings, dozens of them, and a heavy box that I could only imagine was filled with sketches and studies.

Whelan's flashlight moved over the works of art. Some had been taken out of their frames, but all had been covered with a thin plastic sheeting to keep the dust and dampness from compromising the integrity of the canvases. 'This is more than I expected,' I said.

'What were you expecting?' Whelan asked. Shane darted beneath my arm, skidding to a stop in front of a startling blue Monet.

'Not this.'

'What do we do with all of it?' Shane asked, crouching down to get a better look at the Monet.

'Get it somewhere safer, that's what,' I said.

'Portland?' Whelan suggested, wandering into the vault. ' 'Couver? Colorado?'

'I say LV, but all three are possibilities.' I pulled a flimsy square from my back pocket. 'I just hope they're ready with the van.'

Whelan and Shane began shifting the paintings and boxes out into the hall. I knelt down beside one of the sketch boxes, lifting the dusty lid to find a ruffle of cigarette paper to catch the moisture. A layer of parchment paper waited beneath that, and underneath, priceless sketches, each protected from the next. Moritz had done an amazing job. That these had survived so long was incredible; that they had endured in such good shape was even more exciting.

'Good work,' I said softly. 'Really amazing stuff.'

The wrinkled old Polaroid hadn't fared as well as the sketches and paintings. Even so, I put it inside the box, right on top of the cigarette paper, and replaced the lid. He'd get to travel to our next destination in style, on a bed of lovingly preserved masterpieces.

'Yoo-hoo.'

I stood, turning to find Andrea jogging down the lower maze of the bank toward me. She was wearing her pink hat today and it slid to the side as she slowed to a walk. 'Nate's outside. You won't believe the van we found. I think it used to have shag carpeting in the back. We hit pay dirt?'

'All ready to go,' I said. From inside the vault, Whelan and Shane began giggling.

'Probably found the booby paintings,' Andrea muttered, fixing her hat.

She was right. I reached back and banged twice on the vault door. 'Come on, boys. It's time to get the hell out of town.'

Who knows? Maybe Colorado would be pretty this time of year.

ACKNOWLEDGEMENTS

First and foremost, I want to thank my family, for their support and love and for putting up with me typing away on my laptop during holidays. Mom and Pops – thanks for calling and sending snacks. Tristan and Julie – thank you for taking me shooting. Trevor, thanks for cracking the whip and making me kebabs. I'm so glad we got that teaspoon/tablespoon thing sorted. Andrea, Jessy, and Louisa – thank you for reading my work and having the stones to be honest. The Beloit College Library provided a safe haven to work, and I thank them for letting me use their computers when mine died.

I also want to thank everyone at St. Martins/Macmillan, for their hard work and dedication, especially Monique, Holly, and Mallika. To Kate McKean, the biggest thanks of all, for being a miracle worker and friend.